About the Author

Sam Russell is a writer, a blogger and a farmer. Born in London, UK, her family's move to the English countryside ignited a passion for horses and a love of all things rural.

Before farming and writing, Sam worked as a secretary, a bookkeeper and a riding instructor. She spent time teaching in Dubai before returning to the UK to marry a farmer and running her own stables while raising their children.

A Bed of Barley Straw is her debut romantic novel, written when the children were all grown up. She still lives and works on the family farm with her husband and dogs. You can hear more of Sam's story on her *Rustic Romance* blog.

www.russellromance.com

This novel is entirely a work of fiction. The names, characters and incidents portrayed in it are the work of the author's imagination. Any resemblance to actual persons, living or dead, events or localities is entirely coincidental.

A Bed of Barley Straw

Second Edition Printed 2015

Cover: JD Smith Design

A Bed of Barley Straw

Sam Russell

He built a fortress out of straw, on a bed of sand
But the west wind blew in through the walls
Rain fell from the sky
And the ground beneath his feet washed away

CHAPTER ONE

Hettie was a looker. Although at this moment, in muddy yard boots and an oversized, hay-flecked fleece jacket, her beauty could be hard to spot. Her long, wavy copper hair was scrunched under a woollen beanie, and fingerless mittens revealed strong, short-nailed hands (with remnants of purple nail varnish on her fingertips). Her face was exquisite: huge, arresting green eyes set in pretty elfin features. She was beautiful even on a rain-soaked winter's day and without a scrap of makeup. Underneath the layers of work clothes, she had the small but perfect body of a gymnast or dancer (although Hettie was neither of these). Hard work had formed her muscles, shaping her slim lines in all the right places.

Hettie liked to work hard, and at twenty-five, she believed she had the perfect job as yard manager of the stables on the Draymere Estate. The position didn't provide a generous salary; but it did come with a cottage and a Land Rover, and she got to keep her own horse there. In the early summer months, when the hunters were turned away, Hettie took every chance to compete on her mare, Grey Rose.

That's not to say it wasn't damned hard work. In winter, with hunting in full swing and fourteen stabled horses, Hettie worked long hours, six or seven days a week. Two full-time grooms helped her, and Bev from the village worked part time (but somehow managed twice the work of the full-timers). The truth was, though, that Hettie didn't want to do anything else. Even if she won the lottery, she would still spend her days riding and looking after her horses and dogs.

Draymere Hall was a beautiful place to work and to live. Set in rolling Cotswold countryside, the estate included four thousand acres of farmland, woodland, and rivers, which were interspersed with farmyards and cottages. Hettie's own ramshackle cottage was a short stroll from the stables, a quarter of a mile along the drive from Draymere Hall. She was happy there, with Dog and Doris for company. Doris was the most recent addition to her Draymere family, a nutty Jack Russell cross puppy, given to Hettie by Dan the farrier when his Jack Russell surprised him with seven puppies of unknown lineage. The runt of the litter, Doris compensated for her small size with a gigantic ego and too much attitude.

Dog and Hettie had been partners in crime for years; Hettie called him her soul mate. She inherited him when he was a year old (and after begging her mum *a lot*) when their elderly neighbour passed away. Despite Hettie's early attempts to rename him Heart-Star, he refused to answer to anything but Dog, so Dog it remained. The pair became inseparable.

Right now, Hettie was cursing under her breath as she scanned the yard at the end of a long day. Doris had gone AWOL. They had finished work late; Holly the groom had called in sick (for the third time that month). Hettie needed to be at her mum's for dinner in half an hour, with a fifteen-minute drive to the village, and she was still in her mucky work clothes.

"Damn and bugger. Your timing is perfect, as usual, Doris." Maybe if she ran home for a quick shower, Doris would turn up at the cottage. Or she could rush back for another look. But odds were high that the blasted puppy was up at the hall again.

"C'mon, Dog," she called impatiently, and she turned to head home. Dog opened one rheumy eye and heaved himself up from the folded old horse blanket in the corner of the yard. He obediently followed his mistress as she marched up the track, tapping out a text message on her mobile phone:

Hi Mum running late again bloody
doris don't hold dinner up for me you and
Nat start HAPPY BIRTHDAY xxxx

And then she sent a second message.

Hi Grace, have lost Doris again hope she's
not pestering you at the hall will be up in a min
if she hasn't turned up—sorry!
See you tomorrow xx

The cottage was cold, and the water barely tepid. Hettie hadn't got back at lunchtime to fire the Rayburn up. Bloody Holly! As far as Hettie was concerned, if she could manage a full day on the yard with a hangover herself, then Holly should damn well be able to as well. It wasn't as if Holly did much while she was there; she moved at the pace of a snail. At least Jodie was a good worker, even if she rarely spoke a word. And thank the Lord for Bev! Hettie threw on clean jeans and a chunky sweater. Her mum would tell her off for going out "in this weather" with wet hair, but no time for the hairdryer. They could at least be grateful she was clean. As she swept up the keys to the Land Rover and her mum's birthday card, her phone beeped twice:

No rush darling see you when you get here.
Nat only just arrived xx

Doris is here! Alexander says he'll walk her back,
glad of excuse to escape the kids I think, Georgia
has God-awful toddler crush on him
have a nice evening big kisses ps have you met Al?

Alexander? No, she hadn't met him, the middle brother of the three Melton sons. She had met the youngest son, Edward, several times. Everyone had met Ted. Sociable, good fun, and popular, he had often been the local gossipmongers' topic for his antics in the past. The village took a special kind of pride in Ted for his numerous misdemeanors, and he was enthusiastically welcomed at the Fox and Hounds Pub when he visited home. James Melton (good, kind, responsible James) was the eldest, heir to the estate, and Hettie's boss for the last five years since taking over the hall from his father. Hettie couldn't wish for a better boss (Lord Melton had been eccentric and unpredictable, to say the least), and she had become close to his wife, Grace. She was even fond of their children: Artie, Fred, and little Georgia, although as a rule Hettie didn't "do" kids. But the elusive Alexander had rarely been at Draymere in the six years Hettie had worked there. Grace had mentioned he was coming back, something about his career in the army ending.

Awkward, she thought, to be meeting him for the first time when he returned her errant terrier. "Thanks, Doris," she muttered to herself as there was a thud on the cottage door.

The words tumbled out as she greeted the man in the doorway. "Hi, thank you so much! I am so sorry you had to drag down here; it's evil out there tonight—"

Christ, he's bloody gorgeous.

The thought stopped her midsentence. She stared up at the best-looking bloke she had ever seen in her life. Tall and swarthy, with dark tousled hair and piercing blue eyes, he had a strong, chiselled face and the body of a god. Hettie's stunned stargazing was interrupted as Doris, on the end of a length of bale twine knotted to her collar, hit her legs like a crazy champagne cork and scrabbled in a frenzy of excitement. *There go the clean jeans,* Hettie sighed to herself, squatting down to take Doris's head in her hands. "You naughty pup," she said and laughed. "What am I going to do with you?"

"Keep her on a lead?" Alexander drawled sarcastically. He held the twine out, and the smile on his lips didn't make it to his eyes. "Yours, I believe?"

Hettie stood up abruptly. *How rude.* She felt annoyance prickling at his tone. *Rein it in, Hettie,* she scolded herself. *He's your boss's brother; be polite.*

"Thank you, I will bear that in mind," she told him snootily. "I would have been happy to collect her myself, you know. But I'm sorry if I've wasted your time. Now if you will excuse me, I'm going out. Nice to meet you, by the way."

Alexander stared for a second. When he spoke, his voice was low and even. "It's not a matter of who brought her back. This is a working farm, not a park. She shouldn't have been running around loose in the first place. She's only a pup."

He bent to ruffle Doris on the head. Doris squirmed and simpered in pathetic adoration as Alexander barked an abrupt, "Good night," and headed back up the track, leaving Hettie openmouthed with a writhing Doris on the end of the string. "Traitor," she muttered at Doris through her teeth, untying the lead and closing the door with her foot before Doris could make a run for it in pursuit of her new best friend.

Hettie was still simmering as she climbed into the Land Rover. *What an arrogant prick—telling me it's a working farm when I'm the one who bloody well works here, and he hasn't been seen around the place in years. Strutting about like lord bloody muck when he's only been back five minutes.* Throughout the drive to her mum's house, she allowed her righteous anger to smother any guilty thoughts that he might be a little bit right. Doris was only a puppy. It was a working farm and not her land, even if James and Grace were generous enough to allow her unlimited freedom around it. *Just goes to prove,* she concluded the tirade in her head as she pulled up outside her mum's, *good looks count for nothing.*

♦♦♦

Alexander stood at the top of the track, drawing deeply on a cigarette, enjoying the peace of the evening and the damp earthy smell of winter. He glanced toward the cottage as he saw the lights of the Land Rover reversing and disappearing up the drive. *Nice to meet you?* A self-deprecating chuckle escaped him. Hettie Redfern, the star of his sexual fantasies for the last six years, was *pleased to meet him!* She didn't even remember their brief encounter, which had sustained him through many a cold night and casual shag since. If he was honest, he had leapt at the chance to take the dog back so he could sneak a look at her. He was sure he'd be disappointed; no one was as sexy as his fantasies had made Hettie. He was wrong. If anything, she was even more fucking gorgeous than he remembered, and he'd ended up behaving like a tongue-tied teenager and sounding like a total idiot.

Al turned, shrugging his shoulders against the cold, and flicked his cigarette stub to the ground. It was irrelevant anyway; it had been years ago and blown out of proportion in his memory. She had just been the first girl who'd actually made an impression. Probably the only one, if he was honest. But Ted had regaled Al with several colourful stories from home that made it clear that Hettie Redfern was not a nice girl. And while that had been of no importance to his pornographic imaginings, he wasn't going to fall for a home-wrecker. His mother had shown them all how big a mistake that was.

♦♦♦

Nat and their mum were at the kitchen table, halfway through a bottle of red wine, when Hettie burst through the kitchen door with cries of, "Happy Birthday, Mum! Hi, Nat!"

The delicious smell of cooking reminded her that she hadn't eaten all day and was absolutely famished. After hugs and kisses, and with a generous glass of wine in front of her, contentment settled on Hettie. Chatter and gossip flowed back and forth as her mum pulled hot plates from the oven and dished up a steaming shepherd's pie. The sisters fell into their familiar sibling banter.

"Nice of you to dress for us, Het. Did you prewash those jeans in mud before you came out?"

Hettie rolled her eyes. "Don't let us keep you from your meeting, Nat. You must be wearing that power suit for a reason."

"I came straight from work, and *I* managed to get here on time, even with the trains running late and no taxi at the station."

"Work?" Hettie retorted scornfully. "Is that what you call sitting on your butt all day, writing smutty e-mails to Simon?"

"Beats shovelling shit for a living." Natalie grinned triumphantly.

Based on appearance alone it would be difficult to guess that the girls were sisters. Hettie was small, slim, and pale, with a mass of curls falling over her shoulders. Natalie was tall, curvaceous, and olive skinned, with straight, almost black hair cut in a neat, symmetrical bob. They lived very different lives. Nat was driven—her life filled with university, foreign travel, a career in the city, and a long-term, serious boyfriend (with a good job and a nice car). Hettie had never strayed far from the village she grew up in, with the exception of a few Ibiza holidays with mates that she couldn't really remember. Leaving school at the first possible chance, she focused on ponies, then horses (and, of course, Dog). Working with animals was all she wanted, what she knew she was going to do. Plenty of boys had pursued her in her teens, but none of them got anywhere. Since then it had been drunken one-night stands, usually with lads she'd known since school (and most recently with Dan the farrier, which had been a mistake), and quite a few unsuccessful first dates. And the married bloke, of course, but she wasn't going to think about that. An analyst might have suggested that Hettie was avoiding commitment. As far as Hettie was concerned, she was very happy without a man in her life. Her mother, Anna, had managed pretty damn well without one.

Talk and wine flowed comfortably. Nat updated them on her and Simon's frustrating efforts to find a flat they could afford in London. Anna told them about the latest book she had been commissioned to illustrate, and she asked if she could borrow Doris as a model for some sketches.

"Borrow? You can have her!" Hettie retorted, although they knew she didn't mean it. "She humiliated me this evening. Bloody Alexander is back, and he wasn't at all happy about Doris calling at the hall." She chuckled; it seemed quite a funny story now with three glasses of wine and her mum's shepherd's pie inside her.

"Ooh, the gorgeous Alexander is back?" Nat exclaimed. "How long for?"

"I have no idea—hopefully not too long. On first impressions he is a very rude man. Do you know him, then?"

Nat stopped eating with her fork halfway to her mouth. "What do you mean, 'first impressions' and 'do I know him'? Are you kidding, or is this another piece of your history you think you can delete by pretending it didn't happen?"

"Not now, Natalie," Anna scolded her quickly. "It's been a lovely evening so far; please don't spoil it."

Hettie was caught between confusion and anger. She knew exactly what Nat was referring to with her snide remark about deleting the past. But her mum was right, and she had no intention of getting into that discussion. The rest of Nat's sentence was passing her by altogether.

"First impressions. Of Alexander. It's the first time I've met him, and I didn't know you had. He was pretty rude, actually. I have no idea what you're going on about."

Nat threw her head back and laughed out loud. "Hettie! You were drunk, but surely not so drunk that you don't remember! The hunt ball? What, six or seven years ago? The only time I went to one, anyway. Hettie, you must remember. I believe you puked on his shoes!" She dissolved into fits of laughter.

Anna struggled to stop herself from laughing too. "Yes, you did come home in a state that night. Your lovely dress was ruined. You must have been eighteen—your first year at Draymere, wasn't it? And I remember it was 'the gorgeous Alexander' who brought you home. He was sweet. I was very grateful to him."

Hettie was dumbfounded. Of course she remembered her first hunt ball, or at least she remembered most of it. She'd been unable to believe she was actually there, dressed up in heels and a dress, out of her depth and hitting the predinner drinks harder than she should have. She remembered having a great time on the dance floor with Nat and the other girls who worked on the yard, then smooching with a very hunky stranger and being embarrassingly forward in her drunken state—kissing his neck, pushing her hips against his body, and whispering that she wanted to go somewhere private.

"Oh, my God, *that* was Alexander Melton?" Hettie's face was a picture of horror, and a blush reddened her cheeks.

Anna and Nat collapsed into laughter, which became more hysterical as they blurted out their other memories of that night.

"You puked on his shoes! He had to carry you to the car!"

"He carried you in when he got you back, too—and held you over the sink while you puked again! I sat up all night wondering if I should take you to A and E."

"I think you probably puked in his car!"

Oh, my God, oh, my God, oh, my God. That *was Alexander Melton?* The thought went round on a loop in Hettie's head.

"No wonder he kept his distance when he brought Doris back," she said out loud. Anna and Nat fell about laughing again.

Hettie was subdued at the end of the evening. The sisters cleared the table and did the washing up. Nat called for a taxi to the station.

"Are you staying here, Het, or do you want to share a cab?"

"No, I'll drive back over the fields. I can get back without going on the roads from here. James doesn't mind."

"Good-byes" and "see you soons" were exchanged, and Hettie set off up the farm track toward Draymere Hall in her battered Landy. The Draymere Estate extended all the way to the village, and the country route back was much used by estate employees after pub nights or village shindigs.

As soon as she was alone, Hettie's thoughts ricocheted back to Alexander Melton and *that* hunt ball. How had she not known it was him? It seemed incredible, but she hadn't been at Draymere long. There had been a lot of ribbing from the other workers over the following few days, but no one had mentioned Alexander's name. Maybe they had assumed she knew who he was? Thank God she hadn't known at the time. How absolutely mortifying: she would have had to leave! *Christ, Lord Melton had been there that night, not to mention James. And Grace?* Hettie couldn't remember if Grace had been there or not; she hadn't really known her then. Maybe none of them realised that she had gone outside with him.

They had crept out to the hay barn, giggling and stumbling over the uneven ground. She remembered she couldn't keep her hands off him. The drink had made her too brave (or brazen), and she loved the feel of him: his face, his arms, his torso. She pulled his shirt open, kissing his chest and then his mouth. They kissed like they were starving for each other. Hettie couldn't remember ever feeling so needy in her life, before or since.

They slowed momentarily as she lay on the hay bales. He leaned over her, looking into her face. He brushed his thumb over her cheek and her bottom lip, staring into her eyes and at the pale curve of her bosom where it thrust above the fabric of her cream dress. Her long skirt had splits running up each side, and he reached to pull the dress aside, exposing her lace G-string and naked legs in high-heeled sandals. Thinking of it now made her feel horny all over again. His fingers had found and stroked the small horseshoe tattoo on the inside of her ankle. He ran his hand slowly over her calf, behind her knee, and along the inside of her thigh. Hettie gripped tightly to his jacket sleeve and moaned when he reached the top of her leg. She greedily pulled his mouth back to hers, and they were scrabbling at each other's clothes again. Hettie recalled the frustration in her drink-muddled mind as her fumbling fingers tried to release the button and zip of his fly. But eventually she had done it, and she grasped his cock in her hand. As Alexander groaned against her mouth at the feel of her hand there and thrust his tongue deeper, she recalled a flicker of anxiety as she clasped the full size of him. But all thoughts left her mind as Alexander pulled roughly at her G-string. His fingers were between her legs, and it felt oh, so sweet. She was so ready for him…

Suddenly, she knew she was going to throw up: that awful feeling of the walls spinning (in a bad way) and sweat breaking out on the back of her neck. As frantically as she had been trying to pull Alexander near, she was now shoving him away. She remembered shouting, "I'm gonna be sick!" as she gulped for mouthfuls of air and struggled to get up off the bales, with the floor dipping and swaying underneath her. Oh, God. And despite his initial frustrated groan, Alexander had been so kind: helping her up and holding her as she stumbled out of the barn and back toward the house. And then she'd thrown up on his shoes.

The lights were on at the hall as Hettie turned onto the field track that ran past the walled kitchen garden to the yard and her cottage. A shudder passed through her at the thought that Alexander was in there. She wasn't sure if it was a shudder of shame or plain dislike. By the gate to the kitchen garden, she could see the faint glow of a cigarette. She could murder for a cigarette right now; wine always did that to her. Maybe it was Grace sneaking out for a sly one. She'd pull up and say good night, then see if she could filch a spare. The Land Rover had virtually stopped before Hettie realised it was Alexander standing by the wall. Oh, shit! What to do now? Pull away again? Surely that would look worse than saying something. The sight of him was making her cheeks burn, but she would have to brazen it out.

Hettie wound the window halfway down. "Hi. Sorry, I thought you were somebody else." Hettie daren't mention Grace, who tried to keep her smoking habit secret from James. Although Hettie was pretty sure James must know.

Alexander glanced toward her and looked away again. "Yes, apparently you did," he drawled, a half smirk twisting his mouth into a wry almost (but not really there) smile.

Hettie's face flooded with colour. Did he mean what she thought he meant? She should have driven on; nothing could be more embarrassing than this. "Ah, yes, we've met before, of course. You must think I'm mad, what with the dog and forgetting that and this…I am sorry," she babbled, flustered beyond belief.

Alexander stared at her for some seconds before replying without the trace of a smile.

"I have absolutely no idea what you are talking about." Keeping a straight face, he ground out his cigarette and made to turn away. Pausing to turn back toward the Land Rover, he looked along the farm track Hettie had driven, leaned close to the window, and said quietly, "You have made yourself very at home here, haven't you?" before disappearing through the kitchen garden gate.

Hettie gripped the steering wheel and stared straight ahead. Why the hell did she feel like crying? It hadn't been a good day; her period must be due. Why was he being so nasty? He obviously didn't remember her, either. This last thought made her feel more humiliated, which was strange because she knew that it should have made her feel better. She realised she had thought about that night a lot over the years. Their encounter had held so much promise, and she had felt so wanted at a time when she was pretty messed up and vulnerable. Seems it was just another notch on the bedpost with some random girl from the village to him. *Or almost a notch*, she thought wryly. You wouldn't think he'd forget someone puking on his shoes, though. That couldn't have happened too often.

When she let herself back into the cottage, her lovely dogs were there to cheer her up; Doris corkscrewed across the floor in ecstatic joy, and Dog lumped pit-pat across the kitchen with his tail whoomphing back and forth and a grin on his face. Hettie hunkered down onto the floor with her back against the still-cold Rayburn and put an arm around each dog. She should go to bed, early start tomorrow, but she might see if she could find a stray cigarette kicking about first.

Alexander chuckled to himself as he walked back into the kitchen and the welcome heat from the Aga. She had obviously remembered since he'd seen her earlier; her face had been a picture. And that blush! She could have a taste of her own medicine now; buggered if he was going to let her know he'd remembered all along. Damn, but she was pretty, though.

CHAPTER TWO

Mornings in the hall were noisy and chaotic. Grace was a joyful, enthusiastic mother but felt little need to subdue her energetic children. James adapted to the chaos by burying his head in the newspaper and letting the noise wash over him. Alexander was finding the lack of order hard to cope with first thing in the morning. Much as he loved his sister-in-law, niece, and nephews, it would have suited him better to grab some toast and disappear back to his room. In theory the family sat down for breakfast together at the huge kitchen table, but in practice the only person sitting was James. Fred and Artie were playing a hyperactive game of "it," which involved charging noisily around the room, and Georgia, strapped to her highchair, had managed to twist herself round to kneel on the seat. She was now hollering in a fury that the straps prevented further escape, but no one was taking any notice. Grace stood at the Aga conducting an opera of sausages, bacon, and eggs and crying occasional orders:

"Fred! Don't spit at your brother. Georgia, sit down! Eggs are ready! Flossie, *in your bed!*" This last cry was directed at the spaniel, who was glued to Grace's legs with her tongue hanging out, waiting to collect any dropped offerings.

As Grace carried breakfast to the table, the boys scrambled back into their seats and started a tug of war over the one fork that they had reached for at the same time.

James shook and folded his paper with military neatness. Standing up, he firmly righted Georgia in her chair, and with a brisk circuit of the table, he settled the boys with plates of food and cutlery. Georgia pointed and shouted, "Soz! Soz!" at the plate of sausages. Once her request was satisfied, momentary peace filled the room.

Flossie repositioned herself at the foot of Georgia's high chair.

"So, Alexander, what plans have you got for your day?" James asked midmouthful. "I've got a meeting with the accountant this morning, and I'm hoping to visit a few of the farms this afternoon. You're welcome to tag along on either or both if you want to."

Alexander smiled. "Think I'll give the meeting a miss. I thought I'd nip to Swindon and visit poor Digger in quarantine. He must wonder what the hell is going on. I'd like to join you on the farm tour; about time I started making myself useful."

"Gosh, Alexander, you've only been here a few days," Grace piped in. "Plenty of time to work up to that. When is Digger's quarantine over?"

"Two more weeks. Are you sure you don't mind me bringing him here, Grace? Only until I get sorted in the gatehouse. I ought to wander over and take a look at that place, too—see what needs to be done."

"Golly, no, we don't mind having him here, do we, James? The more the merrier," Grace trilled.

"No, no, not at all," James muttered. "Will you hunt with us on Saturday, Al? Grace, can you let Hettie know if Al is joining us?"

"Yes, I think I will. Be good to do something physical." Alexander felt his pulse quicken at the mention of Hettie's name, and the image of her flushed face in the Land Rover last night popped into his mind. He'd like to make her blush like that again. *Good God, man. How old are you—twenty-eight or fifteen?* he rebuked himself.

At eight o'clock sharp, Zofia the Polish nanny arrived to take charge of Georgia. Grace nagged Artie and Fred to find shoes, blazers, and school bags before heading out to the Range Rover for school. By some miracle, at eight thirty they were usually belted in and heading up the drive. Often the car would be back minutes later, though, with Grace swearing vociferously at the wheel, to collect forgotten sports kit or books. This was the one part of the day when Grace liked to be efficient: if she got the boys dropped off on time, she could be back at the yard for breakfast break and a sneaky smoke with the girls.

By contrast, on the yard, they had been working since seven thirty, and all was calm efficiency. Horses were fed, and stables were clean. Hay nets and sweeping would be finished before breakfast break. With Holly back at work, the only fly in the ointment was the constant whining from Doris, who was secured to a tie ring in the corner with Dog. Dog looked morose. Hettie moved at double speed in every job she did. She relished the physical work; it cleared her mind of everything except getting the job done and having the yard tidy and shipshape in time for morning exercise. There would be thirteen horses to exercise today; one was on stable rest following injury. The girls rode one horse and led a second. With Bev staying for first exercise, they would get all thirteen out in two sessions today. When one of them had a day off, Grace often rode to make up the numbers.

As they finished sweeping, Hettie clambered on the tractor to haul the muck trailer off. "Mine's a coffee!" she called. Dog lifted his head nostalgically. There was a time when he would have been in the tractor with Hettie, but these days the scramble up was too much for him. Having tipped up the trailer, Hettie was bouncing back along the muddy track when she saw Grace's Range Rover sweep in behind the stables.

The yard staff room, known as the dugout, was a fug of smoke and chatter when Hettie came in. She stamped her feet to ward off the cold, with Doris still on the lead and Dog following obediently behind. She sat at her place at the table; a steaming cup of coffee awaited. Several packets of open biscuits littered the table. Grace was laughing loudly midconversation with the irrepressible Bev, who was likely telling some bawdy or colourful story about her long-suffering husband or grown-up kids.

"Too much detail, thank you, Beverley!" Grace screamed in laughter before turning to Hettie. "I was telling Bev that I have never been more popular with the local lovelies than I am now, since they've got wind Al is back in the county. They are circling like sharks, poor Al! I will be fighting them off at the door with a wooden spoon."

"An' I was telling her how I used to get rid of the vermin that came calling for our Chelsea. Got plenty of tips for scaring away undesirables, I 'ave!" Bev roared. "That said, it's always nice to 'ave a bit of talent around to spice things up, don't you think, girls?" She guffawed, winking broadly at Hettie. "Grace 'ere tells me you'd never met 'im!"

Hettie went pink and gave Bev a hard stare. Could she detect sarcasm in that last line?

"Ooh, he is so bloody fit!" Holly piped in enthusiastically. "I saw him a couple of nights ago. In the Fox, 'e was. Nearly fell off my stool. Bloody fit, for an old 'un, anyway." She aimed her last comment at Jodie.

"Apparently I had met him before." Hettie tried to keep her voice neutral. "My sister reminded me that we'd been at the same hunt ball years back."

Bev spluttered and choked on her mouthful of biscuit, spraying crumbs across the table. "Met 'im?" she squawked as Grace thumped her vigorously on her back.

Hettie glared warningly through squinted eyes, and Bev, thankfully too busy choking to speak, caught the glare and shut up. *Damn,* Hettie thought, *someone noticed, then.* To steer the conversation to safer ground, she gave Grace an update on Jack, the injured gelding. They agreed that the vet should come out to check him again; hopefully Jack could start being led out in hand.

"That should be fun," Bev interjected. "'E's a bugger to lead, even when 'e hasn't been stuck in a stable. You can schedule that little game for outside of my hours, Hettie. Thank you very much!"

They all laughed. Bev had been around so long that she pretty much wrote her own work rules. And everyone knew that if it was a risky job, Hettie would do it herself.

Hettie glanced at her watch. "Five minutes, ladies!" she called. Bev, Holly, and Jodie all reached for their fags.

"You want one?" Bev asked.

"Trying not to," Hettie muttered, collecting cups from the table and carrying them to the sink. "Holly, washing-up duty, please. And Jodi, you're on Basil. He's lost a boot, so you'll have to find a spare pair in the tack room. Grace, are you joining us this week? Jodie is off tomorrow and Holly on Monday if you're free."

"Love to. Think I can do tomorrow. Let me look in the diary, and I'll text you. I meant to tell you that Al wants to hunt with us on Saturday. He'd be happy with any of the horses, so whatever you think best. And Fred will come to the meet, but Artie wants to go to rugby, which is a nuisance. I'll have to drop him off and beg one of the other mothers to hang onto him afterward."

♦♦♦

At the hall, Alexander ruffled Georgia's hair affectionately before picking up his car key. As he headed for the door, the telephone rang.

"Draymere," he answered.

"Who's that?" a female voice asked. "Fiona Harding here. I was calling for Grace."

"Hi, Fi, it's Alexander. She's not here at the moment, but I can ask her to give you a call back later."

"Alexander!" Fi exclaimed. "I didn't know you were back, you dark horse, you! How terrific! How lovely to hear you! What have you been up to? We simply must catch up."

"Yes, yes, that would be good," Alexander replied vaguely. "Shall I ask Grace to call you?"

"Yes, please do. But I absolutely insist that you and I meet up for a coffee *very* soon. I want to hear all your news, Lexi. Promise me?"

"Of course, give me a call sometime. Or I'm hunting this Saturday. Maybe I'll see you then." Alexander glanced at his watch; he was keen to get off to see Digger.

"Of course! Yes, of course, I will be out on Saturday! How thrilling. It will be like old times! Can't wait, darling."

"Great, I'll see you then."

"Lovely, lovely. Ta-ta for now, Lexi!" Fiona put the phone down with a smug smile on her face. Of course she had known that Alexander was back at Draymere. She had also worked out that if she called around nine, Grace would be on the school run, James would be working, and with luck, Alexander might answer the phone. *Clever girl*, she congratulated herself. *Get in there before blasted Imogen Tatler gets her claws in to him. Now where can I scrounge a horse before Saturday? Best make some phone calls.*

Alexander took the steps down from the front door two at a time and jumped into his Aston. Purring down the drive, he noticed Grace's Range Rover parked behind the stables. He could pass on Fiona's message before he forgot. He pulled over and climbed out.

He rounded the corner to the yard as Jodie, Holly, and Bev spilled from the tack room with saddles and bridles over their arms. The two younger girls stopped in their tracks, Jodie actually emitting a squeak, as they stared at the six-foot Adonis who had appeared before them. Holly would have reached up to stroke back her hair seductively, but she didn't have a free hand.

She improvised by flicking her head, which looked rather odd, given that her hair was knotted up under a blue woolly hat.

"Alexander, you young bugger!" Bev boomed, grinning from ear to ear, "About time you came to bloody see me, you gorgeous hunk of meat!" She rolled her eyes at the simpering ninnies on either side of her.

"Bev!" Alexander beamed back. "Great to see you."

Grace and Hettie came giggling out of the dugout, followed by a waft of smoke, which made it look like they were entering stage right. Alexander eye's locked onto Hettie, and the grin he'd been directing in Bev's direction turned into a smirk as he noticed Doris on a lead. "Ah, on a leash today. Good girl," he drawled with a glint in his eye. Hettie prickled and resisted the urge to immediately let Doris off, satisfying herself with a small, sarcastic laugh, which sounded pathetic even to her. She was buggered if she was going to make any effort to be polite to this man again, though.

"Ah, Grace," Alexander continued. "Fiona Harding called for you; I said I would ask you to call her back."

"Fiona Harding called for *me*?" Grace guffawed. "I hardly think so—haven't spoken to the girl in years."

Alexander looked confused. "Well, yes, that's what she said. Asked that you call her back."

Grace turned to Hettie. "Gosh, aren't men dim!" She laughed and added a conspiratorial aside. "Like I said, the sharks are circling." She turned to Alexander again. "I thought you were off to see Digger this morning, Al. Digger is Al's dog," she explained to the others. "Poor little mite is in quarantine. Al rescued him from Afghanistan."

"Oh, how sweet!" Holly trilled.

"Come on, ladies," Hettie directed. "Time's ticking on. Can we get these horses tacked up, please?" Even Alexander bloody Melton and his good deeds were not going to distract her from the job at hand. "We must be getting on, Grace. Text me later about riding." She headed toward the tack room.

"Yes, of course, darling. Talk later. Oh, Hettie, before you go, do you want Al to have a look at Jack's leg? I can't believe I didn't think of it. We've got a trained vet in the family—captain in the Royal Army Veterinary Corps, no less!" Grace beamed proudly. "Have you got time, Al?"

"*Former* Royal Army Veterinary," Alexander cut in quickly. After a pause he turned to look at Hettie. "Yes, of course, I could take a look."

This was all news to Hettie. *Was he a real vet, then? They had vets in the army?* But she couldn't exactly question his credentials, or turn down the offer of a second opinion on one of her precious charges. If she thought he didn't have a clue, she would call Ewan their usual vet, later.

"Great," she said, unconvinced. "I'll grab his head-collar. Jodie, Holly, can you get my two tacked up?"

Hettie collected Jack's head-collar and walked briskly to his stable. The big chestnut horse glared at her over the door.

"He can be a bit moody from the ground," she threw back over her shoulder. It was tempting to let Alexander find out for himself, but that would probably be taking it too far. "He's a sweetie when you're on his back, though."

Alexander nodded. As Hettie opened the door, Jack swung round and presented them with his huge back end. Hettie chuckled and walked purposely past the threatening back legs to Jack's head to slip his head-collar on. "Well, good morning to you too, Jacko," she said softly. "Pleased to see us again, I see." She called back to Alexander, "Do you want to look at him in here or outside?"

"In here will be fine," he replied. James had said she was good with the horses, and Alexander grudgingly concurred. Not many people he knew would be prepared to walk past the back end of a threatening seventeen-hand horse with that confidence, including most of the lads he'd trained, who must have been twice her height and weight. "Which leg?" he asked.

"Offside hind, the one he's sharpening up for you now." Hettie laughed as Jack stamped his back leg crossly.

So she finds that amusing. Alexander smiled ruefully to himself. "Think I'll come to the head end and introduce myself first, then." He walked to Jack's head, speaking in reassuring tones. "Hey, old fella, what have you been up to? Been in the wars, have we? You gonna stop being a baby and let me have a look?"

Hettie was suddenly aware of how close Alexander was in the confines of the stable and that she must stink of fag smoke and horse muck. She tried to keep her attention on Jack's bared teeth. "He did it in the field," she said. "Not sure how. But he was turned out with a couple of the others, and they were having a bit of a party. Could have been a kick, or he might have done it on the fence. We cold-hosed and bandaged it. It filled slightly, and he was lame but not hopping. Ewan came out to be on the safe side."

Ewan, that name rings a bell, Alexander mused. "That's the trouble with turning these lunatics out together. I'm surprised you turn them out at all when they're hunting. A lot of yards don't."

Oh, here we go, thought Hettie, *more bloody know-it-all criticism.* She launched into a lecture on her pet subject: the importance of allowing horses to behave like horses and giving them some playtime. "It's good for them, you know. All horses should spend time in the field. It's vital for their well-being. It keeps them happy, and it keeps them fresh. And for my money, that is worth the risk of the *very* occasional injury," she finished haughtily.

"OK, OK." Alexander peered up at her from his position hunched down by Jack's back leg. A tingle passed through Hettie as she watched him run his hand firmly down the leg, feeling for any swelling. "You're too prickly, Hettie. I wasn't criticising. Actually, I agree. I wish more people followed your philosophy." He stood and walked back to Jack's head.

Somehow—because he had said her name? because he had actually said something nice?—as he stood beside her, the atmosphere in the stable changed. The air started fizzing between them. They both fell quiet; even Jack stopped chomping his teeth and pricked one ear in suspicion. Alexander stroked Jack's cheek. Unable to help himself, he let his hand touch Hettie's where it was resting on Jack's nose. Neither looked at the other; their gazes remained studiously fixed on Jack. Seconds passed before Hettie, unsure what was happening, was snapped back to life by the sound of horses being led from their stables outside. She squeaked, "So, what's the verdict?" and very obviously moved her hand away.

Alexander was immediately businesslike. "All good. Looks like he's pretty much mended. Lead him out in hand for a couple of days. If he still looks lame, or if you want me to see him trot up, give me a shout."

"Thank you." Hettie spoke quietly. "That's good news." She slipped Jack's head-collar over his ears, and they moved toward the stable door. She knew she was blushing and kept her head down as they came out. Bev would be on Hettie like the Gestapo if she noticed anything. Fortunately the others were busy sorting out and getting on board the six horses now circling the yard. Hettie's flustered state passed unseen.

"No problem," Alexander muttered. He was more rattled himself than he would have liked to admit. He strode purposefully toward the hall before remembering that his car was parked at the back of the stables. Rather than go back, he circled around behind the buildings to reach the Aston without being seen. As he climbed into the car, it came to him. *Ewan Jones! My boyhood mate from the village. And fuck, hadn't he been one of the names Ted had linked with Hettie?* Alexander sped off along the drive faster than was safe or necessary.

Hettie, hearing the speeding car, rolled her eyes in disapproval.

Grace steeled herself and dialed Fiona's number. Grace had no time for the girl and was less than delighted that she was back in contact. But the Hardings were longtime family friends of the Meltons; she would have to make an effort.

"Ah, Grace," Fiona trilled. "Thank you so much for ringing me back." Fiona had to think on her feet; she hadn't had a reason for calling Grace in the first place. With a burst of inspiration, and having failed to secure a horse for Saturday from any of her usual circle, she continued, "I wondered if I could be ever so cheeky and ask if you have a horse I could borrow for the meet on Saturday. My usual mount is lame. Such a blasted nuisance. I would be *so* sad to miss a Saturday meet."

Grace was outraged and flabbergasted at the same time. *Her usual mount?* She couldn't remember the last time she had seen Fiona on a horse, let alone out hunting. The cheek of the girl! Did she think Grace was an idiot? But Grace knew what James would say. Always generous and completely clueless when it came to reading a person's character, James would offer a horse without hesitation. He only saw the best in people. And she loved him for it, of course.

Through gritted teeth, Grace told Fiona she would see what she could do and hung up the phone, irritated.

She fired off a text to Hettie:

hate to be a pain but can you sort
another horse for Saturday? Blasted Fiona
Harding. Tempted to put her on Satan but
Best make it one of the quiet ones—basil
or cora? Ps I can ride tomorrow xx

♦♦♦

In Swindon, Alexander was shown through to the quarantine kennels, where he found a very dejected Digger curled up on the concrete in the corner of his enclosure. He looked a pitiful sight. Not the prettiest of dogs to start with, Alexander saw that he'd lost weight, and his scruffy grey coat was dull and lackluster. Alexander's heart went out to him. Alexander let himself in, and Digger stood up, wagging his tail weakly, with sorrowful, pleading eyes. Al squatted down beside him.

"I am so sorry, mate. You're not enjoying this, are you?" Digger hated being caged. As a stray in Afghanistan, he had never slept indoors, and he still refused to do so. Whining at the door until Alexander let him out, he would settle happily on the ground outside to wait for the morning. Even though Digger was shy and suspicious of humans, he had bonded with Alexander, who had taken him to the veterinary unit after finding him roaming with a gaping wound on his shoulder. Alexander had brought him home at the end of his tour, after jumping through several hoops and completing endless paperwork. Now he was wondering if it had been the right thing to do after all. But he knew Digger would not have been better off set loose to scavenge for food again, and the dog wouldn't go near any of the other men in Alexander's unit.

"Can I take him out for a walk?" he shouted to a nearby kennel hand.

"Yeah, but he'll have to stay on 'is lead," came the reply

"Not really necessary, is it, Digger?" Al muttered to the dog. Digger had rarely strayed more than three feet from Al's legs since they'd found each other. "But we'd better follow the rules, fella. Sorry."

The collar and lead were completely alien to Digger. He looked wary as Alexander buckled them on, though he trusted this man completely. The walk was a faintly hilarious affair. Digger brightened considerably when he was back in the great outdoors with his master. His stumpy legs and overlong tail gave the impression he was a bigger dog walking in a dip. Suddenly playful with excitement, he alternated between leaping about like a puppy and lying on his back in surprised submission whenever he felt the pull of the lead on his collar. Alexander tried to keep up with his antics without letting the lead get tight. The kennel hands looking on laughed out loud at the sight of the big man and the little grey dog running, leaping, and turning in jerky unison.

But Al was in a black mood when he got back to his car. He'd felt like a traitorous shit putting Digger back in that cage and walking away. He missed having Digger around, and he missed the army life. He wondered how the men were doing. Maybe he'd been wrong to get out? *Snap out of it, you bloody girl*, he told himself angrily. *Time to get off your backside and build a life*. He would come to Swindon daily; the two weeks would be over in no time. He would get on with the renovations on the gatehouse, then decide exactly what he was going to do next. Maybe he'd look up an old girlfriend or two; a good shag would sort him out. Blast, but he couldn't even remember the last time.

CHAPTER THREE

Hettie was on the yard at five thirty on Saturday morning. Draymere stables provided a horse for Don, the huntsman, and both he and James, who was joint master, would have second horses taken out to them later in the day. So, with Alexander, Grace, Fred's pony, Gilbert, and now Fiona, that was eight horses she needed to have immaculate and plaited up. Six of them in time for Bert when he turned up with the horsebox, and that was on top of all the usual morning duties.

Jodie and Holly would arrive at six thirty, but for the time being Hettie enjoyed being alone and listening to the horses munching their breakfast. With the lights glowing and gentle noises as horses moved around their stables, it was a welcome little haven in the dark, icy morning. Hettie worked quietly and efficiently. Starting with Gilbert, who as always had finished his breakfast first, she had plaited three horses and was on to her fourth when Jodie arrived. "Morning, Jodie!" she called. Jodie smiled shyly and nodded. "If you want to get started on Cora, I'll make coffee when I'm done here." Hettie liked to do James's, Grace's, and Don's horses herself; no one else's plaits were quite good enough. She flexed her aching fingers before twisting the last plait under, pinching it tight, and threading the needle through to stitch it in place. She glanced at her watch as she led Satan back to his stable; it was six forty-five—where the hell was Holly?

Holly stumbled shamefaced onto the yard at seven fifteen, with last night's makeup smeared across her cheek and her eyes still puffy from sleep.

"Holly, this is not bloody good enough," Hettie hissed through the needle clenched in her teeth as she worked on Gent, horse number five. "I need you here *on time! Every day!* And *especially* on hunting days. You and I need to have a chat, but right now I want you to grab a wheelbarrow and get four stables mucked out *before* eight o'clock."

Holly thrust her bottom lip in petulance. But she moved off to collect a wheelbarrow at a slightly faster pace than was usual, grunting at Jodie as she passed.

Hettie sighed. She knew she'd been soft on Holly all winter, but she actually liked the girl. It was a tricky path to tread between keeping the place running as it should and risking losing a groom in the middle of hunting season. That would be a disaster; decent grooms were hard to come by. Hettie recalled interviewing one girl who had thought she could do the job because she'd kept guinea pigs as a child.

Despite Holly's lateness, all six early horses were gleaming, plaited, and bandaged for their journey to the meet when Bert pulled up in the horsebox just before nine o'clock. Every horse on the yard stuck its head over the door with ears pricked in anticipation when they heard the lorry arrive. Hettie left the girls mucking out and went to lower the ramp and move partitions into place, ready for the first two horses. She loved Bert, who was semiretired now. He was only sixty-two, but his early career as a jump jockey had not been kind to his joints. He had been the yard manager at Draymere for twenty-five years; there was nothing he didn't know about horses, hounds, and the countryside. Hettie could listen to him talk for hours, and he had been a real friend to her when she'd been given the manager's job.

"Mornin', Miss Hettie," he called. "Lovely day for it." This was always Bert's greeting, regardless of whether the sun was shining or the heavens were sending down their worst. "What 'ave you got for me today, then?"

"Busy one, Bert," Hettie replied. "Five horses, one Gilbert, and a hay net for Gil later when Fred finishes up. Don't let me forget the hay net! Keep Gil on the lorry until I turn up with the second horses, please."

"Five!" Bert exclaimed. "And seconds? Blummin' 'ell, 'ow did that happen?"

"Alexander is going, and some girl called Fiona something."

"Harding?" Bert interjected, eyebrows raised in surprise.

"Yes, that's it." Hettie continued, "James is on Satan, Grace has got Gent, and Don's got Belle. I've put Alexander on Patrick—do you think that's all right? And Grace told me to give Cora to this Fiona girl."

"Ah! Be great to see Alexander back out, great to have 'im home safe it is, really," Bert said quietly. "Sure, that boy can ride anything you've got here, so Patrick will be just fine. You'd better write that lot down for me, though. My memory is not what it was."

Hettie laughed. "I've got it right here, Bert." She handed over the note. "And keep your phone switched on! I'll call you before I leave with second horses." Bert would hang around the lorry all day. There was a time when he would have followed the hunt on foot. These days he made do with his binoculars, chatting to old acquaintances and followers, popping into the local for a swift half, or sitting in the lorry with the heating on, reading his *Racing Times* and eating the generous lunch Grace packed up for him.

The horses were led down two by two, each striding eagerly up the ramp to get on with the job ahead. Gilbert, the last to load, was the only one who played up, dragging Jodie off the ramp to get to the grass on the verge. Familiar with his tricks,

Jodie managed to hang on and circle back round, at which point Gilbert capitulated and trotted up the ramp as if that had been his plan all along. The loaded horsebox rumbled out of the yard.

When Bert arrived at the meet, the family and Don were there ready to collect their horses. Fred swung from Grace's arm as the horses were unloaded. Bert searched for the note from Hettie, which he'd left in the cab. By the time he had retrieved it, James was already on Satan, who would only be there for him. Satan hadn't earned his name by accident; he had been known to buck, rear, and refuse to go any direction but backward—often at the same time. But when the hounds were running, he was fast and brave, leaping any obstacle in his path. He had long been James's favorite.

Grace was helping Fred get sorted and onto Gilbert when Fiona arrived in brand-new hunting clothes and full war makeup. She beamed vaguely at the group as she approached.

"Goodness! All the Meltons at once—how lovely," she purred. James responded with a welcome greeting, and the party nodded and said their hellos as they carried on checking their girths and running down their stirrups. With Fred mounted, Grace took Gent from Bert, leaving him holding Cora. Fiona took in the scene and realised with disappointment that Cora was to be her ride. Her face fell. How on earth was she going to look wonderful on *that*? She knew that Imo would be out on one of her mother's stunning show jumpers. She was at Grace's side in an instant, strutting past Bert without bothering to acknowledge him at all.

"Grace, Grace, this is *so* kind, but I *really* should have warned you that I can't ride a *cob.* I had this trouble with my hip, you know, oh, years back now, and I simply *can't* be comfortable on *that.*" She pointed at lovely, patient Cora, who gazed back in bemusement, as did Bert. "I'm sure you won't mind swapping with me, will you? Darling Grace, you are such a dear. I so prefer a thoroughbred."

Grace was so stunned by the rudeness of the girl that she couldn't take in what she was hearing. She stood with her mouth opening and shutting like a fish, as Fiona, with a gushing thank you, took Gent from her and led him over to the ramp to mount. "Gosh," Grace finally managed to splutter.

She and Bert exchanged a long look, voicing all the things they couldn't say out loud. Bert scratched Cora's neck, embarrassed by the insult to her type. "Ah, you'll have a better day with Grace on your back, Cora, and that's for sure," he murmured. "Her father's a lovely man, an' all," he muttered to himself, glancing toward Fiona in confusion.

James and Alexander went to join Don and the hounds in the paddock, and Fiona, having hauled herself somewhat awkwardly onto Gent's back, trotted off behind them, crying, "Lexi! Lexi, wait for me!" Grace, feeling very cross and irritated now, and with Fred on the lead rein, followed sedately behind on calm, wide Cora.

"I'm going to hunt *all day,* Mummy!" Fred shouted, excited that something was finally happening.

"Are you, darling? Lovely." She smiled fondly at him with a sigh. *That's my day buggered, then,* she thought.

With only five horses left to exercise, Hettie sent Holly and Jodie off with four of them while she swept and tidied. It was quicker that way. She decided that as she'd been working since dawn and would miss lunch taking second horses, she would pull Rose out of the field and take her for a ride. She could lead Cloud, Artie's pony. Rose would be put out to have the pony tag along, but it would give her a change of scenery. Since the family members were out, Alexander in particular, she could risk taking Doris and Dog too.

She'd had a chat with Holly, trying not to sound too bossy but still getting her message across. She wasn't sure it had been convincing. She thought she had sounded like a lecturing teacher, haranguing about commitment and putting your studies (horses in this case) first. Now Holly was in a sulk and not speaking. *They'll be having a quiet ride.* She chuckled to herself before realising that they would probably spend the ride bitching about her.

Rose was delighted to be out, striding along with her ears pricked in her long, flowing walk. She was even patient with Cloud, who was as good as gold but had to jog to keep up with the mare. Sun glinted weakly through the bare tree branches, Dog plodded stoically behind them with his tail wagging, and Doris chased pheasants and anything else she came across. *She'll sleep tonight.* Hettie smiled to herself. She wondered how Alexander was getting on, as Patrick could be temperamental. *Quite a good match,* she mused ruefully. Maybe Alexander took after his father. That would be a shame. But what about the way he'd looked after her when she had been so hideous at the ball? If the way her mum and Nat told it was true (she didn't remember that part of the evening, herself), he had been very kind and sweet. Especially *considering.* Hettie blushed and nudged Rose forward into a trot to clear her mind, concentrating on keeping the mare's stride collected so Cloud could keep up.

Back at the yard, Hettie turned Rose out, brushed Cloud, and took the dogs to the cottage, grabbing a packet of crisps while she was there. She would load second horses and call Bert to find out where to park. If she could get close to the action, she would go on her own. But if she had to trek across country, Holly or Jodie would have to come to ride the other horse. *It might be more comfortable with Jodie today,* she thought wryly, knowing that she should take Holly and try to build bridges.

Bert told her it had been a quiet morning. Hounds had circled behind the woods, but were now only a stone's throw from their starting place. If she wanted to park beside him, she shouldn't have far to travel. *Great,* Hettie thought, *I can manage on my own.*

"You two can go for lunch!" she called as she climbed into the cab of the smaller, two-horse box.

It had been a frustrating morning's hunting for most of the followers. The hounds had milled about, failing to pick up the man-laid scent. And when they did start to run, it had been in the wrong direction—toward the village or land the hunt were not allowed to cross. Consequently, there had been a lot of standing around and very little hunting.

Grace, because she was leading Fred, hung toward the back with her good friend Kate, who had her daughter Francesca on a lead rein. At least the slow morning had given them the chance to chat. And it was very nice to be on Cora, who was happy to stand still without fidgeting when nothing was happening.

"There's a good number out today," Kate commented, arching her eyebrows at Grace as they both watched Fiona, Imogen, and a couple of other young women circling Alexander. The same group of girls had made sure to pull up next to him every time they had come to a standstill.

"Yes, I fear Al is the prey today." Grace laughed. "Honestly, it's like something out of a Jane Austen novel!"

Alexander was feeling particularly frustrated. He had come out hoping for a good gallop to blow the cobwebs away and get the blood pumping; instead he seemed to have ended up in a blasted social gathering of ex-shags, who hadn't stopped wittering all morning. His face ached from forcing a smile, and he was fast running out of pleasant responses to their inane comments.

Fiona, on the other hand, was very glad the going was slow. She wasn't long on board her horse before she realised that she was far from riding fit; it must have been a year or more since she had even sat on a horse. This particular damn horse was a nightmare; he only wanted to reverse or turn in circles. And when they had occasionally started moving, he was so slow that she couldn't get to the front of the field where Lexi and blasted Imogen were. Grace on the fat cob and her brat on the pony had actually overtaken Fiona twice. At least, being at the back, no one noticed that she was going round the hedges rather than over them.

Gent, still a youngster and used to having Grace or Hettie on his back, was thoroughly confused and upset by this rider who kept kicking him on and yanking the reins at the same time. He was trying his very best to follow commands, but he couldn't work out what the commands were.

Grace had noticed Gent's confusion and the look of mild panic in his eyes. She was furious with herself for allowing the situation, and slightly nervous about what Hettie would have said if she had been there to witness it. Grace couldn't make a scene right now, but she resolved to have a chat with James and suggest that they didn't lend Fiona a mount again.

Imogen Tatler was a very good rider, and she was riding a very good horse. Imo wouldn't normally have stuck close to Alexander, but her mother, who was also hunting, had insisted she "chat him up." She was very aware of her mother's eyes on her every time she hung back. So Imo had hunted alongside him and obediently joined the group of awful girls around him every time they stopped, eyes cast down in mortification, uttering barely a word. She was having a horrid morning, wishing she hadn't come home at all. Imogen was a model; tall, blond, and lithe, she had been spotted by a talent scout when she was fifteen. It had all been rather surreal. Imogen had gone along with the process, mildly flattered, but mostly because "going along with it" was Imogen's way. She hadn't known what else she could do. Painfully shy, an only child, and cowed by her overbearing mother, modelling had possibly been the worst choice of career for Imogen. But she had been successful despite herself. She hated every moment of it: the bullying, the insults, people prodding and manhandling her. But Imogen was still going along with it. The only pleasure she got was from the horses and riding when she came home, and today even that had been spoiled.

As Hettie pulled up in the horsebox, she could see James and Satan halfway up the hill, less than a quarter mile away. The followers were clustered further away but still in sight, and she guessed Don would be in the covert near James with the hounds. *Perfect,* she thought, waving to Bert and lowering the ramp.

Bert wandered over and held Basil, Don's second ride, while Hettie scrambled up onto Klaus, the biggest horse in the yard. All the Melton men were over six feet tall, so they liked their horses big. And although that didn't always make life easy for five-foot-three Hettie, she usually managed well.

"Been dull as ditch water this mornin'," Bert grumbled, nodding toward the wood.

But the second the words were out of his mouth, they heard the hounds take cry. Horses and people raised their heads, horses tensed, riders gathered their reins, and suddenly they were off, streaming across the hillside at full pelt.

"Uh-oh," Bert noted grimly.

"Oh, shit," Hettie agreed.

Basil and Klaus, who had been standing quietly beside the lorry, began to prance and snort, throwing their heads and flaring their nostrils. Hettie instinctively shoved her feet through the stirrup leathers, the irons being too long to reach, and called to Bert, who was getting shoved about by Basil.

"Best give him here, Bert. If I don't get going while they're still in sight, I'll never catch up."

"I'm sure that's not a good idea, Hettie. Leave Basil 'ere with me an' come back for him."

Hettie looked at Bert, limping around on his "good" leg, getting red in the face with the effort of hanging onto Basil. If she rode off now, Basil would get even more unruly, and she couldn't do that to Bert.

"I will be absolutely fine, Bert." Hettie spoke with more conviction than she felt, knowing that Bert wouldn't let her go with both horses if he thought she couldn't cope. "Give him here; I'm going." She took Basil's lead rein, holding it short so that his head would be tight on her knee, and called, "See you in a minute!" She loosened her reins just enough to allow both horses to break into a smart trot. A few strides on, she passed Grace, Kate, and the children heading back toward the horsebox. Nodding in their direction, Hettie saw Grace's eyes enlarge with mild alarm.

For the first half mile or so, the horses, although keyed up and pulling, behaved themselves and trotted energetically. Hettie forced herself to relax, knowing that if she was tense, they would pick up on it. But as they rounded a corner at the end of a high hedge, the hounds and following horses came back into view, still galloping, in the distance. Klaus, frustrated that he wasn't with them, threw a huge buck and started pulling like a train. Basil broke into a bobbing canter beside him. Hettie cursed and gathered her thoughts. She wasn't going to be able to hold Klaus forever, and it was a long climb up to the crest of the hill. Better to let them break into canter, try to keep steady on the track alongside the field, and hope the hill would take some of the steam out of them. The alternative was a tug of war that she was only going to lose. She tipped forward slightly, taking her weight out of the saddle, and relaxed her fingers around the reins. Klaus immediately upped a gear into long, even canter strides. *Keep the rhythm, keep it steady, and keep it calm.* Hettie chanted inside her head, but she realised pretty quickly that the steady canter was getting steadily faster.

As she flew up the hill, other riders began to notice her. It was quite a sight to behold: the slight girl atop the huge white horse, with another horse by her side, her fiery hair streaming behind as they sped ever faster over the ground. To the untrained eye, it might have looked like a dreamy scene from an advertisement. But those in the know quickly realised this was a dangerous situation. And as she got closer, they saw how often she was leaning back in her saddle and taking a pull on her right rein, and how very little effect that pull was having.

Alexander noticed her the moment before both horses broke into gallop, stretching their necks long as they started to race each other. “Good God!” he barked out loud. Steering Patrick away from the others, he charged toward the top of the field in the direction Hettie was heading. To do what, he had no idea, but instinct made him move.

You fucking, fucking idiot, Hettie chastised herself as fear washed through her. *You'll be lucky to get out of this without two injured horses and a broken neck, you stupid girl.* Her arms were already weak from pulling. She had no choice now but to sit and wait out whatever the end of this bolt might bring.

Alexander positioned Patrick across the track at the top of the hill. He watched in trepidation as the two horses, still going flat out, bore down on him from three hundred yards away. “Whoa, boys! Whoa, there!” he repeated in a loud, calm voice as they pounded closer.

Hettie heard his voice and lifted her head to see him ahead of her, like a knight in shining armour. She knew there was nothing he could do to stop two horses in full flight, but she felt thankful he was there all the same. Alexander's voice began filtering through to the horses. Klaus swivelled an ear, and Hettie felt him check his stride beneath her. Both horses were blowing hard, the gallop up the long hill sapping their enthusiasm. And as they heard Alexander and saw their stablemate ahead, blind instinct began to recede and sanity return. They slowed their pace to canter. Relief and exhaustion flooded through Hettie as she tugged weakly at the reins. Eventually she succeeded in slowing them to trot, and with one last effort and haul on the reins, she brought them to a standstill right next to Alexander and Patrick.

"What the fuck was that?" Alexander growled. "Apart from dangerous, idiotic, and totally un-fucking-excusable."

"It was all of the above," Hettie replied in a small voice, dropping her head. She was pale and shaking.

Alexander cursed to himself and shook his head, his anger the result of fear for Hettie's safety and the adrenaline coursing through him. He tried to get a grip on his emotions as he slipped off of Patrick and walked to her side.

"Are you OK?" he asked quietly, putting his hand on her leg.

Kindness was too much, and a small, breathy sob escaped Hettie. "Are the horses all right?" she asked tremulously.

"I'll have a look," Alexander replied. "You OK up there, or do you want to get off?"

"I'm not sure I could stand up right now. Best stay put for a minute," Hettie answered with a wobble in her voice.

Alexander slowly circled both horses, checking their legs and looking closely for cuts or injuries. Hettie realised that they were being watched from a distance by the rest of the members of the hunt, who were frozen in position a field away. Luckily she couldn't see James or Don, who would be ahead in the covert, or Grace, who had been taking Fred back to the lorry. Hettie took a deep breath, gathered her resources, and swung off of Klaus to join Alexander on the ground. It was a long way down, and she stumbled slightly as her legs threatened to give out underneath her. Alexander grabbed her and held her against him.

"Hey, hey." He laughed. "It looks like you got away with it, so don't fall over now." They stood to the side of Klaus, out of sight of the others. Alexander kept his arms wrapped around her to allow her a moment to gather her senses.

"Such a stupid thing to do," Hettie muttered into his chest. "Are you sure they haven't got any injuries?"

Alexander held her shoulders, moving her away from him he looked into her face. "That was a pretty crap judgement call, Hettie. I can't deny that. But, thank God, you're not injured. And the horses are not injured. The gallop up the hill won't have hurt them; it's no more than they would do on any morning's hunting. But it was risky with all those hooves flying about so close to each other. You put yourself in terrible danger bringing two of them out like that. You had your feet through the stirrup leathers, for fuck's sake! Still—no harm done." He reined his tone back in. "Let's get these nags where they're meant to be and put it behind us. James and Don are in the covert; I'll come with you." He gave Hettie a leg up back onto Klaus's back, then vaulted onto Patrick.

Fiona hadn't taken her eyes off the scene at the top of the hill. She was annoyed that something else had taken Alexander's attention. *Who is that girl?* she wondered. They seemed to spend a long time hidden away behind the horses, and Lexi had been quick to go charging to her rescue. Was it that redheaded slut who'd had an affair with her friend Lucy Greaves's brother? Fiona thought she could remember being told that the girl was working for the Meltons. That cow had caused all sorts of trouble and bother already. Was she trying to get her claws into Lexi? The little tart obviously liked to play above her league.

Imogen had watched the bolting horses in horror, wondering if she should do something to help, but frozen to the spot with indecision. She was very relieved when she saw Alexander chasing off to help them, and even more relieved when it ended without disaster. She knew Hettie's mum from way back. Mrs. Redfern had cleaned their house for years. Imogen remembered her as a very nice lady. Hettie's sister, Natalie, had come to work with her mum sometimes. They had played together while Mrs. Redfern did the cleaning.

Second horses exchanged without further mishap, Hettie and Alexander emerged from the covert.

"Are you sure you don't want me to ride back to the horsebox with you?" Alexander asked.

"Christ, no!" Hettie was adamant. "I've taken up enough of your time. Besides, it's a very different thing taking two tired horses back to the lorry than—"

"Than galloping two fresh nutters across country toward the hounds?" Al interrupted, smiling across at her.

Hettie didn't laugh, but the corner of her mouth turned up slightly. She was still mortified by her actions.

She shook her head. "Thanks for being so nice about it. It's more than I deserve. In fact, I should probably be sacked," Hettie said solemnly.

"I doubt that will happen!" Alexander retorted. "I never hear anything but endless praise from James and Grace about how you run the yard. To be honest, I was sceptical. But I can see the horses are in cracking condition, and you do have a way with them. Usually." He added the last comment with a huge grin on his face.

Hettie did manage a small laugh this time.

"Right, Mr. Melton, I'm going to sod off and let you get on," she said briskly. "Satan is being a puppy. Look." She held his reins up by the buckle so they hung loose down the side of his neck, and Satan continued on his steady, plodding walk. "So it will be absolutely fine. I'm going to cut across here and get back to the road that way." She smiled at him and peeled away to the left, calling, "Thanks again!" over her shoulder.

Alexander felt a twinge of regret as he watched her ride away. "See you at home!" he shouted in reply.

Hacking toward the road, Hettie saw Grace galloping to rejoin the field and noticed for the first time that she was riding Cora. Cora and Grace leapt a ditch on their route, and Hettie could hear her calling the rider of a bay thoroughbred to follow her over. The thoroughbred, spinning and reversing in front of the ditch, failed to follow Grace. As she got nearer, Hettie realised the thoroughbred was Gent. Her eyes narrowed. The girl riding him was jabbing him in the mouth with every kick she delivered, and poor Gent was responding by going backward.

"Drop the bloody reins and give him his head!" Hettie hollered over to her. And the girl, shocked into action by the shouted order, surprised herself by complying. Gent immediately cantered forward, popped neatly over the ditch, and galloped away to catch up with the others.

Hettie sighed. Usually she'd have been as mad as hell at that sort of riding on "her" horses, but having nearly finished off two Melton horses herself that morning, who the hell was she to judge?

CHAPTER FOUR

On Saturday evening, Hettie had plans to meet her old friends, Jade and Hannah, in the Fox. After the day she'd had, she was regretting agreeing to go, but she had let the girls down too often to bail out again. They had been nagging her to come out for weeks. At least tomorrow was her day off; she could stay in bed until lunchtime. Although she would pop to the yard to check on the horses that had hunted today, and she would lead Jack out and do late stables because she was right next door. She quite liked a stroll out with the dogs before bed anyway.

But first she needed to call James. She owed him an apology for what had happened today, and best to get it over with before she lost her nerve. She dialled the number for the hall, which rang for so long that Hettie began to hope they were out and she had been given a stay of execution. Grace answered just as Hettie was about to hang up.

"Draymere," Grace pealed.

"Hi, Grace. It's Hettie. I wonder if I could have a word with James."

"Hettie? Is everything all right?" Grace sounded worried. She couldn't remember Hettie calling James before.

"Yes, everything's fine, Grace. I just need a word with him." She didn't want to involve Grace any more than necessary. Hettie knew Grace would stick up for her, and it wasn't fair to put her friend in that position.

"You're not going to resign, are you?" Grace sounded even more alarmed.

Hettie laughed dryly. "No, Grace! I am definitely not going to resign. Really, it's nothing serious!"

"OK, OK," Grace conceded. "Hang on. I'll give him a shout. James! James! Pick up the phone in the office!"

"Draymere!" James boomed from the extension.

Hettie almost giggled with nerves; she already knew she'd rung Draymere. There was a definite pause before she heard the click as Grace hung up her phone. She knew it would be killing Grace not knowing what was going on; the temptation to stay on the line must have tested her good breeding.

"Hello, James." Hettie had prepared her speech in her mind. "I want to apologise for my actions today. It was very ill considered, and I put your horses at risk, and I wanted you to know that I am very, very sorry, and it will absolutely never happen again. I thought I wouldn't have far to ride, and it was only Klaus and Basil, and they're usually so easy, and I—" She stopped abruptly, aware that she had been babbling.

There was a moment's silence.

"Hettie!" James finally boomed. "Forgive me, but can I know what you are actually apologising for?"

Hettie was thrown. It hadn't occurred to her that James wouldn't have heard about her escapade from Alexander. She hadn't thought of the bit of her speech where she explained what had happened.

"Oh, er, second horses today?" She ventured, but silence from James told her he was still none the wiser. So, taking a big breath, Hettie continued. "I brought out both second horses myself, and, um, well, basically I got buggered off with. It was very stupid of me," she finished glumly. "But thankfully the horses were all right."

"Good Lord, Hettie! Are you all right?" James roared. "Klaus and Basil? That must have been quite some white-knuckle ride."

"Oh, I'm fine. But yes, it was. Alexander was great. He helped me stop and looked the horses over."

"Ah, well, thank goodness for Al. And thank you for your apology, Hettie, but I'm sure it isn't necessary. I have always trusted you with my horses, and I can assure you that one cock-up is not going to change that. Good Lord, we've all got ourselves in a pickle on horseback before! I am just glad you got away with it."

"Thanks, James. I can promise you that it won't happen again."

Hettie came off the phone mightily relieved and feeling much more enthusiastic about her night out.

The Fox was buzzing when Hettie arrived. She spotted Hannah and Jade sitting at the corner table, and she waved over the throng of people as she wriggled her way through a group of braying hoorays drinking cider at the bar. She nodded at the Draymere gardener, spotted Dan the farrier at the far end of the bar (and tried to avoid catching his eye), and turned to grin at Holly and her gaggle of friends when Holly screeched a drunken, "Hetieeeeeeee!" at her and waved furiously. *Looks like a few alco pops have brought Holly out of her sulk,* Hettie thought.

It was lovely to see Jade and Hannah again. They got tipsy fairly quickly, ordered a plate of chips to share, and talked about everything from school days to favourite meals, shoe shopping to bad dates, frequently crying with laughter. Hettie had to lower her voice during the bad dates discussion; most of hers were in the bar. Lots of people came over to say hi, and apart from the woman in the braying group who kept giving her the evil eye, Hettie was having a thoroughly good time. She didn't think she even knew the girl, so Hettie wasn't going to let her spoil the evening.

A couple of hours on, braying group moved to the table next to theirs, and shortly after that Alexander and Ted walked in to the pub. Amid the raucous greetings called from every side, Alexander caught Hettie's eye, waved, and grinned at her.

Hettie's tummy did a double flip as she smiled and waved back. He seemed to get better looking every time she saw him.

Evil eye at the next table stood up. "Lexi! Lexi! Ted! Come and join us!" she called frantically. The men walked to the table and chatted, but Hettie overheard Alexander politely rejecting their invitation. He and Ted settled at the bar.

As the evening wore on, a few people left. Apart from the group on the braying table, chatter noise levels subsided to a low hum.

"Must have a pee!" Hettie told her friends, getting up from the table. As she crossed the room, evil eye's voice rang out, loud enough that everyone could hear.

"Lucy, isn't that the slut who shagged your brother?"

Hettie's step faltered slightly before she lifted her head, squared her shoulders, and walked on. *So that's what the evils have been about*, she thought furiously. *Doesn't this village ever forget anything*?

Alexander and Ted couldn't fail to overhear the comment. Ted shook his head; Alexander clenched his teeth. He might not like what Hettie had done, but rudeness like that from Fiona was plain bad form.

When Hettie got back, Alexander and Ted had moved to sit at their table with Hannah and Jade. Evil eye looked like her head was about to explode.

"We thought we would join you ladies for a drink," Alexander drawled loudly as Hettie sat down next to him.

"That's the second time you've come to my rescue today," she whispered gratefully.

Ted kept them entertained for the remainder of the evening. At some point the braying group left, and none of the people at Hettie's table even noticed. Holly staggered out tipsily, leaning on her boyfriend. Hettie fretted briefly that she wouldn't turn up for work the next day. Dan came over to say good-bye, looking dejected and making cow eyes at Hettie. Eventually only the group of five were left in the bar. Hettie and Alexander joined in the conversation and laughed along with the others, but both were keenly aware of sitting so close to each other: legs almost touching under the table; arms resting beside each other's on the tabletop. They were finding it hard to concentrate on anything else.

"Right, people. I'm about done." Jade yawned. "Hannah, are you ready? Shall I call a cab?"

"I would quite like a cigarette," Hettie piped up. "That is, if anyone's got some."

"I'll join you." Alexander produced a packet from his pocket.

Leaving Ted and Hannah chatting and Jade wandering around the pub trying to find a phone signal, Hettie and Alexander stepped out into the cold night air.

"That was such a nice evening," Hettie mused tipsily, wrapping her arms around herself to stave off the cold.

Alexander leaned back against the wall and held out his packet of cigarettes. "Stand closer if you want to keep warm," he said with a slow smile. As Hettie moved nearer, he took her arm, turning her round so her back was against him. He pulled her tightly to him with an arm around her waist. Flicking a cigarette into his mouth, he lit it and passed it forward to Hettie. They silently passed the same cigarette between them, Hettie resting her head on his chest, Alexander's chin on her hair, until the taxi pulled up.

In the car park, Hettie looked at Alexander's Aston Martin. "How the hell are you going to get back down the track in that?" she exclaimed.

"I'm driving," Ted told her. "I've only had a couple of pints. Do you want a lift, Hettie?" He added, "We could always run you back for the Landy tomorrow."

"No, no, definitely not," Hettie insisted. "It barely takes any longer going the country route. And anyway," she laughed, "I wasn't planning on getting out of bed tomorrow."

A vision of Hettie curled up in bed, with tousled sheets barely covering her, flew into Alexander's mind. He closed his eyes briefly to enjoy the picture.

Ted got into the Aston, but Hettie and Al loitered, feeling strangely awkward but not wanting the evening to end.

"Drive carefully, Het," Alexander said eventually as the Aston purred into life. He felt oddly protective and didn't like the idea of her driving back along the track on her own.

"Yes, of course," Hettie replied, impulsively leaning up to kiss him on the cheek before skittering quickly off to the Land Rover.

Ted was laughing and tut-tutted as Alexander climbed into the passenger seat.

"Well, well." Ted chuckled, shaking his head. "The mighty Alexander has got a crush on the stable girl! Now that's a turn up for the books, not to mention a bit of a cliché!"

Alexander glared at him, but Ted was finding the whole thing very amusing. The glare made him laugh even harder.

"I can't see what's so bloody amusing!" Alexander growled.

Ted tried to get a grip on his humour. "No, of course," he said seriously, "it isn't funny at all. It's nice. She's nice. I've just never seen you acting like a love-struck teenager before. Thought you were above all that!" He was off laughing again.

Al grunted. "Can't deny I seem to have a bad case of the hots for her," he conceded grumpily. "God only knows why. She might be a looker, but she's definitely not my type. I don't much care for women with a reputation."

Ted looked at him sideways. "What sort of a reputation?" he asked. He wasn't laughing any more.

"You know damn well what sort of reputation. You're the one who's taken so much pleasure recounting the juicy details. She's a serial shagger, and worse than that, she doesn't care if they're married. She's a home-wrecker, Ted."

Ted knew by the grim set of Alexander's jaw that they had strayed into dangerous territory. But fuck it. Hadn't they pussyfooted around this subject with Al for long enough?

"Jesus, Al." He sighed. "That was bloody years ago. Surely you can't condemn the poor girl for that. She could barely have been more than a kid. If anyone was to blame in that situation, it was that bastard Greaves. Rumour has it he's done the same thing plenty of times since!"

Alexander didn't answer, so Ted continued. "And as for being a serial shagger, where the hell did you get that from?"

"From you, of course!" Alexander snapped. "Christ, every time you updated me on gossip from home, there was some story about who had just fucked Hettie Redfern."

Ted looked incredulous. "Really?" he asked. "I can't say I remember even mentioning her. To be honest, I didn't know you knew her. So if I dropped her name into a story, it must have been as a byline."

Alexander shifted uncomfortably in his seat.

"Ah." Realisation dawned on Ted. "You've got history, haven't you? You've shagged her before?"

"No! Yes. Well, almost," Alexander spluttered. "Bloody years ago, an 'almost shag.' She barely remembered, so don't go broadcasting the news about in any of your colourful stories."

"She didn't remember?" Ted was laughing again. "Oh, dear, that must have been a massive knock to the mighty Alexander's ego!"

"Yeah, yeah, OK. Thanks for that, bro." Al looked sheepish. "To be fair, she was very pissed. At the hunt ball, the year Dad took her on at Draymere."

"Very gentlemanly of you, Al, shagging the pissed stable girl." Ted arched his eyebrows in mock horror.

"Yeah, well, it wasn't actually like that. And I told you I didn't shag her."

"Christ, she wasn't the girl who threw up in Dad's car?" Ted blurted out.

Alexander grinned. "Yup! Twice! And on my shoes, and at least once when I got her home, too." It felt strangely good to be telling the story. Although if Alexander thought about it, Ted was the last person he should be telling it to. The drink must have loosened his tongue.

"And you still fancy her after that? Bloody hell, it must be love!" Ted was intrigued by the whole thing. Alexander had always been so uptight and self-bloody-righteous. A damn good bloke, without a doubt, but always so cool and aloof, and always in charge. He could come across as arrogant and judgemental. Hell, he was judgemental, there was no escaping that. And transgressions once committed would rarely be forgiven. But this was a side to Al he hadn't seen before. Finding it amusing that some girl he was trying to shag had thrown up over him? Ted was nonplussed.

"It is very definitely not love!" Alexander barked, returning to normal form. "It would, however, be nice to finish that fuck."

"Well, if it's just a fuck you want, Alexander," Ted fired back, "why the hell do you care who she's had before?"

They completed the journey in silence. Ted ruminated on "the incident of the vomit in Lord Melton's car." Their father had always been a stickler for rules, to put it mildly. The law was laid down repeatedly in the lead-up to the hunt ball: *all of them* were to attend, and there would be *no womanising* and *no drinking* (this last rule didn't seem to apply to their father himself, who had rarely taken his head out of a bottle since their mother left). They were ambassadors for Draymere! And as such, absolutely no disrespectful or outlandish behaviour would be tolerated. "Enough shame has been brought on this family!" Lord Melton would shout, going red in the face. "And I will not allow my sons to bring more shame by behaving like thugs and wasters!" Those had not been happy times for any of them.

James had stoically stepped up and tried his damnedest to follow these and all the other crazy orders their father issued. He was loyal to a fault, but spent as little time with their father as was possible. And he felt very grateful to have lovely Grace and his own house to go back to. Ted escaped to boarding school and got clever at disobeying rules and not being caught. And Alexander? Well, Alexander was as angry with their mother as their father was, and that to Alexander meant he was totally on Father's side. He identified with Lord Melton's fury and sense of betrayal. He abided by the rules in support of his father, managing to excuse the old man's selfish, rude, and erratic behavior. He would attend the hunt ball because his father needed him there, and he would abide by the rules to avoid causing him any more heartache. And the rest of the time, he would stay the hell away from Draymere so he didn't have to face the reality of being in the house where his mother no longer lived.

Only, on this occasion, Alexander had not adhered to the rules. Or at least Lord Melton believed he hadn't. The shouting that followed had been excruciating to overhear, Ted thought. So he couldn't begin to imagine what it had been like for Al, shut in the office with his father. The language that Father had used! The sneering comments and roared accusations that their mother had left because of Alexander. Ted shook his head. It was painful to remember, even now. *No father should speak to his son like that.* If Alexander had defended himself, Ted hadn't heard him. Al had packed his bag and left straight after the row. When Ted had stopped him on the front steps to offer sympathy and support, Alexander had been dismissive: "Don't worry about it," he'd said. "I'm not. He's right. I fucked up. And anyway, it isn't me he's angry with; it's her." But Al had come to Draymere even less often after that.

As their car turned into the drive, Ted wondered if he should mention that he'd seen the "her" in question last week. That, as always, she had asked after Al. *Probably not the best time,* he persuaded himself. *Coward,* his inner voice whispered.

Alexander's musings had also turned to his father. He really ought to visit the old man. Not that his father would know him when he got there, or even know he had a visitor. Still, it had been too long since his last visit. The weekly calls he made to the home were a cop-out, and he knew it. It was so damned hard seeing his father like that, though. James visited every week, and Grace, bless her, went frequently. *You need to man up,* he told himself as they pulled up in front of the hall.

Al said good night to Ted but stayed outside for another cigarette. He wandered to the kitchen garden where he had a view along the track. Stepping behind the wall when he saw the lights of the Land Rover bob into view, he kept watch until Hettie pulled up at the cottage. He hung around a little longer, until the light coming on and Doris barking reassured him that Hettie was inside.

CHAPTER FIVE

On Sunday morning, after stumbling sleepily downstairs at seven to feed and let the dogs out (and creeping outside in her pj's and Uggs to make sure Holly was at the yard), Hettie snuggled back into her warm bed and slept for another three hours. At ten o'clock, Doris couldn't stand the lack of attention any longer and leapt onto the bed to wake Hettie by frantically licking her face.

Hettie woke up refreshed and energetic. She turned on the radio while she made herself some porridge and sang tunelessly along to the songs as she planned her lovely, free day. She would take the dogs for a walk, check the yard on the way, and lead Jack out before she went to her mum's for Sunday roast. Heaven! She would take Doris with her so her mum could do those sketches.

In the hall, James questioned Alexander about the incident with second horses. Feeling like a turncoat, Al recounted events as best he could without dropping Hettie in it. James looked concerned as he ate his bacon and sausages.

Ted was late down, and arrived in the kitchen as Alexander was leaving.

"I'm off to Swindon," Al said. "Morning, Ted." And he was gone.

Ted fetched himself a cup of coffee and sat at the table with Grace and Georgia. The boys were long gone, tearing about the hall, burning off the excess energy that food seemed to generate. Ted cleared his throat.

"Grace, ahem, I wonder if I could have a word with you. About something slightly sensitive?"

"Of course, Ted." Grace looked faintly wary.

"Only it's been stewing on my mind all night," Ted continued, "and I know this family is rubbish at talking about things, but, um, it's about Alexander and Mother."

"Ah." Grace sighed. "Yes, Ted, go on."

"Yes, well, I saw her again last week. Um, Celia, you know. She was desperate for news of Al and, well, this whole thing about Mother being the she-devil, and Pa being the heartbroken victim, it's not right and it's not fair, and it's not good for any of us, especially Alexander."

Grace sighed again, distractedly popping bits of sausage into Georgia's mouth. "I couldn't agree with you more, Ted." She spoke carefully. "But I simply don't know what on earth we can do about it. You know yourself that nothing will change Alexander's mind, not once he's decided on something."

"Yes, I know, I know," Ted agreed. "But do you not think we are in some way facilitating it, Grace? I mean, I don't know about you, but I'm too scared to even tell him I've seen her, let alone that she is asking after him. It is breaking Mother's heart, you know. And I know that deep down, it's breaking Al's heart too. That's the worst of it; he loved her as much as the rest of us, if not more. He still loves her; of course he does. That's what all this is about. I mean, do you tell him when Celia visits?"

"No, I can't say that we do," Grace said dolefully. "I mean, to be honest, it hasn't been an issue. Alexander was never here, but now, if he's moving into the gatehouse…I must admit I've been wondering what we were going to do. I had rather hoped James would come up with a solution—talk to him or something. I fear we have all been rather cowardly and buried our heads in the sand."

"Does he read her letters?" Ted asked. "I know she writes to him here."

"I have no idea," Grace replied. "I mean, I always forward them or put them in his room. But as to whether he reads them or burns them, your guess is as good as mine."

"And my guess is he burns them," Ted stated glumly. "Look, shall I talk to James? Or will you? At the very least, we should stop pussyfooting around, and keeping secrets—well, lying, really, about the fact that we are in touch with her. I know it won't be pretty." He finished grimly, "But, hell, it's been fifteen years. Al needs to wake up and smell the coffee."

♦♦♦

It was a beautiful, crisp winter morning. Hettie walked to the far paddocks, past Rose's field, stopping to have a cuddle with her and the broodmares she shared a field with. The youngsters in the next-door paddock looked like a herd of wild ponies, with their thick winter coats and unbrushed tails. They snorted and stared in exaggerated horror as Hettie wandered through their field, glancing a keen eye over them, petting any that would let her near. Bert kept watch on the broodmares and the youngsters, riding up on the quad bike each day to check them while they were turned away for the winter.

By the time Hettie got to the woods, Dog looked like he'd gone about as far as he could manage, so she regretfully turned for home. Everything was under control on the yard. Sunday was the horses' day off. They would be turned out in groups of three or four to play for a couple of hours, so Jodie and Holly were busy putting on turnout rugs. Hettie thought the yard could do with another sweep, but she firmly buttoned her lip.

Moody Jack greeted her with his huge bottom, as usual. She had been leading him out in a bridle, but he had been very well behaved, so today she grabbed a head-collar from the hook outside his stable. He wasn't lame anymore; tomorrow she would give him some gentle ridden exercise.

Jack was angelic until Hettie led him past the hunters turned out in the paddock. The horses chose that moment to start galloping around the field, bucking with the joy of being free. When Hettie reached the main drive, Jack was going sideways, upward, and taking huge leaps forward, with Hettie hanging onto the rope and trying to keep some semblance of control. Alexander, turning into the drive on his way back from visiting Digger, caught sight of them as Jack reared up on his hind legs. Hettie let the rope slip through her fingers in an effort to keep clear of his flashing hooves. He pulled up behind her and, grabbing Digger's lunge rein from the passenger seat, went to lend a hand.

"A bridle might have been sensible," he said, but he was at least smiling this time.

"He's been good as gold until today," Hettie gasped as Jack spun around again.

Alexander struggled to get close enough to fix the lunge rein onto Jack's head-collar, but eventually they both had hold of him. Jack, more impressed by a six-foot bloke than he was ever going to be by a five-foot girl, stopped being quite so unruly and made do with jogging annoyingly, swinging his back end from side to side.

"Thanks," Hettie said. "It seems every time I see you, you have to extract me from some awkward situation. To be honest, it's getting embarrassing."

"Yes, every time," Alexander agreed calmly. "Right back to the very first time we met at the hunt ball."

Hettie's face went scarlet. She was very grateful that Alexander couldn't see her from the other side of Jack's neck.

"Ah, yes," she said so quietly that Alexander had to strain to hear her over the clattering of Jack's hooves on the drive. "Still hands-down the most embarrassing, awkward situation to date."

"Well, we could work on that," Alexander drawled. "And there are some parts of that particular situation I quite enjoy remembering."

My God, Hettie thought. *Is he flirting?* And while her face burned even redder, her stomach started frolicking like the horses in the field. She managed a dry laugh and decided to change the subject.

"Tell me, Mr. Melton, why do you happen to carry a lunge line in your car? Were you a Boy Scout or something?" she said teasingly.

So Alexander told her the story of Digger: finding him, rescuing him, and bringing him home. He told her how shitty it was putting his dog in quarantine, and they laughed when he recounted his efforts to walk Digger on a three-foot lead.

"Anyway," Al finished, "I thought I'd try walking him on a lunge line, and it worked quite well today. That's where I'd been when I came up the drive."

Jack had settled to a steady walk, calmed by their conversation and laughter. Al and Hettie talked easily as they circled the loop of the drive and headed back toward the yard.

"I think this boy is ready for some proper exercise," Alexander said as he unclipped the lunge rein outside Jack's stable.

"I was thinking the same myself," Hettie agreed.

♦♦♦

When Hettie arrived at her mum's, early for once, Bert was there.

"Ah, Miss Hettie!" he cried. "Lovely day for it! I was fetching your mother some vegetables. Have you recovered from yesterday's ordeal?"

Hettie fired him a warning glance, but too late, her mum was on to it.

"What ordeal?" She stopped stirring the gravy. "What happened, Hettie? Are you all right?"

"Yes, Mum, I'm fine." Hettie sighed. "The horses played up, that's all. It was nothing. I didn't fall off. Look." She stood with her arms wide. "No injuries."

Bert mouthed, "Sorry," and winked at her.

The kitchen was full of the smell of roasting beef. Hettie's mouth watered. Doris got busy, head down, checking every corner of the house, scuttling eagerly from room to room without pausing for breath.

"Righto, I'll be off!" Bert said brightly.

"Why don't you stay for dinner, Bert?" Hettie asked enthusiastically. "I'm sure Mum has made enough for an army, haven't you, Mum?"

"I have, actually." Anna chuckled dryly. "Do stay if you'd like to." She exchanged a brief smile with Bert.

Bert had never been married. He'd been shy as a young man, driven by his ambition to become a jockey. Travelling the country wherever the work took him, rarely settling in one place for long, and working every daylight hour, the opportunity for relationships passed him by. He still lived in a cottage on the Draymere Estate, watching over his horses. And for the most part, he was content to be alone. But he wasn't going to turn down one of Anna Redfern's roasts. Especially not when the alternative was an overcooked carvery at the Fox.

Anna served roast beef with all the trimmings: perfectly rare, tender meat; crisp Yorkshire puddings; golden roast potatoes, crunchy on the outside, soft on the inside; and mountains of vegetables. Hettie had taken her mum's cooking for granted when she lived at home; now it was a welcome indulgence. She pestered Bert with questions about the current crop of youngsters. Then realising that all this horse talk was rather excluding her mum, Hettie asked how the book illustration was going, and if she had heard from Nat. Anna was looking particularly pretty, with her strawberry-blond hair curling softly around her face and her cheeks glowing from cooking. Hettie wondered out loud if she'd had her hair done. Anna laughed and shook her head. After apple pie and custard, they were all thoroughly stuffed. Hettie cleared up and chatted to Bert while her mother sketched. Doris proved a perfect model, posing endearingly, to Hettie's wry amusement.

Hettie left before Bert in the end. The TV had gone on, and the pair of them were dozing off in front of a black-and-white film, so she left them to it. Dog would be missing her. He had been deeply put out when she had taken Doris but not him.

Hettie knew she should do some housework, but the dinner had made her lazy. She had a glass of wine instead and sat on the sofa with her laptop, searching eBay for stuff she might want to buy.

At eight thirty, feeling sleepy and realising guiltily that she had worked her way through most of the bottle of wine, Hettie decided to do late stables ahead of time and get an early night. The ground outside was frozen and crunched as she walked. The air seemed to spark with cold. As the lights came on, the horses looked over their doors, blinking sleepily. One by one she checked water and filled any empty hay nets (except Gilbert's, since Gil could get fat on thin air and was on a permanent diet). When she finished, she took pity on him and leant over his door to feed him a handful of hay. Hettie didn't have favourites, but Gil was such a naughty character it was hard not to love him. She stood at the stable door watching the pony, and that was where Alexander found her when he walked onto the yard.

Alexander, outside for a cigarette again, had noticed the lights come on at the yard and walked down to make sure everything was all right. As a rare visitor to Draymere, he wasn't familiar with the yard routines.

His heart skipped when he noticed Hettie. *Christ, you've got it bad,* he scolded himself, wondering if the real reason he'd come down was to see if it was her.

"Hello, there," he said, feigning surprise. "I saw the lights on and wondered if anything was amiss."

"Oh, yes, hello!" Hettie's heart was skittering too, and her answer was slightly breathless. "I'm doing late stables. Earlier than usual—I've had one of Mum's dinners and a glass of wine, so was at risk of falling asleep on the sofa."

Al stood at the stable door beside her. "Who's this?" he asked. "At least we've got one that's the right size for you."

Hettie nudged him sharply in the ribs. "This is Gil." She laughed. "Fred's naughty pony. He's a right character."

"Even more suited to you, then." Alexander grinned.

"Am I a character?" Hettie raised her eyebrows.

"Well, you're certainly not like anyone I've met before." He laughed in reply.

"Is that a good thing?" Hettie narrowed her eyes uncertainly.

Alexander stroked a curl from her face. "I am not entirely sure." He spoke thoughtfully. "But good or bad, I seem to find it captivating."

They stared at each other, and then they were kissing. Hesitantly at first, but the kiss rapidly became passionate. Hettie's hands moved to Alexander's head, her fingers winding through his hair. Alexander held her tightly. When they broke the kiss, both were breathing heavily.

"Is there anywhere we can go?" Alexander asked.

"The dugout?" Hettie suggested.

Alexander lifted her up, pressing her butt against him. Hettie wrapped her legs around his waist. With their faces so close, they couldn't help but start kissing again.

Dog growled a low warning from his rug, and Hettie pulled away from Al to reassure him. "It's OK, Dog. Don't worry."

He gave her a long look and laid his head back down.

Alexander strode to the dugout with Hettie in his arms and pushed the door open with his foot. The room was cold and smelt damp and faggy, but neither of them noticed as they tumbled onto the battered leather sofa.

"I want to feel your skin," he whispered against her mouth as he unzipped her coat and pushed it aside. Hettie moaned softly. Raising himself on one arm, Al stared down at her as he lifted the front of her jumper. He slid it slowly up her body, and his fingers trailing across her skin made Hettie tingle with longing. She wasn't wearing a bra. Alexander's breath caught in his throat as his exploration revealed first one pert, free breast and then the other. His thumb circled lazily over her rigid nipple. And when she moaned again, he dropped his head to kiss her, hard this time, his tongue thrusting into her mouth. She writhed underneath him, her hands pulling at his shirt and his jeans, wanting him naked but trapped underneath him and unable to achieve her aim.

"Patience," Alexander drawled, kneeling beside the sofa. He pushed her jumper higher and took her nipple in his mouth, sucking and teasing with his tongue. He glanced up at her face to drink in the sight of her pleasure. Eyes closed, lips apart, breathless with need, Hettie tried to slow the urges building so strongly inside her as Al rained slow, deliberate kisses over her ribs and down to her navel. With his hand still cupping a breast, he knelt upright and stared into her eyes as he unbuttoned her jeans. Hettie's eyes grew wider. Alexander was breathing heavily, his eyes dark with desire as she gazed into them. He kept his eyes on her as he gently slid her jeans and knickers down, and then he wrenched his eyes away to look at her there. A low, appreciative growl escaped him as he gazed at her slim, pale thighs and the neat triangle of fine, dark hair. He bent to kiss her stomach and her thighs. Sparks of pleasure fired through Hettie; the dark pull of need was becoming almost too much to bear. Parting her thighs with his hands, he moved his head lower and trailed his tongue slowly across her clitoris with a long, deliberate sweep.

"Oh, my God," Hettie moaned, her hands flying to his head, fingers entwined desperately in his hair, as his mouth continued the delicious, torturous caress. When she couldn't take any more, she pulled his head away. "My turn," she croaked, swinging up to kneel on the sofa. Looking into his eyes as she unbuttoned his shirt with shaking fingers, Hettie leaned forward to kiss his neck and chest, nuzzling into him, liking the feel of the hair there against her cheek. She stared hungrily at the thin, dark hairline of promise that led below the waistband of his jeans and at the magnificent bulge she could see pressing against the denim. Letting her fingers press hard against it on their journey to the button of his jeans, she leaned forward and kissed him, darting her tongue into his mouth as she undid him.

They both moaned as his cock came free, and Hettie grasped him with both hands. Sitting back on her heels, she looked down at him, encircled by her hands, rigid and throbbing beneath her fingers. She wanted to kiss and taste, but as she moved to lower her head, Alexander took her shoulders and pushed her gently backward. She could tell by the desperate need in his eyes that he was as close to going over the edge as she was. Laying her back on the sofa, he stretched beside her, cupping her buttocks to pull her close. She could feel his cock pressing against her stomach. They kissed, deeply and slowly, revelling in the anticipation of what was to come, exploring each other's mouths. Hettie's hands trailed over the back of his head, across his shoulders, and gripped his arms. An unwelcome thought popped into her head. *Shit, what about protection?* Every urge in her body told her to ignore it. She didn't want to stop; she didn't want to break this moment. But her conscience argued back. *You don't know where he's been. It only takes once.* Reluctantly she took her mouth from his. Avoiding meeting his gaze, she whispered in a hesitant voice, "Um, I don't suppose you've got a condom on you, have you?"

She felt Alexander still against her, and then he thrust himself up on his arms. "Fuck!" He growled in frustration. "Of course I haven't got a condom! Jesus! I would have thought a girl like you would be on the pill!"

As soon as the words were out of his mouth, he regretted them.

Hettie froze, stunned. She couldn't believe he had said that. "What the fuck do you mean by that?" she hissed coldly.

Alexander lifted a placating arm, but he could see the anger in Hettie was building. "I'm sorry," he said flatly. "That was out of order."

Hettie scrabbled away from him and leapt from the sofa, desperately pulling at her clothes to redress herself. "Fucking right it was out of order!" she roared, almost shaking with fury. *Do not lose it in front of this man. Do not lose it in front of this man,* she recited to herself through the red rage in her head.

Outside, Dog and Doris, hearing their mistress shout, started barking in worried confusion. The horses shifted nervously, heads high, eyes wide with alarm.

Alexander swung to sit on the sofa as Hettie furiously buttoned her jeans.

"I was joking, Hettie," he tried, knowing it sounded weak. "I didn't mean it; it was frustration. I'm sorry. I take it back."

"A girl like me?" Hettie stared at him, her look incredulous and almost imploring. She struggled to fight back the threatening tears of fury and the unreasonable desolation that was engulfing her.

Alexander said nothing. He didn't know what to say. In his mind he was cursing himself for speaking the words out loud. But he'd said it, and there was nothing he could do to change that now.

With hands shaking in anger, Hettie finally succeeded in righting her clothes. Drawing her shoulders back and taking a deep breath, she took a final look at Alexander.

"Stay the fuck away from me, Alexander Melton," she said clearly and evenly. "I don't ever want to see you or speak to you again." She walked out the door of the dugout, slamming it behind her as she left.

Alexander sat quietly in the half-light for a while longer. He felt wrung out, deflated. What a stupid thing to say. She had looked destroyed. *It was only the truth,* the bitter voice in his head argued back. He sighed heavily before standing and fastening his clothes. *Fucking idiot thing to say when you're about to get your end away.* He was disgusted with himself for thinking it.

He walked back to the hall with his shoulders hunched, hands thrust deeply in his pockets. There was a taxi parked on the drive, and Ted was descending the steps with his travel bag. He looked like a rabbit caught in the headlights when he spotted Alexander.

After Ted had spoken to Grace, she had taken his concerns to James. They had all decided, reluctantly, that they should start being truthful about their contact with Celia, no matter how much it angered Alexander. So Ted had resolved to tell him before he left, but having hunted the house and discovered Al was nowhere to be found, guilty relief had washed over him; he could make his escape and call him later in the week. It would be easier to say from the other end of the phone.

"Off then, Ted?" Alexander muttered.

"Yes, yes, just leaving," Ted blustered. They shook hands. Ted walked to the taxi, and Alexander started up the steps.

"Oh, Al." Ted mustered his courage, hand on the taxi door. "I forgot to tell you. I saw Mother last week. She asked after you." He leapt into the taxi, quickly closing the door behind him, resisting the urge to shout, "Drive!"

Alexander stood on the top step, teeth gritted, as a torrent of emotions burst through him. *How dare Ted? How could he mention that woman*? His breath was jagged, fists clenched. He wanted to punch the wall. It took him a long minute to wrestle back control. The violence of his feelings abated, and he could breathe again. He tried to clear his mind of Ted's comment. *Don't think about it,* he told himself. *Well, it proves one thing,* he congratulated himself furiously as he turned to go in the door. *I am well rid of home-wrecker Hettie. What had I been thinking of going back there?*

CHAPTER SIX

The fallout from the row between Alexander and Hettie went unnoticed by anyone else. Life over the next few weeks followed its normal routine.

Hettie considered briefly if she should hand her notice in, but dismissed the idea instantly. She was damned if she was going to let Alexander Melton drive her away from her life, and she doubted he would be recounting the story to anyone. Doris got clingy, and Dog stayed close to her side, both animals sensing her turbulent emotions. She considered seriously whether she ought to move out of the area altogether, wondering angrily if she was going to be able to carry this scarlet woman reputation for the rest of her life. She ruefully acknowledged that her attachments were usually brief, or ended badly, and that her choices were always drunken. But she couldn't see why anyone thought they had a right to judge her for that.

Still thorough and efficient in her work, her gloomy demeanour and snapped orders caused Jodie, Holly, and even Bev to raise their eyebrows at each other and keep out of her way. She bought a packet of cigarettes, then another. Grace looked on with concern when Hettie only stayed in the dugout for as long as it took to smoke one cigarette. Speaking little, leaving the others to it, she got back to the work on the yard. She snapped uncharacteristically at Dan when he came to reshoe the horses and asked Hettie out for a drink. She was off men altogether, she vowed. They were nothing but trouble.

Alexander threw himself into renovating the gatehouse, doing as much of the work as he was able to himself. He spent every spare hour ripping up carpets, tearing out fittings, and clearing rubbish away. Physical activity usually lifted his spirits, but when he returned to the hall after dark each day, his mood got blacker and blacker. Artie and Fred stopped asking him to wrestle with them, and Georgia's bottom lip wobbled whenever he entered the room. James and Grace sighed and put it down to the fact that James had told Al that Celia would be visiting before Christmas, and that if he didn't want to be around her, he would have to make himself scarce. Alexander had left the room without comment. He bumped into Ewan when he was in Cirencester and agreed to meet for a drink, and he finally accepted Fiona's dogged pleas to go for a coffee. The only thing that lightened his mood for a couple of days was bringing Digger home. Digger joined him at work in the gatehouse all day, and he slept in the kitchen garden at night. The family saw little of either of them.

His coffee with Fiona quickly turned into a casual shag. Frankly it was easier than listening to her talk. His urges were sated briefly, but it was a loveless encounter on Alexander's part. It annoyed him how Fiona hollered and threw herself about during the act. And she kissed like a hoover. When thoughts of Hettie crept into his mind, he stamped on them defiantly and concentrated on Fiona's generous bouncing bosom to drag himself back to the moment. Alexander's lack of real pleasure in the experience didn't stop him going back a second time, and then a third. It became a regular occurrence, and he started turning up at her house whenever he felt the need. It cleared his mind of dark thoughts. Digger waited patiently outside the door. He rarely had to wait long.

His evening with Ewan had the potential to be more engaging. They talked about the times they had shared growing up together. Ewan asked Alexander what he was planning to do next with his life. Married now and with a baby on the way, Ewan wondered if he might be interested in setting up a joint veterinary practice. Alexander nodded his interest and tried to sound enthusiastic about Ewan's scheme, but was unable to clear from his mind that Ewan was another bloke Hettie had slept with.

On the one occasion when Hettie and Alexander were in the Fox at the same time (Alexander with Fiona, Hettie with Bev and Holly, who had dragged her out to try and cheer her up), they sat in distant corners of the room and studiously ignored each other. Hettie refused to be cheered, and Alexander listened grim-faced as Fiona bitched viciously about "that little slut" in the corner and the havoc she had wrecked on the Greaves family. Every spiteful detail spilled from her mouth. Alexander decided the only way to shut her up was to take her home and fuck her, so they left.

He was rough with her that night. Fiona seemed to enjoy it and hollered all the more, but Alexander went home filled with disgust and self-loathing.

Hettie hated herself for the painful twist in her gut as she watched them leave together.

Bev observed them both and wondered what the hell was going on.

♦ ♦ ♦

At the end of November, Grace asked Hettie if she would pop up to see James when she had a moment. Hettie went cold with fear. *Has he said something?* she questioned herself desperately, brushing Belle with unusual vigour. *What on earth will James say? Will he sack me?*

She came out of Belle's stable as Grace left the dugout and blurted nervously, "Grace, can't you tell me? Whatever it is James wants?" She could bear it from Grace, but how on earth could she have that conversation with James?

Grace was concerned. She touched Hettie's arm. "Hettie, whatever is it? I can't ever remember seeing you like this before.

Is there something we've done to upset you? Is the work getting you down?" She had mentioned Hettie's low mood to James, wondering out loud if the workload was too much, if it was getting on top of her. But she had no idea why James wanted to talk to Hettie.

"No, no, everything is fine." Hettie rallied. "I just wondered, you know, what James had to tell me that you couldn't pass on instead."

"Oh, gosh, I'm sure it's nothing," Grace reassured. "He didn't say about what. But honestly, Hettie, we are both more than happy with everything you do for us here. You are not to worry. It will be about one of the horses or something. You'll see."

Hettie tried to believe her. But she failed to get any enjoyment from morning exercise on the horses, her mind full of questions about what James would say and how she was going to answer. By the time she put her last horse of the day away and found herself with a moment when she could go up to the hall, she had resolved that if James mentioned *that,* she would leave. There and then. She would pack up and move on, bugger abandoning them mid–hunting season. Alexander could take over the mucking out; he seemed to have nothing else to do except make a God-awful noise banging about in the gatehouse all day and night. Hettie was distracted as she entered the kitchen garden on her way to the back door. She only noticed the unfortunate looking scrap of grey dog when he stood up as she passed.

"Well, hello," she said quietly, squatting down. "You must be Digger. How nice to meet you." Digger stared solemnly, but his tail gave a hint of a wag, so Hettie extended her hand and let him sniff it. Digger sniffed, appeared satisfied, and moved to stand against Hettie's leg. Staring deliberately past her, he allowed her to scratch his chin.

Hettie had just made the connection that if Digger was here, Alexander wasn't far away, when the kitchen door flew open and Alexander came out wearing a dust-covered boiler suit. Hettie jumped up, and Digger, alarmed, shot back to his spot.

"He doesn't like people," Alexander snapped haughtily without breaking his stride.

"No, only snakes, apparently," Hettie spat back, walking past him and into the hall.

Alexander almost laughed. *Pretty good comeback*, he mused before stamping his humour down, irritated by the fact that his pulse had quickened again.

Hettie was glad of the encounter; her adrenaline was up, and she was ready for James and whatever he was going to throw at her. She would bloody well give as good as she got. She knocked sharply on the office door.

"Come in!" James boomed. Hettie entered and nodded at him. "Ah, Hettie. Good. Please, have a seat."

He gesticulated toward the chair opposite him, but Hettie wouldn't have any of it. "No, thank you, James. I would rather stand," she said snootily. "What was it that you wanted to see me about?"

James was mildly wounded by her officious manner, but he mustered his thoughts and ploughed on. "Right, well. Hettie, I've been thinking about that matter the other week, and, well…are you sure you won't sit? I was rather hoping we could have a chat about it."

Hettie lifted her chin and shook her head determinedly.

"Right, well." James stumbled on, confused. "Grace and I have been chatting, well, about your workload, you know, and, well, we are concerned that we expect too much of you, what with the number of horses…"

Now Hettie was confused, too. Did he think she'd ended up in the dugout with his brother because *her workload was too heavy?* Or was this his way of getting around it, saying she couldn't cope with the job so he could fire her? His words kept coming, but they weren't making any sense.

"...and of course, that unfortunate incident. You should never have been put in that position..."

Hettie's face began to glow.

"...so we wondered, really, if it was time to get some extra help on the yard. What do you think?" He stopped.

"What?" Hettie looked at him blankly.

This meeting wasn't going at all as James had expected. He had thought he was passing on good news and that Hettie would be delighted to have an extra pair of hands on the yard. Grace had said she was in a strange mood, but this wasn't the Hettie he knew at all. Good Lord, she almost seemed angry with him. He tried again.

"A couple of days a week, maybe? Hunting days, at least. I know Beverly doesn't work weekends. And, well, you had to take second horses on your own. You should never have been put in that position. Absolutely not. And I know you work long hours and long weeks, and we are eternally grateful for the effort you put in, but someone else, part time? That would make life easier, surely?"

Hettie dropped her chin and looked at him as realisation dawned. *Christ, I've got this really arse-upwards, haven't I?* she thought.

"Oh, James!" she burst out, almost laughing with relief as she dropped into the earlier-offered chair. "Yes! Yes, that would be wonderful!"

James was, if anything, even more disconcerted by this sudden change of demeanour. *I should have got Grace to deal with this,* he thought uncomfortably.

"I am so sorry, James." Hettie sensed his discomfort. "I thought I was here for a rollicking. I probably came over defensive."

James laughed, happy that things seemed to be returning to normal. "A rollicking?" he asked. "Good Lord, Hettie, what could you possibly have done that would make me summon you to the hall for a rollicking?"

He continued to chuckle, failing to notice Hettie's cheeks redden as she shot back quickly, "Nothing, nothing, of course." She attempted to chuckle with him.

They talked about the new role. They would look for someone who could come in two or three days a week, definitely Saturdays and hopefully the midweek hunting days. The person should have experience and be able to cope with morning exercise, and in a perfect world would be up to taking second horses as well.

"There is one thing I must make clear," James interjected. "I do not want you, or anyone else, attempting to take both second horses out on your own again. It is simply too much of a risk. Damn it, I would rather go without a second horse!"

"Yes, James. I understand," Hettie said contritely. "It was a bad call on my part. I'm sorry."

"No, no, I am not blaming you. Not in any way," James went on vehemently. "We've allowed it to continue; it was our fault. Bert told me he'd informed you that things were quiet when you set out, and Alexander said the hounds weren't running when you got on. You know they all spoke strongly in your defence, Hettie, so don't think you were in any way to blame. It was our fault. We've left you overstretched and understaffed, and because you've coped, we turned a blind eye. So *I* am sorry, Hettie. It's me who should be apologising."

James had gone red in the face in his determination to get the point across. Hettie found herself a little bit choked. There was an awkward pause while they both recovered their footing.

"So, I'll put an ad in the local papers." Hettie broke the silence brightly.

“Yes, good idea, and maybe a notice on the Ag college board. Whatever you think best, I’m sure.” James sat up straight and shuffled the papers on his desk to indicate an end to their meeting. He felt rather exhausted.

♦♦♦

Fiona Harding was very pleased with the way things were shaping up. She had certainly whacked that little cow from the stables into orbit. Not that she had ever really been competition. Good Lord, that would be unthinkable. There was just something about her that Fiona didn’t like. Well, everything about her, really, from her pert little arse to her ridiculous red curls. The bitch even had the audacity to insult her riding! She wouldn’t forget that in a hurry. No, Hettie Redfern had better keep out of the way, or Fiona would wipe the floor with her. Fiona had made sure Lexi was fully aware of the sordid details about her dirty little affair, and if she had embellished a bit, well, so what? She had an instinctive distasteful feeling that the girl might be a distraction to Lexi, so she was determined to make damn sure he knew what a tramp she was. With the way that ghastly mother of his had behaved, Fiona was sure he would steer well clear of Hettie when he knew all the “facts” about her. And poor Imogen had well and truly missed the boat. Again! She might be a model, but Lexi had picked Fiona over her! She smiled with satisfaction. Alexander couldn’t get enough of her. He was like a man possessed, turning up at her door all hours of the day or night! Oh, yes, things were turning out very nicely, indeed.

♦♦♦

At the beginning of December, it snowed. Big, soft flakes drifted slowly down and disappeared into the ground. It was pretty enough to make Hettie smile, and it lifted her spirits a little. She loved the snow, despite the fact that if it settled, it would give them all sorts of problems on the yard. Doris was in raptures of joy when they got up a few days later to four inches of snow on the ground. She didn't know what to do first—eat it, dig it, roll in it, or run plunging through the drifts in frenzied circles. Hettie laughed out loud as she watched, then threw a couple of snowballs in Doris's direction. Even Dog hopped up and down playfully and barked a few times.

Alexander cursed at the snow. It would bring his work to a standstill. What the fuck would he do with himself now? He had already made plans to get away from Draymere at the weekend, stay in London with Ted, catch up with mates, and see the architect who was drawing the plans for the gatehouse. *Fuck it. I'll go up early,* he decided impatiently. It would be good to get away from bloody Draymere.

Holly and Jade hung tinsel from the light in the dugout, and Hettie dragged the fake Christmas tree from the cupboard and wedged it in the gap by the sofa, averting her eyes as she did so. A tin of Quality Street sat on the table next to a bottle of Baileys—thank-you gifts from Don, who had also given them generous cash tips in their Christmas cards. Jodie made coffee, and when the others trooped in from the cold, slapping their hands and brushing the snow from their hats, everyone added a dash of Baileys to their drinks and reached for chocolates and cigarettes. Hettie moved to sit facing the sink with her back to the sofa. No one commented; they all shuffled round a chair.

Grace arrived late, complaining loudly about the state of the roads and the time it had taken her to get to Cirencester, only to find out that the school was closed.

"Honestly!" she cried. "A few inches of snow! Roads blocked, school closed, and I daresay there won't be any hunting this week, either. Thank goodness the electricity is still on." She superstitiously touched the wooden table.

"I think we'll be on lockdown today as well," Hettie said. "It's not worth risking the horses on these roads. An extra day off won't hurt them. We'll try to get as many as we can turned out for a couple of hours."

"Ooh, free day!" Bev cackled. "Maybe I'll go home and give me old man a surprise." She grinned wickedly.

Holly giggled, and Jodie looked shocked.

"There's plenty to do around here! Ewan is coming to check the broodmares; I told Bert I would help him with that. The tack room and feed room can both have a bloody good tidy. We can get some clipping done. There's loads of jobs to catch up on." Hettie wasn't letting them off. Despite placing advertisements and putting the word out, they hadn't had a single applicant for the new job. She wasn't surprised. Who wanted to start a new job outside right before Christmas?

Shoulders drooped around the table. Their snow day was sounding like more hard work than the rest of the week. Bev added a second shot of Baileys to her coffee.

"Now, ladies, while I've got you all here," Grace announced, "three bits of news! One, tickets for the hunt ball are going fast, so if you want to come, let me know this week and I can put one aside for you. Two, Christmas drinks as usual at the hall on Christmas Eve—five o'clock sharp—and you are all invited. And three," Grace paused for dramatic effect, "James and I are expecting another little Melton!"

There was an instant hubbub of congratulations and exclamations. Grace beamed happily.

Hettie walked round the table and hugged her friend warmly. "That is wonderful news, Grace," she said, grinning broadly.

They established that the new baby was due in August, that Grace didn't know if it was a girl or a boy, that she felt absolutely wonderful, and that no, Bev, she wasn't puking at all! Hettie felt all warm and glowy. "Will you keep riding, Grace?" she asked, although she already knew the answer. Grace had ridden through all of her pregnancies.

"Yes, of course, for as long as I bloody well can!" Grace cried.

"That's good," Hettie said and smiled. "But I'm going to insist on Cora or Basil from now on. Gent is well ready to have a turn up front with Don or James. It will be good for his education."

Grace happily allowed herself to be told. Hettie had seen her safely through two of her three previous pregnancies, and she wasn't above taking advice.

"And no smoking in the dugout from now on," Hettie carried on. "This place is a dump, and it *stinks.* It will be better for all of us. I'll put a sand bucket out behind the stables, and we'll have to go out there."

A chorus of complaints rose from around the table. Grace tried to insist that she would stop coming in while they were smoking instead.

"No. My mind is made up," Hettie stated. "There's laws against it, anyway. Enough is enough. New baby, new start. In fact," she went on after a pause, "a do-over on this place can be the first job of the day! Everything out, a bloody good clean, and we'll start over again!"

Although gutted at the thought of losing their smoking den, the others got caught up in Hettie's newfound enthusiasm. They agreed that the room was revolting, and with all of them smoking in there, it did become unbearable. Hettie was suggesting they repaint the walls, scrub the carpet and the table, mend the cabinets, and chuck the sofa out.

"Bloody 'ell," Bev cut in. "If we've gotta do all that today, I really am off 'ome."

But there was no stopping Hettie. Before breakfast had ended, she was pushing the old sofa single-mindedly toward the door.

CHAPTER SEVEN

Alexander poked his head around the door of James's office.

"I'm going to clear off earlier than planned," he told James. "This snow has stopped me getting on with the house, so I'm going to shoot up to London for a few extra days."

"Will the trains be running?" James asked.

"I bloody hope so," Alexander grunted.

The trains were running—slow and delayed, but still running. The journey usually took under two hours, but this time it took three and a half. Throughout the trip Alexander stared out of the window, lost in thought, Digger at his feet. He had meant to text Ted from the train to let him know of his early arrival, but he was approaching Ted's flat before he remembered, so he figured he might as well carry on. Ted would be at work anyway. Al would find a café and text him from there. He bought a newspaper and settled in the window seat of a small, uber-cool café across the road from Ted's. He smiled at the pretty but strangely dressed waitress who served his coffee. No one commented on Digger's presence; this was Kensington, after all. It felt good to be away from Draymere. That place could suck you dry. Maybe he had been wrong to go back. In London no one knew you, and no one cared, and that felt oddly uplifting. He keyed a text to Ted:

came up early
hope that's ok
text me when you're through at work
I could meet you somewhere?

Then he called the architects and arranged a meeting for the following day. It was only three o'clock, but the streetlights were coming on. Passing cars swished through slush; London's light snow had melted to a grey sludge on the road. Coffee finished and paper read, Alexander decided to stride to Saville Row and pick up some shirts. It would be hours before Ted finished work. Leaving his paper and a generous tip on the table, he left with Digger trotting behind him.

A woman caught his eye as she exited the building that housed Ted's flat. Something about the way she walked was familiar, but he couldn't see her face beneath her fur hat and turned up collar. When she paused to cross the road, peering carefully in one direction and then the other, Alexander saw her face. His breath left his body as if he had been kicked in the chest by a horse. The pavement moved underneath him. He stepped back, reaching his hand out to feel for the wall. Breathing jaggedly, he was unable to take his eyes off his mother until she disappeared out of sight. Digger whined uncertainly.

Alexander's head was thumping. He lit a cigarette and drew on it deeply. A cloak of grief and confusion settled on his shoulders as he fought the overbearing urge to run after her and call out to her. Why was it that wherever he went, he couldn't seem to escape these fucking emotions? *She* had caused this. It was all her fault. He shook himself. She hadn't changed much, from what he had seen. Still beautiful, he acknowledged, for what that was worth. The sudden thought that she would be fifteen years older than the last time he had seen her scared him. *Christ, how old does that make her?* he thought. *Is she old?* He couldn't bear the idea and squashed it quickly down. A drink, that was what he needed, and then probably a second one. He walked, and Digger stayed close to his heels. Digger knew all about cities, and he didn't like them at all.

Alexander went into the first pub he came to. It was almost deserted, and he chose a stool at the far end of the bar, tucked away out of sight. "A double whiskey for me and a bowl of water for the dog," he directed the bartender, almost adding, "And keep them coming." He glanced sneeringly at the bleached wood décor and painfully arty designer interior as he downed his first whiskey. *What was wrong with being a normal pub or a normal café?* he wondered. He ordered a packet of organic pork scratchings for Digger with his second whiskey. He knew they didn't constitute a healthy diet for a dog, but it was the best he could come up with on the spur of the moment. *And hell, at least they're organic,* he sneered to himself. It occurred to him that he wasn't being fair to poor old Digger and that he hadn't really thought through this trip very well. But he ordered a third double whiskey all the same. His phone vibrated in his pocket. Glancing at it, he saw he had six missed calls from Fiona. Then he belatedly remembered that he had promised to take her for lunch. He turned the phone off and dropped it back into his pocket.

By seven o'clock, when the bar started filling, Alexander was well and truly slaughtered. The bartender was nervous; he wasn't sure he should be serving the bloke any more. But the fellow looked a bit menacing, so he didn't really want to refuse him. What the hell would he do with that funny-looking dog if the man passed out?

"Where do you live, mate?" he tried, thinking maybe he could book him a taxi.

"Nowhere," Alexander slurred, glaring drunkenly. He held out his glass. "Whiskey!"

So the bartender backed off. It wasn't his problem if the guy wanted to get shit-faced.

At some point Al's muddled mind decided he needed to ring Hettie, to tell her he was sorry. He succeeded in turning his phone back on but couldn't find her number. "I need to call her!" he shouted at two women standing by the bar. They moved away and concluded in whispers that the poor guy must be going through a bad break up.

His phone kept buzzing in his hand. He concentrated hard to try and focus on it. *You have four new text messages and three missed calls from Ted,* he read. "Oh, bollocks," he mumbled out loud. It took ten minutes of effort to bring up the most recent text message:

Where the fuck are you bro?

Alexander hit reply and typed FKDDD. *That's what I am*, he thought.

At eight o'clock, he staggered outside and tried to light a cigarette, but struggled to get the end of his fag and the flame of his lighter to meet. A group of fashionable PR types, already outside smoking, tried to ignore his staggering and swearing and continue their conversation, but they quickly finished their own cigarettes and went back inside. After a struggle, he eventually managed to light the cigarette halfway along it. He needed to call Hettie, he remembered. He reached for the phone in his pocket, dropped it, and thumped bottom-down on the pavement when he tried to pick it up. *Fuck it*, he thought, *more comfortable down here, anyway.* So he stayed there. He hurled abuse at a couple walking past who stared at him. Finding himself amused by the panic on their faces, he swore at more people just for fun, chuckling as they looked quickly away and sped up. *That's right*, he thought, *be scared of me. I'm fucking scared of me too.*

The bartender got weary of hearing from every new customer that there was a drunk outside shouting abuse. He called the police.

Ted was back at his flat when Al's text message arrived. FKDDD? What the hell did that mean? He wracked his brain for the name of a street, a bar, or anywhere with the initials FKDDD. He even Googled it, and got a lot of results about heavy metal music, but nothing that helped. *This doesn't feel right.* He tried calling again.

It was pure coincidence that Imogen's route home from yet another humiliating shoot took her past the bar. The cameraman and shoot director had discussed her pictures with jaded disappointment and tried to decide if the photos could be redeemed with a major retouch. She tried to cheer herself up with the thought that she was finished until the end of January now. She had nothing in the diary, and even the January booking was tentative. There was a police car parked ahead of her; she could see two policemen trying to deal with a tramp and his dog. There was a lot of shouting going on, and every time the police tried to move forward, the dog growled loudly. Imogen was turning to avoid the scene when she heard a shout. "I jus' need to fucking call Hettie! Don't you fuckers get that?' She stopped in her tracks. *That sounds like Alexander, but how could it be?* Imogen didn't know what to do. She took a couple of hesitant steps to get a better look at the man, and Alexander spotted her.

"Imo! Imo!" he roared delightedly. "There's Imo!" he told the policemen. "She'll have Hettie's number!"

The policemen looked relieved that a way out of the situation might have presented itself. The older of the two walked toward Imogen, who was still rooted to the pavement.

"Good evening, madam," he said jovially. "Do you know this gentleman? Only he seems to have got himself in rather a pickle."

"Er, yes, I do, actually," Imogen answered nervously. "I think his brother lives around here somewhere."

"Ah, good," the policeman continued. "And do you by any chance have an address or telephone number for this brother?"

"Yes! Yes, I've got Ted's number!" Imogen was energised by the realisation that she could do something after all. "Do you want me to call him?"

"Yes, please, madam. If you wouldn't mind, that would be very helpful."

She scrabbled in her bag for her phone, scrolled through her contacts, and pressed the call button. Ted, thinking it might be Al on the phone, picked up instantly.

"Al?" he shouted.

"No, no, it's Imogen, Ted, but Al is here."

"Ah, thank goodness. Is his phone broken or something? Are you in a bar? Shall I come and meet you?"

"Well, um, he's not exactly in a bar. He's outside the bar, um, on the pavement. I'm afraid he may be drunk. The, um, the police are with him."

"Bloody hell!" Ted exploded. "I'm on my way." He started dashing toward the door. "Tell them to hang on for me. I'll be as quick as I can. What's the name of the bar?"

"Er..." Imogen craned her neck to get a view of the sign. "It's called the ZenBah," she said.

"Right, I know it." Ted hung up and flew down the stairs from his flat.

"He said would you hang on for him, please. He's on his way; he will be as quick as he can," Imogen recited to the policeman. She glanced apprehensively at Alexander, who appeared to have fallen asleep, and wondered if she could escape. Alexander was scary sober, let alone drunk. "Is it OK if I, like, go now?" she asked.

The policeman noticed her nervousness and wondered if she was the reason for the guy's binge drinking. Although, he kept going on about Hettie, and that obviously wasn't this lady. Ah, well, none of that was his problem. All he had to worry about was getting the bloke off the street without being bitten by the blasted dog. "If you wouldn't mind hanging on for a moment," he said, "until the brother gets here. Can you tell me the gentleman's name?" He nodded toward Alexander and took his pad out of his pocket. Ted came into view, sprinting around the corner, slush splattering his suit trousers with every stride.

"Ah, there's his brother now!" Imogen pointed excitedly. "That's Ted. That's his brother."

Ted arrived and bent over, holding his knees to try and catch his breath. He struggled to take in the scene: Al, dishevelled and apparently out cold on the dirty, wet pavement, with an unfamiliar grey dog sitting on his chest; one copper standing guard next to the body; and another copper twenty feet away taking a statement from Imogen. It all seemed surreal.

"Is he hurt?" he asked the younger policeman. "Has someone hit him? Has anyone called an ambulance?" He had never seen Al this drunk. Well oiled occasionally, yes. Bleary eyed and swaying, more than once or twice. But passed out cold? No, surely not.

"No, no, sir," the young copper reassured. "Are you the gentleman's brother?" And in response to Ted's nod: "The barman informs us that your brother has been drinking double whiskeys since three o'clock this afternoon, sir. That he and his little dog here left the bar approximately forty minutes ago, and that since that time he has been sitting outside on the pavement shouting offensive language and abuse at passersby. He seems to think he needs to call someone by the name of Hettie. He fell asleep approximately"—the policeman glanced at his watch—"six minutes ago, sir, after the young lady over there arrived." They both glanced toward Imogen, but she was walking quickly away. The second policeman was moving back to join them.

"Christ!" was all Ted could manage.

"We were attempting to move him on, sir. Ted, is it?" the older policeman asked. Ted nodded again. "But, unfortunately, the dog appears not to like the idea."

Ted had concluded that the dog must be Digger. He'd listened to Al talk about him, remembered him saying that Digger didn't trust people and could get defensive. It was one of the reasons Al hadn't wanted to leave him behind when he left Afghanistan. "Do you mind if I have a go?" he asked the policemen. "I know the dog was a stray; he might be feeling intimidated. Maybe you could back off a little and let me try?"

The policemen looked at each other. They had spent too long here already; all they really needed to do was make sure the drunkard was moved from outside the bar.

"We'll let you give it a try, sir," the older policeman said eventually. "You can have five minutes to get him moved on, but after that I'm afraid we'll be putting in a call to the dog warden and hauling your brother away on a drunk and disorderly. We'll wait in the car."

Digger growled as Ted approached. This obviously wasn't going to be easy. He tentatively sat on the pavement himself, a couple of feet from Al. The cold slush immediately soaked through the bottom of his good suit trousers, and he cursed under his breath.

"Al, time to wake up," he said. Digger watched, but didn't growl. Al made no response at all.

Ted shifted nearer, chatting to the dog. "You see, the thing, Digger, is this. Me and you need to look after him, and right now I need you to cooperate and let me get close enough to wake him up. Now I don't want to upset you or anything, but if we don't manage this between us, old son, things are going to get a whole lot uglier." Ted kept his voice low and inched closer to Al's side. He wasn't animal mad like the rest of his family, but Ted had grown up with animals around and knew how to handle them.

Eventually he was right next to Al. Digger cocked his head suspiciously. Ted's five minutes were up, but the watching policemen could see progress was being made and decided to wait it out.

Ted nudged his thigh against Al's shoulder. "Al, wake up!" No response. He tried again, a harder nudge this time. Al turned his head and grumbled in his sleep. Digger seemed to be tolerating him, so Ted risked it and aimed a hefty body blow at

Alexander's side, which finally brought him round, cursing like a pirate. He spluttered upright, grasping his head, and catapulted Digger from his chest to his knees.

"What the fuck?" he muttered.

"Al, you're pissed," Ted explained. "And if you don't get up off your arse right now and come with me, those policemen over there are going to arrest you for swearing at strangers."

Al looked at him, bleary eyed. "What?" he shouted.

Ted sighed heavily. Standing up, he put his arm through Al's and attempted to haul him to his feet. "Get up, Al! Up! Come on now. Up!" It was like trying to lift a corpse.

"I wanted to call Hettie, that's all," Al mumbled moodily.

Ted didn't bother to question why the hell Al felt he needed to call Hettie from the pavement in the middle of London; he saw a chance and took it.

"You can call her from mine, Al! That's where the phone is. My place. Look, over there. Up you get. Let's go and call Hettie, shall we? Hettie's waiting for your call! Off we go! Up we get!" Ted babbled like a lunatic, and Al, slowly but surely, struggled ogre-like to his feet.

Ted needed to keep the momentum going. He kept hold of Alexander's arm and pushed him in the direction of his flat. He raised his hand in thanks to the policemen sitting in their car, then replaced his hold quickly when he felt Al sway away from him. Every time Al slowed, Ted pushed him on and told him they needed to get to the phone. Digger followed, close behind but not too near to Al's feet, as he couldn't work out where Al's feet were going. It took the sorry-looking trio half an hour to make it to the flat.

Ted was shattered. Getting Al up the stairs had been the final insult. At one point he'd been trying to hoist him forward with an arm round each shoulder and a knee under his backside. He hoped neither of them remembered that in the morning. Al was now lying prone, half on and half off the sofa with his head hanging uncomfortably off of the end. It would have to do. Ted didn't have the energy to move him another inch. Ted consoled himself with the thought that if Al chucked up, he wouldn't choke on it, and found a takeout carton in the kitchen to place under Al's face. He poured himself a glass of wine and sat at the table with the post and his laptop, intending to check his e-mails. But he was distracted by concern about what had happened to make Al turn up early and go off on a bender and why Hettie's name kept coming up.

He sent a text to Imogen:

thanks for calling me earlier
Alexander safely installed at mine
come for a drink with us in the week so we
can say a proper thank you

And then he sent one to Grace:

hi Grace, have you got Hettie's
phone number?

He wasn't planning to call her, but it felt sensible to have her number just in case.

Restless and unsettled, Ted gave up trying to work and decided to turn in for the night. He threw a duvet over Al and stood a pint glass of water on the table. He shuffled through his post to see if anything needed his urgent attention and found a handwritten note from his mother, scribbled in pencil on a scrap of paper torn from an artist's pad.

Teddy, called by on the chance that you were working from home. In town for two days Christmas shopping before I go on to Draymere; would love to see you! I do not have my phone. (!) Call or leave a message at the Grange on Langham St. Vous tenir toujours dans mon coeur, Mama x

Ah. Ted couldn't begin to think how this fit in with today's drama, but instinct told him it wasn't a coincidence. He decided wearily that he had better work from home tomorrow and rattled off an e-mail to his secretary before closing his laptop down.

Alexander surfaced in the early hours. His neck was painfully cricked, his head was pounding, and his mouth was parched. It took a few long minutes for him to work out where he was. He shifted uncomfortably as memories of the previous day filtered back, and squeezed his eyes shut in an attempt to force the return of oblivion. It was no use; his crashing head and full bladder drove him from the sofa. He crept unsteadily out of the room, feeling the walls and furniture rather than turning on a light, and located the bathroom. Holding his head under the basin tap, he gulped greedily at the water. He went to the kitchen in search of painkillers. He rifled through the drawers until he found something that felt like boxes of tablets. He carried them to the living room, sat at the table, and turned the desk lamp on, shading his eyes with his hand and squinting painfully at the boxes. Bingo, ibuprofen. Alexander threw four tablets into his mouth and swallowed. Then he rested his elbows on the table, his head in his hands, and closed his eyes.

He sat like that for fifteen minutes, letting the pain wash through him and trying not to think, because thinking was too hard. As the pounding in his head slowly reduced to a more manageable thumping, Alexander let his eyes fall open and wondered if he could make it back to the sofa without too much pain. He glanced at the table and saw the note. Another minute passed before he reached gingerly to turn off the lamp. Rising slowly, he shrugged off his clothes and settled back on the sofa in his pants and socks, pulling the duvet around him. "Vous tenir toujours dans mon coeur," he mumbled as he closed his eyes.

CHAPTER EIGHT

Celia checked at reception on her way to breakfast to see if Teddy had left a message, but was disappointed. If only she had remembered her phone, or written down his number. Celia had always been forgetful and disorganised; she had been born that way. Artistic, romantic, and loving, she charmed all who met her, and she found herself equally interested in and charmed by others. Born in France, to a French mother and English father, she enjoyed an idyllic childhood. She loved to read, draw, and paint; she relished poetry and baking; and she spent endless happy hours wandering in the warm vineyards around her home, picking flowers, collecting insects, and dreaming. She was the apple of her father's' eye. A surprise late and only child, she was pretty, endearing, and affectionate. Her mother loved her too, but would frequently roll her eyes heavenward at her daughter's fanciful ideas and dreamy forgetfulness.

Celia met William, soon to be Lord Melton, when she travelled to England with her father. He had to go on business and offered to take her sightseeing in celebration of her success at art college. Celia hadn't completed sufficient work to actually pass her exams, but she had received wonderful comments from her tutors.

Celia fell in love with London; it was full of promise, dreams, and opportunities. She fell in love with the gentle English countryside and the grand country houses. And she fell head over heels in love with William Melton. He was tall, handsome, gallant, and temperamental: everything the novels she had read described how an English gentleman would be. He was also twenty years her senior.

At forty-three, William knew he had left it late to get sorted with a wife and some offspring. He couldn't believe his luck when this enchanting little virgin skipped into his life with her eyes full of adoration. She was so fresh and sweet and naïve, a far cry from the overeducated, moneyed, and sophisticated women who made up his usual circle.

Their forced separation after a whirlwind three-week romance confirmed Celia's devotion. Back in France she cried for her English love, wrote him letters and poetry, and begged her father to allow her to go back. They married a year later, and Celia happily discovered she was pregnant three months after their wedding day.

Before James was even born, William's gallantry became more like opinionated bullying. His temperamental nature made him prone to shouting and sulking. Celia found life in England lonely, and she missed her parents terribly, but she adored Draymere. Every day, whether William was working or hunting or shooting, she would take her sketchpad and leave the gatehouse to go roaming, sketching the scenes and animals that she found on her wanderings. She made friends with the gardeners, then with the grooms, and when her meanderings took her further in the long days of summer, she stopped to chat with the farm workers and villagers walking their dogs. Time-keeping was not one of Celia's skills, so although she set out for just a short walk and intended to be back to cook a delicious meal for her husband, William often returned to an empty house. Celia, strolling in dreamy and weary, would find him sitting at the table waiting for his dinner, and a dreadful row would ensue. To Celia's credit, she didn't allow the loneliness or the rows to bring her down. She loved being pregnant, loved the countryside and the life all around her, and escaped to her drawing. When James arrived, her happiness and love were all consuming. William, proud of his newborn son, became for a while at least tolerantly affectionate toward his pretty young wife as he observed her showering their son with love. Her parents visited from France. Lady Melton made the short walk from the hall, the first time she had called at the gatehouse since Celia's arrival. Although she declined to hold the baby, she peered at him keenly and expressed herself satisfied, which made William even prouder.

Their life together ticked along pleasantly enough. Celia sang around the house and pushed James in his pram when she went for her walks, making even more friends when the strangers she met stopped to coo at the baby. The walks were shorter—James's hunger and her full bosom compelling them back to the house—but her time spent talking to the gardener inspired her to start nurturing her own garden. With the pram parked beside her, she sketched baby James and her blooms instead. She took baskets of produce to the hall, visited her mother-in-law, and shared recipes, gossip, and baby cuddles with Mrs. Gilder the cook.

Celia wanted a houseful of children. Five, six, seven, maybe even a dozen. And William seemed happy to oblige with his part in the process. But each successful pregnancy was followed by a handful of miscarriages. And when she lost her pregnancies, William found Celia's misery impossible to cope with. He distanced himself from the details and endless weeping, until eventually Celia stopped telling him at all. If he noticed the quiet sobbing and the long walks recurring, he made no comment.

When James was old enough to go to school, Celia was very happily pregnant again. She was adamant James would not be sent to board at the school William had attended. And for the first time in her life, she was enraged enough to shout at her husband and her mother-in-law, usually in French, which confounded them. She found strength and a drive she had not possessed before as she trawled the local public schools, demanding facts and figures on their achievements and results.

When she presented her findings in report form, she finally won her argument. It broke Celia's heart the first time she delivered her darling boy to school, trussed up in uniform and uncomfortable shoes, when he should have been barefoot and playing in the garden with her. But James thrived and ran happily into school each morning and out again each afternoon, full of excitement and bursting to tell her what he had been doing. Within months of losing her first baby to school, Celia was overwhelmed with love all over again on the happy, safe arrival of a second little dark-haired boy, with huge eyes and a serious, thoughtful face. They called him Alexander.

♦♦♦

Ted called and left a message at The Grange, speaking quietly from his bedroom while Alexander was still asleep. He left his phone number so Celia could get in touch. He noticed the box of ibuprofen on the table and guessed that Al had been up in the night. He was relieved to see both the plastic tub and the sofa were clear of any aftereffects from the marathon drinking session. He made himself a coffee and worked quietly at his table until Al opened his eyes.

"Good morning, brother!" Ted laughed brightly.

Alexander shut his eyes again.

"I was about to run to the deli and get myself a bagel for breakfast. Do you fancy anything? Do you want a cup of coffee?" Ted asked.

"You don't need to run around after me," Al grumbled, pushing off the duvet and sitting up. "Why aren't you at work?" He realised he felt surprisingly well; Ted's mention of breakfast had made him feel suddenly very hungry.

"I thought I might be needed here, given the state of you yesterday." Ted had resolved not to let Alexander scare him, although that was easier said than done.

Alexander said nothing for quite a long time, finally growling, "Is that all they sell around here, then? *Bagels?*"

Ted laughed and closed his laptop. "Yes, at the deli, and there's nothing to eat here. Good bagels, though. Bacon bagels, egg bagels, sausage bagels—you name it."

Al peered at him through bloodshot eyes. "One of each of them, then," he said.

"Digger's on the balcony, by the way, when you realise he's missing. He whined until I let him out there, and then he wouldn't come back in." Ted reached for his jacket from the coat stand. "I'd offer to take him with me, but I don't think he'd come. I gave him the last of the Brie from the fridge and a couple of crackers."

Alexander actually chuckled. "I hope you buttered those crackers," he said flatly. "There's nothing worse than a dry cracker. Poor little bastard. God knows what that will do to his stomach. I'll take him out when I've had a shower. I smell like a fucking distillery."

"There's a reason for that," Ted said, then let himself out of the door.

Al said good morning to Digger and left the balcony door open. He had an energising shower and wondered if he should get one like Ted's for the gatehouse. It was nice to find a shower he could actually get under. He searched for his bag until Ted got back, and they worked out between them that it must still be at the ZenBah, so Ted trudged back down the stairs and out again. Al made coffee and wolfed back all three bagels before Ted returned with his clothes. Then he left for the park and his architects meeting. Ted worked, and prayed his mother would ring while Alexander was out.

It was late afternoon before both men were in the flat together again. Ted leaned back in his chair. "So are you going to tell me what yesterday was all about?" he said pleasantly, glancing at Alexander.

"What are you? My shrink or my dad?" Al tried to joke in reply, but Ted wasn't playing.

"Did you see Mum when she came by the flat? Is that what brought on the drinking?"

Al stood up from the sofa and walked to the window—the furthest point in the room from where Ted was sitting. "What the fuck is this?" he growled dangerously. "The fucking Spanish Inquisition? Since when does getting pissed need a reason? Bit rich, coming from you! I've picked you up off the floor totally bladdered more times than I care to remember. I don't recall grilling you on the *reason*. You've lived in this city too long, Ted. You're turning into a girl."

The room was silent as the words of his tantrum settled. Al knew he was being a juvenile dick. Ted noted he hadn't said no to the question.

"You did see her, then," he said quietly.

"Not to talk to," Al snapped. "I saw her walking away." *Again,* his mind added to the statement.

"You know, she asks after you. Every time I talk to her."

"She left us, Ted." Al looked at him and spoke through gritted teeth. "She left us all for another *man*. She can ask after me all she likes. How can you forgive her for that?"

"She left *Dad,*" Ted stressed. "*Fifteen years* ago. And even you must see that was hardly a match made in heaven. She's here now, in London. She would cut her own arms off to see you. Just meet her, for Christ's sake. What bloody harm can that do?"

"I've done without her for fifteen years. Why the hell would I see her now?" Al shot back. "Nothing's changed. She deceived us, deceived Dad. *Left* us, him, Draymere. All for a passing fancy and a quick shag. Jesus, she wasn't even with the creep for two minutes after she went. Hardly true love that wrenched her away from us all, was it? You might have forgiven her, mummy's boy, but I can promise you I never will."

"And how is that panning out for you, bro?" Ted growled back, growing angry himself now. "You arrogant, self-righteous bastard! Working out well, is it? Running away, fucking women you hate, raging at the world, and drinking yourself into a coma."

If anyone else had said those words, Alexander would almost certainly have punched them. But Al was so shocked to hear it from his easygoing, mild-mannered brother, he found himself rendered speechless.

The drawn-out silence was terrible. Ted, half expecting Al to come at him from across the room, waited in trepidation and got ready to run. Then Al started laughing, and his laughter built until Ted couldn't help but laugh with him. For whatever reason, they didn't know, but the pair of them were falling about.

That night they ate out with friends of Ted's, some Al had met, some he hadn't. They enjoyed good food and good company. Al was in jovial mood and became the new fantasy figure for more than one of the women at the table. Ted got a call from Celia and was easily able to take his phone outside to talk to her; they made plans to meet for lunch. Ted didn't mention it to Alexander. He figured enough had been said for now. Digger relaxed into city life; it seemed that if Al was there, people didn't kick him or throw stones. The three of them returned to the flat in good spirits, and each slept well that night.

On Friday, Ted was back at work. Al ran two circuits of the park with Digger. Then he called a very irate Fiona and apologised sarcastically for changing his plans. He shopped for shirts and a jacket. He went to his club for lunch with a mate from the RAVC and rode the top of the bus back to Ted's to take in the lights on Oxford Street with Digger. At the flat he checked his e-mails on Ted's laptop, looking briefly at the architect's suggestions for the flooring and kitchen at the gatehouse. They all looked much the same, and outrageously expensive, so he stopped looking and decided to ask Grace when he got back to Draymere. Bored and restless, he turned on the telly and worked through the channels, settling for American football. He ruminated on what Ted had said. *Arrogant and self-righteous?* Yes, that was probably fair. He knew he came over too full of himself at times. *Raging at the world?* Yes, possibly that too. He had no patience with idiots, and not much more even with those who weren't. That was something he needed to work on. *Running away?* Never! He hadn't run from anything in his life, and drinking himself into a coma had only happened once, and it wouldn't happen again. Did he really only fuck women he hated? No, surely not. He'd fucked a lot of women he didn't like very much, Fiona included, but surely there must have been a couple he'd been fond of? He wracked his brain but could only come up with Hettie. He reminded himself that he didn't hate her, only what she had done. There was a difference. *Ah,* the voice in his head taunted him, *but you haven't actually fucked Hettie, have you?*

Thinking of Hettie left him frustrated and horny. He scrolled through his phone looking for Candida's number. She lived not too far from Ted.

Candida said, "Of course, I'd love to see you. Bring wine—I've got the whole evening free."

Alexander sneered at the easiness of it all as he hung up the phone. He collected Digger and his jacket, and then he scrawled a note to Ted and left it on the table:

Gone for a drink with Candida

Candida sent a text to the group of friends she had made plans to go out with.

sorry girls, killer headache
won't make it tonight
have fun will miss u all xoxox

Then she hurtled to the bathroom to shower. By the time Alexander arrived, she was clean and shaven from the armpits down, had blow-dried her hair into sexily tousled, and applied just a hint of lipstick and mascara. Chanel No. 5 and her skimpiest, thigh-length strap top completed the look. When Alexander arrived with a bottle of red, Candida greeted him demurely.

"My goodness, that was quick, Lex! I'm nowhere near ready! You can come in, but you'll have to take me as I am."

"Taking you was what I had in mind," Alexander drawled smoothly. Candida giggled.

The dog was a shock; she didn't like dogs at the best of times, and this mutt was particularly ugly. She ushered him into the garden, regained her composure, and fetched two glasses for the wine.

Alexander sprawled on the sofa and prepared to endure her well-rehearsed routine. She complimented him on how well he was looking and asked about his exercise regime. Flicking her hair and leaning forward, she told him she wanted to hear about "every detail" of his life. She sat at the end of the sofa, curling her long legs seductively between them, "accidentally" brushing her toes against his thigh. She left her glass of wine on his side table and had to kneel up and lean across him to collect it. Every third sip from her glass was punctuated by a little drawing of her white top teeth across her bottom lip, sometimes with an accompanying suggestive giggle. Alexander wondered if she'd taken classes or if she practiced her techniques in front of a mirror. He found it amusing that he'd only come for a shag, and she still thought she needed to seduce him. He grew bored of her voice and the obviousness of her, then annoyed by the dishonesty of her game. If she wanted a fuck as much as he did, why didn't she get on and do it? He thought about walking out, but his imagined picture of her indignant face aroused him more than she had. Abruptly he leant forward and grabbed her left tit, hoping to provoke an honest reaction. "Shall we get on with it?" he drawled.

Candida simpered and giggled. "Oh, Lex, you're keen today! I think you must have been missing me."

So he put down his glass and flipped her over, sliding his hand in the leg of her knickers. She gasped as he inserted his finger.

"It seems you've performed sufficient foreplay yourself," he whispered harshly as his finger slid easily into her. "Do you want me to stop, or can we just get on with this?"

Candida moaned, her first unorchestrated noise of the evening. She was finding his crudeness wildly arousing and for once was unable to answer. Al smiled in satisfaction and, withdrawing his finger, pulled her knickers down to her knees.

"Answer me, Candida," he demanded, dragging a finger slowly up the back of her thigh. "Do you want me to stop, or shall I fuck you?"

"Don't stop," Candida gasped.

Al unzipped his jeans and bent over her back. "So what is it you want me to do?" he asked, letting the end of his cock nudge against her.

"Fuck me," she whimpered weakly.

"Good girl," Alexander grunted as he pushed his cock inside her. "If you'd said that earlier, you could have saved us both a whole lot of acting."

But Candida didn't hear him; she was lost to sensation overload and making too much noise herself.

Alexander didn't hang about long afterward. Ironic politeness made him stay to finish the wine, but he really wanted to get out of there. He was nearly back at the flat when his phoned buzzed:

after work curry at brick lane

join us if you want to?

He diverted to Brick Lane.

Candida looked at the clock on her wall and wondered if she could reinstate her plans for the evening. She sent a tentative text:

feeling heaps better will try to make
the effort hate to let my gorgeous
girls down see you all later xoxoxo

On Saturday, both men slept in following their late, boozy Friday. Ted had arranged for them to take Imogen out for lunch. Al was moody and uncomfortable about it. He didn't really want to think about Wednesday, let alone thank anyone for "saving" him.

Imogen didn't want to go, either. She found the Melton men hard to be with; they were so self-assured and overpowering, Alexander in particular. But Ted had asked more than once, so she'd had to go along with it. At least it was just lunch, and she had an excuse to get away; her train for home left Paddington at three o'clock.

Alexander sulked outside the Italian restaurant with a cigarette while Ted went in to greet Imogen. If Ted wanted to apologise for his behaviour, he could bloody well do it without Al in the room. Shortly after he joined them, he realised he shouldn't have worried; this was Imogen after all. It was hard to coax two words out of her on any subject, so there was little chance she was going to say anything about Wednesday. *She's a good-looking girl,* he thought, *but it's hard to find much character.* He emerged from his sulk as his efforts to engage her in conversation became animated. He finally struck gold when he asked about show jumping and the family's horses. Imogen lit up, chatting happily about how much she was looking forward to getting back and doing some riding, about her favourite horses and their successes in the ring. Al talked about the hunters and dropped into the conversation that if she fancied some extra riding while she was home, they were desperate for someone to ride out at Draymere. Imogen said she might be, although it would only be for a few weeks. Did he think that might be possible?

"I'm sure it would," Alexander said. "Frankly, I think they would snatch your arm off. They've been advertising the post for weeks now and haven't had one taker."

Imogen felt hopeful and interested for the first time in years. "Gosh," she said. "Who should I talk to? Shall I give James a call?"

"No, better to speak to Hettie," Al replied, surprised to find himself liking the sound of her name coming from his mouth. "I would give you her number, but I haven't got it. Or call by the yard when you're home."

"I've got her number," Ted cut in. "Hang on, it's on my phone."

Al scowled as Ted searched his phone. *Now why has my brother got her number when he doesn't hunt and lives in London?* Maybe Ted hadn't been filling him in on *all* the gossip after all.

Imogen took the number eagerly, then made her excuses and hurried away. The brothers were left at the table with half a bottle of wine.

"Call her often, do you?" Al had returned to his sulk. He wanted to punch himself, but the question was already out.

"Who?" Ted asked, surprised. "Imo? No, haven't spoken to her in months. She's not exactly a stimulating conversationalist!" He tried to lighten the mood.

Alexander didn't reply. He looked away, reaching for the wine, and topped up his glass without filling Ted's.

Ted was fed up with this. Having Al to stay was becoming more and more like inviting a teenager into the house. Al had been such a laugh when they were younger; Ted would have called him his best mate as well as his brother. Ted hated to think it, but with each passing year, Al seemed to get more and more like their father.

"What, Al? Speak to me!" Ted blurted in exasperation. "What the fuck is going on here? One minute you're all up and firing, and the next you disappear!"

Alexander didn't say anything, and he knew he was being a prick. He was mystified as to where these moods came from, and they sickened him. But he wasn't going to explain that to anyone else. He grunted a sarcastic, "Huh."

In Al's head his grunt conveyed everything: that he knew what was going on and that he wasn't going to be made a fool of. But Ted was none the wiser. He steered his thoughts back through the conversation to try and work out what Alexander was angry about, then tested a couple of suggestions.

"Are you talking about Mother? Do you fancy Imo and think I'm shagging her? I can tell you I'm not, if that's the case! Who am I meant to have been calling? Or are we back on Hettie? For fuck's sake, Al, it would help if you spoke fucking English!" He spotted that Al reacted when he mentioned Hettie's name. It wasn't much, but Al had lifted his chin and gritted his teeth. *Is that it?* Ted thought, sighing.

"Hettie, then," Ted stated flatly. "What's the obsession there? And why the fuck you'd think I called her, I can't begin to imagine."

"You've got her number, so there must be some reason to call her." Alexander glared.

"Yes, you stupid fucker, I got her number from Grace. When you were ranting about needing to speak to her for two fucking hours on Wednesday. Jesus, Al, I—"

"Christ, you didn't let me call her, did you?" Al was out of his seat, a look of horror on his face.

Ted couldn't help but start laughing. He was tempted to make Al sweat, but given his current mood, that was possibly a dangerous idea.

"No, no, you didn't call her. I got the number in case. Why did you want to call her, anyway?"

Al sat back down, mightily relieved and shaking his head to clear it. "No fucking idea," he said. "I didn't tell you I had another 'almost' with her, did I?" he added, grimacing wryly. "Maybe it was something about that."

"What, like why the hell can't we seem to finish a fuck?" Ted was well on the way to another bout of hysterics. "Surely she didn't throw up on you again! If she did, I think you should take the hint!" He fell about at his own humour. Al tried hard not to join in but couldn't help a reluctant chuckle.

"No, she didn't throw up this time. And there won't be a next time; I'm damn sure of that." Al brought the mood down glumly. "But thank fuck I didn't call her when I was out of my head and ranting. That would have been too much to bear." He shook his head again.

"Too much to bear?" Ted laughed. "Come on. That's stretching it, isn't it? What in God's name happened this time? Is that why you came up early?"

"No, I came up because it snowed, and there was fuck all to do. This happened weeks ago. I said something she didn't like, that's all. It's not a big deal. There's a limited talent pool in the village; I limited it by one more."

Ted could tell by the way he was avoiding eye contact that it was a bigger deal than he was letting on. "What the fuck did you say?" he asked.

Al sighed. "I asked her if she was on the pill."

"And that's it? So she wasn't? And that was why you couldn't carry on? Well, the girl's got some sense, anyway. You're right. That's not a big deal. But why does that knock her out of your 'talent pool,' as you call it?"

"No. It wasn't quite like that, to be honest. I, er, I said I would expect a girl like her to be on the pill, or something along those lines. It didn't go down too well." Al was looking anywhere but directly at Ted now, and he actually looked sheepish.

"'A girl like her'? Ah," was all Ted said.

They were quiet, self-consciously drinking their wine.

"Seems to me you've got a problem with this girl," Ted said eventually.

Al grunted and looked away.

"So maybe it's a good thing that, you know, *that* isn't gonna happen. Maybe you can be friends?"

Al looked at him incredulously, as if Ted had grown two heads. Friends with a girl he wasn't fucking? Well, that had never happened before! He was barely friends with the ones he was.

"I don't need any more 'friends,'" he snapped.

CHAPTER NINE

Alexander was pleasantly surprised by the lift in his spirits when he turned into Draymere drive. More snow had fallen on Gloucestershire. The hall and gardens looked like a scene from a Christmas card. Fred and Artie were outside, catapulting carrots at a snowman. They greeted him excitedly, pink cheeked from the cold, and clamoured noisily for attention.

"Uncle Al, we built a snowman!"

"Uncle Al, Uncle Al, no school today!"

"Uncle Al, look what Mamie got us!" They held out catapults for inspection. Alexander took them, laughing.

"Well," he said after serious consideration. "Those are pretty special. Perfect for very special boys."

Digger celebrated his homecoming with excited laps through the snow.

The boys begged Al to join their game, and he was happy to oblige. He threw snowballs at the snowman while they catapulted carrots, which Digger rushed to eat. Fred's bits of carrots were falling out of his catapult before he shot them, but he either hadn't noticed or didn't care. Al patted his head. "Good shot, buddy." He smiled. They were good lads, he thought, and he was glad they knew their mamie. The game turned into a snowball fight, and ended abruptly when Artie got overenthusiastic and pushed a snowball into Fred's face. Al saw Fred redden with fury, his bottom lip starting to wobble, so he scooped the child up off the ground. "Hot chocolate and biscuit time!" he hollered, tucking Fred under his arm and running up the steps to the hall. Artie and Digger bounded after him.

Al threw himself into Draymere life over the next week: helping to decorate the Christmas tree and keeping the kids from under Grace's feet when she had a million things to do. He drove to the farms in James's Land Rover to deliver Christmas hampers and cheer. He enjoyed chatting to the farmers, usually in their kitchens with tea and a slice of cake, and walking the farms to look over the stock. He was introduced to numerous wives, children, and dogs, and ended the day with a Land Rover full of homemade cakes and preserves.

Grace asked him if he could spare some time to help exercise the hunters. It seemed churlish to refuse. Grace was run off her feet organising Christmas and the hunt ball, and trying to fit that around snow days, carol concerts, and Georgia's numerous tantrums was running her ragged. The girls were stretched to breaking, she said, with no hunting for over a week and fourteen horses to ride every day. So Al said of course he would, then wondered if Grace had cleared it with Hettie first.

Outside for a cigarette later that night, he thought about what Ted had said—that awful line about "being friends." Even saying it in his head, he put the words in sneering quote marks. Ted was becoming too much of a new man for Al's liking. But Ted was right about Al having a problem with Hettie; he had to admit to that. An unhealthy, lust-filled ambition that wasn't going to be fulfilled—that was his problem, and he wanted to get over it. It must be his failure to shag her that had caused it; he'd never let any woman get under his skin before. So maybe Ted had a point. Now that they both knew "that" wasn't going to happen, he should put it behind him and move on. He needed to get the relationship back on a professional footing, at least, and preferably before he joined them on exercise and she put him on Gilbert for revenge. He would call her tomorrow and arrange to meet for a chat—clear the air, wipe the slate, and all that. Al was pleased with his plan and with himself for being so adult about it. He stamped out his cigarette and headed for bed.

Hettie was also being run ragged. It was OK when there were four of them to ride, but with the grooms' days off and Grace so busy, that was only two days a week. With hunting off, they were riding three exercise sessions a day, which left very little time for all the other jobs that needed to be done. She hadn't finished before eight o'clock for days and was getting up earlier and earlier to start in the morning. After work she couldn't find the energy to do anything but sleep. And her diet was terrible; she was virtually living on crisps and mars bars, supplemented with Quality Street and Baileys (plus the wine and the fags, of course). She knew she ought to get her act together, but she couldn't find the time.

Her phone rang when she was taking the dogs back to the cottage before morning exercise. Dog was feeling the cold on the yard, so she had started stoking the Rayburn when she got up and taking him back to the warm for the day. She didn't recognise the number and nearly didn't pick up. Then she remembered that they were still advertising for the illusive new groom, so she answered hopefully.

"Hettie Redfern."

"Hettie, hello, it's Alexander Melton." He wasn't sure why he used his second name, but it seemed more businesslike somehow.

"Who?" Hettie questioned coldly, although her heart was instantly racing.

"You know who I am, Hettie." Alexander sighed. She wasn't going to make this easy for him, but he'd known that would be the case.

"What do you want?" she snapped. "I'm busy, so make it quick."

"I thought we should maybe meet up for a chat."

"Why?" She sounded so horrified by the suggestion that Alexander almost laughed.

"Because Grace wants me to help with morning exercise, because we didn't get off to the best of starts, and because you live here and I live here and it would make sense if we got along."

It did sound sensible when he put it like that. Hettie couldn't think of a smart reply. She would quite like to put the "incident" behind her, and the help with morning exercise was too good to turn down, even if it was from Alexander.

"OK," she agreed reluctantly. "I might be able to spare ten minutes, but I'm working seven days at the moment and not getting done till eight, so you work it out."

"Fine, eight thirty tonight. I'll pick you up at the cottage."

"Pick me up? Why? Where are we going?"

"Can you think of somewhere here you want to talk?"

Hettie thought about that for a second and decided he was probably right. "I'll be outside at eight thirty." She ended the call.

Hettie didn't bother to change after work, she didn't really have time, so she was still in jodhpurs, wellington boots, and her yard coat when Alexander arrived in the Aston. She enjoyed a little smug satisfaction when she climbed into his nice, clean car covered in horsehairs, straw, and mud. Alexander almost passed comment, but he bit his tongue. They made do with a curt nodded greeting. Al drove past the Fox and on through the village to the Nag's Head, which didn't have a good reputation and was therefore usually empty. Hettie sat hunched, uncommunicative in her seat, and wished she'd got in the back. She hated that she wanted to punch him but still could have snogged his face off.

The Nag's Head was deserted. The paunchy landlord was disgruntled to have customers and hauled himself reluctantly away from the TV to serve them. Hettie reached into her pockets and realised with horror that she hadn't brought a penny out with her. "Nothing for me, thanks," she mumbled awkwardly. The landlord scowled and shook his head.

"I'll have a beer," Al said smoothly, "and an orange juice for the lady who I think has forgotten her purse."

Hettie glared at him. "I said nothing, thank you. I don't need you to buy me a drink, and we won't be here long enough to work up a thirst."

Al looked at her as the landlord drew his pint. "This is meant to be a 'working out how to get along' meeting," he said quietly. "Surely you can let me buy you a drink?"

Hettie looked away, but didn't argue when he paid for the drinks and carried them to a table.

Al watched her as she followed and sat down. She had scruffy yard clothes on, her body language was screaming "fuck off," and she'd come into the pub and refused to buy a drink. If it was anyone else, he'd be embarrassed by now, but all he could think was how fucking sexy she was.

Hettie knew she was behaving ridiculously, but she couldn't seem to stop. She tried to get a grip on herself and this bloody awkward meeting by being the first to speak.

"So, Grace wants you to help out with exercise, and I take it, as you're here, that you've agreed." She still sounded petulant, but she had to start somewhere.

"Yes," Al replied smoothly. "She's run off her feet at the hall. And what with the hunt being grounded, she thinks you could do with some help."

"*I* can manage quite adequately. But if *you* want to help, I'm sure we can find you something to ride. We exercise twice every morning, at ten o'clock and eleven forty-five, and the horses need their routines, so it's important we get out on time."

Al was pissed off by her bossiness, but he was enjoying the behavioural upper hand too much to let it slip now. It wasn't a situation he often found himself in, after all. "Yes, that's fine," he said brightly. "And Grace usually does what—two or three days a week?"

"Yes, she covers the girls' days off when she can, on a Monday and a Friday. Tuesday, Thursday, and Saturday, we usually have horses out hunting, although not at the moment, of course. And Wednesday and Friday, the ones that have hunted have an extra day off. Again, not at the moment."

Al realised it must actually be manic on the yard. He hadn't really thought about it before.

"Has Imogen Tatler called you?" he asked.

"No, why would she?" Hettie queried.

"I had lunch with her in London, and I mentioned the vacancy here. She's off work until the end of January; she sounded keen on some extra riding."

Fiona and Imogen, Hettie thought, *and he's passing judgment on my currently nonexistent sex life.*

"I would have thought she had plenty to ride at home." Hettie had often admired the show jumpers that came out of the Tatler yard. She couldn't imagine why someone with Imogen's horses and money would turf out of bed three times a week for cold morning exercise.

"Well, she seemed keen, anyway. Said she would give you a call. Maybe she changed her mind, but it might be worth ringing her, if you want the number."

Hettie grudgingly took it. She was fast running out of options. And Imogen was a bloody good rider from what she'd seen of her.

There was another awkward pause after they had exchanged the number. They had leaned close to each other without thinking, and it put them both on edge. Hettie was remembering the mortifying experience in the dugout, and Al just wanted to shag her.

"So!" he ventured bravely. "Do you think we can tick along?"

"I guess we'll have to." Hettie sighed.

Al heard the door to the pub swing open and felt the blast of cold air, but he had his back turned so didn't see who came through. He did see Hettie pale, though, and the look of panic in her eyes. She dropped her head and started fumbling with her phone.

"Time we were off," she said quietly.

Al was intrigued to see who had caused her reaction. He could hear two or three men talking but didn't recognise the voices. When the men reached the bar, Hettie got up and almost ran for the door. Alexander took his time following, turning to look at the group as he rose. He didn't know two of the men, but the third was Julian Greaves, although he hadn't aged well, Al thought. He had filled out a lot and was losing his hair—looked a bit pasty too, like someone who was drinking too much. Al didn't know Julian well; he was nearer to James in age, possibly older. His sister Lucy had been in Al's school year, and if he remembered rightly, there had been a couple of other Greaves siblings between them. Julian was a horse dealer, a dodgy one, Al had heard. The Meltons had certainly never bought any of his horses.

Julian caught him looking over and nodded hello. Alexander lifted a hand in reply and turned for the door. *Is there anywhere in Gloucestershire you can go without bumping into someone she's fucked?* he thought bitterly.

Julian Greaves had noticed Hettie, looking scruffy, he thought. *He* wouldn't have been seen out with her dressed like that. She needed taking in hand, that girl, always had. He wasn't going to call her attention when she was out with her boss, not much sport to be had there. If she'd been on her own, now that was different. They could have had a nice chat, relived some pleasant memories. Very pleasant memories. Julian smirked into his beer.

Hettie had been fifteen when she first met Julian. She was riding one of the riding school ponies at a local show, and he had sought her out. Said he'd seen her riding and was impressed. He had a lot of youngsters he brought over from Ireland and competed locally. Wondered if she would be interested in riding some of them for him, and maybe competing them.

Hettie was ecstatic; she couldn't believe her luck. She had seen Julian and his string of ever-changing horses out at shows. He was a big-time dealer or something. Would she be interested? You bet she would!

Her mum was less enthusiastic. Julian wanted her to ride every day after school and compete on Saturdays. Anna worried about her schoolwork and Hettie getting overtired. She was only a year away from her final exams. But she knew that Greaves was a well-known name in the village and that Hettie would be following her passion. Anna didn't know where this obsession with horses had come from; she had always kept a respectful distance from the beasts herself. It must be from her father's side. And if so, it was about all he'd ever given her. After two days of Hettie's tearful pleading, Anna finally capitulated. She said Hettie could "give it a try and see how she got on."

Hettie flew in from school every day and straight out again on her bike, with Dog running beside her. She spent every hour of the summer holiday at Hardacre Farm. Anna barely saw her. When their paths did cross, Hettie could talk of nothing else: she'd ridden five clear rounds, Julian was giving her lessons, Julian was letting her help him break the three-year-olds, Julian had a new horsebox. And she told a million stories about the horses: the funny things they'd done, who had bought them, and where they'd gone.

When the autumn term began, Julian suggested he pick Hettie up from school so she could have more time for riding. So she lugged her boots and jodhpurs with her and changed in the girls' loo, until Julian told her to leave her stuff at the farm and get changed in the tack room.

Hettie was flattered and deliciously thrilled when he started touching her leg in the car when he picked her up. He was her idol: he had a stable full of horses, an indoor arena, and a big car.

He was good looking, and he fancied her! Hettie's fifteen-year-old hormones were raging, and she didn't need much encouragement.

They kissed and cuddled at first. Julian would follow her to the tack room and tickle and kiss her while she got changed. Occasionally his hand would brush her boobs, sparking needles of excitement inside Hettie. When she rode he would give her a leg up, sliding his hand up her thigh so she ended up sitting on it. They laughed at his trick. As her sixteenth birthday approached, Hettie was wandering the school in a daze of hormones and daydreams, wishing the day away so she could be at Hardacre Farm. Her grades began dropping significantly, and the school gave her mother a call. Anna and Hettie had their worst, and only serious row when Hettie returned from riding that day. Anna said the job had to stop, and Hettie stormed out of the house. She walked all the way back to Hardacre and knocked on Julian's door.

Julian wasn't pleased to see her, which upset and baffled Hettie. He said he was having his dinner, but if she waited in the tack room, he would drive her straight back. Hettie heard him shout as he left his house, "I'll be back when I've sorted this mess out, Carol."

He came into the tack room angry. Hettie had seen him get mad, but it had never been with her before. He ranted about her misbehaviour, upsetting her mother, and not working hard enough at school. When Dog started grumbling at Julian's tone, he kicked him out of the room. Hettie, miserable and lost, started crying then. Julian calmed down and gave her a cuddle and kissed her. Then he was pulling at her jodhpurs, squeezing her boobs, telling her it was going to be all right—that he would look after her, but she needed to learn to behave. Somehow they were on the cold concrete floor of the tack room. Julian was between her legs, grunting and thrusting. Hettie felt cold and discomfort, then pain. When he'd finished, Julian stood up.

"Right, get dressed. I'll take you home," he said.

In the car he said he was married, so if she wanted to keep riding his horses, she had better keep this quiet. That, anyway, no one liked a girl who slept around. When she got out, he drove away. Hettie went inside; she didn't know what else to do. Anna held her for a long time while she sobbed and said she was sorry.

Anna sent a note to Julian, thanking him for bringing Hettie home. Julian's Toyota pickup was outside Hettie's school again the next day.

He was different after that. Sometimes he acted like the same old Julian, praising her and teaching her new skills with the horses. At other times he was bullying and critical, sneering and shouting at her. When he had been angry, he always wanted sex, usually in the tack room or sometimes in his car. Once on the ground behind the stables and on another occasion in the horsebox when she hadn't done well at a show. Hettie dreaded the walk to his car after school, not knowing what mood he would be in. But she still loved the horses and riding the youngsters, especially the trickier sensitive ones. She noticed that Julian wasn't straight with the people who came looking to buy. He sold a particularly difficult youngster to parents looking for a pony for their novice daughter, and a cob with tendon problems to a woman looking for a hunter. And he lost his temper *a lot,* often with the horses, which Hettie couldn't bear to see. Hettie didn't speak out; failed sales or criticism put him in a rage. They didn't cuddle or laugh anymore. But sometimes he was good to her; after one session in his car, he kissed her and said, "You're a good girl, Hettie. If you want that psycho mare you're obsessed with, she's all yours."

Happy for the first time in weeks, Hettie ran into the house to tell her mum that she had been given a horse.

CHAPTER TEN

Hettie finished her phone call to Imogen and concluded that the girl must be dippy. It wasn't an easy conversation, and she still wasn't sure if Imogen was keen or not. They had, at least, decided that Imogen would ride tomorrow to see how it went.

Work became slightly less hectic. Alexander was reliable and capable, exercising two horses each session on three days a week. He arrived early for his first morning and gazed around the dugout in dismay. The room had been painted mint green (Bert found the can of paint in his garden shed). The cabinets were adorned with spotty sticky back plastic, and the battered leather sofa had been replaced with a once-bright floral one (Holly's aunt had been planning to chuck it out). The carpet was almost clean. Grace had sourced some less forlorn Christmas decorations. And Hettie completed the makeover with pictures of the horses: she took some photos on her phone and got Nat to print them on glossy paper. The Quality Street was long gone, but a second bottle of Baileys graced the "nearly new" chintz tablecloth, and Bev had arrived with mince pies (only Tesco value; they had gone down very well). Even the overflowing ashtray and smog had disappeared.

Hettie managed to avoid speaking to Al most of the time. He knew to look in the daybook to see which horses he was riding and leading. Bev showed him where everything was, and Holly fluttered around him, trying to be helpful in any way she could, which made a nice change from her ususal behaviour. Hettie put Al at the front and herself at the back of the ride, or vice versa, depending on which horses they were riding. If he was near Bev, no one else got a word in, which suited Hettie perfectly. The only prideful vanity she allowed herself was that she wouldn't ride the ponies when he was there; it would be too humiliating. Because of her height, she often rode Cloud or Gil, but on Alexander's days, she passed them over to Jodie or Holly. Jodie was unperturbed; Holly was horrified and sulked all day. *Tough*, Hettie thought. *For once my injured pride is more important than yours.*

Imogen also agreed to come and ride three days a week. She slipped onto the yard like a guilty stalker and slipped out again without a word when exercise was done. Even Jodie was ruffled by how little she spoke.

Hettie was amazed to have work breaks again, and she started finishing at a reasonable hour. They caught up with clipping and rug cleaning and a hundred other jobs that had been getting out of hand. When another thick covering of snow settled on the day of the ball, Hettie sent the others home early and told them to take the day off. She would give the horses a snow day in the field. When Alexander turned up to ride, she was rugging up horses in the yard, preparing to turn them out.

"Sorry, I should have called you," she said over her shoulder. "We can't take them out on the roads in this. I've sent the others home to turn themselves into Cinderellas for the ball. They're mad with excitement, so they weren't being much use here."

"Would you like a hand turning out?" Al asked, and Hettie, surprised by his offer, said she would.

So she rugged and he led the first horses to the field. They led the second lot out together. They laughed at the hunters snorting at the snow, pawing the ground, and trotting high-kneed like dressage divas.

"One of the best sights in the world," Hettie said in an unguarded moment, "watching horses play in the field."

"You can Cinderella yourself when this lot come in?" Alexander asked. He was looking forward to the ball. He couldn't remember the last time he'd gone dancing, and Ted was coming with some of his crowd. Grace had been working so hard; Al was determined to make it a good night for her sake.

"Oh, I'm not going," Hettie stated matter-of-factly.

"Not going to the ball?" he cried in mock horror. "You really are Cinderella, then!" His earlier enthusiasm ebbed.

Hettie smiled but said nothing.

Alexander cleared his throat. "Right, if I'm not needed here, I'd better go and make myself useful shifting tables or something. Deck the hall and all that."

He took out his cigarettes and offered Hettie one. She accepted in the spirit of ticking along together. She'd had all sorts of grief from Bev, Holly, and Grace for not going to the ball. She told them she was worn out and just couldn't face it this year. She hadn't even started her Christmas shopping yet, and she had no desire to add dress shopping to the list.

Alexander hesitated when their paths split. "You're not staying away because of me, I hope. I thought we were friends now." He pulled a face to indicate that he knew this wasn't true, but he waited for her reply.

Hettie sighed. She didn't know what to answer. *The truth would be yes, I am, but not in the way you think. Not because you insulted me when we were making love (because that is what I was doing, even if you weren't). Not because I hate you for that, although sometimes I think I do. But because I don't trust myself, and I seem to have developed feelings. Because, despite knowing what you think of me, if you asked, I would still snog you. And at the ball, with the wine and the atmosphere, you probably wouldn't need to ask. So I'm staying away for self-protection. But yes, because of you.*

"No, no, not because of you, Mr. Melton," she said and walked on toward the stables.

It was an easy day, even though it did feel rather flat and un-Christmassy to Hettie. She decided to go to her mum's that night rather than sit in the cottage listening to the merriment coming from the hall. She took a long bath—the cottage was toasty warm now with the Rayburn burning night and day—called her mum, and loaded the dogs in the Landy. Best to take them with her in case the noise upset them. But she had to lift Dog into the car these days, and it somewhat wounded his pride.

The drawings of Doris that Anna had done were brilliant. Hettie asked if she would do one of Dog when the book was finished. They spent a low-key evening drinking hot chocolate in front of the TV. When she got back to the cottage, it wasn't even eleven o'clock; the party was in full swing. The hall was lit up like a Christmas tree, music blared, and the drive was packed with cars. Hettie could see partygoers outside under the lights, smoking or snogging, some of them staggering drunkenly. She wondered who Alexander was snogging: Fiona? Imogen? Someone else altogether? *Snap out of it, and stop being so bloody pathetic,* she scolded herself.

Alexander wasn't having the best of evenings. There were a lot of people he wanted to catch up with, but he couldn't shake damned Fiona. Every time he thought he'd escaped, she was back, butting in on his conversations, asking him when he was going to dance with her, wanting him to get her a drink. She was hanging off his arm like a limpet. If it hadn't been Grace's do and old man Harding, who he liked a lot, hadn't been in attendance, he'd have told her to fuck off once and for all. He escaped outside for a cigarette and saw the lights of the Land Rover pull up at the cottage. He wondered darkly what, or who, Hettie had been doing in preference to the ball. Ewan was outside with his pretty, very pregnant wife, Clare. He introduced Al, who offered congratulations to the couple. Clare joked that she'd thought dancing might get things moving, but it seemed to have induced a hot flush, so they'd come outside to try and cool her down. Al and Ewan agreed to meet in the New Year to talk more about Ewan's plans; Clare was enthusiastic.

"No Hettie tonight?" she asked Alexander. "We missed her moves on the dance floor! She's not poorly or anything?"

Alexander said he didn't think so; she'd been working that day and seemed fine.

"Well, tell her from me, if you see her, that all work and no play makes Hettie a dull girl!" She laughed. "I'll give her a call," she added. "See if I can drag her out for a night."

"She works too hard, that girl," Ewan said. "You're bloody lucky to have her."

I'm not the one who's had her, Al thought irately. He hadn't known she was friends with Ewan's wife. That was a bit freaky, wasn't it? His overactive imagination wondered briefly if they'd had some sort of kinky threesome, but he pushed the thought down as being ridiculous, even for him, and berated himself for being so keen to leap to the worst conclusion.

Clare and Ewan decided to call it a night. Clare waddled off uncomfortably, saying she needed to pee and would meet Ewan at the car.

"Of course, you dated Hettie, didn't you?" Alexander couldn't help himself; the question asked itself.

"Me?" Ewan asked, raising his eyebrows. "I think 'dated' would be stretching it."

Fucked, then, Alexander thought gloomily. *Serves you right for asking.*

"No, no." Ewan was still talking. "We had dinner a couple of times. She's a sweet girl, but you could say she wasn't sweet on me." He laughed. "She introduced me to Clare, actually. They've been friends since primary school. And the rest, as they say, is history!" Ewan grinned like the cat who'd got the cream as he turned to walk to his car.

Al lit another cigarette and mused awhile longer. He would definitely get together with Ewan in the New Year; the idea of a shared veterinary practice had started to sound quite exciting. He saw the lights go out in the cottage and wondered if Hettie would get much sleep with this music blaring out. *You don't know she's trying to sleep,* the devil in his head reminded him.

Fiona was having a horrible night, and she had been so looking forward to the ball. Her dress had cost a fortune, and she'd had her hair and nails done. She wanted Lexi to be proud of her at their first ball together. But he'd been distant and off since his trip to London. The night visits had become infrequent, and try as she might, she couldn't persuade him to go anywhere with her. Tonight was no different. The harder she tried, the more he shrugged her off. They hadn't even shared a dance, although he'd danced with Imogen, who looked stunning in her slinky turquoise dress. He'd danced with Bev as well, though, and Grace, and a few other girls she thought worked at Draymere, so she told herself they were only duty dances. At one in the morning she devised a plan to get his attention back. Sidling sexily up behind him as he sat with Ted and his crowd, she leaned down and kissed his neck, nuzzling his ear.

"I've got the most awful headache," she whispered conspiratorially. "Time for bed, Lexi darling."

Alexander's face registered irritation. He didn't turn around. "Poor you," he shot back, deadpan. "Good-bye. Have you called a taxi?"

Fiona was heartbroken and humiliated. She finally got it, and her eyes filled with tears. She lifted her chin and went to find her father. "Daddy, I'm not feeling very well," she whined. "Can you take me home?"

"That was a bit harsh, mate," Ted said quietly.

Alexander didn't care, and his evening warmed up after that. He had another dance with Imogen. She didn't say much, but she was looking bloody good tonight. Then a mob of them, including Ted and Bev, tore up the dance floor to all the cheesy classics the DJ put on. Grace and James decided to turn in.

Alexander gave Grace a happy hug and told her what a great night it had been. He had a good chat with Bert about the horses, but he made his excuses when Bert started singing Hettie's praise; he didn't want her name spoiling his night. He had a third dance with Imogen and let his hands roam over her naked back. She stiffened under his touch, but he wasn't sure if that was from pleasure or not.

By two thirty only the young and the hard core were left. Dan the farrier had a fight with Holly's boyfriend, while Holly screamed from the sidelines. Jodie slipped in spilled drink and landed awkwardly on her hip. Imogen helped her back to her seat, and the pair became involved in a deep and drunken discussion. Don the huntsman found his wife snogging one of the farmers and marched her smartly home. Bev boogied hard and rarely returned to her table, where her slight husband Colin sat single-mindedly nursing his beer. Ted and his crowd engaged in ever more ludicrous drinking games. All in all, it had turned out to be a vintage hunt ball.

Hettie hadn't slept a wink. She tossed and turned in her bed, getting crosser and hotter as the hours ticked by. She had just drifted halfway off when a thump from downstairs jolted her awake again. She lay still for a moment, wondering if she should stop trying to sleep and get up. *Maybe I could start mucking out early,* she thought, *and come back to bed when they've shut the fuck up.* The second thump made her jump, and her heart started racing. Was there someone down there? What was that noise? She slid out of bed and pulled on the pyjama bottoms she had thrown off earlier. She was reaching for her jumper when she heard Dog's yelpy groan, a terrible noise that she had never heard him make before. Hettie dropped the jumper and ran. She found Dog on the kitchen floor, and he looked like he was fitting. His eyes were rolled back, and a foamy froth had collected at the side of his mouth. "Oh my God!" Hettie said in horror. She panicked for a moment. *What to do? Call the vet.* She glanced at the clock on the wall. *No, just take him there.* They would be shut; she needed to call, where was her phone? *Ewan would be at the ball!* This final thought struck her—he was here, at the hall, and so was Alexander. Filled with dread, she took Dog's blanket from his bed and wrapped it around him. He was jerking, and his breathing was loud and raspy, and a sob escaped her as she hoisted him up into her arms and ran for the door. She didn't register the cold snow on her bare feet or the cold air on her arms. She just ran.

"Ewan! Alexander!" she screamed as she got in sight of the hall, "Ewan! Alexander! Alexaaaaander!" Her screams got more desperate as she felt Dog slipping away in her arms.

In the hall no one could hear her; the music was thumping at full volume. Holly, outside making up and making out with her boyfriend, was the first to notice her. A faint cry made her look in Hettie's direction, but she looked away again. *Someone off their head and playing in the snow,* she thought distractedly.

Hettie almost made it to the hall. Her last desperate scream for Ewan, Alexander, or *anyone* finally made it to Holly's ears, and Holly saw with horror that it was Hettie screaming and that she was carrying Dog. She flew into the hall and to the table where Al was involved in a drinking game with Ted.

"Hettie, Hettie, Dog," she gasped, gesticulating toward the door.

Alexander took one look at her face and leapt up. Ted and a few others followed, hot on his heels.

But it was too late for Dog. Hettie had collapsed to the ground. She sat in the snow, holding him on her lap. Dry sobs wrenched her body; she buried her face against his too-still head.

The group of onlookers hung back as Alexander walked quietly over and squatted down where she sat. He gently pushed the blanket from Dog's throat and felt for a pulse. Nothing. He put the blanket carefully back in place and wrapped his arms around both of them. He stayed there, holding them, until

Hettie's sobs began to subside. Then he stood and walked back to the others.

"Go back inside, guys," he said. "It's cold out here, and I've got this."

A few of the girls were crying; Ted helped Al usher them determinedly away. Hettie had stopped crying when he got back, but she was still sitting in the snow—with bare feet and pyjamas on, he noticed. He took off his jacket and draped it around her shoulders. "Shall we get you both back to the cottage?" he said. Hettie nodded, but she struggled to get up with Dog in her arms and shook her head when he tried to take Dog from her, so he stood behind her and lifted her to her feet.

He couldn't bear the sight of her small, cold feet walking through the snow, but he didn't want to leave her alone, and his shoes would be like boats on her feet. He consoled himself that they didn't have far to go. They walked in silence, a few feet apart. Hettie's tight shoulders and averted head warned him off further comfort. The cottage door was still open, but Doris had uncharacteristically stayed inside. Alexander shut it behind them, and they both stood in the kitchen, unsure of what to do next.

"Do you want to put him back in his bed?" he ventured softly.

Hettie nodded and lowered Dog down. She arranged his blanket around him and stroked his head. Alexander could see it was taking a huge effort for her to hold back more tears, so he busied himself by putting the kettle on and then hunting the cottage for something she could put on her feet. He found her furry Uggs and went upstairs to search for a sweater or dressing gown. The jumper lay inside the door, on the floor where she'd dropped it. Al held it to his face and inhaled as he walked back down the stairs.

He made tea and searched the cupboards for sugar, adding four teaspoons to Hettie's cup. She thanked him when he passed it to her and pulled a face at the sweetness.

They sat in silence at the table. Al didn't really know what to say. *He was an old boy? He had a happy life? He went quickly?* All true, but they seemed like meaningless platitudes to him.

"Would you like me to call your mum or anything?" he tried eventually.

Hettie rallied. "No, no, I'll be fine. Thank you for helping us back." She paused. "Haven't got a fag on you, have you?" There was almost a sad little smile.

"Yes! Of course, here." Al proffered a packet and his lighter. He found a saucer to stand on the table. He nearly used a dog bowl but realised in time how that might appear tactless.

"I, er, don't know what happens next," Hettie said quietly. "You know, what do I do with him now?" Her voice wavered slightly.

"Well, you can bury him," Al answered. "Or the vets would take him for cremation, if you preferred that."

"Where would I bury him?" she asked. *Are there dog cemeteries?* she wondered.

"You could bury him here, at Draymere, if you like. If you think he was happy here."

Hettie nodded, and a solitary tear rolled down beside her nose. "Yes, thank you. I would like that. He's been very happy here."

"Well, we can sort that out tomorrow. Think about where you'd like him to be. A favourite walk, or your garden. Wherever you think, really. Um, the ground is frozen at the moment, which might be the only consideration. Somewhere we could get the digger to?" He sounded apologetic for mentioning it, but it needed to be said.

Hettie nodded. "Yes, thank you again. So he can stay with me tonight?"

Al thought his heart might be breaking for her. "Yes, of course," he said gently. "I'll come down first thing. We can deal with it then." *Although first thing in the morning is only a few hours away now,* he realised.

Hettie ground out her cigarette and stood up. "I'm keeping you from the ball," she said. "You get back. I'll be fine. I'm sorry to have interrupted your night."

Al took her cue and stood up. "You're not keeping me from anything important," he said. "I'm just sorry I couldn't help." He nodded toward Dog, and Hettie nodded back briskly, not trusting herself to speak. He put his hand on her shoulder and briefly kissed the top of her head before he left.

Hettie sat down on the floor next to Dog with her back to the Rayburn. Doris, unusually subdued, climbed onto her lap.

CHAPTER ELEVEN

Neither Hettie nor Alexander went to bed for the rest of that night. Hettie brought her pillow and duvet downstairs and lay on the floor next to Dog's bed. She dozed fitfully, and got up red-faced and sweating at a quarter to five.

Alexander went back to the ball and chatted to Ted for a while. The drinking games had ended, and the mood had come down. People drifted off home to bed. The DJ played end-of-night love songs, and a few couples continued to dance, draped wearily against each other. At half past four, Al helped the DJ pack up, collected empty bottles, and stacked tables for an hour. He called the nearest farm tenant, Jim, at half past five and asked if he could get his digger to Draymere Hall by six. Jim had been at the ball and had been hoping to sleep in. But he liked Hettie and was sorry to hear the sad news about her dog, so he willingly dressed and set out. James got up at six, and Al went to check with him that it was OK to bury Dog at Draymere.

"Yes, yes, of course," James said sadly, stroking Flossie's head absently as he spoke.

When Grace came down, Al told the story again and asked if she would call Hettie's mum. Grace was upset. Dog had been a sunny fixture on the yard for years, and they were all fond of him. Her pregnancy hormones were playing seesaw with her emotions. Alexander patted her on her back and gave her an awkward cuddle before walking down to the cottage and knocking on Hettie's door.

Hettie answered in her yard clothes, ready for work. She was pink from her shower and fully back in control.

"How are you?" Al asked. "Have you had decided where you want to put him? I've got Jim coming over from the farm with his digger."

Hettie said she was fine. She had thought about where to put Dog and had chosen a spot up by Corner Wood, with a view over the village and Draymere. They walked to the wood together, so Hettie could point out the spot, and then she went back to the yard to get on with the morning's work. Her mum arrived and hugged her, and the girls hugged her too. Grace came down and got upset again. Hettie got her head down and worked even faster than usual, but her stomach fell when Alexander walked on to the yard. She put down her fork and in response to his lifted brow said she would bring Dog in the Landy and see him there.

There was quite a gathering at the graveside: Bev, Holly, Jodie, her mum, Grace, and Al. Bert had appeared from somewhere, and Jim stood a distance away beside his digger. Hettie focused on breathing and fighting off the threatening tears. She asked Bert to lift Dog from the Landy and lay him in the ground. Holly and Grace sniffled, and Anna hugged her again. No one seemed sure what to say. Hettie didn't trust herself to speak at all.

"Right, you lot," she managed bravely as she walked back to the Landy. "Stables to muck out and horses to ride!" She climbed in and quickly drove off.

Hettie got through the day somehow, although she felt truly awful. On top of her grief, she seemed to be running a temperature: hot and sweating one minute, cold and shivering the next. Her legs ached, her eyes stung, and her head throbbed with a dull, aching pain. She put it down to sadness and lack of sleep and battled on, hoping that she wasn't going down with a cold.

The next morning Hettie could barely drag herself out of bed. Her throat was raw, she couldn't stop shivering, and she was panicking about how she was going to get through the day. Bev told her she should go home, that they could manage very well without her, but Hettie shook her head. Imogen asked if she wanted her to stay on so Hettie could take the afternoon off. She said the help would be welcome but stayed on the yard anyway, weakly trying to get through her jobs, stopping every two minutes to try and catch her breath. She did let Jodie do the evening stables shift, praying she would feel better the next day.

She didn't. She almost crawled out of the cottage the next morning; her feebleness made her want to cry. Holly tut-tutted and swore at her for being an idiot, said she should go home before they all caught it for Christmas, but Hettie obstinately hung on. She'd never taken a sick day in her life; it was incomprehensible to her that the yard could function without her.

Alexander walked onto the yard as Hettie was lugging Belle's tack weakly toward the stable. He took one look at her and immediately relieved her of the saddle.

"You look like death, Hettie. Go home," he snapped.

"I'm fine, thank you," she replied tightly, swaying woozily from the effort of trying to take the saddle back.

"You are very obviously far from fine." He hung onto the saddle; he didn't think there was much chance of her winning it back. "And you are not indispensable. Now are you going to go quietly, or shall I get Grace down here to order you off the yard?"

Holly cheered from the next-door stable. "Bloody right!" she said.

Hettie's shoulders dropped as she finally accepted defeat. The thought of her bed was suddenly irresistible. She passed Belle's bridle to Alexander and weaved her unsteady way off the yard without another word.

Christ, she must be sick, Al thought. He put the saddle and bridle down and got out his phone. "Grace," he barked, "I've sent Hettie home. She looks bloody awful. I wonder if her mum should come and pick her up. I'll leave it with you, anyway. Sorry, I know the timing's not great."

Grace got in the Range Rover and headed down to the cottage. She found Hettie crashed out on her bed still in her jodhpurs and boots and almost had to carry her to the car. She threw a few of Hettie's clothes into a carrier bag and put the bag and Doris in the back. They drove to the village and parked outside Anna's. Grace knocked on the door. Together Anna and Grace managed to coax Hettie upstairs. They dragged off her boots and clothes and tucked her into bed.

"Don't let her come back to Draymere until she's completely recovered," Grace told Anna as she waved good-bye.

Good Lord, however are we going to cope? she thought as she climbed back into the car. Three days before Christmas, no hunting, no school, and no staff. *Please, God, let Hettie get well quickly,* she offered in guilty prayer.

Hettie didn't get better quickly. For the next five days, she barely knew night from day as she sweated and tossed and ached her way through every painful hour. Anna called the doctor, who diagnosed flu but only suggested painkillers. Doris stayed on her bed. At Draymere, Alexander stepped up and worked full time on the yard. His muscles ached for a few days as he got accustomed to the work, but he slept like a baby at night.

Nat and Simon arrived at Anna's on Christmas Eve. Hettie wasn't aware they were there, and she missed Christmas drinks at the hall, which was always a highlight of the year. Ted was at Draymere for Christmas and had invited a girlfriend to join them on Boxing Day. Al ribbed him ruthlessly until he succeeded in winding Ted up. Ted had never introduced a girlfriend at Draymere before, but then, Al realised uncomfortably, neither had he.

By tradition the Meltons did the horses on Christmas morning, although Hettie usually popped over to help (she actually redid everything behind them). Despite Hettie's absence, the Meltons carried on the tradition and did their best. Fred and Artie threw droppings at each other, and Georgia toddled from one messy disaster to another. The yard looked like a typhoon had passed through a muck heap when they left, but they pretended not to notice. Drinks and the turkey called.

At her mother's, Hettie caught vague snippets of merriment from downstairs. Bert peered around her door to ask how she was doing, but only got a groan in reply. Her mum brought in water, painkillers, and soup that she couldn't face.

The snow had melted in the days before Christmas, so the traditional Boxing Day meet at Draymere Hall would go ahead. The Melton horses, always the best turned out, would have been immaculate for the Boxing Day meet under Hettie's watch. But if anyone noticed the wonky plaits, or the stable stains on the horses' flanks, there was no comment. The whole family, barring Ted, who hadn't ridden for years, was mounted at the meet. Even Georgia was led out briefly on thirty-six-year-old Snoop, who was dragged out of retirement for the occasion. Al was delighted to see him; he'd had his first day's hunting on Snoop. He held Georgia's lead rein from Satan's back and beamed at the gathering crowd. Gilbert was in high spirits and bucked Fred off before the day even got underway. Onlookers came from miles, joining the locals to see the hunt off. Mince pies and port were passed round, a rogue hound tracked the offerings hopefully. Anna fielded well-wishers asking for news of Hettie. Imogen was out on one of the Draymere horses, Fiona noticed resentfully, and they hadn't put *her* on a cob. Fi had come as a spectator with Lucy Greaves and her beau, but she was fed up and bitter and wishing she hadn't bothered. Jodie and Holly were riding. Bev had been offered, but she declined on the grounds that, "My poor old body is still recovering from the ball—you ask my 'usband!" She ended with a dirty cackle. Ewan hadn't made it. Clare had gone into labour in the early hours; he was currently in Cirencester Hospital, listening to a torrent of profanities he hadn't known his wife could pronounce.

A taxi pulled up, and Ted eagerly went to meet the attractive girl who climbed out. Both of them sported foolish grins as they vanished into the hall.

When the huntsman blew his horn, all the small talk stopped. Reins were gathered and horses' heads raised. Port glasses were deposited, and hard hats patted into place. A splendid procession followed the hounds away; over fifty dapper horses and riders trotted smartly along the half-mile Draymere Hall drive. Onlookers clapped and raised their glasses, hearts full with tradition and pride. As the riders reached the gate, they forked right into open countryside, breaking into canter as they touched the soft ground and streamed across the valley. The last view of Cora and Grace cantering elegantly away showed Gilbert bucking furiously alongside and Fred hanging on for grim life.

The day after Boxing Day, Hettie dared think she might be feeling slightly better. She managed to shower, sipped three spoonfuls of soup, said good-bye to Nat, and slept soundly for twenty-two hours.

On day seven she managed a whole bowl of soup, an hour in front of the telly, and grilled Bert for every detail about the yard when he stopped by. Grace visited the next day, bringing Christmas gifts and gossip, including the news that Ewan and Clare had a little girl. Hettie said she would be back tomorrow, but Grace glared and told her a draft would blow her away and to stay home and build up her strength.

Alexander sent her a photo of the stables via a text message, which simply said:

See—we're coping!

Hettie laughed.

Bev, Holly, and Jodie called by and wore Hettie out with talking until Anna ushered them away.

By day ten Hettie was bored and starving. She decided enough was enough. Still weak as a kitten, she concluded that she wasn't going to get stronger lying in bed and informed her mum she was going back to Draymere. Anna protested weakly but was secretly relieved; Hettie wasn't the easiest of patients, and it had been a lot of years since she'd had to run around after a child. She was thrilled to be getting her life back. After Hettie had consumed a full English breakfast, Anna cheerfully drove her, Doris, and two bags of groceries back to the cottage. She drove away singing along to the radio.

The cottage felt sad and abandoned, with no Dog and the Rayburn burned out. Her mum had been in to vacuum and tidy. Her clothes were washed and ironed, and the bed newly made up. It was all rather disconcerting; Hettie realised with shock that the year had changed without her even noticing.

She was back on the yard the next morning, and she told Alexander he could go home.

"I think I'll hang around for a few days yet," he drawled, looking her up and down. Her eyes looked huge in her gaunt face, and her watch hung off her wrist.

It was as well he stayed. Hettie had underestimated how weak she had become and struggled to get back into full swing. She hid her horror at the state of the yard and Alexander's attempts to muck out. She had to concede it was amusing to have him around. Breakfast had become quite lively for a start; the banter between him and Bev was so blue that Jodie spent the entire break scarlet with embarrassment. Even Holly blushed a couple of times. Imogen had crept out of her shell and stayed on after morning exercise to help out, and Holly was a woman transformed with a man on the yard to play up to.

January remained icy cold, but there hadn't been any more snow. As Hettie got stronger, Alexander backed off his work on the yard. He was surprised to find he had enjoyed it. But the gatehouse was calling; the builders had started work. He continued to ride out on the morning exercise sessions.

He tried to seek Grace's advice on the plethora of samples the architects kept pestering him with, but she loudly professed herself "useless at all that stuff."

"I moved into Draymere as it was, and I haven't changed a thing!" she admitted and laughed.

So he took some samples to the dugout and got four different kinds of advice: Holly liked everything shiny or gold; Bev said, "Shag pile," and winked; and Hettie picked out the most colourful samples and got in a huff when he asked her sarcastically if the dugout was all her own work. Only Imogen hesitantly put forward some useful ideas, suggesting colours and textures that would work together and laying them next to each other on the table so Al could see that she was right. She became his design guru by default. He would trot to the yard to ask her opinion on every new sample he received. Hettie simmered enviously, but it was good to see Imo blossom as her confidence grew. Hettie liked having Imogen on the yard; she was good with the horses, polite, and always willing to help. Before long Alexander was dragging Imo off to look at baths or door handles. Hettie concluded that Fiona had been replaced.

The builders found an old leather suitcase tucked under the eaves in the attic. The case was packed full of drawings, so they carried it down to Al, who sat on a stack of floor tiles in what would be his kitchen, looking slowly through them. They were incredible—so many poignant pictures of him and his brothers as babies and growing children. She had captured their expressions perfectly: concentration from James as he studied something in the garden, mischief in Ted as he sat in the pram, and one of Alexander grinning cheekily from Snoop's back that made him smile. *There must be more than two hundred drawings,* he realised in awe. Flashes of their life, the garden, and Draymere were recorded in these simple sketches. He admired portraits of Bella the cat, basking in the sun; dogs and horses they had owned; and so many pictures of the three of them, although not one with his father. Al packed them carefully back into the case and carried them up to the hall.

James and Grace were enthralled; they all three sat in the kitchen looking through the pictures again. They chuckled at memories the drawings inspired and tried to recall the names of horses and dogs Celia had drawn.

"If it's OK with you and Ted, I might put a couple of them up in the gatehouse when it's finished," Alexander said as he left.

James and Grace raised their eyebrows at each other.

By February Grace's bump was beginning to show. The gatehouse was progressing in leaps and bounds, and Alexander and Imogen spent ever more time together. Al was slightly baffled that he hadn't made a pass at her yet. Imogen was attractive, and underneath the shyness, she was actually a really nice girl. They were spending a lot of time together, and he hadn't seen Fiona since the ball. He put it down to the fact that she was impossible to flirt with; he couldn't read any signals. He was used to his women being more obvious and chalked that up as a point in her favour. Anyway, he decided cynically, it would be a shame to screw things up before the house was finished.

Hettie was back to her old self, physically at least: eating and working like a horse and trying not to look at the empty space where Dog's bed had been. Hettie told Imogen they would miss her when she went and that she had been an asset on the yard.

"Are you sure you don't want to jack in the modelling and stay?" she joked laughingly.

But she nearly fell over in shock when Imogen replied, "Yes, thank you. If you mean that, I will."

So Imogen started working three full days a week, much to Alexander's annoyance. He had become accustomed to having her at his beck and call. Now when he appeared at the yard wanting her immediate assistance, she told him she was busy and to call her later. Hettie couldn't begin to understand why Imogen would chuck in a glamorous modelling career to shovel shit in the cold, until it dawned on her—Alexander, of course. Imogen wanted to stay near him. Hettie couldn't blame her for that, but it would be difficult watching their courtship from close at hand.

In an effort to drag herself out of the doldrums, Hettie accepted Clare's offer of a night out with Clare and her brother Steve. It wasn't Clare's first attempt at matchmaking the pair, but Hettie, who couldn't think of anything worse than a blind date, had repeatedly declined. This time Clare said she would come too, so it wouldn't really be a date, and it wouldn't really be blind either, since Hettie had met Steve before.

Dan the farrier came to shoe the horses, and Holly started behaving weirdly.

"Am I imagining it, or is Holly hiding in the hay barn?" Hettie asked Bev as they cleaned saddles in the tack room.

"Ha!" Bev exclaimed. "Bit of a canoodle between Dan and Holly at the ball." She grinned. "Followed by a punch-up with Holly's young man!" Bev cackled delightedly.

Hettie laughed. "Oh dear, the hunt ball strikes again! They should ban that bloody event, you know."

"I don't know, but you would." Bev grinned. "Didn't you and Dan have a thing one time?"

Hettie glared at her. "No, we did not have 'a thing,'" she shot back. "I overplayed a forfeit in some stupid drinking game, and things got out of hand." She looked glum. "And I think I've paid fairly heavily for that, so don't go calling it 'a thing.'"

Bev wasn't the least bit ruffled by Hettie's glare. "You certainly 'ave!" she cried. "Not only 'as the poor boy been moonin' around like a lovesick bullock ever since, but you ended up with Doris!"

Hettie allowed herself a small smile. "Well, with luck he'll be mooning after Holly now. Wish I'd thought of hiding in the hay barn."

Alexander, standing outside the tack room door with his saddle, eavesdropped on the exchange. He upped his efforts to flirt with Imogen later that day, but wasn't convinced he was making any progress.

♦♦♦

Alexander called Ewan to arrange a meeting to discuss the practice. He could hear baby Charlotte yelling over the line, and Ewan sounded frazzled.

"Yes! Come over now!" Ewan shouted. "Clare's gone out, and I'm babysitting. I could do with the support, if I'm honest!"

Alexander didn't see how they were going to get much discussed with the baby hollering like that, but he couldn't really refuse. Ewan sounded desperate.

Charlotte was still bawling when Alexander arrived. Ewan opened the door with the baby on his shoulder, bobbing up and down and frantically patting her back.

"I can't get her to take the bloody bottle." He sighed in despair. "Clare's been gone less than an hour. She expressed some milk, but Lottie isn't used to a bottle. She's been screaming ever since Clare walked out the door."

Alexander didn't think he could be much help. "Can't you call Clare?" he asked, dismayed.

"I could!" Ewan shouted from the kitchen over the noise of Charlotte's cries. He was walking laps of the floor, still bobbing up and down. "But it's the first time she's been out since the baby was born. I can't give up in less than an hour, can I?" he asked beseechingly as the volume of the screaming intensified.

Alexander could see the problem. "What would you do if it was a lamb?" he called after Ewan, who had exited the kitchen via the back door and was now circling the garden. The shock of the cold air had some effect in disrupting the pattern of screams, but the silence was short-lived.

"Squirt the milk in its mouth!" Ewan shouted back, jubilant at the thought that there might be a solution. He jogged back into the house.

They got themselves in position, Ewan on the sofa, holding Charlotte against his chest so she wouldn't choke, while Alexander knelt on the floor in front of him with the bottle. Every time she opened her mouth to scream, Al pinched the teat and squirted a few drops on to her tongue. The first couple of tries, Charlotte screamed even louder, and the two men shared fearful glances. On the third attempt, Charlotte paused momentarily to purse her lips, and stared deeply at Al for a second before resuming the screaming again.

"She doesn't know my face." Al panicked, squirting more milk. "Maybe we should swap places?"

So they changed places and tried again. Little by little, Charlotte started to get the idea. She licked her lips, looked at her dad, and tried sucking, but spat the unfamiliar teat back out. Once, twice Ewan popped it back into her mouth, and *finally* Charlotte latched on. Ewan and Alexander relaxed their shoulders in relief and grinned. Alexander took the bottle and let Charlotte drift sideways into the crook of his arm as she suckled furiously.

"Tea? Beer?" Ewan whispered, standing up.

"Tea will be fine," Al whispered back. He chuckled softly at the strangeness of finding himself sitting in Ewan's living room feeding a six-week-old baby girl. She was pretty bloody cute, he thought sentimentally.

Charlotte zonked after her bottle. Ewan placed her gingerly in her Moses basket as if she might be about to explode. "Phew!" he exclaimed to Alexander. "Shall we sit at the kitchen table so we don't disturb her again?"

"Clare's out on a blind date with Hettie," Ewan went on conversationally as they sat down. "Well, Clare's not on the blind date, obviously." He laughed. "She's been trying to get her brother and Hettie together for years. Hettie finally caved."

Ewan didn't notice Al clench his teeth or the dark shapes he began doodling on his notepad.

They spent an hour discussing costs, venues, legal necessities, and general ideas for the proposed new veterinary practice. Alexander drew up a list of things they needed to research, and they allocated out the jobs.

Clare arrived home cheerful. She peered in the Moses basket and mouthed, "Well done!" to Ewan, who grinned like a Cheshire cat.

"I've left them to it." Clare smiled conspiratorially at him. "Used the baby as an excuse to let young love bloom!" They laughed. Ewan offered Al more tea.

Alexander stood up. "No, no, I'll leave you lovely people to it," he said, packing up his notes. "I'm sure you need all the sleep you can get at the moment! Congratulations, Clare, by the way. Charlotte is really beautiful."

He drove straight to Fiona's. She was petulant and off with him, but eventually obliged, as he knew she would.

CHAPTER TWELVE

Alexander decided he needed to get away from Draymere. He would go up to London again. The architects wanted to meet face-to-face, and he could catch up with Ted and have a look at some furnishings.

"If you wanted to delay it, Celia is visiting again at the end of March," Grace said gently, seizing her opportunity.

"I should be in the gatehouse by then," Alexander replied nonchalantly, leaving Grace to wonder if he would stay there during the visit. *Progress*? she wondered hopefully.

He wasn't sure what to do about Digger. Ted's flat had been far from ideal with only a balcony. Digger had become a new dog over the last few months. He adored Artie and Fred now. But he still kept his distance from Georgia, which Al thought was wise given the way she dragged Flossie around by her ear. Grace and James were permitted to touch him, and he didn't need to be next to Al at all times; as long as he saw Al often enough through the day, Digger was happy. When Imogen offered to let him crash at her place in London, which was standing empty, it sounded like a good solution. She had a two-bedroom terrace with a small garden there, and Digger still insisted on sleeping outside.

"Come with me!" Alexander suggested, then regretted the idea as soon as he'd said it. She wasn't exactly stimulating company, and he didn't seem to be any nearer to getting his wicked way with her. It was almost becoming a challenge. Besides, he'd been looking forward to time out, and taking

Imogen would be like taking Draymere along. But she could look at furnishings with him, which would be useful.

Imogen blushed. "Um, I couldn't be away for three days," she said. "But I could possibly join you for one of them."

That sounded like a result to Alexander; he could drag her around Selfridges and Liberty for a day and have the rest of the time to himself.

"Great!" he enthused. "I'll take you out to dinner to thank you for your help. Stay a night, at least." *Well, you never know,* he thought gamely.

Imogen blushed even harder. "Um, OK," she agreed. "But, er, I would need to stay…um." She stopped, looking panicked.

"What, Imo? Spit it out." Alexander was losing patience with the conversation; he had things to be getting on with.

"Er, different rooms," she whispered.

Al wasn't sure if it was a question or a statement. "You want different rooms? Or you don't want different rooms?" he asked bluntly.

Poor Imogen looked like what she actually wanted was for the ground to open up and swallow her, but for once she held her nerve. "I want different rooms," she said more convincingly.

"Of course," Alexander barked. *Bloody hell, is the girl a born-again Christian or something?* he wondered irritably.

Grace rode exercise while Alexander was away, though it wasn't actually necessary any more. They had Imogen now, and with hunting on again, all the horses were out at least once a week. But the weather was clement, and Grace was fed up with being stuck in the hall. She knew she would only be comfortable on a horse for a few more months.

It was nice to have her back, although Hettie did wish she would stop talking about Alexander and Imogen and quizzing them all about whether they thought the relationship was going anywhere.

"I doubt it!" Bev said ominously, then pressed her lips together when Jodie glared at her. Grace chatted on, oblivious, but Hettie noticed the exchange, and her curiosity was piqued. She nabbed Bev as they came out.

"What was that about?" she hissed, but Bev shook her head.

"I'm sworn to secrecy, Hettie! You can cut my legs off, but you won't get a word outta me!" she muttered mysteriously.

Hettie didn't quiz Jodie, as that would have felt like bullying.

Imo's place was really nice, Alexander thought appreciatively as he gave himself a tour of the rooms, pulling himself up sharply when he realised he was stroking the kitchen units. *You're turning into a fucking metrosexual, you ass,* he scoffed silently.

Ted and Anju had invited him for dinner. Alexander wasn't sure how he felt about that; usually he and Ted went out and hit the town. And as Ted never had any food in his flat, Al couldn't think what they were going to cook. Anju seemed nice enough, from what he'd seen of her, which hadn't been much. He'd hunted most of Boxing Day, and Anju had sat at the far end of the table during dinner, so they hadn't got past the pleasantries. Ted had gone to bed not long after Al got back from evening stables, he remembered with a grin. He wasn't sure if he liked the idea of her taming his little brother, though.

He got to Ted's place at seven, carrying a bottle of wine and an attitude about how grown-up it all felt. The flat smelled amazing, though. His mouth started watering as soon as he walked through the door. Anju kissed him, on both cheeks, which put Al on his guard again. He could never get the hang of that two-kiss thing; there was always an awkward fumble in the middle. Ted poured him a drink, and he was relieved to see they hadn't put nibbles out. That would have been the final straw. Al thought the flat looked different, but he couldn't put his finger on why. Anju flitted between the kitchen and sitting room as they talked, sharing an occasional shouted comment.

"She's a bloody amazing cook, aren't you, Anj?" Ted said, raising his voice.

"Yes, I am," she called back.

Alexander relaxed a bit as the wine took hold and the food came out. Ted was on form, and Anju was great, really. Funny, bright, and engaging, she asked lots of questions and was interested in his replies. Al found he was enjoying the evening, despite himself, and even became slightly envious of the way Ted and Anju were together. They laughed a lot, ribbing each other constantly, and Ted was right: she was a bloody amazing cook. It was the best meal he'd had in a long time. The dinner plates were mismatched, Anju was drinking her wine from a mug, and the salt and pepper were in boxes. Al decided it wasn't so grown-up after all, although possibly a little bit bohemian.

Dinner over, Anju jumped up. "Right, I'm going to leave you boys to play," she said. "You can clear up, Ted." She laughed, swatting him on the head.

"She's off clubbing," Ted told him. "Buggered if I can keep up with her."

"Don't you mind?" Al asked as the front door closed behind her.

"Mind what?" Ted countered.

"Her going clubbing without you? You can go if you like; it won't bother me."

"Of course I don't mind. Why would I? She's going dancing with a few of her mates. We don't live in each other's pockets."

"I know, I know." Al tried to back down. "But, well, she's a good-looking girl."

"I'm very pleased you think so." Ted laughed. "But as you're here, I don't think womankind is in much danger out there tonight. Bloody hell, Al, sometimes I think you were born in the wrong century!"

He got up to fetch another bottle of wine. "Open another?" he asked, holding the bottle up. "Or would you rather go out?"

"Open it up," Al said. "That meal and the first bottle have made me lazy."

"She made me visit Dad, you know, when she was down at Draymere," Ted said quietly after he'd poured the wine.

"About bloody time," was all Al replied. He knew Ted hadn't been to the care home before, but that wasn't his business. He didn't go enough himself to pull a guilt trip on anyone else.

"Anj came in with me," Ted went on, "and Father hollered, 'Get that bloody darkie out of my room!' when we walked in."

He'd got Al's attention now. "Fucking hell! Shit! What in God's name did you do? What did she say?"

"She laughed," Ted said, chuckling himself. "I was fucking mortified. There she was, trying to do the right thing, reuniting me with my father, building bridges and all that shit. And he called her a 'darkie.' I could have turned his oxygen off there and then, to be honest."

Al still looked aghast. "Did you leave?" he asked.

"I wanted to!" Ted snorted. "She wouldn't. Said I was being ridiculous. That he's an old man who's had so many strokes he doesn't even remember his family, so how could he remember his manners? We stayed for nearly an hour. She was good with him, really nice. Which is more than I was."

They sat in silent contemplation for a moment.

"You didn't tell her he didn't have any manners to start with, then?" Alexander finally drawled. And released from sentiment by his question, they both fell about laughing.

They opened a third, then a fourth bottle of wine. Alexander went to the loo and noticed there were two toothbrushes in the bathroom.

"I know what's different about the flat!" he shouted, swaying a little on his return "It's been womanised! My little brother is living in sin!"

Ted laughed uproariously. "Almost, but not quite. She's still got her own place. I just keep her here whenever I can. How's your place coming on, anyway?"

"Really well, actually. I'm pleased." Al was getting more pissed by the minute, and Ted wasn't far behind. "I've had Imogen doing stuff for me. She's bloody good, actually."

"You've had Imogen *doing stuff for you?* What the fuck does that mean?" Ted found the statement hilarious for some reason.

"Samples, stuff, you know—*things*. Choosing them and whatnot. Not that sort of *stuff,* you dirty bastard. I don't seem to be getting any of that," Al finished grumpily. "Although we're staying in the same house tomorrow night, so you never know." He tried to wink, but ended up shutting both eyes.

"Imogen Tattler? Meek as a mouse and nearly as interesting Imogen? I find it hard to believe she's resisted your charms." This conversation was getting funnier and funnier as far as Ted was concerned. "You managed to get rid of Fiona, then?"

Alexander had the grace to look sheepish, even in his drunken state. "Sort of," he mumbled.

"You dog!" Ted almost shouted. "Not getting any of that? How many women do you want at one time?"

Al laughed, albeit a little self-consciously. He wasn't sure he liked the way this discussion was going now.

"No, I'm not with Fiona." He put the record straight. "I had a single transgression. And I am *not* with Imogen, although the prospect is slightly intriguing."

"The prospect is slightly intriguing? Are you tryin' a land yourself a virgin, bro?" Ted quipped, in an accent possibly meant to be Deep South American but wasn't. "You really are Victorian! You are an imposter in our time! What about Candida and Hettie?"

"Candida is an occasional amusement, and not a very amusing one at that. And Hettie, well, I haven't had her, but it seems about every other man in Gloucestershire has."

"Christ, can you hear yourself, Al?" Ted stopped laughing and poured them both another glass of wine, shaking his head.

"Yeah, I'm a bastard, aren't I?" Al replied matter-of-factly. He had heard himself, and he knew his words were ugly. "I didn't mean every man. That was out of order. Just some of them. But the bit about Candida is sadly true."

"Sometimes you shock me," Ted said quietly. "It's hard to know if you really mean it or not."

"I shock myself," Al admitted gloomily. "I wonder if I'm turning into Dad."

"No, you're not," Ted insisted. "But I can't help thinking that your fucked-up opinions of women have got a lot to do with Mum."

Alexander was silent for a long time. Ted thought he might have overstepped the mark again.

"Have I got fucked-up opinions of women?" he asked finally.

"Well, yes, you have. The ones you sleep with, anyway, or the ones you want to sleep with. You get on pretty well with all the others." The drink was making Ted untactfully honest.

Alexander thought about this for a moment, but his woozy mind couldn't find a decent argument to deny what Ted was saying. "I've slept with quite a few women I didn't know well enough to have a fucked-up opinion of," he tried finally. But he realised as he said it that it wasn't really a ringing endorsement of his character. "I don't hate Imogen," he tried again.

"No, but you don't really like her, do you? And you don't really want to sleep with her. You only think you should because you could. And she's got no 'history,' which you're finding 'intriguing,' as you put it."

"Has she really got no history?" Al cut in. "That's a bit odd, isn't it?"

"Damned if they do, and damned if they don't." Ted sighed.

"No, that's not fair," Al protested. "It's not history that bothers me; it's the number of colours I can't deal with."

"I take it we're back on Hettie?" Ted asked. "OK, then, how many 'colours' do you know about in Hettie's past?"

"Quite a few!" Al growled.

"More than you?" Ted countered.

That shut him up.

"Name them, then," Ted challenged. "All of the men she's slept with."

Alexander glared. "I don't know their fucking names, do I? Julian Greaves—there you go. That's name enough!"

"And there we have it!" Ted shot back. "Condemned for eternity because 'she slept with a married man'! And you ask if you've got a fucked-up attitude to women! She wasn't the married one—he was! Go and get some therapy, Al, for fuck's sake," he said quietly.

"Apparently that's what I come here for," Al muttered back.

Hettie's birthday was coming up in March. She decided to make herself celebrate with birthday drinks at the Fox. At break she told everyone they were to spread the word, and she called some friends, and Nat and her mum. It would be good for her to have a knees-up. She was restless and frustrated—stuck in a rut.

"I need spring to get here," she told Bev as they stood by the sand bucket smoking a cigarette.

"You need a man, that's what you need!" Bev told her. "A man and a bloody good—"

"Yes, thank you, Bev!" Hettie cut in. "But actually that's the last bloody thing I need. They bring more trouble than I can be bothered with!"

"Ah, you're far too young to be so cynical," Bev scolded her. "Now, when you get to my age, you'll be right to be cynical. But at twenty-five you should be goin' out there without a care in the world, shakin' the buggery out of life."

"I'm nearly twenty-six," Hettie mumbled sulkily.

"Oh lor'!" Bev screeched. "Forget what I said, then. You settle yourself down and get a couple of cats to keep you company in your old age. Bugger me, Hettie, it's not like you to feel so sorry for yourself, and that's a fact."

"I'm not feeling sorry for myself," Hettie protested. "I'm feeling, oh, I don't know—"

"Un-bloody-shagged!" Bev interrupted, then grinned triumphantly. "Don't you worry, girl, we'll get you mated up with someone at your birthday party." She cackled delightedly.

"Don't you fucking dare!" Hettie laughed.

Imogen arrived in London the following afternoon. Alexander had booked a table for dinner, as promised, and in a moment of inspiration asked Ted and Anju to join them. It was a relief when they said yes. Al wasn't sure he could maintain a conversation with Imo for a whole evening on his own. As it turned out, it was a congenial night. Imo chatted happily to Anju, and Al wondered if it was only him she couldn't talk to. They went back to Imogen's after dinner, and Anju exclaimed excitedly at the décor of the house.

"And you did this all yourself?" Anju kept asking.

Imogen nodded and smiled self-consciously.

"I've got friends who would kill for a place like this, and they would definitely pay for your help creating it. You should be an interior designer, Imo!" Anju enthused.

The praise was getting too much for Imogen to handle now.

"She's got work at the moment!" Al called. "Your friends will have to wait until my gatehouse is done."

"And how much are you paying her?" Anju shouted back. "Or do you count having your company as payment enough?"

"Ouch, that hurt." Al looked offended. "You've definitely been spending too much time with my brother." But her comment did make him wonder if he'd been taking advantage of Imogen's doormat nature.

Al took Digger for a walk after Ted and Anju had left to give Imo a chance to get through her bedtime routines without him being awkwardly present. She was tucked up in bed with her door shut when he got back.

They made progress the following day. Imogen was a real asset. Alexander even took her to his architects meeting, and the architects were delighted to find someone who spoke the same language as them past the point of plumbing and joists. They got questions answered, decisions made, and furniture perused. Imo was almost assertive once or twice. Al saw her off at the station with a brief but grateful hug.

CHAPTER THIRTEEN

Hettie was excited about her birthday drinks. Loads of people had said they would come, and it was too long since she'd had a good blowout and let her hair down.

After morning exercise on the Thursday before, Imogen was edgy. She followed Hettie from job to job until Hettie couldn't stand it anymore.

"Did you want something, Imo?" she asked impatiently.

"Er, I, er…can we have a talk?" Imogen stuttered back.

Shit, she's going to hand her notice in, Hettie thought. *I knew it was too good to be true.*

"Yes, of course." Hettie climbed off the bucket she had stood on to brush Klaus's mane. *Maybe she's going back to modelling,* she mused. *Or maybe she's got what she stayed for.* That thought formed a knot in her stomach.

"What can I do for you?" Hettie was brisk, but Imogen wasn't finding it easy to spit whatever it was out. Hettie tried to avoid looking at her watch.

"Imo, just say it. It can't be that bad." She tried to sound encouraging, but wasn't entirely successful.

"I wondered if I could bring my girlfriend to your birthday drinks," Imogen blurted in a rush, going very pink in the face.

"Of course you bloody can!" Hettie laughed. "It's in a *public house,* Imo! Bring as many friends as you want. The more, the merrier!" She turned to get back to her grooming.

"No!" Imogen stopped her. It had taken a lot of will to get this far, and she wasn't backing off now. "I, I didn't mean, er, like that. *My girlfriend*, Hettie." She stressed the words and stared determinedly at the wall.

As the real meaning of Imogen's question hit home, Hettie thought for an awful, hysterical moment that she was going to erupt into giggles. She fought with every ounce of her will to bring her insensitive reaction back under control.

"Oh, Imogen, of course you can! That would be lovely!" she gushed, laying her hand on Imogen's shoulder in support—and then, concerned that the gesture might count as inappropriate touching now, took it away again. *I'm way out of my depth here*, she thought. "How great! Good for you!" she finished weakly. *Good for you?* Her mind mocked her for the ridiculous choice of words.

Imogen, still pink, looked shyly relieved and as keen to get away now as Hettie was. They parted in awkward silence, with Hettie doing her best to offer an encouraging smile.

Hettie realised guiltily that she was actually thrilled by this news. Wicked grins kept escaping her as she finished brushing Klaus. She wondered if Alexander knew; she would *so* like to be a fly on the wall when that conversation took place.

There was a shocked discussion around the table when the subject came up at breakfast the following day (raised by Bev, who said, "She told you, then!"). Jodie, who had already known, wasn't saying much, of course, but she was quietly very relieved that the secret was finally out. Bev was purse-lipped with disapproval. "I'm the last person to judge 'ow people live their lives," she said. "But they do need to make their bloody minds up."

Holly said, "Ew," and professed herself disgusted. Nobody knew who the mystery girlfriend was. Hettie said they should remember that Imogen was their friend, but was still struggling to think about it without giggling. When Alexander joined them, they flashed warning looks at each other and abruptly shut up.

Al was on sterling form, grabbing two biscuits as he sat down to join them. "What has the boss got in store for us today, then, girls?" He beamed at Jodie and Holly. "More bullying and tyrannical overwork, I daresay?"

Jodie looked scared. Holly nodded solemnly in agreement with his assessment.

Alexander winked at Bev.

"All at the Fox tomorrow, then? For Hettie's birthday drinks! Getting on a bit now, Hettie, aren't you? Are you excited?" he teased.

"Yes, I am, actually," Hettie said smartly. "Lots of people are coming, and I intend to get pleasantly pissed."

"Don't get too rat-arsed," he retorted. "You might end up throwing up." He winked at Bev again.

Oh, we are on form today, aren't we? Hettie thought crossly. "Imogen's bringing her girlfriend," she said out loud. "I don't know if you know her. Do you?" The devil in her had escaped. Bev narrowed her eyes, Jodie's head sunk into the collar of her coat, and Holly's mouth fell open.

"Can't say I know any of Imo's friends, but another model, I hope?" Al grinned, lifting his eyebrows in suggestive question.

"I don't know. None of us have met her," Hettie drawled casually. "We didn't even know Imo had a girlfriend until she came out to us."

Alexander's face was a picture. Hettie was so busy enjoying his look that she failed to notice the horrified faces of the others.

"Christ!" Alexander exclaimed quietly.

Hettie couldn't hold back the hysteria any longer. She dissolved into uncontrolled giggles, clutching her hands to her stomach.

Bev, Holly, and Jodie shuffled painfully in their seats.

"Ah, that'll do, Hettie," Bev said sternly.

Alexander was silent as Hettie's hysteria died down, and the slow realisation crept over her that no one else was laughing, or even close to it.

"I think Hettie and I will have a word," Al told room in general. Bev, Holly, and Jodie were quick to get up and get out.

Hettie felt slightly sick as she realised what she'd done. Suddenly it didn't feel very funny at all. *Oh, shit.* She closed her eyes and leaned her face on her hands. "Oops," she offered weakly.

"I seem to have missed the joke," Alexander drawled. "What exactly about Imo shagging girls is it that you find so amusing?" He knew full well that everyone thought he and Imogen were an item. He hadn't seen any reason to disillusion them, but was regretting that right now. Hettie was enjoying making fool out of him rather too much for his liking.

Hettie kept her eyes closed behind her hands. She couldn't think of a thing she could say to justify her announcing that his girlfriend was cheating with another woman, *and then laughing at his reaction.*

Alexander waited in moody silence. They heard horses being led out of the stables. Bev must have decided that getting on with morning exercise without them was the best course of action. Hettie thought miserably that she had no one to defend her now.

The silence dragged painfully. She had to say something. "Shall I get my coat?" She made a feeble attempt at a not-so-funny joke from behind her hands.

"Oh no. I'm not letting you off that easy. I asked you to explain the joke, and I'm waiting. Or maybe *I* am the joke?" He leaned back in his chair and folded his arms to demonstrate that he was there for the long game.

Hettie kept her head firmly down. "No, no, of course not!" she protested. "I'm really sorry. Believe me, you don't know how sorry I am. I don't know why...I don't know what I was thinking. Nothing is funny. Nothing is funny at all. Definitely not you." *Especially not right now.*

Alexander leaned forward and pulled her hand away from her face. "You enjoyed making me look like a fool," he stated matter-of-factly. "What was that, Hettie? *Revenge?*"

"No!" she protested. "I just didn't think before I spoke. I don't know why I laughed. I can't excuse it. I don't know where it came from myself." She deliberated miserably in the silence that followed, then exhaled a defeated sigh. "Christ, maybe you're right. Maybe I did want revenge. And what 'sort of a girl' that makes me, I don't even want to know. I'm sorry. Sorry that I said it, and double sorry that I laughed. Can we stop this now? Say what you've got to say and let me get out of here."

"Christ, you sure know how to hold a grudge," Alexander said, almost admiringly.

The grudge is the easy bit, Hettie thought wearily. *It's the torch that's wearing me out.*

"All right, apology accepted, if that's the best I'm going to get." Al abruptly stood up. "If making me look an idiot is how you get your kicks, I'll just have to watch my back. But don't expect me to forget in a hurry." He walked over to look at the daybook. "Looks like it's just me and you left to exercise on our own." He smiled at her unpleasantly.

Great, Hettie thought. *The torture goes on.*

They reached for the door together. Alexander couldn't help himself. He could smell the shampoo in her hair; they were so close all he had to do was turn her around. When he dropped his head, Hettie's mouth was already lifted to meet his. He held the back of her head, threading his fingers through her curls, and pressed his lips hard to hers, plunging his tongue into her mouth, bruising her lips with the passion of frustrated desire. Hettie's arms flew to his neck, and she pulled him even harder toward her. Matching his kiss and accepting his tongue, she felt desire surge. They pressed their bodies together, breath catching, loins aching, plunging their tongues into each other's mouths with equal need. Hettie was lost to everything else; at that moment, this was all she wanted.

After what felt like an age but was only seconds, it dawned on them both that they were standing at the door of the dugout, snogging each other's faces off again. Their lips parted, but Alexander kept hold of her head and Hettie's arms remained wrapped around his neck. Alexander was fighting the urge to pick Hettie up and christen the floral sofa when she spoke again.

"I know I've fucked up royally today," she gasped into his chest, "but I don't think being your revenge on Imogen is going to help either of us very much."

Al sighed jaggedly, dropped his arms to Hettie's shoulders, and pulled her into a hug. She was right; this wasn't going to help him very much. And there he'd been thinking he was dealing with this fucking obsession quite well lately. *Literally a fucking obsession.* His mind laughed wryly at his own joke. *You said you weren't going back there*, he reminded himself, releasing the hug and moving away. But he was damned if he was going to tell her that he and Imogen hadn't been an item in the first place.

They saddled Satan and Gent and left the yard in surprisingly companionable silence. The frosty air and the long loping gait of the horses beneath them were refreshingly mind clearing after the complicated passions of the dugout.

"We could take the north bridle path," Hettie ventured, "as neither of us are leading. Give them a leg stretch up Long Hill and a change of scenery." Still mortified by what she had done, she needed to make an effort to get through this.

Al nodded his agreement, and they rode on, trotting where the ground was good, walking over frozen furrows drawn by tractors through the earth. The north bridle path led them along narrow, hedged avenues where they had to ride in single file. Hettie, riding behind on the smaller horse, Gent, couldn't help but admire Alexander's handsome physique in front of her. Her groin still ached. *I should have just got on with it,* she thought moodily. *I was already a scarlet woman, and now I'm a total bitch, so what have I actually got to lose?* But her conscience fired back, *Your heart and your morals, Hettie. That's what you've got to lose.*

When they emerged from the avenue, Long Hill was in view ahead. The horses knew where they were going now and jogged with impatient anticipation. Alexander couldn't help but notice Hettie's thighs on the saddle as Gent repeatedly nudged her almost against his leg. *What I actually want to do,* he thought, *is pull her off that horse and shag her right now on the frozen ground.*

As they approached the turn to Long Hill, the horses pulled and plunged to get away, refocusing their attention.

"Do we let them go?" Al shouted a few strides from the turn.

"Yes!" Hettie called back, grinning wickedly as they swung onto the hill.

Gent and Satan were swift into gallop; they were thoroughbreds, and they were fast. As the horses stretched long, Hettie and Al crouched forward; the ground flew past, hedges blurred, and hooves thundered on grass as muscles bunched beneath them. Hettie whooped with exhilaration as they galloped side by side. Alexander flashed an elated grin.

At the top of the mile-long hill, the horses and riders eased back. Al and Hettie grinned cheesily and chuckled as they brought the horses back to walk. They allowed them stretch their heads low to catch their breath.

"I'll call Imo later," Hettie said bravely while the adrenaline from the gallop was still up. "Tell her that you know, and apologise for being a shit-stirrer. I know that doesn't mend things, but I don't really know how I could."

"Ah." Al was caught out by the statement. *That will be an interesting conversation,* he mused. "If she's bringing this girl tomorrow, she must have figured I'd find out sooner or later," he muttered.

Hettie shot him a lopsided smile. "You've been good to me, Alexander. Please don't think I don't know that. What with sorting Dog out, and taking over the yard when I was ill. That was a shit thing I did in return."

"Forget it," Al retorted sharply. "I think enough has been said." He had actually been feeling quite smug that there was a reason Imogen hadn't fallen for his charms, until Hettie complicated the situation again.

They consciously changed the subject. Hettie asked him how the gatehouse was coming on, and he told her that he planned to be in by the end of the month, although it wouldn't be completely done. He studiously avoided bringing up Imogen's name. They talked about Grace and her growing bump, which led them on to Ewan and Clare's baby. Al noted grimly that she didn't mention Steve. He shared his and Ewan's plans for the veterinary practice. Hettie was enthusiastic about the idea. She asked him how Digger was settling, and he asked how Doris was getting on without Dog. All in all, it was a thoroughly civilised conversation.

"Grace tells me your mum is visiting again soon," Hettie said.

Al glanced at her sharply, but the words had been spoken candidly, and he couldn't believe she would say anything to deliberately antagonise him again. Not today, at least.

"Yes, at the end of March," he replied cautiously. "Have you met her, then?"

"Only briefly," Hettie replied. "She came down to the paddock to sketch the horses in the snow. Her pictures are amazing," Hettie enthused. "I told her Mum would love to see them; my mum's an artist too. She does book illustrations. She's drawn some great pictures of Doris. I wanted her to do one of Dog, but well, turns out we ran out of time."

They chatted the length of the drive, but Hettie was brought down to earth with a bump when she pulled up in the yard. Bev glowered ominously from behind her wheelbarrow. Holly and Jodie couldn't even look at her. "The wicked witch is back." She sighed as she slid off Gent and took him back to his stable.

Bev marched over as soon as she came out. Hettie held up her hand to ward her off the inevitable onslaught. "I know, I know," she hissed. "It was a terrible thing to do. I've apologised to him, and now I'm going to ring Imogen and apologise to her too. I don't know what else I can do, Bev. If I could turn back the clock, I would."

Bev pursed her lips. She could see that Hettie was sorry, but she still needed to say her piece.

"That was wicked, Hettie, and it wasn't your place to say anything. And from you? I'm shocked, I am. I'd have said you were better than that. Hasn't that poor boy had enough heartache in his life without the likes of you addin' to it?"

Hettie didn't know what heartache Bev was talking about, but she'd had enough for one day. To have Bev, who was usually her staunchest defender, turn on her was the final straw.

"It isn't me who cheated on him, is it?" Hettie spat from the corner she'd backed herself into.

"No," Bev said flatly. "And you can rest assured I will be 'avin' a word with that Imogen as well."

Al came out of Satan's stable as the exchange came to an end. He saw Bev marching away and Hettie looking upset. He sighed and followed Bev. Bev's mettle was up, and she started as soon as he caught up with her.

"All I can say is that that girl is usually the nicest person I know. I don't know what got in to her, I really don't. No excuses, I know, for that kind of behaviour, but it was out of character, and that's a fact. She must have the hots for you, Alexander; that's all I can think. I can't think of any other explanation for it. She's been moody and all out of odds with herself…"

Alexander also held up his hand to try and slow Bev down.

"Bev, Bev, it's all right," he said. "We've sorted it out. Calm down."

"It is not all right." Bev was off again. "I've had words with her, and I'll be 'avin' words with that Imogen too, for leadin' you on like that."

Oh, Christ, Alexander thought wearily. *I've cooked up a right shit-storm here.*

"Beverly," he said sternly. "There is absolutely no need for you to speak to Imogen, or to think badly of Hettie. Imogen and I, we were never, well, we weren't—"

"Exclusive?" Bev asked. Al barked out a laugh.

"Yes, if you like, exclusive. Imogen hasn't done anything wrong. And as for Hettie, well, she's got her reasons for wanting to knock me down a peg or two, and they are probably justified as well. So let's leave it at that, shall we?" he asked her hopefully.

Bev's eyes narrowed as she stared at Al and slowly shook her head. "Humph," she grunted eventually. "You young'uns wear me out. It was easier in my day. You shagged 'em, and you married 'em. Straightforward as that. You be careful with that girl," she muttered. "She's 'ad trouble enough."

Al felt shattered as he walked away from the yard, but his step regained its spring when he remembered that Bev thought Hettie had the hots for him. And that Imogen was gay.

Hettie went out to the sand bucket for a much-needed cigarette and called Imogen while she was there. She said she'd "let slip" the fact that Imo was seeing a girl. It wasn't the truth, of course, but she couldn't bring herself to say that she seemed to have done it deliberately to get a reaction from Al. She came off the phone completely befuddled by Imogen's take on the world. She had refused all Hettie's apologies and thanked her instead for "getting that ghastly conversation over with on my behalf."

CHAPTER FOURTEEN

The Fox was packed on Saturday evening, with Hettie's friends swelling the usual local crowd. Hettie was chuffed at the number of people who had turned out. And as everyone who arrived to celebrate her birthday insisted on buying her a drink, she had easily hit her pleasantly pissed mark by nine o'clock and she still had half a dozen drinks lined up. James and Grace called in, Nat had brought Simon along, and even Ted and his girlfriend were there (Hettie realised Ted hadn't actually come back for her benefit, but it was still really nice to see him). Bev was back to her normal self, which was a massive relief, and Holly was being surreptitious in the corner with Dan. Having Dan distracted was almost as much of a relief as having Bev back on her side.

Clare and Ewan brought Steve, who kissed Hettie's cheek platonically in greeting. They actually had quite a laugh on the unblind date, after Clare had gone home and they both agreed there wasn't going to be a second. Hettie had worked out she wouldn't be interested in anyone else while she still had a yen for Al, even if she hadn't yet worked out what she would do about the yen. Hannah and Jade were doing shots at the bar with him now, and even that was making her jealous, despite the fact that both of them had brought their significant others. *Am I the only one here who hasn't got a significant other?* Hettie thought in sudden panic. Jodie didn't count because she was only nineteen. Then she remembered her mum. Anna hadn't had a significant other in forever, in fact not since her father, as far as Hettie knew. Jodie and Bev, along with Imogen and "the girlfriend," were sitting at the table next to them. Hettie had avoided looking at Alexander since those two had come in. She gave Imogen credit for having some guts—more than she would have had. Particularly for being brave enough to introduce the girlfriend to Bev. Hettie decided she wasn't going to join that table in a hurry. Nat and Anju were hitting if off, and Ted and Simon were chatting. Ewan and Clare had joined Alexander at the bar. Hettie wanted to be with them, but she didn't dare get that close to Al at the moment. She knocked back another drink.

Alexander was aware that Hettie was avoiding him, but he couldn't help keeping an eye on her all the same. He'd clocked the familiar kiss from Steve, and the hugs that Ewan and Dan had given her when they'd come in. But the shots were taking the edge off, so he hadn't minded Bert hugging her at all. She looked fucking gorgeous tonight, he thought, with her heels and those skintight trousers. He could see the outline of her midriff through her silky blouse, which was making him uncomfortably horny. He could also see that she had passed the point of pleasantly pissed about forty minutes ago and was starting to enjoy herself just a little too much.

Del and Tricia, the landlords, turned the music up after ten. They served chips 'n' dips for the tables and brought out the birthday cake that Hannah had dropped off. Hettie blushed happily as a raucous chorus of "Happy Birthday" went up across the pub. She blew out her single candle and threw back a couple more drinks.

Imogen and Nat rekindled their childhood acquaintance and were reminiscing with Anna when Fiona Harding walked in with Lucy and Julian Greaves. Word was out that the long-suffering Carol had finally left him. Whispered comments scurried around the room. Lucy had brought her brother out for a drink to lift his spirits, and Fiona had persuaded them to revisit the Fox. She told Julian he shouldn't be taking the blame for that sordid little affair and that everyone knew Hettie Redfern was a slut, so why should he be the one to suffer? Julian, fired up with bitter and self-righteous indignation at the way the women in his life had treated him, agreed. Buoyed up by Fiona's conviction of his innocence, he conveniently forgot the countless affairs he'd had in the intervening years and concluded that his wife's leaving was entirely Hettie's fault.

Fiona pursed her lips with proved-right smugness when they arrived in the bar to see Hettie dancing with abandon in the middle of the room.

Alexander, leaning on the bar between Ted and Ewan, was enjoying Hettie's dancing too much. There was a small copper curl bouncing against her neck and he wanted to push it aside to kiss her in exactly the place where it was touching her skin. He dragged his eyes away for long enough to notice Fiona and Greaves come in. He glanced back at Hettie to see if she was aware. She was laughing and dancing with her school mates and Anju and obviously hadn't seen their arrival. Anna and Nat had, though, Al thought, as they visibly tensed in their seats. Natalie glared openly, and Anna leaned forward and put her hand on Nat's arm. They appeared to be sharing a heated discussion, but Al couldn't hear what was said.

The arrivals found a corner beyond sight of the dancing crowd. Julian simmered into his beer as Fiona stirred his grievances.

Anna quickly decided she'd had enough for the night, so Bert offered to walk her home. She hugged Hettie, made her good-byes, and fired a warning look at Natalie as she left.

Jade invented some party games, and they spent a hilarious hour drunkenly trying to follow the rules and participate in them. Even Al had downed enough to join in and make a fool of himself. When the games were over, Hettie tottered happily to the bar and used Alexander's leg to propel herself onto the stool next to him.

"I'm having such a good evening!" she announced. "But I want to know you've forgiven me for being such a bish yesterday." Her words overlapped in her tipsiness.

"You are completely forgiven." Al laughed. "As long as I am equally forgiven for my own ill-timed and bad-form comment. I am sorry that I said it," he finished more seriously.

"Then I guess I will have to forgive you too!" Hettie beamed happily. "Look at us, all happy families! You know it was never really the comment that set me off," she whispered conspiratorially. "I've got used to that sort of shit, I can promish you. It was knowing that you thought of me like that, like everyone else in this village. That was what really got to me." She smiled a little sadly, then swayed and giggled tipsily as her elbow slipped away from her on the bar.

Al was about to protest that he didn't think badly of her at all when Fiona thrust her head in his face.

"I hope you weren't fucking that when we were together," she spat viciously, indicating Hettie with a nod of her head. "If you were, I think we both need a visit to the clinic. She's been around, you know."

"Fuck off, Fiona!" Alexander snarled. "And take your nasty mouth with you."

Fiona glared back at him, swung her hair defiantly, and flounced off.

"See?" Hettie said brightly, forcing a tight smile, although the two red spots forming on her cheeks and her glinting eyes belied it.

"Don't take any notice of Fiona," Al said. "She's being a bitch because she's jealous."

"Ah, another broken heart chalked up to Alexander Melton," Hettie slurred, smiling ruefully. "I might even feel sorry for her now. She's lucky Nat wasn't in earshot, though, cos she would have had her eyes out."

"I'm sure there's no need for your sympathy," Al interrupted curtly. She'd misunderstood his comment. He meant jealous of Hettie's looks, not the fact that she was sitting next to him.

"How are you coping with *that?*" Hettie tried to whisper again, and nodded her head woozily in Imogen's direction. "It can't have been easy for you this evening."

Al chuckled dryly. "I refuse to answer that question on the grounds that my suffering might cause you to get hysterical again. And you would be at serious risk of falling off that bar stool and injuring yourself."

That did give Hettie the giggles, and he couldn't help but laugh with her.

"A pee and a fag!" she announced when her giggles eventually subsided.

"Do you need a hand down from there, by any chance?" Al smiled.

Hettie grinned and nodded. And when he put his hands on her waist, she closed her eyes in pleasure. "Maybe I should just sleep with you and get it over with," she muttered almost to herself as she landed.

"It's not meant to be an ordeal!" Alexander cried, mock offended, as she tottered off in the direction of the ladies' room.

Hettie was coming back from the loo when she came face-to-face with Julian. She froze, and a chill washed down her spine. Julian was smirking nastily; Hettie knew that look too well. She tried to walk past him in the narrow corridor, but his hand shot out and grabbed her arm.

"Well, well," he sneered. "If it isn't little Hettie. How very fitting to bump into you, of all people."

His breath on her face smelled of stale fags and booze, and the rest of him reeked of BO. His eyes were gleaming dangerously, and fear rooted Hettie to the spot. She instantly became her sixteen-year-old self again. Her heart was racing, and the hairs on her arms stood on end. Everything in her screamed to get away, but she couldn't make her muscles listen.

"Let go of my arm, Julian," she tried, bravely lifting her chin. But her voice came out weak and wavering, and she cursed herself for that.

"You don't sound very pleased to see me, Hettie," Julian said. "And after everything I did for you, as well. But then you always were an ungrateful little brat."

Hettie was beginning to think she might actually be in danger. Julian was obviously drunk and even nastier than she'd known him to be before. Her mind raced. If she called out, no one would hear her; the music was playing too loud. She could run, or she could try to fight him off. Surely someone would be out in a minute, and she could get away from him then. Her eyes went hopefully to the back door of the bar.

Julian followed her gaze. "Yes, you're right. Good thought," he said. "Not very private here, is it? Let's go somewhere a little more secluded, where we can have a nice chat." He pushed her toward the exit door to the car park, walking closely behind, holding both her arms.

"Julian, I'm not going out there," Hettie said firmly. "I've got friends and family waiting for me in the bar. If you want to talk, we can go back in there."

Julian laughed and kept pushing her until they were standing outside in the car park. Then he shoved her backward against the wall. Holding her wrists by her sides, he leaned his body into hers, pinning her in place.

"What I want to hear," he snarled, "is you saying how sorry you are for fucking up my life."

Hettie closed her eyes and pressed herself into the wall.

"Enough now, Julian," she said. "You're drunk, and you're obviously upset. But this is a very bad idea. Even you must know that." Her voice sounded shrill and desperate.

Julian glared at her furiously. *Snooty little bitch,* he fumed. His life was in ruins because of her. She'd been the first one who'd led him astray with her sly, lithe body and her adoring puppy dog eyes. And now she was telling him enough? He slapped her hard across her face, and the pained little yelp that escaped her as his hand connected with her jaw gave him a rush of satisfaction.

"Enough?" He growled, "I say when it's enough, Hettie. Surely I taught you that much."

Hettie started to struggle. Her ears were ringing, and she was literally seeing stars. But the pain of the slap had woken the fight in her, and she was determined to get away now.

Julian forced her arms behind her, laughing darkly at her struggles. He pressed his groin against her front. Hettie struggled on, trying to get her arms free, turning her face determinedly away from his. But tilted backward as she was, with his weight on top of her, she couldn't get enough purchase to shift him. She tried to head-butt him, but even in her heels, she wasn't tall enough to do more than bang her head ineffectively against his chin. She could feel the evidence that her efforts to fight were exciting him. The thought made her panic, and Hettie started to scream.

In the bar, Nat had been searching for Hettie for nearly five minutes. Al had told her she'd gone to the loo, but she'd checked there. And she looked outside the front of the pub where everyone went for a smoke. No one seemed to know where she was. She noticed that bastard Greaves was missing from his seat, and that worried her. She turned back to double-check the ladies' room.

Alexander was heading for the loo when he thought he heard a noise in the car park. He peered out of the window and saw a couple out there snogging. He found that amusing for the second before he realised who it was. A wave of disgust and jealousy hit him. *She's been fucking the bloke all these years.* The thought turned his stomach.

Then things seemed to happen in slow motion. He saw Hettie raise her knee and deliver a punishing kick to Julian's groin. And as his mind tried to readjust to that, Natalie pushed past him and flew out through the door. He heard Nat shriek like a banshee as she ran at Hettie and Julian, "Get your hands off her, you fucking pervert!"

Alexander charged out behind her. Nat's scream had distracted Julian long enough for Hettie to get a hand free. She grabbed his hair, twisted to the side, and smacked his head into the wall. When Alexander got to them, both girls were attacking Julian with their fists, and he paused for a second, unsure how best to help. Then he caught site of the blood on Hettie's lip and raged into the action. Julian stepped back and raised both his hands when he saw Alexander coming for him.

"All right, mate, no need for you to get involved," he wheedled. "Just having some fun with Hettie."

Alexander drew back his fist and landed a punch squarely on Julian's jaw. Julian was out cold before he hit the ground.

The three of them stood for a moment, staring at Julian on the ground, before Natalie went to Hettie and took her in her arms.

"You're hurt," she said. "What the fuck has the bastard done this time?"

Hettie shook her head and took a step away. She was seriously shaken and couldn't control the shivering that was creeping over her.

"Nothing of matter," Hettie said firmly. "Get me home, Nat, please. I don't want anyone in there to know about this. You'll have to think of an excuse, but get me out of here."

Alexander stepped towards her. "You're bleeding, Hettie," he said quietly. "Are you sure you don't want someone to take a look at that?" He turned to Nat. "Should we call the police?" he asked.

"No!" Hettie shouted at them, then collected herself before she spoke again. "No police. Get me home, and don't let anyone know what's happened. If you want to help me, you'll do that," she added determinedly.

Nat sighed and looked at Al, and he looked at Hettie, standing in the car park with blood on her face, shaking like a leaf. He shrugged.

"All right, we'll take the Landy," he said. "Hettie, is it locked? Where are your keys?"

"It's not locked. They're in my handbag. It's still in the bar," she answered.

"Nat, can you go and find Hettie's handbag? Tell anyone you need to that you've had to take Hettie home, that she's not feeling well or something. And can you tell Ted that I'll see him back at the hall?"

Natalie nodded and went back to the bar. Al put his hand on Hettie's shoulder and directed her toward the car. She was shivering visibly now, and a bruise had begun to develop along her jaw.

"Are you sure…" he started, but her glare stopped him short. He opened the passenger door, and Hettie climbed in.

Natalie came back with the handbag. Al took the keys. He reached for his phone as they reversed out of the parking space. He rang Fiona as they crossed to the track.

"Your friend seems to have passed out in the car park," he said when she picked up. "You might want to go and sort him out."

In the bar Lucy sighed. *Not again.*

They took the country route in silence. Hettie's shivering slowly subsided. She got a tissue out of her bag and dabbed at her split lip. She could feel Nat simmering beside her with the rage she wanted to vent and was thankful that Alexander's presence was forcing her to keep quiet.

When they arrived at the cottage, Hettie thanked Al and told him she'd be fine with Nat. But he climbed out of the Landy and followed them in anyway.

Hettie put the kettle on for want of something to do while she waited for the onslaught from her sister. She leaned against the kitchen unit. "How are you going to get back?" she asked.

"Are you going to pretend that didn't happen?" Nat countered the question belligerently.

Hettie rifled in her bag for her cigarettes, got one out, and lit it. "We've got company, Nat." She nodded at Al. "This isn't the time. A drunk jerk tried a fumble in the car park, and now he's got a broken jaw. Incident over, problem sorted. Go home, or back to the pub if you like. You too," she said and looked at Alexander. "Thank you both for your help, but I really want this forgotten. And people must be wondering where you've got to."

Alexander didn't say anything. He could feel the tension in the room, and every time he looked at the bruise on Hettie's chin, he was overwhelmed with self-hatred. The thought that he had been raging against her morals while he was watching her being attacked was truly awful. He could have got to her quicker if he hadn't been fixated by his vicious, twisted assumptions. He wanted to go back to the car park and pound Julian Greaves into the ground.

"Right, I'll call a taxi," Nat said. If Alexander hadn't been there, she would have had a lot more to say. But Hettie was right, now wasn't the time.

"I can take you back," Al said, "if Hettie doesn't mind lending the Land Rover." He looked at Hettie, so brave and brittle it nearly broke his heart. And she'd been having such a good time before that bastard had ruined her night. It made him sick to his stomach, but he felt helpless and didn't know what to do.

"Yes, of course. Thank you again," Hettie answered. She wished with all her heart that Alexander hadn't been there to witness that. She wanted him to go now, while she was still holding it together.

"You're sure you're all right?" Nat asked. "I can stay here with you, if you like. Simon wouldn't mind."

"I'm absolutely fine, Nat. Please don't fuss. Don't mention this to Mum, or to anyone, will you?" She glanced at Al, hoping to include him in the request.

"Of course, sis; whatever you say." Nat sighed and kissed Hettie on the cheek. "Call me if you need me. I'll speak to you tomorrow."

Hettie nodded.

"Or me," Al added. "I'm minutes away, and my phone will be on."

"Thank you," Hettie said again. She wished they would go; she was worn out with being thankful.

She went outside with Doris when the Land Rover had driven away and smoked another cigarette. There were texts on her phone from the girls, asking if she was OK. She turned the phone off; she could deal with that tomorrow. She locked the kitchen door and took a knife out of the drawer, which she carried up to bed with her. Breaking her own house rules, she beckoned Doris to follow her up.

Nat's simmering boiled over the minute she was alone with Alexander.

"I shouldn't be saying any of this in front of you," she started. "Hettie would never speak to me again if she knew, but I'm so fucking wound up and angry. She should have called the police! She should have called the police ten years ago, and she should bloody well call them now. The bastard attacked her in a car park! There's laws against that, and there's laws against what he did before! I would call them myself if I thought for a minute she would talk to them. He spent two years hurling abuse at her in the street, and he wrote her threatening letters—did you know that? No, no one knows that," she answered her own question indignantly. "That fucking evil family spread so many rumours that Hettie came out of it as the villain! She was—" Nat stopped abruptly, aware she'd said too much and was about to make it worse. "I'm sorry," she added less furiously. "None of this is your business or your problem, and I shouldn't have said any of that."

Alexander was computing years in his head, absorbing Nat's comments, and his feelings of sickness and self-disgust were getting worse. He'd been one of the people who had made Hettie the villain, hadn't he? What the fuck kind of man did that make him?

"It's OK," he told her, wiping his hand across his face. "I can pretend I didn't hear it." He wished he hadn't, really. "She's lucky to have you as a sister," he added gently. "But you can only follow Hettie's lead on this, Nat. You know that."

"I know." Nat sighed. "That's why I'm ranting at you instead."

They were silent for a while.

"You landed a right corker on him, though." She grinned wickedly. "With luck he'll be eating through a straw for a while at least."

They might not look anything like each other, Al thought, *but that grin is pure Hettie.*

Hettie was up early the next morning, although it was actually her day off. She gave the horses their breakfast feeds and picked up the copy of *Horse and Hound* magazine, which was in the dugout. She took Doris for a long walk, stopping to say hi to Rose in the field and calling at Dog's grave before walking on through the woods for a couple of hours. Alexander called at the cottage to make sure she was all right, but he didn't get an answer when he knocked.

Back at the cottage after her walk, Hettie made coffee, lit a cigarette, and fired off a round robin text in reply to the ones she'd received last night. She sent it to Nat and Alexander as well, so they would know what she had said.

oops birthday girl had a few too many!

sorry to abandon you early :-/ but I had fun! :-)

Thanks for celebrating with me! See you all soon xxxx

Nat worked it out in an instant, but the breezy message confused Alexander. He thought he would go back to the cottage later to check on her again.

Hettie sat with the *Horse and Hound,* smoking a second cigarette. She circled three job advertisements in the classifieds: one in Norfolk, one in Cumbria, and a third in Saudi Arabia. Then she put on her riding boots and went back to the yard for a head-collar to catch Rose in from the field. When Holly and Jodie exclaimed in dismay at her bruised face and split lip, she determinedly laughed it off. "Don't ask! I am never drinking again! Bit of a fight with the bathroom floor, and I think I lost!"

"It was a bloody good night last night, though, wasn't it?" Holly said, laughing.

"One of the best," Hettie agreed as she grabbed Rose's head-collar and made a run for it.

Alexander knocked on the cottage door for the second time that day, and when he still didn't get an answer, he thought he'd better make sure Hettie wasn't lying unconscious in there. That text had been worryingly strange. He went in and checked every room. Hettie wasn't in there, but the *Horse and Hound* was lying on the kitchen table, open to the page with the circled job advertisements.

He tried the yard. "Is Hettie about?" he asked Holly.

"No, she's gone to get Rose from the field," Holly answered. She called after him as he walked away, "Wait till you see the shiner she's got on her cheek! That girl needs to learn how to hold her drink! She fell over in the bathroom!" Holly chortled happily.

Hettie saw him walking up the track as she was leading Rose back down, Doris trotting beside them. *Oh, shit,* she thought. He was the last person she wanted to see, but she couldn't really avoid him now.

"Hi," Alexander called. The bruise on Hettie's check had turned a nasty shade of purple; he had to look away when he saw it. "How are you feeling?" he asked, falling into step beside her.

"Fine, never been better," Hettie snapped.

"That cheek not hurting too much?" Alexander persisted, although he was conscious from her body language and the shortness of her reply that she didn't want to talk about it.

"I've worked with horses for ten years; I've had worse than this." She was silent for a moment before continuing hesitantly, "Um, I told Holly and Jodie that I got the bruise—"

"Yes, I know. You fell over in the bathroom," Alexander cut in, sighing. "And what was with that weird text you sent me this morning?"

"I sent it to everyone. You know, everyone who was asking where I'd got to last night. I don't expect you to lie for me, but I thought you needed to know what I was telling them, that's all."

"No one will hear about it from me, Hettie, if that's how you want it." Al was getting exasperated. "But I can't for the life of me understand why you're protecting that bastard."

"I'm not protecting him; I'm protecting myself," Hettie bit back.

"From what?" Alexander asked.

"From rumour, from innuendo, from people thinking badly of me."

"Why on earth would anyone think badly of you?" Alexander was incredulous.

"I don't know, Alexander; you tell me. Why would someone think badly of me for gossip and rumour they've heard around the village?" Hettie knew she shouldn't be turning on him, of all people. He was only trying to help. But she didn't want to talk about it. His questions were making her defensive, and she hadn't failed to notice that he couldn't even look at her now.

"I thought I was forgiven for that," Alexander said sadly.

"Apparently I was lying," Hettie spat.

She had a lovely ride on Rose. Doris came too. She was nervy and clingy again, so Hettie didn't think she would stray at the moment. It was a mild, early spring day. The trees were in bud, bluebells brightened the woods, and everywhere Hettie looked, there were signs of new life waiting to burst out when the warm spring sun offered encouragement. It was hard to think she would be leaving all this soon. The beautiful countryside, her horses, the cottage, even Rose, she thought sadly. Rose would have to be sold; not many jobs let you take your own horse. And besides, it was time to put all the reminders of that episode of her life behind her. *Enough*, she told herself determinedly. *It's time to move on.*

CHAPTER FIFTEEN

Hettie had telephone interviews for the jobs in Cumbria and Norfolk. She decided against trying for the post in Saudi Arabia. She wouldn't be able to take Doris, and she wasn't sure she was brave enough to go that far away. The woman she spoke to in Cumbria sounded slightly mad. But Cynthia from Norfolk was nice, so they agreed to meet for a second interview. Hettie was clear that she wouldn't be leaving her current job until hunting was over and a replacement had been found. "My dear girl," Cynthia cried, "with a statement like that, you've landed yourself the position, as far as I'm concerned! But come and see us in Norfolk. Make sure you like the place. Meet the horses and the girls. Then make your mind up."

Hettie came off the phone, gathered her courage, and walked reluctantly to the hall to inform James and Grace. James accepted her news with sad resignation, but Grace was devastated. She wanted to know what they could do to make Hettie change her mind. Hettie spent a painful half hour declining Grace's offers of more money, more time off, or pretty much anything else she wanted.

"My mind is made up, Grace. I'm sorry. Please don't think this is down to anything you've done. I couldn't work for anyone better than you and James, but it's time that I moved on. I want to work with eventers—that's always been the dream. If I don't do it now, while I'm young, free, and single, I never will. You've made me too comfortable here, Grace," Hettie finished sadly. "I want you to know that it hasn't been an easy decision. I will miss you terribly. I'll miss the horses and the yard, and I will never stop being grateful for everything you and Draymere have given me." Hettie stopped talking before the emotion got too much for her.

"But you won't be here for the baby!" Grace wailed. She knew she wasn't being fair. Hettie had every right to change jobs, but she *really* didn't want her to go.

"I'll be back, Grace. Of course I will. You're my mate! My mum lives up the road. I'll probably be home every weekend! We can text and talk on the phone. I'll put pictures on Facebook, and you can as well!"

"You're rubbish on Facebook, Hettie; you haven't been on there in years," Grace said petulantly.

"I'll be better, you watch. I'll probably be Facebook stalking you when I'm miles away and homesick." Hettie went on more brightly, "Anyway, it took months to find Imo. I've told Cynthia I can't take the job until you've got a replacement, so I'll probably be here for ages yet!"

"I hate this Cynthia already," Grace muttered, but she smiled ruefully as she said it.

That whole week was traumatic. Everyone who heard the news tried to make Hettie change her mind. Everyone except Alexander; she didn't hear a word from him. In fact he didn't seem to be talking to her at all unless it was unavoidable. Out of all the people she spoke to, only her mum and Nat were happy and offered encouragement. It was almost a relief when Sunday arrived and Hettie set off for her visit to Norfolk. She left early and took Doris with her. Doris being welcome was part of her criteria for accepting the job.

Flintend Farmhouse was an attractive, ramshackle place. Cynthia greeted her warmly and welcomed Doris and Hettie into the big, disorderly farmhouse kitchen, where Hettie counted at least three other dogs. Cynthia was funny, down to earth, and gritty; Hettie warmed to her immediately. She was given a tour of the house, including the generous en suite bedroom, which would be Hettie's own. The dogs had free roam of the rooms, and there were pictures of horses on every wall. The dining room table was littered with paperwork, out-of-date horse magazines, and an assortment of leather saddlery.

"It's rather untidy!" Cynthia cried, waving her hand dismissively each time they entered a room. And it was, but the house felt warm and well lived in. Hettie could see herself being comfortable there.

"Now the important bit!" Cynthia said, slipping her feet into mucker boots as she opened the garden door out of the utility room—the untidiest room so far with only a narrow path remaining through the coats, boots, and dog beds—and led them along a brick path, which wove through half an acre of overgrown garden. "That's the pool house over there, by the way, although we haven't filled it in years." Cynthia indicated a flint barn conversion with glass patio doors. Hettie thought she could see a ride-on lawnmower and some hay bales through the glass. A procession of dogs followed them through the garden and on to the stable yard. The contrast from the house was a shock; Hettie found herself in an immaculate American barn stable block, with five stables running along each side, eight of them housing horses who looked over their doors when they arrived. Through the open far end of the barn, Hettie could see two further horses being ridden in a large outdoor arena surrounded by manicured post and rail-fenced paddocks. The stable tour took much longer than their quick flit around the house. Cynthia introduced each of the horses and gave Hettie a lengthy rundown on their characters, ages, training levels, and competitive careers.

"The ponies are in these end two boxes. We'll meet them when you meet the girls; they're riding them at the moment." She nodded in the direction of the arena. "It's a bonus you're short. I look ridiculous on them, as Harriet delights in telling me!" Cynthia laughed. The tack room was clean and tidy. Polished saddles and bridles hung in regimented, orderly rows, and the feed room looked more like a science lab than any feed room Hettie had ever seen.

"I'm a bit OCD about my feeding regimes," Cynthia explained.

Hettie was impressed with the facilities and the quality and condition of the horses and excited by the cross-country fences she could see running alongside the paddocks and disappearing into the trees.

"Right, my delightful daughters next. I've saved the best until last!" Cynthia said (ironically, Hettie thought). "Harriet's thirteen—we communicate mostly through grunts—and Jessica is nine. Girls, come and meet Hettie!" she shouted as they reached the fence of the arena. "Hettie? What's that short for, Henrietta?" she asked distractedly as the girls obediently stopped what they were doing and rode in their direction.

"Close," Hettie replied. "It's actually Henriqueta; my father was Portuguese," she added by way of explanation.

"Was?" Cynthia raised her eyebrows.

"No, is, I think," Hettie corrected. "I don't know. I've never actually met him."

Harriet and Jessica introduced themselves and their ponies politely and returned to their riding (they rode very well, Hettie thought). Cynthia gave her a lengthy lowdown on the ponies they were sitting on.

"Right, that's about the sum of it," Cynthia said as they leaned on the fence, watching her daughters. "Harriet! Outside rein! All your meals and use of a car. Every weekend off. Harriet! More leg, girl, legs! Don't sit there and expect him to do all the work for you! You won't be a nanny or a cleaner; I don't expect housework or cooking. When you're finished on the yard, that's you done. I'm training clients most days a week; you can join the lessons when it's practical. There might be a chance to compete if I decide you're up to it. Say yes, please. You're by far and away the best I've interviewed so far. Harriet! I shouldn't still need to tell you! Lean back and sit on your blasted bottom!" Jessica galloped round the arena and flew over a couple of jumps.

"Yes," Hettie said, "if you're still prepared to wait for me. I would very much like to take it."

"Excellent!" Cynthia beamed, turning away from the fence. "I've bumbled along for the last six months since their blasted father ran off with the last girl. I'm sure I can hold out awhile longer now. Get yourself up here as soon as you can, and keep me updated on progress."

"Oh, I'm sorry to hear that." Hettie spluttered, not sure how to react to that sort of bombshell from a woman she barely knew.

"Don't be." Cynthia laughed. "I'm not! Although losing a groom is always a blow."

"That must have been hard on the girls," Hettie tried again.

"God, no," Cynthia retorted. "They see more of him now than they ever did before, if that can be counted as a blessing."

Hettie was emotional on the long drive home. There was no question in her mind that the job was a good one; the hours were better, the pay was amazing compared to what she was getting now, and she would be working for a renowned rider who had competed at national level and had even said she would train her. But it was all feeling too real now. And after seven years at Draymere, the thought of leaving felt like walking into an abyss.

Alexander was working flat out to get the gatehouse into a state he could live in. With the plumbing and electrical work finished and most of the flooring down, he decided that when the kitchen and bathroom were functioning, he could make the move and let the builders work on around him. He had taken advantage of James and Grace's hospitality for too long. He could do the decorating and finishing touches when the mood took him, which it really wasn't at the moment. Ewan was pushing to get moving on their plans, and James had offered a redundant barn complex on the estate. With a lot of work, it could be converted for their practice and surgery. They were looking at it that afternoon, but the thought of further renovation work wasn't improving Al's mood. He needed to get away, he thought, and put some space between himself and Draymere. He couldn't seem to shake the black cloud that had been hanging over him since that incident at the pub. He walked through the house to look at the work the builders had finished: a covered outdoor area where Digger could sleep and have access to the house and the garden. It looked good; Digger would be more than happy there. He called Imogen.

"Imo, order me a bed, a sofa, and a telly, would you? No, I don't care about colours or styles. You choose. King-size, I guess. Superking? Never heard of it, but if you think it will fit in. Big telly. Oh, and I need the bed by next week, and all the sheets and stuff. What? No, I've already told you, Imogen. You choose."

He would look at these barns this afternoon, visit his father on the way home, then bugger off somewhere for a few days to try and clear his head. Not Ted's—the last thing he needed right now was more Ted-induced navel-gazing. It didn't matter where, as long as it was somewhere other than Draymere. They would have to do without him on morning exercise. Grace was still riding, and he'd done it for long enough. It was only meant to be for a few weeks in the first place. What did it matter now, anyway? Hunting was nearly over, and Hettie was leaving. Probably due to people like him judging her and making her life a misery. He pushed the thought away. He didn't know that was the case. Maybe she was bored. Bored with Draymere, bored with him. He knew he was. He'd asked James how old Julian Greaves was. James thought forty, possibly a few years older. So he would have been thirty-plus ten years ago, then—older than Al was now when Greaves was messing about with a sixteen-year-old girl. Al was disgusted by the thought, and disgusted with himself for thinking badly of Hettie for that sordid situation. She was right not to forgive him; he couldn't forgive himself.

The barns had huge potential; there was no question of that. Ewan, fired up with enthusiasm, started expanding their plans to include an equine clinic and operating theatre, with a stable block attached so they could have horses as inpatients.

"Whoa, whoa." Al tried to slow him down. All he could see was a shitload of work and expense. He was beginning to wonder if his heart was in it anymore. "Neither of us are equine surgeons, Ewan, and have you got any idea of the sort of money we're talking about? I mean, I've got a bit put aside, but it wouldn't get close to covering the scale you're thinking along."

"We always knew we would have to borrow funds," Ewan argued. "And James donating the premises will save us a heap of money. We've got to think big! It's just a question of how much we borrow. The accountants are working on our projections, and then we can go to the bank. It doesn't all have to happen at once. We can start small, get the place going, and then build up and take on a surgeon when we start getting some income."

"Humph," Al retorted, burying his hands deep in his pockets. "All right. I guess seeing what the banks have to say can't do any harm."

"Great!" Ewan enthused. "I think we have made a decision on the premises for 'The Melton and Jones Veterinary Practice,' or maybe 'The Jones and Melton!'" He grinned. "I'm seeing the accountants on Monday—you should come with me."

"I can't," Al said shortly. "I'm going away for a few days."

"Anywhere nice?" Ewan asked. He didn't know what was eating Alexander today, but something obviously was.

"I haven't actually decided yet—somewhere, anywhere, away," Al muttered uncomfortably.

"I've got a mate in East Anglia who works in a practice like the one I'm envisaging. If you go that way on your travels, I could give him a call, get him to give you the tour. He's a good bloke, Tom. We were at veterinary school together. Cracking place they've got there, too."

I could have a look at East Anglia, Al thought. *It's not as if I've come up with anywhere better. Wasn't Hettie going somewhere up there?* He was pretty sure Grace had said Norfolk, although he'd been trying not to listen. He had a couple of uni mates in Norfolk too. He could look them up if he ran out of things to do.

"Yes, all right. Good idea," he told Ewan. "Give him a ring and let me know."

Grace was astounded when she got a call about Hettie's job before they had even advertised it. The ad had been placed in the *Horse and Hound* but wouldn't appear until the following week. The woman, Siobhan, said she was local; she worked at Hardacre Farm and had heard on the grapevine that a position might be coming vacant. Grace agreed to interview her that Friday. She came off the phone and sighed. With any luck the girl would be totally unsuitable. Most of them were. Hardacre, wasn't that the Greaves place? Not a hunting yard, then, which would probably prove to be a deal-breaker. Grace cheered up a little bit.

Hettie panicked when Grace told her they had someone coming in for an interview on Friday. She hadn't expected things to start moving that quickly. It hit her that whoever got this job wouldn't only be taking over her work. The person would get her horses, her cottage, and her Landy too, basically moving into her life. Then Grace mentioned that the woman was working at Hardacre. And Hettie, who still felt a chill at the mention of the place, hardened her resolve that moving on was the only option left to her.

Siobhan was a mature, stocky woman in her forties. She had a tattoo on her wrist (Grace couldn't work out what it was) and a staid, somewhat slow manner about her. When she first arrived,

Grace was convinced she was going to be a nonrunner. But Siobhan answered their questions with obvious knowledge. She had worked with hunters in Ireland for several years before moving to England four years ago, and had been at Hardacre ever since. There were currently forty horses under her care, and she was the only full-time paid employee.

"I say 'paid,'" Siobhan added, "but he hasn't actually paid me a penny in over two months. Rumour is the bank has foreclosed. He's shedding the horses for cash at rock-bottom prices. I believe my job to be as good as gone. Not a minute too soon, mind you. If it hadn't of been for Carol, I'd have been out of there long ago. The man's an eejit, but she's a good woman is Carol, a very good woman indeed."

"Goodness," Grace said in surprise. "Forty horses and just you—how is that even possible?"

"Ach, most of them live in the field, to be fair, and he has a lot of…um, volunteers."

"Can we give you a call?" Grace asked. "When we've had a chance to chat."

"Of course," Siobhan replied, slowly standing up. "I can tell you I'm honest, trustworthy, and loyal, and I will take every care with your horses. Carol will be happy to confirm that, even if the eejit's not."

Grace found herself in a dilemma after Siobhan had left. James said they wouldn't do much better and that they would be lucky to fill the post so quickly. Grace was reluctant to agree. They continued their discussion in the kitchen, where Alexander was watching Georgia for them.

"It's all too quick," Grace was muttering. "We should wait to see who applies when the advert comes out. I know that Hettie has said she's going, but I'm still hoping that she might change her mind. If we take on the first person who turns up, we're not giving her a chance to do that."

"Grace, Hettie has handed her notice in," James replied. "And wishing she hadn't isn't going to change that. We can't *not* employ someone on the off chance that Hettie has a change of heart."

"Well, she didn't speak too well of her previous employer, and that always sets off alarms," Grace responded heatedly. "All that about the bank foreclosing, and him being an eejit! It could be us she's talking about like that if we take her on."

"She sounded very fond of his wife," James countered, "and he hasn't paid her in two months, to be fair. We all know that Greaves is an idiot, so it's not as if she's telling us anything that isn't already common knowledge. She's got the experience and the knowledge we're looking for, Grace, and you know that."

"The Hardacre horses have never looked particularly well turned out. Bit of a sorry bunch, if you ask me." Grace was indignant and clutching at straws.

James sighed.

Alexander couldn't help hearing their conversation, and although he wouldn't usually interfere in a marital dispute, their comments captured his attention. Grace was hoping that Hettie would decide not to go, and this woman was apparently no friend of Julian Greaves. Any enemy of Greaves was a friend of his, he thought. He was with Grace in hoping that Hettie might stay but didn't see how they could force her to by refusing to fill the post. That would be unfair.

"Why don't you let Hettie decide?" Al said. They both looked at him. "After all, if you think she might change her mind, Grace, introducing her to her replacement might be the catalyst for that."

Grace called Hettie that evening. "She wasn't too bad, this Siobhan," she said. "Not perfect, but not too bad. I said we should wait for the ad to come out, that things were moving too fast, but Alexander thinks we should give her a go, a second interview at least. A tour of the yard and a meeting with you, if that's all right. I would very much like to hear your impressions and see what you think of her."

♦♦♦

Alexander took off on his trip the following day. He had booked a hotel in Blakeney, right on the Norfolk coast. His room had a courtyard attached for Digger, and he was looking forward to going on some long runs on the Norfolk beaches with him. Ewan had spoken to Tom, and Tom was keen to give Al a tour of his place and said Alexander should call when he was in the vicinity. Al had discerned by discreet questioning of Grace that the woman Hettie was going to work for was called Cynthia Briggs-Johnston. Googling her name almost by accident, he found her eventing and training website, which showed him that she lived just a few miles north of Blakeney. He might take a drive past the place, he thought, just out of interest.

His hotel room was large and luxurious, with a massive bed, sumptuously dressed in starched white cotton, dominating the room. *I wonder if that's a superking,* he thought as he allowed himself to imagine Hettie being here with him and what he would do to her in that bed. And in the en suite bathroom, and on the sofa in the corner, and out in the small, grassed courtyard adjoining the room. He shook himself back to reality. Jennifer from uni lived half an hour away. He hadn't seen her in years, but maybe he could persuade her to meet him for dinner.

He took Digger for a long walk and tried to call Jennifer, but his phone didn't have any signal, and he couldn't be bothered to walk any further to try and find one. He contented himself with dinner in his room and watching the telly on the sofa with Digger.

Rising early the next morning after a restful night in the comfortable bed, he went for a six-mile run before breakfast and worked up quite an appetite. He found a hilltop where his phone would work and called Tom. If Al was about tomorrow, Tom said, Sunday was their quietest day, and he could give a more extensive tour then. Alexander agreed on a time to meet Tom, then tried Jennifer's number again.

"Alexander Melton!" Jennifer exclaimed. "Well, there's a blast from the past. How the hell are you, Al?"

"I'm well, Jennifer, thank you. How are you? I'm visiting Blakeney, actually. I wondered if you wanted to meet up."

"I'm good, Al," Jennifer answered tentatively. "When you say meet up..."

"You know, coffee, dinner, or a drink. I'm killing time, really. I've got a meeting nearby tomorrow, and your name came to mind. It's been a long time, Jennifer."

"Yes, it has," Jennifer agreed. "Look, can I be frank with you, Al? If you're looking for dinner and a catch-up, I would be delighted to agree. But if it's recreational sex you're after, well, I gave that up years ago."

Al was taken aback, but he laughed it off good-naturedly. "Dinner and conversation, I promise. It really would be nice to chat."

"That's exactly what you always used to say, but I will give you the benefit of the doubt," Jennifer replied. "I'm engaged now, Alexander, so don't try to lead me astray."

"As if I would!" Alexander cried, laughing even more. He managed, after some persuasion, to get her to agree to come to his hotel that evening.

"Only if you're paying, though," she said. "I can't afford their prices."

Al was surprised by how pretty Jennifer was looking. He had remembered her as being rather plain and plump. She had lived down the corridor in halls, and when the group had moved on to shared digs, Jennifer had come along. To be fair, he had rarely seen her since uni; they had all gone out into the real world and drifted apart, of course.

"Happiness," she said, tartly, in response to his compliments.

Jennifer was witty and entertaining over dinner, if maybe a little sharp at times. This was another surprise. He had known she was super bright but didn't recall her having much character at all. As the main course progressed, they ordered a second bottle of wine and laughed about parties they'd held in their digs and numerous outrageous events that peppered their uni years. Al couldn't actually remember Jennifer being present at the occasions they reminisced over, but she must have been there if she recalled them so well.

"Top up?" he asked, lifting the wine bottle.

"Yes, please!" Jennifer grinned in reply. "Phillip is picking me up, so I can drink as much as I like."

"Ring him up and tell him not to bother," Al said. "I've got a bed the size of a ship in my room, plenty big enough to share. You wouldn't even know I was there." He grinned wickedly.

Jennifer was horrified to find herself tempted, even now. After all these years, and with a good, kind fiancé whom she loved and who had responded to her news that she was going dining with an ex by offering her a lift. There and back.

"I won't be doing that," she said. It sounded prudish, even to her.

Al forced a laugh. That was something else that had changed, then. He couldn't remember needing to ask her twice before.

"What happened to mates with benefits, Jen?" he said, mock hurt.

"Oh, Alexander," Jennifer said sadly. "You never really got it, did you?"

"Got what?" he asked, midmouthful.

"That you had a mate with benefits, but that I was actually in love," Jen replied, curling her mouth up sadly. "Why do you think I followed you to every rented house we had? Trailing along like a puppy, with you barely noticing my presence. For four years!" she added, shaking her head. "God, what a sad bitch

I was. Watching you bring home one girl after another and *still* happy to step in when you had a slack night. So, no, Al. Sorry, I won't be doing that. Phillip is a good man. He loves me and I love him, and it's so, well, *nice* when it happens like that."

Al was stunned. "Christ, Jennifer, no," he said. "Don't tell me that. We were housemates. We shagged now and then. That's what uni is all about."

"Well, it certainly was for you!" Jennifer laughed. "Don't fret; it was years ago. Water under the bridge and all that. I shouldn't have said anything; it was my problem, not yours. You were doing what horny young men do, if they're given the chance."

"Acting like a total shit, you mean. Honestly, I never knew you had, well, feelings—"

"Head over heels in love!" Jennifer exclaimed. "You broke my heart, Melton. But it's nicely mended now, and I definitely don't love you anymore." She laughed again. "But I must admit that I spent years fantasising that you would fall devastatingly in love with someone who didn't give two hoots about you. That hasn't happened, I suppose?" She started to chuckle but stopped when she saw his face. "Oh, Al, it has. I'm sorry. I was trying to make a joke. I wouldn't really wish that on anyone, not even you."

"No, no, no," Alexander protested (too much). "I'm not in love with anyone. I get unhealthy obsessions occasionally, but that's the best I can offer, I'm afraid." He tried to smile, but this whole conversation had thrown him off kilter.

"I'm not buying that. Spill the beans, Al." Jennifer folded her arms and rested them on the table. "I've waited a long time to revel in your misery, so I won't be giving up easily."

"All right," Al said, "but there's not much to it, I'm afraid. There's a girl, a woman, I can't stop thinking about. We've come close to, you know, once or twice, but I acted like a total shit. Again." He smiled ruefully at Jennifer. "And I've blown it once and for all, so the obsession has gone, er, unrequited, shall we say, and that doesn't seem to be doing me much good at all."

"I'm trying very hard not to smile," Jennifer said. "But I'm so glad I came tonight. Can you thank this girl, if you see her, for exacting revenge on my behalf?"

Al laughed. The waiter offered coffee, and they sat in companionable silence as it was served.

"I am sorry, Jennifer. Really, I am," Al said seriously when the waiter left. "You are a really nice person, and, well, I never had any idea. I'm afraid I may have treated women rather badly in the past."

Jennifer looked at him contemplatively. "Why am I here, Alexander?" she asked. "An unrequited love, or obsession, if you prefer, and suddenly your former easy lay from university gets a call? That's not rocket science, Melton, and it's not actually in the past either, is it? To be honest, I don't know if I envy this girl or pity her."

Al wiped his hand across his face. "OK, OK, I get it," he said, suddenly cross. "You only came out to glory in what a nasty bastard I am."

"And you asked me out in the hopes of a shag with no strings attached," Jennifer shot back. "So at least one of us got what we came for." She smiled, got out her phone, and sent a text to Phil.

"Thanks for dinner," she said. "And, honestly, I really came out to catch up. It's been nice to see you again after all these years. Strangely, it really has. I hope you get the girl, Al, and I'm being honest again. If she can hold out against the Melton charm, she must be one tough cookie. Tougher than I was, anyway." She smiled and kissed him on the cheek. "Oh, and Al, apology accepted. Thanks," she added as she left.

CHAPTER SIXTEEN

Hettie didn't like Siobhan, but she knew in her heart that wasn't Siobhan's fault. She didn't like that Siobhan was older and taller than her. She didn't like that she worked at Hardacre, and she resented the way Siobhan was asking stupid questions, with a lift of surprise in her voice at the end of each sentence.

"So you've only got fourteen horses?"

"Do they always get this much bedding?"

"You get two breaks *every* day, then?"

Hettie felt as if her management was being questioned. Her replies were defensive and guarded; she could hear it herself.

"Of course, if you get the job, you can make any changes you like," Hettie said, syrupy sweet. Wasn't this woman taking enough off of her without rubbing it in?

Siobhan redeemed herself slightly when she said the dugout looked nice. She obviously knew her horses. Her CV, as Grace had described it, suggested she would be perfectly able to do the job. *Just not the way I do it*, Hettie thought sullenly.

"It will be nice having horses that hang around long enough to get to know them," Siobhan said wistfully as she patted Cloud over his stable door.

Bit presumptuous, Hettie thought. *You haven't got the job yet, and the horses won't actually be yours.*

But she informed Grace later that she couldn't see any reason why Siobhan wouldn't be OK for the job.

"You've been at Draymere longer than me, Hettie. However am I going to do without you?" Grace wailed with a hand on her bump.

Alexander returned reenergised and full of enthusiasm for the new practice following his tour with Tom. He felt physically refreshed from hours of running followed by long, restful nights. He was still irritated about his evening with Jennifer; it felt like everyone had a gripe with him at the moment. He called Imogen, and he shouted when she told him the bed wouldn't be delivered until the following week. And his mood wasn't improved when he got a call back from Imogen's girlfriend, Helen, who gave him a sound telling-off for "taking advantage of Imogen's sweet nature" and called him a rude cunt. He borrowed the mattress from his room at Draymere and moved into the gatehouse anyway.

The final day of hunting, and Hettie's last day on the yard, would be April first. *Fitting*, Hettie thought. Siobhan was starting next week; they would be working together for a while so that Hettie could show her the ropes.

"Although she won't be moving into the cottage until after you've gone, of course," Grace reassured. Which was meant to make Hettie feel better, but didn't at all.

She really needed to sell Rose. Time was going so fast, and she needed to buy a car to get her to Norfolk and back. It was all very well having use of the family car, but that wouldn't get her home when she needed to be here. The train journey took over five hours, and she would never be able to carry all the stuff she needed to take.

The subject of the Hardacre horses came up at break. Holly said Julian was flogging them off for a hundred quid a pop now. Trailers and horseboxes trundled through the village daily on their way to or from Hardacre farm.

"I might buy one," Jodie said quietly. "I've wanted my own horse for so long."

"Don't buy a horse from that man!" Hettie blurted, louder than she had intended. She didn't want Jodie going anywhere near Julian Greaves. "Buy Rose!" she added in sudden inspiration. "Then she can stay here!" She checked herself and looked at Grace. "Well, that is, if James agreed, of course."

"Well, I can't see why not," Grace said thoughtfully. "Siobhan isn't bringing a horse. Although I would have to ask him, Jodie, so don't raise your hopes."

"Oh, I couldn't afford Rose, Hettie," Jodie said sadly. "She's far too good for me."

"Don't talk daft," Hettie said. "You're a good rider, Jode. It would be the perfect solution. Rose would get to stay at Draymere, and you would get a half-decent horse, as opposed to whatever poor waifs are left standing in the fields at that place."

"I can barely scrape together the hundred quid for one of the poor waifs," Jodie said awkwardly, sinking down inside her coat.

"Have her, she's yours!" Hettie burst out impulsively. "I can't think of anyone I would rather give her to. If James lets you keep her here."

James agreed to Rose staying, and Hettie was over the moon. "I want to see lots of pictures!" she told Jodie excitedly. But it didn't solve the problem of a transport, and when she looked at train tickets online, it seemed a return journey to Norwich cost nearly as much as she had been planning to spend on a car.

Hettie started packing up the cottage as Alexander began moving his things into the gatehouse.

Celia arrived at the end of the month on a four-day visit to Draymere. Alexander had been warned of the times and the dates, so he kept himself out of the way and steered clear of the hall. He had plenty to keep him busy. With Ewan still working full time and dealing with the baby, Alexander was tasked with getting planning permission for the barns. He even attended a couple of meetings with the accountants. He called Imogen and apologised for his behaviour (which embarrassed Imogen more than his shouting had), and she joined him again on his hunts for the never-ending list of items the house seemed to need. Helen the girlfriend came once. She was standoffish at first, but Al turned on his charm, and she came around in the end. The evenings weren't easy. Al brooded in his half-decorated house. Knowing that his mother was only a stone's throw away made him moody, uptight, and restless. He nearly called on Fiona, but her association with Julian Greaves and bitchiness toward Hettie stalled him. Digger settled down well, paradoxically spending more time indoors now that he could get out whenever he wanted to.

Bert called at the gatehouse one morning and asked Al if he would walk with him to look at one of the youngsters. There was a lump on the filly's flank that he was concerned about. They walked to the paddock slowly, to allow for Bert's dodgy hip, and chatted companionably. Alexander always took pleasure from time talking to Bert. The lump didn't look too ominous, so they agreed to keep an eye on the filly. Then Alexander saw his mother as they came back out of the paddock. She was walking along the track with Artie and Fred. All three of them were carrying sketchpads. His mouth went dry. He didn't know what to feel or what to do, so he stopped and stood. Celia hadn't seen him. She was peering into the hedgerow, pointing something out to the boys.

Bert took quick stock of the situation; he was one of the few people who knew about Alexander's ongoing rift with his mother. Bert had seen at close hand what the boys and Celia had been through with that ugly separation. He had witnessed the fallout as well. Alexander had taken it particularly badly. Bert figured fifteen was a tricky age to be dealing with that sort of thing. He couldn't let Celia bump into the boy without any word of warning. Lord knows what that would do to the poor woman when she'd been through so much already.

“Mornin’, Miss Celia, lovely day for it!” he called loudly before muttering to Al. “Stay here if you have to. I’ll head her off.”

Celia looked up with a smile and started to raise her hand. She froze with her hand half lifted when she realised who was there. Her face drained of blood and her eyes filled with tears as she saw Alexander standing there: so near, so heartachingly beautiful, and so heart-wrenchingly far away.

Bert hobbled toward her as fast as his hip would allow. Artie and Fred, spotting Bert and their Uncle Al, came running over to see them. Celia didn’t move; she didn’t even drop her hand. The boys ran on past Bert and bounded up to Al. They had missed him since he’d moved out, and bowled into his legs enthusiastically.

“We’re doing drawing, Uncle Al!” Artie said. “Mamie’s going to take us to the wood!”

“Look! Look at my bug picture!” Fred waved his pad.

Alexander tried to give them his attention, but he was finding it impossible to drag his eyes away from Celia. Bert was with her now, holding both her hands. She was still staring at him, though, over Bert’s shoulder.

“Come and see Mamie,” Artie said. Both boys took hold of his arms and attempted to pull him forward.

“She’s probably got a pad for you too,” Fred added by way of encouragement.

Alexander shook himself. “Not now, boys. I’m sorry, I can’t. You go and do your drawings. I’ll come and see them soon.”

The boys pleaded noisily and swung from his arms in an effort to change his mind. “Not now,” Al snapped, sharper than he had intended. They let go and wandered dejectedly off toward Bert and Celia. Al went back into the paddock. He stood behind the nearest yearling and made a show of checking her over. When Celia remained in sight, he moved on to another. He felt a complete fool, hiding behind the horses and pretending to be busy. But his throat was thick and his head full of emotions he didn't know what to do with. He stayed in the field until Bert came back to the gate.

"They've gone on up to the wood," was all Bert said.

Bert didn't speak again until they were almost at the yard. "She wouldn't have left you if she had any choice," he stated abruptly, as if he had taken some time working himself up to it.

Alexander glared at the ground. He didn't make any comment.

Where the path split away to the gatehouse, Bert stopped and stood his ground. "I've kept my mouth shut fifteen years now, boy. But I reckon it's time you stopped thinkin' 'bout what she's done to you an' per'aps started thinkin' 'bout what you've done to her." Bert nodded his head decisively, once, stuck his hands in his pockets, and hobbled toward the yard.

Grace announced that there would be leaving drinks for Hettie at the hall after work on the first. Hettie had known it was inevitable but couldn't think of anything she wanted to do less. All the good-byes and emotion: she wasn't up to it. Still, at least it was being held after work and before most people's dinner. Hopefully no one would hang around long; her last week was already proving hard enough. Every time she brushed one of the horses or took in a view across Draymere, she found herself welling up at the thought of leaving it all behind. She was grateful that her last day was too busy to allow time for any misgivings. They finished the yard at seven, and Hettie belted on her bravado as they all walked up to the hall.

Grace had decorated the kitchen with balloons, and the boys had made a banner reading, "Good Luck, Hettie" in very wonky letters. There was champagne and a cake on the table; all of the

Draymere staff were there. Grace started crying as soon as Hettie came in.

"It's my blasted hormones," she explained to anyone who came near. Champagne corks popped, and the cake was cut and passed out. James gave a farewell speech lauding Hettie and her management of the yard, interrupted occasionally by rude comments from Bev. Bert got misty-eyed. The boys stuck their fingers in the leftover cake and flicked it at each other. Georgia toddled happily from person to person, demanding to be picked up so she could smack the balloons. Hettie held it together when she got the massive card, signed by all of them, wishing her good-bye and good fortune. She would read their comments later, in private, she thought. She nearly lost it when James presented her with the title to the Landy. "No, no, not at all." He dismissed her protests that it was too much. "It's knocking on, might be a gift horse yet. Best reserve your thanks." Alexander sat in the corner, one heel resting on the knee of the other leg, and glared into his champagne glass without speaking a word. Hettie managed to excuse herself soon after eight.

"So much packing to do!" she said brightly. "I can't thank you all enough. I won't do a speech and bore you but, well, I've had the best of times at Draymere, and that's down to all of you."

She exited rapidly and cried all the way back to the cottage. She was spending her last night there, dropping in at her mum's in the morning to get rid of the rest of the stuff she had loaded into the Landy. *My Landy*, she thought. Her mum had offered a lift to the station, but that wouldn't be necessary now. She regretted her decision to stay; the cottage, empty and cleaned, didn't feel like home anymore. All that was left were the covers on the bed, her clothes for the morning, some teabags, and half a pint of milk. Still, she could have a bath and adjust her packing now that she could take more. Then a nice early night ahead of a long day tomorrow.

She was putting her pj's and sweater on when she heard the knock on the door. Doris started going crazy; she was thoroughly upset by the changes going on and driving Hettie mad with her neurotic behavior. *Someone else saying good-bye?* she wondered wearily as she trudged down the stairs. Alexander was at the door, with an unopened bottle of champagne in his hand.

"I was antisocial at the hall," he said. "Thought I should say good-bye properly."

"Oh, right," Hettie replied awkwardly. They had hardly spoken in weeks. "Er, do you want to come in?"

Alexander nodded and came through the door. Digger, growing in confidence, trotted in behind him.

"I'm, um, in my pyjamas, I'm afraid." Hettie, flustered, tried to laugh. Her heart was racing again. "I wasn't expecting company and, well, everything else is packed."

Al recognized the pyjamas from the night that Dog had died. He didn't laugh with her, but sat at the kitchen table and plonked the champagne bottle down.

"I've only got paper cups," Hettie apologised.

"It will taste the same," Alexander drawled. He quietly popped the champagne cork and got out his cigarettes.

"Er, we ought to go outside, really, if you want to smoke. Only it's not my house anymore." She poured two cups of champagne, away from the table so that he didn't notice her shaking hands.

"Bugger that," Al said, lighting his cigarette and looking at her fully for the first since his arrival. He pushed the cigarettes and lighter toward her by way of invitation.

Hettie passed him a paper cup, took a cigarette, and sat down on the opposite side of the table.

"So, Norfolk tomorrow!" Al tried valiantly. He didn't know why he was there. He wanted to say, "Don't go! Stay here!" but that wasn't going to happen.

"Yes, off tomorrow!" Hettie replied brightly. "Fancy that!" *Fancy that?* Her mind queried, *What the fuck are you talking about?* She gulped some champagne and drew on her trembling cigarette. *Tell me not to go and I'll stay,* she thought miserably.

"What's this place like, then?" Al tried. "The one that you're going to." His voice was too angry for normal, idle chitchat.

"It's very nice," Hettie said. "Nice horses, nice stables. They ride on the beach!" she added with surprise. "I've never ridden on a beach, or in the sea, so I'm looking forward to that."

"Humph." Al downed his champagne, stood up, and got a refill.

Why is he here? Hettie thought. *He can't bear to look at me, and he doesn't want to talk to me. I don't understand this at all. Unfinished business? Injured pride?* She held out her glass for a refill. *Oh, fuck it. Who cares?* she decided. *He's here. So what? And I don't want him to leave.*

They had a few more stabs at conversation over their second drink. The champagne was working its magic on Hettie, and she was upset when he stood up again and chucked his cup in the sink. "Don't go," she whispered to his back. Al stood, head bowed, gripping the edge of the work top. She walked up behind him and rested her head and her body against his back. She could feel his breathing become jagged, but he didn't move a muscle. So she took his hand in both of hers and led him up the stairs. Somehow she knew that he wanted this every bit as much as she did.

They didn't turn the light on, but the outside lamp over the kitchen door illuminated the room with a soft, orange glow. Hettie slowly took her jumper off and stepped out of her pyjama bottoms. She didn't look at Alexander but was rewarded by his low, throaty exhalation of appreciation. He moved to stand behind her, tracing a finger down her neck and slowly across her shoulder.

"I need you naked too," she whispered tremulously.

Her back felt cold and abandoned when he stepped away. She could hear him shedding his clothes, but she didn't turn around. She closed her eyes and focused on the feelings building inside her. When Alexander moved close again, Hettie was shivering with need. He wrapped his arms around her and laid her on the narrow single bed, stretching his length out beside her, not quite touching, millimeters apart. They stared into each other's eyes. Al traced her eyebrows and cheekbones with a finger, and Hettie reached up to stroke his bottom lip, moistening her own lips, wanting his to be touching hers. She moved her head to his, kissing him softly on the mouth. He clasped her head and held her there. They kissed tenderly, Alexander breaking away to kiss her chin, her neck, and her throat. Hettie moaned as she felt urgency building in her, but Al hushed her and stilled her roaming hands. Holding them in his own, he carried on teasing her lips and her mouth with gentle, fleeting kisses. He slipped his tongue into her mouth, withholding it again as she eagerly sought to accept it. Hettie thought she might come without their bodies even touching. She moved nearer, and her nipples brushed his chest, shooting darts of pleasure.

"Alexander," she moaned, "I need you now."

"Patience, Hettie," he whispered, but he released her hands and ran his own hand down her back. Cupping her bottom, he pulled her closer, lifting her thigh across his hip. Hettie held his head and kissed him greedily, flicking her own tongue into his mouth, moving her body to encourage his fingers that were resting inside her thigh. She felt his cock against her leg and moaned again, louder this time. Her hands reached to feel him, but Al caught hold of them again.

"No touching yet, Hettie," he said huskily, eyes dark with lust. "Not if you want me to last."

"I want you *now.*" Hettie moaned into his shoulder in frustration.

He rolled her gently onto her back and raised himself on one arm. Bending to take a pink nipple in his mouth, he sucked hungrily, flicking the tip with his tongue. His free hand, flat on her stomach, dropped down and stopped on her pubic bone. Hettie bucked against his hand. Her fingers dug into his shoulders, and she groaned loudly again.

"Don't make me wait any longer." She sighed. He slid a finger inside her without releasing her nipple from his mouth. Hettie felt pleasure burst in her with a force she had never experienced before. Al lifted his head and watched her face as wave after wave of ecstasy flooded through her. She trembled as she came back down. Al kissed her gently as his fingers continued to move, slowly withdrawing and plunging back in, trailing across her clitoris with slow, deliberate intent. Hettie felt pressure and need start building again.

"Oh, my God," she moaned. "What are you doing to me?"

He moved her legs apart and knelt between them, stroking her breasts, gently pinching her nipples, then watching his own hands as he lazily circled her clit with his thumb and slid two fingers deep inside her. Hettie whimpered and arched her back to meet him, spreading her arms and gripping the sheets in her fists.

"Now, Hettie?" he asked, withdrawing his fingers and holding himself above her.

"Yes, now!" she cried desperately, raising her hips to meet him. Alexander pushed his throbbing cock into her, stretching her, filling her like never before. A low groan of pleasure escaped him. Closing his eyes, he paused for a second, holding himself together, trying to keep control as Hettie's legs wrapped around his waist. Then he was thrusting rhythmically, trying to be tender, but it was taking every ounce of his reserve not to bury himself deep inside her. He opened his eyes and looked at Hettie's face. Her eyes were bright with longing, her face was flushed, and her lips parted breathlessly.

"Alexander," she whispered, "I'm not made of glass. I want this as much as you do. Don't hold back on me, please."

"I'm scared I'll hurt you," he said jaggedly. "You're so small and so tight—"

"You won't hurt me," Hettie interrupted. "Please, Al, I trust you."

A second groan escaped him at her words. His thrusts began to build, and their eyes locked together as Hettie met and matched him. Her hands flew to his shoulders; she arched and cried out his name as he finally, beautifully fucked her for all he was worth. At the moment of his orgasm, he bent his arms and took her mouth as well, thrusting his tongue in, bruising her lips as they groaned, spent, against each other. They lay entangled and sweating, breathing heavily. Alexander rolled off of her, and she curled up inside his arms, burying her face under his chin. As their breathing returned to normal, Hettie giggled.

"That was funny?" Al asked, raising an eyebrow in question.

"I don't know what the hell that was," Hettie pealed. "But I've certainly never done it before."

Alexander smiled into her hair and kissed the top of her head, pulling her tighter into his arms. *I wish that was true.* The thought darted into his head, but he pushed it quickly away.

Hettie squirmed deliciously against him and stretched her legs.

"Do you want anything?" he asked her.

"I think I want to do that again." She grinned her wicked grin.

"Ah." He laughed, about to add, "You might need to give me minute." But as her hands travelled down his torso, he felt his cock stiffen again, so he kissed her instead. Her hands closed around him, and she gave a small sigh of pleasure.

They were leisurely the second time. Hettie knelt on all fours and pushed Alexander onto his back, kissing his shoulders, his chest, his ribs, her head moving slowly down his body. The small gasp that escaped him when she took him in her mouth sent a shiver of pleasure down her spine, and the taste of her still on him intensified her desire. When her tongue and lips started leading him further than he wanted to go, he took her shoulders and moved her gently away. He placed soft kisses all over her body, finding her nipples again. Then, parting her thighs with his hands, he took her to unimaginable heights with his tongue until she crashed into waves of splintering orgasm. He held her as she trembled, then entered her again, moving with slow, building strokes that made her cry out with unhinged pleasure.

Twice more that night, as they lay kissing and holding each other, their urges reignited and they pleasured each other again, in every way they knew how, until Hettie, sated and exhausted, fell asleep in his arms.

Alexander lay awake beside her, watching her sleep. His arm beneath her went numb, but he didn't want to move. Finally drifting off briefly himself, he woke as the dim glow of predawn filtered through the window and lay with his face pressed against her hair, lost in thought. He felt drained, wrung out, washed clean. Unwelcome thoughts and questions butted into his mind. *She had given herself so totally; was she always this insatiable? She had initiated their night; how did he feel about that?* He knew his thoughts were unfair and unreasonable. Hope and reason argued that their incredible union had simply been a meeting of equal passions. But he hated the way his mind was working, and he hated himself for his thoughts. Gently extracting his arms and moving away from her, Al got up and dressed. Taking a last long look at Hettie lying still asleep, he fought the urge to climb back into the bed, wake her up by kissing her, and take her all over again. If he didn't leave now, he thought he might never let her go. So he padded quietly down the stairs, carrying his shoes, and put them on in the kitchen before he left. If he noticed the peculiar fact that Digger was still in the cottage, asleep in the dog bed with Doris, his mind was too full to register it as anything out of the ordinary, and Digger followed him out.

Hettie stirred an hour or so later, stretching like a contented cat, a smile playing on her face. She rolled onto her back and blushed as memories of the night filtered into her consciousness. Disappointment settled when she realised that Alexander was no longer in the bed, and then she felt a touch fear when she remembered what day it was. She got up and looked hopefully in the kitchen for a note as she let Doris out and put the kettle on. She checked her phone. Then she showered and got dressed, trying to shake the nagging thought that he had only come round for one thing, and she wouldn't be seeing him again. *He might turn up in a minute,* she told herself. *What was it he said when he arrived?* Her mind threw back, *"I thought I should say good-bye properly." Was that what he'd been doing?* She put her last few things in the Land Rover and swept the kitchen floor, taking longer than necessary in case Alexander returned. But it was past nine when she was ready to lock up and leave, and there was still no sign of him. She took another look at her phone as she opened the door of the Landy to let Doris jump in, and absentmindedly checked the pads on Doris's feet to see if there were any injuries to explain the small blood spots she'd found on the kitchen floor. She made sure her phone wasn't on mute.

Sadness settled in as she drove through the Draymere gates for the very last time. She didn't stay long at her mum's. Bert was delivering vegetables. She hugged them both, said her good-byes, and left with her mum's instructions to call the minute she had arrived. Hettie stopped briefly in Cirencester and called in at the chemist. She bought a morning-after pill and took it straight away. The dragging pains and bleeding she suffered over the next few days perfectly fitted her mood.

CHAPTER SEVENTEEN

Hettie threw herself into the new job with determined vigour. Cynthia couldn't believe her luck: the girl worked like a demon, was neat and tidy on the yard, and barely stopped, even for lunch. Before Hettie's second week was over, Cynthia was frequently yelling, "Stop working for five minutes and go and eat something, for heaven's sake, girl!" Her riding impressed as well. Cynthia didn't hesitate to let Hettie ride her top eventers and included her in training sessions, even using her on occasion as an example to her paying clients of "how it should be done."

Under her veneer of efficiency, Hettie was floundering. Everything was new and strange, she was terribly homesick, and she hadn't spoken to anyone from home apart from the odd text. She didn't trust herself to speak on the phone. She took herself off to her room every evening and watched rubbish on the little TV there or listened to music on her iPod until a song made her sad and she had to turn it off. She even seemed to have lost her appetite. She spent a long, lonely weekend driving around Norfolk with Doris, trying to keep out of the way of Cynthia's family time. "At least you've settled in," she muttered to the little dog as Doris trotted placidly beside her on the beach. Doris was very content; her outlandish behaviour during the move had morphed into lethargy since their arrival in Norfolk. She was even putting on weight. Hettie put it down to the fact that Doris liked having other dogs for company again, which led to thoughts of Dog and made her sadder still.

When her second Friday loomed, she thought about going home for the weekend but wasn't sure she would be able to make herself come back.

"Pieter has got the girls this weekend!" Cynthia boomed as they finished on the yard. "I'm taking you out on the town, Hettie. I'll show you around, and we can go out on the razz on Saturday night."

Hettie tried to protest, but Cynthia wasn't having any of it. "No, you've done nothing but work since you arrived. And I thought *I* was OCD! You need some fun. I'll take you out and introduce you to my crowd. Granny Briggs will stand in on the yard."

Pieter arrived at Flintend after dinner (their usual fare of fish fingers and oven chips, which, along with the alternate dish of chicken nuggets and oven chips, had been Cynthia's only offerings so far). The girls were delighted to see him. Harriet, who had barely spoken in Hettie's presence, ran up and hugged him, talking nonstop for the next fifteen minutes. Jessica sat on his lap and sucked her thumb. He stayed for a cup of coffee. Hettie was relieved that he and Cynthia appeared to be on reasonably good terms, chatting and laughing amiably with each other. Pieter wasn't at all like Hettie had imagined he would be. Cynthia was tall and muscular, almost masculine, with her short-cropped hair and her no-nonsense manner, whereas Pieter was short, stocky, and balding. Dressed smartly in an expensive-looking suit, he was polite and quietly spoken.

"Thank heavens for that!" Cynthia cried as the front door shut behind them. She pulled a bottle of wine from the fridge and poured a glass for them both. "Poor Pieter, a whole weekend with the girls in London. I almost feel sorry for him!"

Hettie wasn't sure if she felt sorry for him because he had to look after the girls or if it was the being in London that had evoked her sympathy. "He lives in London?" she asked by way of conversation.

"Yes, he always kept a place down there, saved him the commute. Now where are my fags? At least I can smoke in my own bloody house now there are no children here!" she barked. "Now, tell me about you, Henrietta!" she continued after lighting her cigarette. "You've been here two weeks, and I don't know a thing about you."

"Oh, there's nothing much to know," Hettie offered hurriedly. "Grew up, lived, and worked in the same village. And now I'm here!" She smiled.

"Humph," Cynthia retorted, but she didn't push it. "Pieter's South African, you know. Came here for university. Met me, Harriet came along—bit of a shock, that—and the rest, as they say, is history."

"Do the girls enjoy their trips to London?" Hettie asked. "Is he, er, still with the last girl?"

"God, no!" Cynthia barked with laughter. "Poor Pieter, he didn't really want to go with her in the first place. She was dim, that girl, but persistent. Far too pushy for Pieter." She laughed again. "But the girls? Well, yes, I think they do, actually. Change of scenery, you know. Break from their bossy mother." She grinned. "They were both always daddy's girls, really," she finished wistfully.

"I don't mind working this weekend." Hettie steered the conversation onto safer ground. "I know the girls usually help at weekends, and, you know, I'm around."

"Absolutely not!" Cynthia roared. "I've still got Granny. She likes the work, says it keeps the weight off! But if you want to ride on Sunday, we could take them to the beach. They've forecast good weather. And didn't you say you've never ridden in the sea before?"

♦♦♦

Alexander took off for London the day after Hettie left. He asked Imogen if he could crash at her place again, and Imogen of course said yes. He stayed for two nights and shagged Candida twice, although he nearly changed his mind when she asked him to "talk dirty, like before." His brain kept throwing up images of that last night with Hettie, which made him horny and frustrated, so he needed to clear his head. He still found time to spend a boozy evening with Ted, attend meetings with several banks, pound miles around the park with Digger, and watch too much bad TV. He made one last visit to his own bank before catching the train for home. He planned to put the two letters he was carrying into his deposit box—with the rest of them. But he changed his mind at the last minute, and taking the thick wad of letters out, he bundled them into his holdall.

Back at Draymere, he concentrated on getting the house finished so he could give his full attention to the barn conversions when planning permission was granted and the loan from the bank came through. His heart skipped a beat every time he heard the horses leaving for morning exercise, but he gritted his teeth and worked harder. When he noticed the cottage lights coming on in the evenings, he had to remind himself that Siobhan was living there now. He hadn't been in contact with Hettie since that night. He didn't know what on earth he could say to her. That he couldn't cope with the way she made him feel? That she brought out the worst and the best in him? That he was too jealous and too fucked up to ever be a nice guy? That she was undoubtedly better off without him?

Grace said the boys were missing him, so he began spending time at the hall, falling into the habit of going there for his Sunday dinner and a couple of evenings a week. Grace told him she'd had texts from Hettie and had tried to call her more than once without success. "I know the signal in Norfolk is unreliable," she said. "But I hope it is only that, and not that she's feeling too homesick to talk to anyone." Al didn't say anything, but his mind told him that Hettie was too busy living it up in her new life to want to talk to them.

The letters stayed in his holdall on the bedroom floor. And when the bag kept catching his eye, he put it away at the back of the cupboard under the stairs.

♦♦♦

Hettie had a better second weekend. Cynthia drove her to town to look around the shops and the market. They had coffee outside Starbucks. It seemed most of the people who walked past knew Cynthia, so they stopped to talk and introduce themselves. She made Cynthia visit the supermarket and bought supplies for a Sunday roast with her first generous paycheck. "I'll cook for us tomorrow," she said, "to thank you for all the lessons." She was craving proper food and vegetables, like one of her mum's dinners.

They went to the pub in the evening and ate with a crowd of Cynthia's friends, who were very welcoming if a little overconfident for Hettie's immediate comfort. As far as she could work out, everyone at the table had slept with one of the others. She became wary of speaking in case she made a gaffe, not that her reticence was noticed; they were a loud and boisterous lot. She received a lot of attention from the men, and several propositions, which felt overly forward for a first meeting.

"Bit of an incestuous mob, that lot." Cynthia confirmed her suspicions as they got back in the car. "Bloody good fun, of course. Best wear your chastity belt, Hettie! You were the star attraction tonight, and they like new blood." She laughed loudly.

Hettie hung nervously onto her seat belt throughout the return journey. She was fairly sure Cynthia had knocked back the best part of a bottle of wine. One of the men from dinner (Hettie couldn't remember his name) arrived at Flintend about ten minutes after them. Cynthia winked broadly over her shoulder at Hettie as she led the man off to her room. Hettie went to bed with her earphones in and her iPod turned up loud.

Sunday dawned sunny and bright, a perfect day for a ride. Hettie was at least enjoying the riding; she had never ridden such well-bred, well-schooled, athletic horses before. They rode through woodland to the coastline, where miles of sand and crashing waves stretched out in front of them, and cantered the full length of the beach, right at the water's edge. Hettie grinned with pleasure for the first time since her arrival and whooped when they rode into the waves. She asked Cynthia to take a picture of her sitting on this beautiful horse, knee-deep in the surf, with the sun and the sand behind her. She beamed happily as the picture was snapped and posted it on Facebook when they got back.

Her Sunday roast was a triumph, not to her mum's standards but certainly an improvement on Cynthia's. Cynthia smacked her lips and said she might have to relax her no-cooking rule. When Pieter returned with the girls, Hettie left them to it and went up to her room to phone her mum, Grace, and Nat.

"Oh, it sounds so lovely!" Nat wailed. "Beach and sun and sand. And I'm stuck in bloody London. When can I come up and see you?"

"Come next weekend!" Hettie said excitedly.

Grace told Alexander that Hettie had called and showed him her picture on Facebook. When Alexander left the hall, he drove straight to Fiona's house.

Ted and Anju visited Draymere again. Anju went into raptures when she was shown around the gatehouse and called right away to ask Imogen to take a look at her place when she was next up in London. Jodie fell in love with Rose and sent so many pictures that Hettie had to delete some from her phone when her memory card became overloaded. Alexander stayed clear of the yard and avoided Bert. It wasn't hard; most of his time was taken up trying to persuade the banks that their venture was a worthwhile proposition, and his efforts to secure funding got ever more time consuming. Grace's bump became onerous and obvious, and Holly dumped her boyfriend, transferring her love to Dan the farrier. Bev and Siobhan developed an earthy rapport. The yard continued to thrive, albeit not quite as tidily as before. Holly still believed she was put-upon and sulked for three whole days when Siobhan told her that if she was late again, she would be issued with a written warning. She sent a text to Hettie, saying Siobhan was a bitch and asking when Hettie was coming back. Hettie posted messages and endless pictures on Facebook—of the horses she was riding, the jumps she was jumping, and action shots of Cynthia competing. Nat loved Norfolk after her weekend visit, and she said she would come back soon. And Cynthia's crowd adopted Hettie as one of their number. Hettie continued to bat off the frequent unsubtle passes that came her way. As Hettie and the girls became closer, she spent more time with the family and very little time in her room.

Cynthia and Hettie were putting on their boots amid the usual gaggle of dogs waiting patiently to follow them onto the yard when Cynthia barked, "You realise that bitch of yours is about to whelp?"

"What?" Hettie looked at her blankly.

"Doris!" Cynthia cried. "Those puppies are about to drop, I think."

"Puppies? She's not having puppies. She's only…" Hettie stopped and looked at Doris. She was looking plump, and she had been slow and lazy for weeks. "How could she be having puppies?"

Cynthia roared with laughter. "My God, girl. I know you're a prude, but surely even you must know how puppies are made!"

"But she's only a baby herself!" Hettie was shocked. "She hasn't even had a season! I would have kept her away from your lot if she'd been in season."

"Can't have been any of my lot. I had them all done as a bogof deal when we got to seven bloody dogs. Girls kept talking me into keeping one out of every litter, and poor Pieter said he'd had enough. No, it must have happened before you got here. Nipples are proud; wouldn't be surprised if she drops them in the next day or so."

Hettie was stunned, but as she stared at Doris, she couldn't believe she hadn't worked it out before. "It must have been Digger," she said almost to herself.

"Well, you'd better let Digger know he's going to be a daddy." Cynthia chuckled as they walked toward the yard.

"What do I do now?" Hettie asked. "Does she need to see a vet? Should I be feeding her anything different? Oh, my God, what am I going to do with puppies, Cynthia?"

"Waste a lot of hours staring at them and even more cleaning up behind them, in my experience." Cynthia chuckled. "But the girls will be delighted; we haven't had puppies in the house for years!"

"Should I tell the father?" Hettie asked stupidly.

"Ha! Not unless he wants to raise them himself! Or pay puppy maintenance!" Cynthia mused.

"Well, I suppose I meant the father's owner, really," Hettie said as they reached the stables and were greeted by a round of whinnies from horses anticipating their breakfast.

"Oh, yes, you must tell them!" Cynthia cried as she hoisted a couple of feed buckets onto each hip. "Share the joy! There's nothing quite like puppies." She hummed happily as she distributed the feeds.

Oh, shit, Hettie thought. She stewed all day about whether, and how, to tell him. She knew if the roles were reversed, she would want to know. Imagine if Dog had been a father and no one had even told her. That was unimaginable (and impossible, as Dog had been done before she got him). She decided she had to tell him, but she still had to think about how. E-mail would be easiest, but she didn't know his e-mail address. Writing a letter would just be odd, but there was no way she was calling him. They hadn't spoken in two months, and she didn't want to speak to him now. She could send him a text. Or she could get Grace to tell him! She settled on that option with relief. When she cuddled Doris on the bed after work she rested her hand on the little dog's bulging stomach, then rushed downstairs excitedly to tell Cynthia and the girls that she had felt the puppies move. She called Grace straight away.

"Grace! Doris is having puppies!" she shouted down the phone.

"Oh, good Lord, that's wonderful, Hettie. Is it?" Grace asked.

"Well, it's a shock, Grace, to be honest. She still only seems like a puppy herself, bless her, and I didn't even know! But I felt the puppies moving, Grace! It was amazing. And Cynthia thinks they'll be born in the next day or two. Imagine that!"

Grace laughed at Hettie's excitement. "Oh, Hettie, didn't you know she'd done the dirty deed? Oh, I wish Doris was having her puppies here. I miss you so much, and Siobhan is, well, not you. We could do with some fun at Draymere."

"Grace! You're having a baby! How much excitement does a girl need?"

"Yes, yes, I know." Grace sighed. "But I'm surrounded by noisy boys and moody men. You were my escape, Hettie, my lifeline in this place."

"Grace, that's the hormones talking. You know you always get grumpy in your third trimester."

"It's not me that's grumpy; it's everyone else," Grace muttered. "James is shut in that bloody office all day, some problem with the legal stuff and his father, and Alexander only wipes the scowl off his face when he's talking to Digger. What is it with that man and communication? I'm at—"

"Er, talking of Digger," Hettie interrupted. "I think, um, he's the father."

"What?"

"Digger. I'm pretty sure it was him that did the dirty deed with Doris, you know. Would you let Alexander know when you see him next?"

"Digger? But he never leaves Al's side. Surely it can't have been Digger. Alexander would have stopped him. How would Digger and Doris have got it together?"

"Oh." Hettie hadn't thought this through. "I expect Doris escaped and visited the hall. Digger was probably there. She must have been in season when I left, and what with the packing and everything, she probably went missing."

"Your leaving drinks! That must have been it, when you were both up here."

"Yes! Exactly!" Hettie breathed a sigh of relief. "I didn't realise she was in season, you see."

"Oh, dear." Grace laughed. "What a pickle."

"Anyway, Grace, I'll call you soon for a proper catch-up, but Cynthia is yelling so the oven chips must be done. I wanted to share the news. And you'll tell Alexander?"

"No, no, you call him, Hettie. It's lovely news, and I'm sure he'd be pleased to hear it from you. I won't rain on your parade. He adores that dog; he'll be over the moon. Go and eat your oven chips and call me soon. And come home and visit us! It's been much too long!"

Well, that didn't work, Hettie thought as she came off the phone. She typed a quick text before she gave herself any more time to think.

Doris having puppies. Must be Digger's.

She pressed send and went downstairs to find out if it was fish fingers or chicken nuggets with the oven chips tonight.

When Alexander called, she was at the kitchen table with Cynthia, Harriet, and Jessica. She got flustered when his name came up and answered instead of rejecting the call.

"Hettie? What do you mean, they must be Digger's?" he barked without greeting.

"I mean they must be Digger's," Hettie said, going pink and getting up from the table to take the call somewhere private. But she knocked over her glass of water in her panic, so she started hunting for a dishcloth instead.

"Don't be bloody ridiculous!" Alexander almost shouted. "He never leaves my side. I would know if—" He stopped abruptly. Hettie was in full blush as she mopped ineffectually at the spilled water with a piece of kitchen towel. Cynthia took it off her and waved her away.

She heard Al's chuckle down the line, and it made her heart somersault. "Ah," he said. "Yes, of course. Clever Digger. Why the fuck didn't you tell me she was in season? I could have shut him outside!"

"I didn't know she was in season," Hettie hissed. "There weren't any signs." *Although, strictly speaking, that isn't really true.*

"Anyway," Hettie went on tightly, "I thought you should know, and now you do. I will tell Grace when they're born and—"

"Has she seen a vet?" Alexander barked. "Is she getting sufficient nutrition?"

"I only found out today!" Hettie was trying to keep her cool and resisting the temptation to hang up on him.

"Right, I'm coming up," Alexander stated.

"No," Hettie tried, but he'd hung up. "I don't want you here," she said to her phone instead.

She rejoined the table, still pink in the face, and avoided meeting Cynthia's questioning eyes. *He'll have to call back,* she thought. *He doesn't know where I am.* "He's coming here, the daddy dog's owner," she spoke to the table in general. "I hope that's all right. I tried to say no, but he's coming anyway."

CHAPTER EIGHTEEN

Alexander left Draymere at seven, and Doris went into labour at nine.

Cynthia sent the girls to bed, telling them it would be a long night and they had school in the morning. She promised to wake them up when the puppies were born. Doris paced and panted and glanced at her sides in puzzlement, then appeared to change her mind and go off the idea.

"Could be hours," Cynthia said. She dragged a big box in from the pool room, and they cut one of the sides down, lined it with blankets, and tried to encourage Doris to choose it as her nest. Cynthia opened a bottle of wine as they sat to wait it out. Hettie glanced nervously at Doris and began to feel reassured that there was a vet on his way. She barely sipped her wine in case she had to face an emergency.

"Tell me," Cynthia said boldly, "the man on the phone, the dog's owner, is he an ex?"

"No. Yes. Sort of," Hettie replied. "A mistaken one- or two-night stand."

"One or two?" Cynthia queried. "You must remember, surely?"

"Oh, I remember," Hettie said grimly. "Although I try very hard not to."

"Ah," Cynthia said. "Bit tense, then, him coming here. Do you want me to call him and tell him he's not welcome?"

"No." Hettie sighed. Sadly she really didn't want Cynthia to do that, although she knew she ought to. "He's a vet," she added by way of excuse. "He might come in useful."

"A vet!" Cynthia exclaimed. "Bloody useful, I would think. Could save yourself a fortune, marrying a vet. It's a shame you've gone off him."

"I don't think it was ever going to end in marriage!" Hettie laughed. "And I didn't exactly go off him. It was more the other way round. He's a bit of an arsehole, really."

Cynthia smiled. "My dear, most of them are. What's his name, this arsehole?"

"Alexander," Hettie answered. "Alexander Melton."

"Melton? The lot you worked for?"

"The brother." Hettie nodded.

"So money and a vet? Good God, girl. Can't you find a way to get him interested again?"

Doris started panting and pacing again, so Hettie was saved from having to reply. She moved to sit on the floor, petting Doris when she passed on her circuits of the kitchen.

"Daddy dog is a stray, from Afghanistan," Hettie said. "He's very shy and funny looking, bless him. I expect you'll meet him later. Those two are never far apart."

"A vet with money and compassion for dogs. If you don't want him, I might have him myself!" Cynthia joked. Hettie didn't find it funny.

Doris whined at the door, so Hettie let her out. She circled the drive, peed a few times, then came in and found the box. She pulled the blankets out, moved them under the kitchen table, and lay down there instead.

"So, you and Pieter," Hettie said, looking up from her position on the floor. "You seem to still get on well, despite what he did."

"Oh, I love him to bits," Cynthia said. "We're not compatible, though. Pieter is one of the few who is not an arsehole." She smiled. "But poaching my groom was pushing his luck too far."

Doris began straining in earnest. Cynthia turned down the lights, and they crawled under the table. The first little scrappy grey pup arrived at ten fifteen. Hettie had tears in her eyes as she looked from the puppy to Cynthia in wonder. Doris did everything she was meant to do, attending to her baby as if she had done it a hundred times before. She settled for a few minutes before starting to push again. They heard the sound of tyres on the gravel drive.

"I'll go," Cynthia whispered. "You stay here."

She heard the door open and Alexander making polite introductions before they both appeared under the table with her.

"They're being born," she said to Alexander in amazement. He nodded his head and smiled.

They watched in silence as a second little grey pup arrived, followed quickly by a third—brown and white this time. Doris lay back contentedly on the blankets.

"Is that it?" Hettie whispered, sniffing back a tear.

"It might be," Al whispered cautiously. "Let's give her half an hour. If she isn't showing any signs, I will check her over then."

They reversed quietly out from beneath the table.

Hettie couldn't stop smiling. Al was grinning too. He really wanted to hug her, but he wasn't sure that would be well received, so kept his distance.

"Cup of tea and a fag, I think, to toast the babies heads," Cynthia said quietly. She made three mugs of tea, which they took outside to the drive.

"Good Lord, is that Daddy?" Cynthia exclaimed as Digger stood up to greet them. "Well, those puppies certainly won't be winning any awards at Crufts, will they?" She laughed.

Hettie chuckled quietly, but Al took offence.

"You made good time." Cynthia turned to him. "If you left after you called here. That's quite a drive from Gloucestershire."

"There wasn't much traffic," Al mumbled.

Hettie peered through the kitchen window as she smoked her cigarette. She could keep an eye on Doris that way, and even with the excitement of the evening, being near Alexander was making her uncomfortable.

Cynthia and Al, discussing family and hunting, were finding acquaintances that they had in common. When they moved to return to the kitchen, Al held Digger back.

"Oh, he'll be all right," Cynthia told him. "Doris will keep him backed off in no uncertain terms!"

She was right. Digger heard the puppies squeaking and approached the table with interest, but Doris sat up and gave him a look that perfectly illustrated the saying "shooting daggers from her eyes." Digger stealthily reversed.

After half an hour, the puppies and Doris were deep in contented sleep. Al crawled back under the table and gave Doris a thorough check-over.

"No more puppies," he said, emerging back out. "Two dogs, one bitch, and Doris is absolutely fine. What a clever little mother she is."

Hettie wanted to hug him, but just smiled instead.

"Do you mind if I wake the girls?" Cynthia asked. "I won't let them hang around."

"Of course not," Hettie said. "It's your kitchen, Cynthia, and I'd love the girls to meet them."

The room felt awkward as soon as Cynthia left. They started talking at the same time, and then both stopped again.

"I'm sorry, Hettie," Al said eventually. "I'm sorry I didn't call."

Hettie was quiet for a moment. "I don't think sorry will do it this time," she said sadly.

"You could have called me," he reminded her.

Hettie sighed and said nothing.

Harriet and Jessica came into the room dressed in their pyjamas, rubbing sleepy eyes. They bobbed under the table with

Cynthia and oohed and aahed in excited whispers. Hettie leaned down and grinned at them. When Jessica asked which were the boys and which was the girl, Al joined them on the floor and gave a brief biology lesson.

Cynthia popped up and raised her eyebrows at Hettie. "He's fucking gorgeous," she mouthed.

Hettie smiled weakly and shrugged.

The girls were ushered reluctantly back to bed. "They'll still be here tomorrow," Cynthia told them firmly.

Al leaned under the table and stroked Doris's head. "Right, I'd best be off," he said.

"All the way back to Gloucestershire?" Cynthia asked, glancing at her watch. "Stay here, man, my bed is big enough!" She winked at Hettie. "And I would enjoy the company!" She grinned.

Alexander looked uncomfortable. Hettie might have found his embarrassment amusing if she hadn't been so horrified by Cynthia's suggestion herself.

"No, no, I've booked a room," he muttered hastily. "At Blakeney. I've stayed there before."

"Worth a try." Cynthia grinned. "Come back and see us tomorrow, then. Visit your grandpuppies and all that. Come for dinner!"

Alexander glanced at Hettie. She sat with her chin on her chest and her shoulders hunched. She obviously wasn't enamoured with the idea of him coming back, but he would very much like to see the puppies again before he left. And Hettie too, if he was honest.

"I would like that. Thank you," he said.

Hettie rolled her eyes and crawled back under the table.

James came out of his office looking grey and drawn. It was after midnight and Grace had gone to bed hours ago. He poured himself a whiskey and knocked it back before trudging wearily upstairs for another sleepless night.

♦♦♦

Hettie woke with the dawn and ran excitedly downstairs. The puppies were feeding, and she sat with them for nearly an hour, gazing in awe as she petted Doris and stroked the puppies' silken backs. She had to carry Doris out for a pee, and Doris darted immediately back to her squealing babies, sniffing them all with concern before snuggling back down. Hettie topped up her water bowl, put food within her reach, and went to get dressed for work. She thought she would be looking forward to the day more if Alexander hadn't been coming back, then admitted to herself that this wasn't really true.

Alexander stretched in the big white bed and let himself think about that night with Hettie, until his thoughts forced him to get up. He went for a long run with Digger and took a cold shower.

♦♦♦

Grace decided enough was enough. James was moody and uncommunicative; he had barely spoken to her for the last three weeks. He was either out (at the solicitors, he said) or in that blasted office with the door firmly shut. She would have to confront him; there was nothing else for it. Whatever was going on with him (and she was thinking the worst), it was time to have it out. The prospect of raising four children on her own did make her consider briefly if she could be one of those women who swept these things under the carpet. She rapidly dismissed that idea.

"Right, James," Grace announced bravely, walking into the office and sitting down opposite him. "Whatever it is that's going on, I want to know about it."

James jumped and looked up, surprised, before sighing heavily and slumping back into his chair. "I would rather not trouble you with this, Grace," he said wearily. "What with the baby and everything."

"Not trouble me?" Grace asked crossly. "How untroubled do you think I am by the fact that you have barely spoken two words to me in the last three weeks? And that's when you've been here! Is it another woman?"

"God, no!" James exclaimed. "I wish it was that easy."

"Are you ill?" Grace asked, her face registering horror.

"No, no, I'm not ill. All right, I'll tell you. I'm sorry that I've caused you worry, but I was hoping to spare you this. I thought I could sort it out, you see, but—"

"James, tell me!" Grace almost shouted. Her phone beeped, but she was too scared to register the noise.

"It's about Father, and this place, Draymere," James started. "It's been a nightmare with cash flow since his strokes, as you know. He didn't have a power of attorney, so I only have access to funds created directly from profits, through the business, as it were." He sighed again. "All the properties, and the backup funds, are still in Father's name. You know all that, of course," he went on, "but, with the aim of transferring the title deeds for these barns to Al, I approached our solicitors to see what could be done." He paused for a moment and took a deep breath before carrying on. "But the answer is that nothing at all can be done. Father has a codicil attached to his will stating that if any of us resume contact with Mother, we are not to inherit a thing. Draymere will not come to us."

There was silence as Grace attempted to digest the full magnitude of his words. Her eyes grew bigger and her hand flew to her mouth.

"Oh, my God," she finally whispered. "And you've been shouldering this all alone? James, why on earth didn't you speak to me sooner?"

"I thought I could sort it out." James was close to tears. "I didn't want anyone to think badly of Father, and I didn't want Celia to know. The whole thing is an awful fuckup, and our future is fucked as well. Grace, I am so very, very sorry. I can't tell you how sorry I am."

Grace had never heard him use the F word before. She walked around the desk and held his head against her bump. "No," she said. "No, James. That isn't true. And you have *nothing* to be sorry for. Our future is you, me, and four healthy children. Wherever we might be. But we will fight this, James. I know you don't want to think badly of your father, but that is a mean and wicked codicil intended purely to spite Celia and hurt you all in the process. When was this will drawn up?"

"Seven years ago," James said miserably.

"But Alexander hasn't had any contact with Celia." Grace brightened at the thought. "If Al gets Draymere, that would be all right. We could move into the gatehouse; I would be quite happy—"

"I thought of that," James interrupted. "They said the onus of proof is on us, and if Celia and Alexander have been present in one place at the same time, or even if there has been correspondence, it would be considered contact."

"But I don't believe he even read the letters!" Grace cried. "And as for being in the same place, well, that's only just happened, and it's not as if they met. They were never in the same house, for God's sake."

"I know, I know." James sighed. "It might still be our only option; everything else has failed. But how do I tell Mother that she can't come here anymore? Or even write to Alexander? Or tell him he can't stay in his house when Mother is visiting us? I can't do that, Grace, not on top of the damage that has already been done."

"But to keep Draymere?" Grace asked helplessly. "Surely if we explained?"

"That's exactly what I've been sweating over for the last three days." James smiled weakly.

"Well, one thing I do know," Grace said stoutly, "is that you can't deal with this on your own. Alexander and Ted need to know, and the sooner, the better. Call a family meeting, James. We'll work this out together somehow. It is too much of a load for you to carry on your own. And if we end up in a council house in the village—so be it." She tried to laugh, but the noise came out rather strangled.

"Is there still such a thing as a council house?" James asked weakly as they embraced each other. He felt the awful pressure of the last few weeks abate just a bit.

"Out of interest," Grace asked, "if none of you get it, what happens to Draymere then?"

"It all goes to Bert." James laughed ruefully. "Lock, stock, and barrel."

Alexander returned to Flintend on his very best behaviour. Smartly dressed, he brought flowers and wine for Cynthia and offered to help with the dinner. He chatted sweetly to Harriet and Jessica, asking them about riding and school. Harriet became tongue-tied and shy, but Jess revelled delightedly in the attention and got overexcited. Cynthia shouted at her when she started demonstrating cartwheels across the kitchen floor.

Hettie was embarrassed that Cynthia had cooked fish fingers again, then annoyed with herself for caring what Alexander thought. Alexander said, "School dinners! Yum!" And helped himself to eight.

They talked puppies, dogs, and horses. "Hettie is bloody amazing!" Cynthia proclaimed. "A real diamond. You lot must miss her at Draymere." Hettie blushed, and Alexander nodded noncommittally. "She's competing one of my youngsters next week, aren't you, Hettie? First groom I've trusted to do that in years!"

"Do you girls compete?" Alexander asked them.

"Jessica takes every chance she gets," Cynthia answered for them. "But Harriet keeps telling me she wants to do *dressage!* You're a bit of a wuss, aren't you, Harriet?"

Harriet blushed scarlet and glared at her food.

"There's a lot of skill in dressage," Al cut in mildly. "I know I couldn't do it. I don't have the patience or the ability. Anyone can jump; you just hang on and kick."

Cynthia was taken aback, but she barked with good-humoured laughter. "Fair point, dear boy. I probably deserved that."

Harriet fell in love.

The girls were packed off to do homework in the study.

"It's a lovely evening," Cynthia said. "Let's take a bottle of wine out to the garden."

"Coffee for me, but I'll make it," Alexander said. "Long drive ahead."

Hettie persuaded Doris to come out with them, but the little dog was back in the kitchen before they even sat down.

"She's being such a good mum," Hettie said proudly.

"So far!" Cynthia boomed. "It will wear off when they're teenagers!"

"Cynthia! Harriet's a lovely girl; it's just a tricky age," Hettie admonished her jokingly.

"Yes, yes." Cynthia sighed. "And I expect she's missing her father."

"Is your husband away?" Al asked.

"No, he ran off with the last bloody groom," Cynthia told him. "Eight months ago. Couldn't keep it in his pants." She laughed.

"I am sorry to hear that, Cynthia," Al said sincerely.

"Oh, don't be, old boy. To be honest, we were both at it constantly. Throughout the marriage, really, and before—in my case too." She mused, dragging on her cigarette. "Last one was the final straw."

Al looked so shocked that Hettie had to fight the urge to giggle. She had become accustomed to Cynthia's outrageous comments and somewhat decadent lifestyle.

"So the girls don't see him now? Because of the other woman?" Alexander questioned doggedly.

"Gosh, no, they still see him, every other weekend and half the school holidays. *She* didn't last much longer than the end of the drive!" Cynthia laughed again.

"Oh, I see," Al muttered, but he really didn't look like he did.

"Now." Cynthia stood up. "Alexander, do you want to meet the horses?"

"Yes, I would very much like that," he replied.

"Good. Hettie, show him round. I'm going to do the dishwasher."

"Let me do that for you." Al stood up too.

"No, I won't hear of it. Go and visit the nags, you two. I'll leave you in peace for a while." She strode off back into the house.

"Great," Hettie muttered under her breath, rolling her eyes.

Al looked at her and laughed, which annoyed her even more. He couldn't help but be impressed by the immaculate stable block and impressive horses, and took a special interest in the partitions between the stables and the well-planned layout. *I must ask Cynthia who designed this,* he thought. Something like this would work well for their equine block—if they ever managed to secure the bloody funds.

Hettie didn't talk much, but she pointed out the cross-country jumps and the horse she would be competing.

"Right," she said when the brief tour was done. "I expect you need to get off now."

"Keen to get rid of me, Hettie?" Al asked dryly.

"I think it was the other way round, if I remember rightly," Hettie muttered crossly.

"No, that's isn't true," Alexander shot back. "You're the one who left."

Hettie looked at him in amazement. "You left my bed," she hissed.

Alexander sighed, and Hettie couldn't find the words to tell him how much he'd hurt her by disappearing like that, when she'd given herself so completely. She didn't understand; one minute they were making love, and the next they weren't even talking.

"Will you keep me updated on the pups?" Al asked eventually.

"Call me any time," Hettie shot back dismissively.

CHAPTER NINETEEN

Ted was visiting Draymere regularly now. Anju insisted he see his father at least once a month. James and Grace decided they could schedule the family meeting when his next visit was planned and shouldered the bad tidings for a while longer by themselves.

Alexander grew increasingly frustrated as bank after bank refused them loans. He knew that he and Ewan would make the practice successful, but convincing the banks of that was proving impossible. He would have to speak to James; it was only a loan they were after. He had hoped they could do it without further help from Draymere. The estate had provided the barns, and it didn't feel right to take money from his father while the old boy was still alive but in no position to approve it. He was convinced by the accountant's projections that they would be able to make the repayments plus interest inside the first five years. He took his projections and business plan to James.

"I'll have to stop you there," James said wearily before Al had even got going. "I would love to say Draymere could back you, but the truth is there is no cash, Al. Not that we can access. In fact, it is even more complicated than that. Er, I was planning to call a family meeting this coming weekend, while Ted is about. I can explain in more detail then. I am sorry, Alexander. I really am."

Alexander noticed how tired his brother was looking. He was embarrassed that he'd brought his problems to James without thinking it through, made assumptions without knowing the facts. That was his own fault. James had often tried to involve him in the running of the estate. The truth was that until recently all this accountancy stuff had been like a foreign language to Al. It was only in his efforts to get the practice up and running that he had taken the time to understand it. He was ashamed of himself now. James obviously had serious cash flow problems, and Al hadn't offered any support to his brother.

"No, I am sorry, James," Al said. "You've obviously got enough on your plate. If I'd paid attention, I wouldn't have brought this to your door. Is there anything I can help with? I've got some cash myself, if it's cash flow that's the problem. Just say the words, James. Anything I can do, anything at all."

"We'll discuss it at the meeting," James said firmly. "But in the meantime, Al, thank you for that offer. And good luck with finding your investment."

♦♦♦

Hettie came off the phone to Alexander. He was calling her every day now, sometimes more than once. It was funny, she thought, how they could talk about anything on the phone but didn't seem able to communicate when they were actually together. He had wanted to hear all about her recent competition, and Hettie was buzzing to tell him. Then he told her about progress with the practice, or more specifically the lack of it. She went and cuddled the puppies. *Their eyes should be opening any day now,* she thought excitedly as she relayed parts of her conversation to Cynthia, who was putting trays in the oven for dinner. *Roll on Sunday,* Hettie thought as she saw the oven chips going in, *when Granny Briggs cooks for us.*

"So, anyway," Hettie babbled, "he's got amazing plans for this practice—an equine clinic and everything. But they can't get funding; the banks keep turning him down."

"Tell him to speak to Pieter," Cynthia said. "That's his sort of thing. Entrepreneurial funding, or something, I never really understood it. He's coming here next weekend, staying with the girls so I can compete. Granny Briggs is off to bloody Spain or somewhere. Or give him Pieter's mobile number. I'll text it to you."

"You know, I could mind the girls," Hettie said. "I'm here minding puppies, anyway, and it's not as if they're any trouble."

"No, it's not your job!" Cynthia boomed. "That's the slippery slope to slave labour, Hettie, and you should value your skills higher than that. I pay you to be a groom. It will be nice to have Pieter in the house anyway," she mused. "For the girls, of course."

Hettie sent a text to Alexander later that evening.

About your money—you should talk to Pieter
he does entre something funding. I'll
send you his number, or he's staying here
next weekend

She got a text straight back:

Who is Pieter?

So she sent another one.

Cynthia's ex. Works in the city
one of the big banks I think

Alexander scowled. *So that would be the ex who had "been at it" throughout the marriage and run off with the last groom?* He dialed Hettie's number.

"I meant to say when we spoke that it would be good to see the puppies again, if their eyes are about to open. I'll come up next weekend, when this bloke is about. I can talk to him then. Kill two birds, as it were."

"All right," Hettie said.

Alexander walked up to the hall to see if Grace was on her computer. Hettie had said the pictures of her competing were on Facebook.

♦♦♦

Ted turned up on Saturday, without Anju, who was away on a girls' weekend. Al managed to avoid passing comment.

"Fox tonight, Al? After I've visited Father?" Ted asked.

"Of course." Alexander grinned.

He regretted the decision when he saw that Fiona and her braying clique were eating in there, but the Nag's Head wasn't appealing, and they were there now, anyway.

"What's this mysterious meeting all about, then?" Ted asked.

"Cash flow problems, I think. All the money still being in Father's name. We've let James try to handle too much on his own, or I have, anyway. It can't be easy with Pa as he is, trying to keep control without really having any. How was the old man today?"

"Much the same," Ted said. "Isn't he always? It's a funny old thing; they look after him brilliantly in that place. Attend to his every need, pump him full of antibiotics if his temperature so much as flickers. And yet to all intents and purposes, he's already gone."

Alexander nodded solemnly, and they gazed at their pints in silence. Fiona's shrill voice carried across the room.

"Of course, *he's* shagging the redhead slut now. God help him, is all I can say." She followed it up with a snigger.

Alexander covered the distance between them in seconds. Grabbing Fiona's arm, he propelled her out of her chair and into the corner.

"If I *ever,*" he whispered savagely, "hear you mention her again, or find out that you have been bitching about Hettie, I will make damned sure that this entire village knows exactly how rough you like it—that you squeal like a pig as you beg me to spank you. I am warning you, Fiona; I can make your life a misery, and I will."

Fiona turned a strange shade of puce as she tried to think of a comeback. "And *I,*" she managed eventually, "will tell them how tiny your prick is."

Alexander threw back his head and roared with laughter. "Tell them what the fuck you like, Fiona. I'm immune to your vicious tongue." He glanced slowly around the group at her table before adding complacently, "And I think you'll find that most of your *friends* have got firsthand experience of the size of my prick."

He let go of her arm and chuckled as he returned to sit with Ted.

"The Hettie saga continues?" Ted asked, raising his eyebrows.

"No, no. We're just, er, mates," Al replied.

Alexander and Ted registered the shock on their faces when James had concluded his explanation of the reason for the meeting.

Grace, sitting beside James, reached out and squeezed his hand. She had suggested she shouldn't be at the meeting, but all three of them had wanted her there.

Alexander was reeling. His world had shifted on its axis, and nothing seemed to make sense.

"And you've looked at all the legal options for getting around this?" Ted queried the point again.

They had simply assumed that James as the eldest would inherit Draymere, and life would carry on pretty much unchanged. The idea of that not being the case was incomprehensible.

"Yes," James said sadly. "I'm afraid I have. The only options left open to us are to establish that Father was unsound of mind when he wrote this will, which simply isn't true, or to provide irrefutable proof that Alexander has not had any contact with Mother, from the time of her departure from Draymere until the time of Father's death. Whenever that may be."

"Should we talk to Bert about this?" Ted asked.

"Well, yes, personally, I think we should. Bert has been like a second father to us and, well, any action we take to revoke this will would of course deprive Bert of a fortune."

"Not having contact on principle is one thing, but not having contact for *money?*" Alexander suddenly burst out with passion.

"I know, I know," James soothed. "The whole thing is a moral catastrophe."

"He didn't intend Bert to inherit Draymere," Grace said tightly. "His intention was to keep Celia away."

James patted her hand absently.

"No, I'm sorry, James," Grace went on, "and I wouldn't say this outside the room, but what your father has done is evil. He deprived a mother of seeing her children grow up, and that is unforgivable." Grace pressed her lips together tightly to stop any more words getting out. Angry red spots had formed on her cheeks, and she was close to tears. Not one of the brothers refuted her assessment.

"Did Celia know about this?" Alexander struggled to speak.

"Not the will, I don't believe," Grace replied. "But he told her when she left that if she saw any of you, he would write you out of his will. She didn't want you to know, but I think we've passed that point now. She said she'd hurt your father enough." Grace almost sneered, which was not like her at all.

"So why didn't she stay put?" Alexander asked beseechingly.

"He didn't give her that option," Grace replied shortly. She had probably said too much, but why anyone would want to protect William Melton's good name was currently beyond her.

"We should talk to Bert," Ted said, "before we take this any further. He needs to know what's going on and, well, whether we're going to challenge it."

"How can we not challenge it?" Alexander said, running his hand across his face.

"The letters from Celia, Alexander," Grace cut in softly. "Can you prove that you didn't read them?"

Alexander stared angrily at the table. "They are all in my cupboard, still sealed. But I can tell you I am not comfortable with this at all. And that is an understatement. There must be a better way, for God's sake!" he exploded. "Can't we get Father to rewrite his will? I'll hold his hand to sign the fucking thing."

Nobody answered, and Alexander knew he was talking utter rubbish.

"Anyway," James concluded. "We do need to decide our next course of action."

"Talk to Bert," Alexander said with finality. "We can't do anything else until he knows the situation."

"And pray Father doesn't die in the meantime," Ted added.

"All agreed, then. I'll talk to Bert, or should we do that together?"

"I'll come with you," Alexander said.

"And you need to decide, Alexander, if you would be prepared to prove no contact. I know it doesn't sit well with you, but it may be our only option." James sighed.

Alexander gritted his teeth. "Bert saw me not fifty yards from her when she visited in March."

"We're back to talking to Bert then. But you can all put your minds to any bloody thing you can come up with that might get us out of this God-awful mess." James ended the meeting.

When Alexander got back to the gatehouse, he had to fight the urge to rip open Celia's letters and read every single one.

Granny Briggs was, if anything, even more outrageous than Cynthia, but she cooked a decent dinner. *Not up to Mum's standard,* Hettie thought. The gravy was too thick, the vegetables were too soft, and the potatoes were a little soggy, but it was a definite improvement on oven chips.

"So you worked for William Melton?" Granny Briggs questioned after discussion about the puppies had led to Alexander's and Hettie's previous employers.

"Yes, for a couple of years before James took over," Hettie said.

"Nasty bastard, that man," Granny Briggs muttered.

"He was OK when I was there," Hettie interrupted. He had been something of a tyrant, but the Meltons were like family, and she couldn't let that sort of comment pass without a rebuttal.

"Awful man," Granny continued unperturbed. "Married that French girl, can't think what her name was. Little slip of a thing. She was never going to be a match for Melton. Ugly divorce, if I remember rightly. Forbade her from seeing the children."

"No, that can't be right," Hettie cut in determinedly. "Celia visits Draymere often. I've met her myself; she's an artist. She did some great sketches of the hunters out in the snow. I was talking to Al about it just the other week."

"Must be thinking of someone else," Granny muttered. "Seen a lot of ugly divorces."

"Yes, and three of them were your own!" Cynthia crowed cheerfully.

CHAPTER TWENTY

Alexander left for Norfolk on Friday afternoon, having booked a room in Blakeney for a two-night stay. They hadn't spoken to Bert yet, dreading the conversation and shying away from airing the family laundry, even if only with Bert, who almost counted as family himself. And Alexander still hadn't come to a decision over the dilemma of proving no contact with his mother. It felt like blackmail, and for the first time in years, he let himself consider what that might do to her. Bert's reproof had found its mark. Al knew, of course, that his refusal to see her must have hurt her a lot. But the idea of losing Draymere was awful to contemplate, the estate had been in the Melton name for centuries. So the terrible quandary circled around in his head without him ever getting closer to an answer. He resolved to put it from his mind for the weekend. They would talk to Bert next week, and what was to be would be. His bloody father had caused immeasurable turmoil by hanging onto his bitterness for all those years. That he was sure of.

Al didn't hold out much hope for this meeting with Pieter, either. If the other banks had turned them down, there was no reason why this one would be any different. He suspected Pieter was just giving it the big "I am" in an effort to impress the latest groom, which made him unreasonably irritable about the idea of talking to him at all. He had packed his paperwork, though, on the off chance.

Cynthia had left with the horses early on Friday morning, taking one of her crowd along to groom for her. Pieter arrived at Flintend in time to pick the girls up from school. He entered the kitchen laden down with classily packaged groceries and asked Hettie if there was anything she didn't eat.

"I eat everything." Hettie laughed. "But you don't need to cook for me, Pieter. I can sort myself out."

"I would like to, if you would let me," Pieter told her in his quiet, unassuming way. "Cooking is one of my pleasures, and I enjoy sharing food."

Hettie watched the goodies coming out of the bags and accepted happily. She and Jess went out to the stables, leaving Pieter and Harriet to cook.

When they sat down to dinner, Hettie noticed with amusement how different the house felt without Cynthia or Granny there. Pieter was so softly spoken and quiet compared to both of them. Harriet, finally able to get a word in edgeways, chatted eagerly about school. Hettie didn't speak much; she was too busy enjoying the wonderful meal Pieter had prepared. The puppies mewed and squirmed contentedly under the table, and Jess played with her phone until Pieter took it from her with a quiet remonstration. Hettie leaned back in her chair and sighed with stuffed satisfaction.

Harriet jumped up and answered the door when Alexander knocked. Going red in the face, she sat back down hurriedly when she realised who it was.

Hettie stretched, smiled a hello, and introduced Pieter, who stood up and to shake his hand.

Quite the cosy scene, Al thought moodily.

"Right, I'm clearing up, Pieter. That was an amazing dinner." Hettie patted her stomach.

Pieter smiled graciously in acceptance of her offer.

"Look at the puppies, Al. You won't recognise them. See how much they've grown!"

Alexander found himself in the uncomfortable position of having to crawl under the table that Pieter was still sitting at. Jess scurried under with him and picked each puppy up to tell him what names she had given them.

They were adorable, even if Al wasn't bowled over by the choices of names. He shot out quickly when he saw Pieter's legs moving across the kitchen to where Hettie was.

"Homework, girls. I will join you," Pieter announced, clearing plates from the table.

"I haven't got any," Jess declared quickly.

"Well, come and sit with us anyway," Pieter went on mildly. "Bring your books, Jessica. Show me what you've been doing at school."

Jessica emerged willingly enough from underneath the table.

"He's a really nice man, Pieter," Hettie said when they had gone. "I hope he can do something about your loan. Wouldn't that be great?"

Alexander grunted and went back to the puppies.

"Cynthia's mother knows your dad," Hettie chatted on happily. It was nice to see him again, especially now they were friends. "She's a character, Granny Briggs." She laughed. "I was telling her about your mum's drawings, the horses she did in the snow, when she visited you."

Alexander froze. It was an unknowing remark, but if Hettie was making comments like that, so was the rest of the village. They had been so discreet about the real situation; it stood to reason people would assume that Celia's visits had been to all of them. He relaxed his tensed shoulders and chuckled softly. Decision made, then. It felt like a burdensome weight had been lifted. He wouldn't deny his mother, not even for Draymere.

"What are they doing?" Hettie smiled, coming over to see what he was laughing at.

"Being cute," Al replied.

Hettie didn't join him under the table. They were getting on so well at the moment, she didn't want to spoil it by reminding herself of the other feelings she still had for him.

Pieter took Jessica to bed. She hugged Hettie and Alexander good night, and Harriet went upstairs to her room because she couldn't stay in the kitchen while Alexander was present without blushing and stumbling over her words.

"I think she's got a crush on you," Hettie whispered and laughed.

"Poor kid," Al replied. "I can remember what crushes are like."

Hettie didn't like that answer; she felt ridiculously jealous of whoever had been the focus of Alexander's teenage passions.

When Pieter came back downstairs, Al wondered if it was time for him to leave. He really didn't want to go. He accepted the wine that Pieter offered and scowled when Hettie did too.

"Cynthia tells me you have a business proposition," Pieter said. "I would be happy to hear about it, if you think I can be of help."

"I doubt you'll be able to," Al muttered. "All the banks have turned us down, so I don't expect yours will be any different.

"I deal in private investment," Pieter continued, unruffled. "You would be surprised at the number of private investors who are looking for tax breaks by investing in entrepreneurs. But, of course, that may not be a route you wish to go down."

"These private investors," Al asked, his interest piqued, "do they have decision-making powers and interests above that of a normal loan?"

"Rarely," Pieter answered. "Some get more involved than others. But of course, all of that is settled in writing at the time of the agreement."

"Maybe you should take a look," Al murmured, slightly reluctantly. "I've got my projections and business plan, if you've got time now."

"Yes, of course," Pieter said. "It would be my pleasure."

Hettie left them to it and went to check on the horses. It was strange, but having Al around made her homesick for Draymere and the village. She must spend a weekend at home soon. Her mum and Grace kept asking when they would see her, but they had been so busy eventing, and now there were the puppies to consider.

Alexander came to find her before he left, animated and full of optimism about the doors his discussion with Pieter had opened. He had left his business plan for Pieter to read through that night. *With luck, that will keep him busy,* Al thought dryly.

"I'll see you tomorrow," he said. "Have you got any, er, plans for the day?"

"No, nothing planned." Hettie smiled. "Laundry and maybe some shopping. That's my usual Saturday. I might ride out with the girls if either of them wants company."

"Come to Blakeney," Al said. "We could take Digger for a walk. I'll buy you lunch."

"OK." Hettie nodded, feeling weirdly shy as Al pulled her into a parting hug. Her heart rate betrayed her, and they hung onto each other for longer than was strictly normal for mates.

"See you tomorrow, then." Al said, clearing his throat as he stepped away. "You'll be, er, going to bed now, will you?" He wanted to add "on your own," but checked himself in time. If he was honest, he hadn't seen any hint of flirting or chemistry between them. And Pieter was a nice bloke, not at all what he had imagined from Cynthia's comments. Anyway, the girls were here, in their mother's house. Nothing was going to happen, was it? He was just being paranoid and obsessive. *Again,* his mind chided him.

Saturday dawned bright and warm. Hettie was excited to be going to the seaside. She found Pieter and the girls already up in the kitchen. Pieter was making pancakes, and she ate a couple greedily when he offered.

"I will watch you girls riding," Pieter told his daughters. "And then maybe we will go to the pictures or something this afternoon."

"I can show you my flying changes," Harriet said excitedly.

"And I can show you how high I can jump," Jessica added, her mouth full of pancake.

"Hettie," Pieter said, "get Al to give me a call. Or is he coming back here later?"

"I expect he'll want to see the puppies before he goes," Hettie told him. "But if you're out, I'll get him to ring you." She had dressed in her denim shorts and halter-neck top, with her bikini underneath in case she felt brave enough to venture into the sea. The early summer heatwave was forecast to continue. Hettie was already golden brown from working outside, and the horses had begun staying out overnight to enjoy the cooler temperatures. She threw a towel and her trainers in the Landy, in case Alexander was planning to trek for miles.

Al was leaning against the wall outside the hotel when she pulled up and parked. He was wearing loose running shorts and a white T-shirt. *He looks bloody gorgeous,* Hettie thought, ruffled. She fiddled about in the Landy for a moment to collect her thoughts, and they grinned stupidly at each other when she got out.

"Do you want a drink or anything before we set off?" Al asked.

"No, I've got my water." Hettie waved her bottle. "Let's get going."

They took the costal path toward Wells-next-the-Sea. The water glittered under the sun as they wound along the coast. Digger chased around them in enthusiastic circles. Al thought he had never seen Hettie looking sexier, with her curls piled up on her head, her brown shoulders bare, and those sexy legs beneath her shorts. And that tattoo on her ankle always did him in. He struggled to concentrate on the sights she kept pointing out.

"I should have brought my sun cream," Hettie said as they emerged from forest into the sun. She slipped off her flip-flops to feel the sand between her toes.

Al took her hand. "Let's climb that sand dune," he said.

"Race you!" Hettie cried, snatching her hand away and running off. Digger barked excitedly as Al sprinted after her; he caught up easily but stayed behind to enjoy the view. They reached the top of the sand dune laughing and out of breath.

"Beat you!" Hettie crowed.

"I let you!" Al laughed.

They flopped down on the sand. Hettie knew what would happen next if she allowed it to, and she knew that she wanted it to as well, almost more than anything. The chemistry between them was strong and the pull irresistible. But she wasn't going to risk getting hurt like that again.

"I'm going in the sea." She jumped up. Digger followed as she ran down to the water's edge, but Al stayed where he was lying on the dune and watched as she stripped off her shorts and top and waded into the waves. Digger stood at the edge of the sea barking joyously while trying to avoid wetting his feet in the breaking waves.

Alexander continued to watch as Hettie dived under the water and resurfaced to wave at him. He didn't wave back. She was only in the water for minutes—the sea was icy cold in contrast to the warmth of the day—and after pulling her clothes back on, she wandered contentedly back to the dune.

"Bloody cold!" she said.

"Are you deliberately trying to tease me?" Al growled, his eyes fastened on the horizon.

Hettie stopped smiling and looked at him in dismay. She found her towel and wrapped it around her shoulders.

"No, I'm not," she replied in a small, tight voice. "If anything, I'm trying to resist you."

He scowled even more and shook his head. "I don't like games, Hettie."

"Games?" Hettie said, "So now I'm a *player*, as well as a *one of those girls?* Christ, Alexander, you bastard. I never know where I am with you from one minute to the next. And you think *I'm* the one playing games? I bloody well knew this would happen. We should have stuck to talking on the phone, or not talking at all," she finished miserably.

"Knew what would happen?" Al asked.

"This!" Hettie almost shouted. "As soon as we get close to…well, as soon as we start getting on, *this* happens and you bloody well turn on me. Or drop me and walk away."

"So you dance about in front of me, half-fucking-undressed!" Al shouted back. "And then tell me you are trying to *resist me.* What the fuck is that?"

Hettie wanted to hit him. She was shaking with anger now.

"That," she said slowly, "is the result of you being a total wanker."

"So it was deliberate," he drawled.

Hettie snatched up her bag and walked away before she lost it altogether. Digger was confused and ran between the two of them, barking frantically.

She reached the edge of the forest before she realised that she had left her flip-flops on the dunes and her trainers were still in the Landy. But she was close to tears of fury now, and no way was she going back. Alexander caught up with her twenty feet into the wood, as she was picking her way precariously over the wood-chip path. He laid a hand on her arm, and Hettie rounded on him, swinging her arms and landing punches on his chest. He stood and took the punches until she had worked her fury through before pulling her into a hug.

"I'm sorry," he whispered against her wet hair. "At the risk of sounding like a cliché, it's not you; it's me. I am being a bastard."

"Every time I trust you," Hettie raged into his chest, "you judge me and hurt me. I can't deal with this. I don't have to deal with this, and I don't see why I should."

Alexander sighed heavily and kissed the top of her head. "Give me another chance, Hettie, to be someone you can trust," he said. "I'm screwed up, I know, and judgemental, even when I'm wrong. But I do want to *try*. I would like to be a better person for you."

"But do you *really* think of me like that? The things you accuse me of? I don't know, why would you say things like that if you didn't really believe them?"

"I don't believe them," he answered. "Not when I'm being rational. I get angry and jealous. I'm not good with…well, feelings and all that shit. I say things that come into my head. I can't explain it. It's not something I'm proud of." He pulled her tighter into his arms, embarrassed at his own rare honesty.

"All right." Hettie sighed. "One more chance. But I can't be always thinking about how I'm acting when I'm with you. I'm just me, Alexander. What you see is what you get. I don't play games. I'm not that bloody clever. If you can't trust me too, we might as well give up."

"I can do that," Alexander said stubbornly, not really sure that he could. He rubbed her shoulders with the towel and kissed her head again. "You must be cold. You're soaking wet and we're standing in the shade. Let's walk back, get you dry, and I'll buy you that lunch I promised.

Hettie sat on a log to dry her feet and put her sandals back on. Alexander held out his hand as she stood, and they walked back hand in hand.

Surprisingly, Cynthia was at Flintend when Hettie returned after lunch. She'd had a fall in the cross-country phase and been eliminated. She had hurt her ankle quite badly as well.

"Did you drive the horsebox back like that?" Hettie asked as Cynthia limped around the kitchen.

"Yes, only my left foot," Cynthia barked. "Didn't affect my braking."

"Alexander wants to take us all out for dinner," Hettie told her. "The girls as well. To say thank you for putting up with the puppies, and to thank Pieter for looking at his business stuff."

"Where are the girls?" Cynthia asked. "I'm sure they'll be delighted. No need to thank us for the puppies, though. Having them here is a pleasure. Was Pieter able to help him?"

"I don't really know, but they both sounded fairly positive after they'd been through the business plan, and I think Pieter has taken the girls to the pictures." She ran upstairs for a shower to wash the sand and the salt away before Alexander turned up to see the puppies again.

He arrived at the same time as Pieter and the girls. His offer of dinner was greeted with thanks from Pieter and excitement from Jessica, who shouted "McDonald's" repeatedly.

"We'll see," Pieter murmured quietly.

"Wherever you like, Jess." Al beamed. He was casually dressed in jeans and a shirt, looking sun kissed, relaxed, and handsome.

Harriet blushed.

They had a raucous time in McDonald's. Alexander was back on form, and Cynthia was merciless in winding up Pieter about his disdain for the food. Pieter smiled and took it with good grace.

"You got a chance to look at our plans?" Alexander asked him in a quiet moment.

"Yes, come back to the house and I'll run through things with you. I can't see any problem with securing the funding. None at all."

Hettie and the girls played a game on the side of Jess's Happy Meal box.

Back at Flintend, Pieter and Alexander disappeared off to the study.

"Beats me why you're not staying at that hotel with him," Cynthia said as soon as the room was clear.

"Oh, no," Hettie said quickly. "We're just friends now."

"Humph," Cynthia retorted. "I'd like to say I admire your restraint, but if it was me, I'd be over there shagging the hell out of him." She laughed loudly.

I wish I could think like that, Hettie mused wistfully.

"I'll say good-bye to these puppies, and then I'd better be off," Al said when he returned.

"Come for Sunday lunch tomorrow?" Pieter asked.

"No, I'm leaving early in the morning. There's something I need to do before a meeting next week."

Hettie was disappointed. "I'll see you off," she said, following him out to the car.

"Good news from Pieter?" she asked.

"Sounds very promising. I need to speak to Ewan and get the ball rolling now."

"Have you seen Clare and baby Charlotte?" Hettie was missing home even more, knowing Al was going back there.

"Yes, she's very sweet." Al smiled. "She's smiling and laughing now. Clare keeps asking when you're going to visit, and she's not the only one. Grace gave me orders to nag you."

"I'm stuck puppy-minding now, but I am missing home. It would be good to get back for a visit."

"I'm sure Cynthia wouldn't mind looking after the puppies. She seems very, er, laid back."

"That's one way of putting it." Hettie chuckled. "But well done for not being judgemental."

Oddly, the thought of passing judgement on Cynthia had never entered his head. *Only the ones you sleep with*, Ted's words came back to him. *But how could he not want to sleep with Hettie?* he thought, looking at her standing there.

"Can I at least kiss you good-bye?" He grinned.

"You think we can stop at a kiss?" Hettie laughed. "History would indicate otherwise, and, well, don't you think we should work on trusting each other first?"

"Huh," Alexander said grumpily. "You're killing me, Hettie Redfern."

"No more than I'm killing myself," she answered with regret. She hugged him briefly, forcing herself to step away again. "Drive carefully, Alexander Melton. I'll call you with regular updates."

"You're calling me?" Alexander smiled. "That's progress, at least."

CHAPTER TWENTY-ONE

Alexander only returned to the hotel to settle his bill. His day spent with Hettie and the meeting with Pieter had left him restless and wired. Fired up with energy, he knew he wouldn't sleep, so he decided to drive home through the night instead. It was three o'clock in the morning when he got back to Draymere. He parked the Aston in the garage, closed the doors behind it, pulled the blind, and drew the curtains in his study. After pouring a large whiskey, he took his holdall out of the cupboard and sat at his desk in a pool of light from the desktop lamp.

With the exception of the two most recent, Celia's letters were secured in date order. Selecting the oldest first, Alexander starting reading. Her early letters were doggedly upbeat and cheerful. His mother asked about his riding, his rugby, and school. She included anonymous snippets about her own life: a book she was reading or a drawing she had done. There were funny little sketches around the edges of each page. She said she was missing him and that she loved him and always would. Every letter was signed with her familiar good night refrain from their childhood: *vous tenir toujours dans mon coeur, Mama x*

Alexander had to leave the study several times. He paced the downstairs rooms, staring at the floor, fighting to get his emotions back under control before pouring another drink and returning to his desk.

He read her excited congratulations on the successes in his life and of her concern at times when he had been injured or unwell. *How did she know all this?* he thought. There was no mention of other friends, or men, which Alexander had dreaded. She apologised often for the hurt she had caused, without ever mentioning her reasons for leaving. Her letters always asked about Draymere and his life and included anecdotes and memories of her own times there. She wrote of how sad she was on hearing that their father was ill, and said she wished she could comfort them all with what they were going through.

The letters asking for forgiveness, with tentative suggestions they might meet, started around the time of his first overseas posting. The pages remained determinedly cheerful, but the dread she was suffering seeped out of her words. On one letter Alexander found what he thought was a teardrop smudge. Leaving the study, he paced again, and went outside for a cigarette.

Dawn was breaking when he read the last, most recent letter. Then he went upstairs and fell onto the bed fully dressed. After sleeping fitfully for a couple of hours, Alexander showered, shaved, dressed, and returned to the study. He sat down to compose the toughest letter he had ever written. He asked Celia to forgive him for taking so long to get in touch, and told her that she had nothing to apologise for. If she still wanted to meet him, he said, he would very much like to see her.

He strode to the village with Digger, over tracks and footpaths packed hard by the sun. Draymere land stretched around him at its most beautiful. He passed still-lush meadows and cattle grazing contentedly in the weak morning sun, wildflower-flecked hedgerows, and trickling streams. Birdsong filled the air from every leaf-laden tree, and insects and butterflies flitted and bumbled nearby. He posted his letter in the village, then turned for home to face the day and tell James of his decision.

James was choked when he told him. He patted Alexander awkwardly on the shoulder. "I'm proud of you, Al," he said gruffly.

Grace pursed her lips when James passed the news on to her. She knew it was the right thing to do, but this was her home they were talking about. Alexander was plain bloody ornery, she thought resentfully. Fifteen years without contact, but now there was actually a reason to keep it going, he had written to his mother! She rebuked herself for her mean-spiritedness and blamed it on her hormones. She forced herself think about how she would feel if it was Artie or Fred or Georgia in the same situation, and made herself cry with her thoughts.

Al walked from the hall to Bert's cottage. He was thoroughly ashamed of himself for avoiding Bert and embarrassed to be calling on him now. But Bert never held a grudge against anybody.

"Mornin', Master Al. Lovely day for it," Bert called in greeting as he came out of the cottage when Al arrived. "Just off for my Sunday dinner," he added, patting his stomach.

"Anywhere nice?" Al asked.

"Oh, yes," Bert answered mysteriously, which rather stumped Al for follow-up conversation.

"Bert, er, James and I," Alexander said, cutting straight to the point, "wondered if you would come up to the hall for a meeting next week. Any day that works for you would be fine."

"Not turfin' me out, are you?" Bert queried.

"No, no," Alexander reassured him, almost laughing at the irony. "It's not bad news, just something we need to discuss with you. Nothing to worry about."

"Well, that's all right, then." Bert smiled. "I'll be up tomorrow mornin'. Make it eight o'clock so the curiosity don't have a chance to kill me first." He chuckled. "You've been up to see Hettie?" He carried on, "How's that young'un doing? It's takin' some getting used to, not seein' her about the place."

"It is, isn't it, Bert?" Al agreed. "But she's doing very well, I think, enjoying the competing. And the puppies are growing fast."

"Aye, they'll do that." Bert nodded.

"I don't want it," Bert stated adamantly when the brothers had finished their speech. "What would I be doin' with four thousan' acres? At my age an' all. No, you can keep it, if you don't mind. That wouldn't be right. No, not right at all."

James smiled at him wearily. "I'm afraid it's not quite as easy as that, Bert. You see, it's Father's will. None of us have the power to change it. If we have been in contact with Mother, and all of us have..."

Bert didn't say anything, but his gaze moved briefly to Alexander.

"...then the estate will come to you. Unless Father was unsound of mind at the time he wrote it, which he wasn't—"

"Debatable," Bert muttered.

"And we would have to prove that in court to get the will overturned. Which would be a terrible business, of course, on top of everything else."

"And you should realise, Bert," Alexander cut in, "that we are talking about a large estate. You would be able to live very comfortably for the rest of your life."

"I'm very comfortable now, thank you," Bert retorted. "Happiest I've been. No, I don't want it, and I shan't take it. There must be a way."

"At the very least," James stressed. "You should take independent advice. You need to speak to a solicitor. Have a think about this. The last thing we want to do is deprive you of what is yours. You're like family to us, Bert, and this dreadful business must not change that."

"I'll not talk to them solicitors," Bert said adamantly. "Bunch of thievin' crooks, they are. No, I'll not be dealin' with them."

Alexander and James glanced at each other in dawning realisation of how difficult this was going to be, despite Bert's magnanimous statements.

Bert sighed heavily. "Right," he said. "I'll tell you something now which you may not like. It was me that kept your mother in touch all these years. Called as regular as clockwork, she did, on a Sunday evening. It was breakin' 'er 'eart, leavin' you boys. She tried to move to the village, but 'e said that weren't far enough. I'll have no truck with this," he finished quietly. "It weren't fair then, and it ain't fair now, an' it's mainly down to me that you boys could lose this place. I couldn't live with that."

Bert looked so miserable that Alexander patted his shoulder. "Don't feel badly for that, Bert. I'm sure you did us all a favour."

James nodded his agreement.

"So what do we do?" Bert rallied. "Can't I leave it all back to you in my will or whatever? You boys are like sons to me, an' I've no other relatives. An' in the meantime, if 'e goes before me, we'll jus' carry on as normal. I'll sign anythin' you tell me to sign, James. Will that straighten' the 'ole thing out?"

James and Alexander stared at him, struck by the generosity and simplicity of the suggestion.

"Good Lord," James said eventually. "You know, I think it could."

They tried again to persuade Bert to seek legal advice, and repeated every point to make sure he understood exactly what he was offering and what he would be giving up.

"All of this," Alexander said, waving his arm expansively. "All of this could be yours, Bert. You understand we feel uneasy taking that from you?"

"You're taking nothing," Bert said crossly. "It shouldn't be mine to give. But if that's the way of it, well, who else would I give it to? Draymere has been my 'ome. Happiest years of my life I've spent here. That's reward enough. You get it written up, James, and I'll sign the blummin' thing. The sooner, the better, I say. Get this bloody feud put to bed for once an' all. There was never any good gonna come of it."

Exhausted by his speech, he got up to leave.

"I'll do a draft," James said, "and you can read it through. Think on it some more. You can change your mind, Bert, if you have second thoughts—"

Bert scowled at him darkly, so James shut up.

"One thing I will say," Bert muttered when he'd almost reached the door. "This will, my little bit of savings should, er, go to Anna Redfern. That doesn't leave this room." He scowled at them both again. "She never wanted the children to know, an' I respect that, so I do."

James and Alexander sat openmouthed when he'd gone.

The solicitors thought it improper that James and Alexander were acting on Bert's behalf. Especially given the circumstances and the beneficiaries of Bert's will. So Bert put on his Sunday suit and marched into their offices with his electricity bill, driving license, and an untidily scrawled note on a piece of scrap paper.

I heerby authorise James William Melton and Alexander Henry Melton to act on my behaf in all matters purtaynin to me will. Signed Herbert O'Brien.

"Will that do you?" he asked the receptionist belligerently.

James felt like the weight of Draymere itself had lifted from his shoulders.

Summer grew even hotter. The ground began to crack, and meadows paled beneath the never-ending sun. The streams over Draymere ran dry, and the media talked endlessly of climate change and drought. The days at Flintend turned topsy-turvy; they rode in the early mornings or late in the evening, although it was too hot even then. Competitions were cancelled because of the hard ground. The horses spent their days in the shade of the stable and their nights out in the field. Pieter became a regular weekend visitor; the city was just too hot to bear. They cleared out the poolroom and filled the swimming pool. Cynthia booked lessons for Harriet with a local dressage rider. The instructor told her that her daughter was gifted. Hettie amused Alexander with the puppies' first adventures and wobble-legged explorations, taking video on her phone and posting it on Facebook so he could watch it on Grace's computer. He thought about setting up his own account.

A letter arrived from Celia, the shortest one to date:

Enough apologies, Alexander, from both of us. I would adore to see you anytime, anyplace, anywhere. Call me, Mama xx

So he picked up his phone, and Celia, who hadn't put her mobile down since she had mailed her reply, answered instantly and cried at the sound of his voice. They met in a small café near her home. They didn't hug, but Celia took his hands, held them across the table, and couldn't let them go. Their coffee got cold as they talked for hours.

"I will be at Draymere soon, to meet the new baby," Celia said as they parted. "But *anytime* you want to see me, Alexander, I am here." Alexander hugged her good-bye and walked away before she noticed the tears in his eyes.

On August second, at two o'clock in the morning, Grace went in to labour. Alexander, called to the hall to mind the other children, sent a text to Hettie:

Baby Melton on the way

Hettie woke Cynthia, knocking on her bedroom door, and realised with embarrassment that Pieter was sharing the bed.

"Go, go!" Cynthia said groggily, waving her arm. "Take a few days. We can manage perfectly well."

Hettie kissed the puppies and flew out the door, sad to be leaving them but excited to be going home, back to Draymere.

Sophie Celia Melton was born at 3:47 a.m., weighing seven pounds and nine ounces.

"I'm an old-hand now!" Grace cried, elated and exhausted, as James ushered her and the baby into the hall a few hours later.

"Bloody impressive!" Alexander grinned. "Hello, Sophie Celia Melton." He peered at the tiny face peeking out of the pink blanket. "Welcome to Draymere. I think you will be very happy here."

Hettie parked the Landy at the front of the hall. Running up the steps, she knocked loudly on the door.

Alexander let her in. "They're in the living room." He grinned, hugging her in greeting.

Artie, Fred, and Georgia were playing pass the parcel with Sophie. All three of them lined up on the sofa stiff backed with their little legs stuck out in front of them.

"We got a new sister, Hettie!" Fred told her when she walked in.

"You clever things!" Hettie said as she bent and hugged Grace tightly. "And you too, you clever, clever girl," she whispered in Grace's ear.

"I've bloody missed you," Grace whispered back.

Hettie hugged James and bubbled with happy congratulations and compliments on the baby, only pausing long enough to accept an offer of tea from Al.

"A quick one," she said. "Before I go to Mum's. If she knows I'm back and haven't called, I'll never hear the last of it. I'll come back later." She interrupted Grace's protests. "It will give you a chance to get some rest." She stared at Grace pointedly.

"Nothing wrong with me," Grace replied. "I'm full of energy. She gave me a nice, easy time. Didn't you, Sophie?"

"Did she come out of your bum, Mummy?" Artie asked her as he gazed, entranced, at the baby. Georgia leaned over and poked a finger gently up Sophie's nose. "You mustn't do that, Georgia," Artie admonished her.

"Sort of," Grace replied vaguely. "Ask Daddy; he'll explain it."

James pulled a mock-horrified face and laughed.

Hettie enjoyed her visit home so much. Out every evening with the girls from the yard or Jade and Hannah, and sharing her days between Clare and baby Charlotte, Grace, her mum, and the horses. She rode out with Jodie and Rose, and with Alexander. The weather stayed hot and dry, the nights uncomfortably so. Flowers and lawns withered under the effects of a hosepipe ban. Celia, Ted and Anju, and Grace's own mother were installed at Draymere when the time came for Hettie to leave. She promised to visit again soon and left with sad goodbyes but eager to get back to Doris and the puppies.

At Flintend, Cynthia greeted her enthusiastically. "They've been a bloody nightmare!" Cynthia laughed, nodding toward the puppies. "On the go nonstop. Even Doris is fed up with them. And watch where you tread—they're going everywhere but on the newspaper."

Hettie got out her phone and filmed some video for Alexander. The puppies were hilarious, play-fighting, climbing on anything they could find, and charging around on far-from-stable legs. She showed Cynthia and the girls her pictures of Sophie. Harriet thought she was lovely; Cynthia and Jess glanced briefly and made appropriate noises but were less impressed.

"Never liked my own at that age much, let alone anyone else's," Cynthia said. "You get better as you get older, girls," she added quickly. "Talking of puppies," she went on (which they hadn't been at the time), "have you had any thoughts about where they are going?"

"Oh, I can't even think about that," Hettie said. "I can't keep more than one, but the thought of sending them away is just too hard."

"Well, if SpongeBob is up for grabs, the girls and I would love to have him. Even Pieter seems keen," Cynthia told her.

"That would be brilliant!" Hettie was thrilled. "If I can persuade Al to have Dora the Explorer, that would leave Peppa Pig for me!"

"He'll have to have Digger done, if he takes the bitch," Cynthia mused out loud.

"Yes, I've got a feeling that might be a sticking point." Hettie laughed. "But she is his favourite. I'll see what he says."

Alexander was astonished to get an invitation to Jennifer's wedding. She had written "plus one" with a smiley face next to his name. He thought he might ask Hettie, as she was in the area anyway, and the more he thought about it, the better he liked the idea.

When they spoke later that day, they both came off the phone conflicted. Alexander had said he would love to have Dora, but was outraged at Hettie's suggestion of chopping Digger's balls off. And Hettie, initially thrilled about the wedding invite, immediately started panicking about what on earth she should wear. She hadn't been to any weddings except for Clare and Ewan's, and being a bridesmaid at that one, she hadn't chosen her own outfit. Alexander hadn't been any help. "A dress, I think," was all he said.

"Granny Briggs will take you shopping," Cynthia said when Hettie told her about the dilemma. "It's not my area at all, I'm afraid. But Granny goes to at least eight weddings a year, and she used to be in fashion. She's got an eye, I'm told, whatever on earth that means. I must have been a great disappointment!" She laughed before musing out loud, “It’s very short notice. Alexander must have been an afterthought.”

Granny was thrilled. “Oh, yes, you’re little but perfectly formed, Hettie. I will have great fun dressing you. That galumphing daughter of mine would never wear anything but jodhpurs. It was like World War Three getting her wedding dress. Worst shopping experience of my life,” Granny muttered darkly.

“Thank you,” Hettie murmured politely, not sure how else to respond, and wondered if this was a good idea after all.

CHAPTER TWENTY-TWO

By late August the endless heat was getting on everyone's nerves. The pool at Flintend was in continuous use. Hettie only felt comfortably cool while she was swimming and for a few minutes after she got out. Before she got back to the yard, she was hot and sweating again. They were taking the puppies into the garden to play in the evenings, but even then the temperature barely dropped, with the baked earth radiating back the heat it had absorbed through the day. The temperature didn't dampen the puppies' energy, though. They played and tumbled constantly, spreading puppy food and mishaps in their wake. Cynthia was right: Doris was fed up with their endless clamour for attention and sneaked out with Hettie at every chance she got. Which made the chaos and clamour even louder when they returned. Despite their best efforts, the kitchen floor became a minefield to be navigated with care.

Grace told Hettie over the phone that she couldn't cuddle Sophie nearly as much as she yearned to. By the time the poor baby had fed, she was hot, pink, and sweaty, so she to be put back down with a fan constantly blowing over her cot. "And I have to fight Artie off her first!" She laughed. "Bless him, he is totally smitten. It's as well Fred and Georgia got bored of her so quickly. It is a terrible thing to say, but I will almost be glad when they're back at school and I can have her to myself."

Al was going to take Dora home with him after the wedding. Hettie was dreading it, and he still hadn't done anything about Digger, refusing to even discuss it. His investment funds had come through. Pieter travelled to Draymere to meet Ewan and take a look at the project and had organsed the loan efficiently. "Top bloke," Alexander commented. "And I get the impression we're small fry compared to his usual investments. The builders have started—same lot that did the gatehouse, but a bigger job this time. At least this dry weather will give them a chance to get on. Have you sorted your dress?" he added as an afterthought.

"No, not yet. I'm shopping with Granny on Saturday," Hettie told him.

"Shopping with Granny?" Alexander laughed. "I look forward to seeing you in a crochet two-piece, then."

"Granny is very trendy, actually." Hettie laughed too. "But I must admit I'm worried; her determination is slightly intimidating. What are we doing about a present? Have they done a list or anything?"

"I've done it online," Al said. "Got them some kitchen knives. You just have to tick it off the list and give your card details. It was really easy." He sounded genuinely surprised.

"Bloody hell, Al, are you joining the twenty-first century?" Hettie jibed.

"Ha bloody ha," he replied.

Hettie went for another quick swim before bed. Even with no cover and every window open, she was too warm to sleep. Not a breath of air made it into the room.

Granny laid down the rules for their trip as soon as Hettie was in the car, and she drove so aggressively that Hettie was too busy gripping her seat to put up any fight.

"No fussy patterns, not on your small frame. Those tits of yours need help. A push-up bra and a flattering neckline will do it. Nothing too crass and obvious, of course. Although that would be impossible with your little tits!" She laughed loudly. "Simple classic jewellery, heels, of course, but in proportion to your height. We don't want you looking like Minnie Mouse. And a nice subtle colour to bring out that copper in your hair.

Your legs are lovely and brown, so we can do without stockings. I absolutely abhor fake tan. Shouldn't be allowed."

"That's quite a shopping list!" Hettie laughed. "I hope you've remembered this is my budget we're working with."

"Yes, yes," Granny answered. "That won't be a problem; they do some good stuff on the high street. And I know a few independent boutiques where the prices are fair."

Granny proved to be a very efficient shopper. She bossed the assistants in Top Shop and Zara, Whistles, and Cos. She knew exactly what she was looking for, and Hettie only tried on two dresses. She had looked at dozens of others, but Granny dismissed them all. They found the second dress to try on in a vintage boutique. It was perfect: a silver silk sheath with a loose sash belt knotted at the waist. It fitted Hettie's body like a soft glove, and the Wonderbra was amazing. Hettie hadn't realised she could look so curvy, the simple soft neckline of her dress showed a subtle, sexy cleavage. She grinned delightedly at her reflection. Granny selected a jewelled clutch bag from a high street shop and completed the outfit with a crushed velvet shawl in midnight blue, found in a hidden boutique that Hettie hadn't even known was there.

"Shoes must be decent," Granny stressed. "Cheap shoes can ruin an outfit, and they scream tacky." They found a gorgeous pair of rose-gold stilettos, with a thin strap that buckled around the ankle. The sandals cost more than the rest of the outfit put together, but Hettie couldn't resist. She handed over her credit card with a guilty thrill and tried not to look at the number the assistant rung up on the till.

"No necklace," Granny stated. "That bosom is pretty enough. But some beaten silver drop earrings, I think. You'll be wearing your hair up?" She didn't wait for an answer. "Yes, hair up, pile those beautiful curls on top. No hat, the hair is statement enough. Maybe a velvet flower to tie in with the shawl." And she was off hunting again.

Hettie was shattered by the time they had finished, but Granny was still on fire. She was in her element and selected earrings and a flower clip without even asking Hettie, which suited Hettie just fine. It was too hot to make decisions, and she'd had more than enough of shopping by then.

Cynthia smiled and nodded with feigned interest when they got back and showed off their bags of bounty, but Harriet joined in excitedly and asked if she could to do Hettie's hair and nails.

"Say yes," Granny directed as she sipped her tea and cuddled Peppa Pig. "She's a dab hand with a hairbrush."

"Thank you, Harriet. I'll say yes, then, on Granny's advice." Hettie laughed. "With all this attention, I feel more like the bride than just a random guest."

"If you don't snare the man in that outfit, you never will," Granny said bluntly.

Although it hadn't seemed possible, it grew even hotter as the day of the wedding approached. Alexander had said he would pick her up at one, after driving up in the morning and changing at the hotel.

Hettie left it as late as possible before taking a tepid shower, and even then she knew it would only be minutes before she was too hot again. Harriet had painted her nails a soft silver grey, filing them all into shape, chatting excitedly.

"You're really good at that." Hettie admired her shaped and painted nails. They didn't look like they belonged on her hands at all.

"I'd like to do beauty or fashion," Harriet said. "Like Granny did."

At one o'clock, Hettie gave a twirl in the kitchen, trying to fight the puppies off of her expensive sandals as she did so.

"Bloody hell!" Cynthia exclaimed. "I'm not a man, but even I could fancy you in that getup."

Hettie smiled. "It's all Granny and Harriet's work." She suddenly worried that Alexander might think she was leading him on again. "Is it too much, do you think?" she asked, too late, as they heard his car pull up outside.

"Too much? Don't be ridiculous!" Cynthia boomed. "If you've got it, bloody use it, that's what I say. He won't be able to keep his hands off you." She winked as Al knocked on the door.

Oh, shit, Hettie thought before all thought abandoned her at the sight of him in his suit.

"Fucking hell." Cynthia growled appreciatively. "Don't touch those puppies!" She shouted as he went to bend down. "Dora's got shit on her feet; I saw her run through one. Get out, the pair of you, before you ruin your outfits. I won't wait up!" She grinned lewdly at Hettie.

Hettie smiled apprehensively at Alexander. "You'll be hot in that suit," she said to him as they walked toward the car. Beads of sweat had already broken out all over her.

"At least you won't have that problem," Alexander drawled, looking her up and down.

"Is it too much, my outfit?" Hettie asked again as she tottered precariously over the gravel in unfamiliar heels.

"Too much?" Alexander growled. "I don't think so, do you? If you wore much less, you'd be virtually fucking naked."

Hettie stopped. "Right, I'll get changed," she said angrily. "I haven't got a burka, I'm afraid, or a nun's surplice, but would a sheet be cover enough?" She thrust out her chin and glared at him before turning back to the house.

"I'm being an arse again, aren't I?" Al said grumpily, putting his hand on her arm. "Hettie, you look fucking stunning. Don't change a thing. I'm just wondering how I'm going to get through the day without dragging you back to the hotel and ravaging you."

Hettie turned back and looked at him. He was smiling wryly. "Is that tantrum over for today, then?" she asked archly.

"Yes, I promise." Al grinned. "Absolutely best behavior from now on. See if I can charm you back to the hotel instead." His grin developed a wicked tilt.

"If you want me to come back with you, I will," Hettie said flatly. It was going to happen anyway, with him wearing that suit. Unless she avoided him all night and kept off the booze as well. In which case she might as well not go at all. "But last chance, Melton. If you turn on me this time, I'm done."

"Straight to the hotel, then?" he asked hopefully.

"No way." Hettie laughed. "I'm showing off this fucking outfit before I take it off. This took a lot of effort, you know!" But she had to admit that having agreed to sleep with him, the anticipation was already making her weak with lust.

"Christ," Alexander swore as he opened the car door for her.

The big church was refreshingly shadowed and cool. Hettie even used her shawl, which she had nearly left behind. The bride looked gorgeous, rosy faced and glowing, which Hettie thought gave a pretty flush to her cheeks. Her dress was beautiful, and she looked so blissfully happy, it was easy to get into the spirit of the service even though they had never met.

"Shown that dress off enough yet?" Alexander raised an eyebrow as they stood in shade outside the church watching the photographs being taken. The poor bride was getting pinker by the minute, and one of the bridesmaids was sitting on the grass being plied with water by the best man.

"Patience," Hettie hissed.

Alexander traced a finger gently down her neck, pausing above her cleavage, and grinned when she flushed and her quickening breath gave her away. "Two can play at that game," he whispered, bringing his head down close to her ear and dropping a kiss on her shoulder before standing upright again.

It was a relief to get in the car after they had let it run for ten minutes with the air conditioning on. Alexander didn't mention the hotel again, and Hettie resisted the urge to lean over and snog him there and then. There were too many people about. They drove to Jennifer's home, where a large marquee in the garden welcomed them. The lawn was suffering the effects of the drought, but at least the women didn't have to worry about their heels sinking in. Hettie gulped thirstily at her champagne.

"Steady," Alexander warned. "I want all your senses on full alert later." Hettie wasn't sure she could cope with her senses being any more fired up, but she exchanged the champagne for orange juice, aware that she hadn't eaten yet and that alcohol wasn't the best idea in this heat. Inside, the marquee was a musky swamp. The beautiful flowers had wilted pitifully despite the two noisy fans struggling to move the heavy air.

"Well, I asked for sun!" Jennifer laughed when they reached her in the reception line. She was flushed but elated, with her carefully curled hair clinging damply to her face.

She roared with laughter when Alexander said, "You look absolutely beautiful, Jennifer. Phillip is a very lucky man."

"Yes he is!" she answered happily. "Looking handsome and cool as ever, Melton. How are you managing that in this bloody heat? Now introduce me to your lovely guest."

"Hettie," Hettie said, holding out her hand. "Alexander's friend. Thank you for including me in your day. It's been wonderful so far, and I adore your dress."

They moved on up the line, meeting Phillip and the parents, making small talk, trying not to let thoughts of the night ahead distract them. They were seated at a table with a crowd of similar ages, a couple of whom Al knew. Hettie tensed when the man to her right started flirting outrageously, but Al smiled politely and chatted to everyone while running his hand over the top of her leg and dropping his fingers deliberately onto the inside of her thigh. His touch scorched her already hot skin. She sipped her water and tried to follow the conversation. The meal looked delicious. Alexander managed to down every dish with gusto, but the heat and her lust had killed Hettie's appetite. She twizzled a stray curl in her fingers distractedly through the speeches, and when Alexander's hand rested back on her thigh, she shifted in her seat to encourage his fingers onward. He gazed at her knowingly, a faint smile playing on his lips.

"One dance," Hettie said under cover of the clapping. "Then we can go."

"Patience," he whispered back with a smirk.

The heat in the marquee reached an unbearable level, and as soon as the speeches were over, guests started spilling outside to try and find relief in the darkening night. Hettie and Al went too. The lawn lit up with a thousand sparkling lights, and the backdrop of trees was illuminated in shades of gold and purple.

"It's beautiful," Hettie said. "But I'm just too hot!"

"Yes, you are," Al agreed.

Hettie laughed. "Beats me how you still look so unruffled in trousers and a shirt, when I'm bloody boiling and, quote, 'virtually fucking naked.'"

"I didn't say that!" Alexander protested, nuzzling her neck. "I said if you took anything else off. I'll demonstrate virtually fucking naked on you later if you like."

Hettie would have laughed, but his lips on her collarbone were distracting her too much.

Music started in the marquee, so they moved back to the door and watched hand in hand as Jennifer and Phillip performed their first dance to Shania Twain's "From This Moment On."

"May I have the pleasure?" Al grinned at Hettie when other couples moved on to the floor.

"Yes, you may." Hettie smiled.

"This brings back memories," Al said as they moved against each other to the music. "Although maybe not for you, as you didn't remember who I was."

"I didn't know who you were!" Hettie protested. "I remembered a hunky stranger." She grinned.

"Hunky stranger?" Al laughed. "Mm, I think I can live with that. As long as you were remembering me at all the right times."

"Oh, yes," Hettie whispered breathily against his ear. His hands tightened their hold on her back.

They danced a couple more dances. Alexander's shirt grew damp where Hettie was pressed against him. "I love the smell of you," she told him truthfully. Alexander kissed her, but they had to drag their lips apart when the kiss quickly became too enthusiastic for general viewing.

"Shall we go?" Alexander asked.

"Yes," Hettie answered. They had nearly made it to the bride to say their good-byes when the master of ceremonies announced the cutting of the cake. So they joined the spectators and watched that before nabbing Jennifer and Phillip on their way back to the dance floor.

"Don't be strangers!" Jennifer shouted over the now thumping disco beat. "Next time you're both in Norfolk, look us up. Phillip's got a boat—we'll take you out."

"That would be great!" Alexander shouted back. Jennifer swung her hips and sashayed to the dance floor.

As they walked back to the car, fireworks cracked and popped, and white showers of stars burst in the sky.

"And I haven't even started yet." Al grinned at Hettie.

"Big talk!" she exclaimed. But she was suddenly feeling weirdly shy, and apprehension filled her.

"Are you OK?" Alexander asked, sensing her change of mood as he started the car.

"Absolutely fine," Hettie said brightly.

"We don't have to do this, Hettie. It's not compulsory. If you've changed your mind, tell me."

"Now if I did that, you would be justified in calling me a tease." She tried to laugh.

Alexander pulled over at the side of the road and turned the engine off. "Hettie," he said seriously, "if you want me to take you back to Flintend, then that's where we'll go. I might spout some awful shit when I'm in one of my moods, but I would never expect you to do something you didn't want to do."

"I do want to do it." Hettie blurted quickly, "I don't know what's come over me. Last minute nerves? I'm not drunk enough."

"Charming." Alexander smiled. "If you need to be pissed to sleep with me, that might still be a no."

I need to be pissed to sleep with anyone, Hettie thought miserably. But she wasn't going to tell him that.

"The hotel," Hettie said determinedly.

"All right, hotel it is." Alexander turned the engine back on. "We can order coffee, watch some of telly, have a cuddle on the sofa?" He glanced sideways at her, and Hettie laughed.

When they got out of the car, the oppressive heat hit them like a heavy blanket. Thunder rumbled in the distance, but it had been doing that for weeks with no wished-for storm to break the drought and bring relief.

True to his word, Alexander called at reception and asked them to send coffee to the room. Hettie wished he'd ordered alcohol. She slipped off her sandals with grateful relief and padded around the soft carpet appraising the room. "Nice," she said appreciatively. Al opened the French doors wide, but the temperature in the room didn't change. A carafe of fresh coffee arrived, filling the heavy air with its aromatic scent. Hettie busied herself serving it.

"Do you mind if I shoot in the shower?" Alexander asked.

"Give me a minute and I'll come in with you," Hettie said quietly. She was furious with herself for turning this into a big deal. Here she was at twenty-six years old, acting like a nervous virgin because she hadn't downed enough drink. It was ridiculous and humiliating, especially considering the hours she had spent thinking about this happening with Alexander again.

Alexander was confused. He didn't want to push her, but he didn't understand what had happened to change the mood of the evening. Although something obviously had. She looked like she was steeling herself for an ordeal.

"What's going on, Hettie?" he asked, sitting down beside her.

"Nothing!" She shook herself. "This is lovely. Lovely evening, lovely room, lovely to be here with you."

"That's a lot of lovelies." Alexander sighed. "But I can't help feeling you've gone off the idea."

"I haven't," Hettie said firmly. She curled against him on the sofa. Alexander put his arm around her and tried to look at her face, but she tucked it into his chest.

"I'll still be here in the morning," he tried. And then to lighten the mood, he added, "I'll have to be; I've got to pay the bill."

Hettie chuckled and stood up. "Come on, Melton." She tugged on his arm. "I thought we were going in the shower before we die of heatstroke."

"I've heard better chat-up lines." But he stood up and walked to the en suite still holding Hettie's hand. He pulled the light cord, then turned on the shower.

"Can we leave the light off?" Hettie asked.

"No, we fucking can't," Al said. "I like to see what I'm getting, and what I'm doing to you."

"Right," Hettie said and stepped under the cold shower with her dress still on. The cold was a shock but felt like bliss. She pulled off her earrings and chucked them on the floor.

"Ha!" Alexander snorted, undressing slowly. "If you are suddenly too coy to let me see you naked, you had better get out of that shower, because when I get in, one way or another that dress is coming off."

Hettie stood her ground. "It cost a lot of money," she said. "I'm getting my money's worth." The wet silk was clinging even closer to her skin, and her nipples, hardened by the icy water, pressed tightly against the fabric.

"That dress wet is more revealing than naked anyway," Alexander told her as he stood behind her in the shower of water.

"That's not what you said earlier," Hettie retorted smartly. She tried to let herself succumb to Alexander's touch as he cupped her breasts and kissed the back of her neck. She forced herself to relax as he pulled the pins from her hair, and slid the zip of her dress slowly down her back. She trembled as he pulled it over her head. "Do you want this water warmer?" he asked, undoing her bra and turning her around to face him.

"Maybe a little," she answered. "A degree or so up from freezing."

"I could ask the same of you," Al said gently as he adjusted the temperature.

"Please don't stop," Hettie said. "I want this, I really do. Just give me a chance."

"Has this got something to do with what happened at the Fox?" Alexander asked, holding her shoulders and looking at her face."

"No, it hasn't," Hettie snapped. "And I can't have this conversation standing naked in a fucking shower."

"And I can't fuck someone who so obviously doesn't want me to," Al shot back.

Hettie dropped on to her knees and buried her face in his groin. He tried halfheartedly to pull her back up, but the feel of her mouth on his cock and the view of her head there undid him. He groaned with months of unspent lust as her lips closed around him. Hettie felt a welcome flicker of desire at the sound. She ran her hands up his thighs and cupped his balls before moving them to his cock, leaning back on her heels to watch her hands pleasuring him.

Alexander growled and pulled her up. Kissing her hard, he slid his hand inside her knickers, but she was tight and unyielding. "Don't stop," she ordered again against his mouth when she felt him hesitate. He picked her up and carried her out of the water. Grabbing the corner of the duvet as he passed the bed, he dragged it to the garden and threw it on the parched patch of dusty grass. He laid Hettie on the duvet and settled down beside her, pushing her away when she tried to kiss him and catching her hands when she reached out for him. He gently smoothed the wet hair away from her face, studying her. Her eyes were shut as his fingers stroked her cheek, siding down her neck to her collarbone and slowly circling a breast. Her lips parted slightly when he brushed her nipple, but a small frown appeared when his hand dropped lower.

"You won't tell me what's going on?" he whispered softly. Hettie shook her head and reached for him again. He let her this time. He accepted the kisses she pressed onto him and watched her deliberately brush her nipples across his chest as she leaned over him, working his cock in one hand, kissing him tentatively. Finally her breath became jagged, and her breast rose and fell with increasing rapidness. She pulled her knickers off and, kneeling up, took his hand and pressed it between her legs. This time she yielded when his fingers found her soft, moist flesh, and she whimpered and gasped as his finger found its path and entered her. She pushed him onto his back and climbed astride him with her eyes still closed, a look of purpose on her face.

"Hettie…" Al tried to stop her, but she shook her head angrily again and, holding his cock, lowered herself over him. The entry was painful, but it was a familiar pain. Hettie knew how to breathe her way through it, and this time at least the pain was tinged with accompanying pleasure. She arched backward and leaned on her arms. Alexander felt his cock throb at the vision of her in front him. He cupped her breasts, thumbing her nipples, and a second moan escaped her as she started moving cautiously over him. Alexander kept a tight rein on his growing urges and let Hettie set the pace. It took all of his self-restraint not to throw her on her back and take his fill. He dropped a hand, and his thumb found her clitoris. Her own hand flew to his and held it there as her speed of movement grew and her breath came shorter. She was gasping now, and he felt her open to accept him fully. His own breath grew jagged as she thrust against him. "Oh God, yes," she moaned, eyes still shut. Alexander lost himself as he felt her muscles clench around him and then spasm as she groaned in the throes of a fierce, splintering orgasm. Grabbing her hips, he drove into her as his own orgasm was dragged forcefully out of him.

Hettie swung off him and curled at his side, lifting his arm and pulling it around her shoulders. She pressed her face against his still-heaving ribs and squeezed away the tears that inexplicably filled her eyes. She trembled slightly against him from the aftershocks of her orgasm. They lay in silence, their bodies glistening with sweat, as Alexander softly stroked her mussed-up hair.

The first heavy raindrop splattered onto Alexander's chest. They lifted their heads and looked at each other in surprise. They laughed as a second and third drop landed on them and then gathered up the duvet and ran for cover as the heavens opened and a deluge fell from the skies. They stood at the French doors, surveying the downpour in awe, and watched Hettie's abandoned knickers disappear in a flash flood of water that found a shallow gulley and streamed through the courtyard. Hettie tried to wrap the duvet around her.

"It's still too hot," Alexander said, pulling it from her and throwing it into the room. They moved back from the window when the lightening startled them and the splash from the flood began hitting their legs.

"What have you got in your mini bar?" Hettie asked, curling up on the bed, gathering the duvet on her way. "I'm cold," she said when he gave her a long look. But he walked to the mini bar and opened it.

"A half bottle of champagne, gin and tonic, some beers, and spirits," he called over to her.

"Champagne, I think," Hettie said.

"What are we celebrating?" Alexander asked, but Hettie didn't answer. He carried the champagne to the bed and climbed beside her, on top of the duvet. She snuggled next to him, and they watched the storm, swigging from the bottle. A cool draft ruffled the curtains and sent a welcome breeze through the room. Alexander looked at Hettie as she sipped from the bottle, with the duvet tucked up under her arms. He wanted to know what the hell had just happened, and cursed his own contrariness for doubting her when she was willing and doubting her when she wasn't. He couldn't understand why that had felt like shagging someone else altogether. As the champagne on her empty stomach gave Hettie the freedom from thought she craved, she pushed the duvet lower to enjoy the cool air on her skin. Alexander turned appreciatively to face her, absently caressing her breast and placing a kiss on her temple.

"Maybe you don't quite trust me yet?" he asked.

Hettie didn't want this conversation, not with anyone, and definitely not with him. She pointedly changed the subject.

"How are the barns coming on?"

"Very fast," Al said. "It's amazing what can be got through in a day with continental weather. Are you visiting home again soon? I'll give you the tour."

"I'd like that," Hettie said.

"Really like it or pretend to?" Al was suddenly irritated.

"Are you turning on me?" Hettie snapped.

"Are you turning off on me?" Al shot back.

Hettie didn't say anything, but she swigged more champagne. Kicking the duvet away from her legs, she pressed herself against him. Putting the bottle down, she took his head in her hands and kissed him deeply, thrusting her tongue in his mouth. The kiss aroused him instantly, and this time when his hand slid to her hip, she arched her back in encouragement and kissed him harder still. A sigh escaped her. She ran her fingernails down his back and moaned against his neck when he dropped his head to take her nipple in his mouth. Still impatient and confused, he pushed her onto her back and sat up to look at her naked. She smiled and stretched seductively under his gaze, returning his stare and letting her own hands run down her body. He groaned and moved her legs apart when her fingers dipped between her thighs.

"Hunky stranger time," Hettie whispered and laughed.

He pulled her hands away when the urge to touch her there himself got too strong to resist. "You're back, then," he whispered as he dropped his head, and she bucked against his tongue and cried out his name the instant his tongue made contact. They made slow love, wrapped around each other on the bed, kissing each other tenderly as they moved languorously together, the kiss growing harder with the need building in them. The rain continued to deluge from the sky, and thunder rumbled distantly as they came simultaneously in the same glorious moment.

They made lazy love again, spooned together, before they slept. Alexander woke her in the early hours, dropping kisses on her neck and along the length of her spine. When he reached the small of her back, Hettie turned around and welcomed him again.

They smiled, weak and sated in each other's arms, as they watched the sun rise. The earth steamed with thankful gratification.

CHAPTER TWENTY-THREE

Once the rain had started, it was reluctant to stop. Farmers with crops still in the field peered from their windows and worried, while those who had finished harvest rubbed their hands in pleasure.

Hettie made a brief one-night visit home early in September, bringing Doris and Pig with her this time. She visited Dora at the gatehouse, and Alexander gave her a tour of his house. He showed her Digger's penthouse suite and wondered out loud if it had been such a good idea now that he had Dora. He had no way of keeping her off the sitting room rug, which had become her favourite place to do her business. "She doesn't like going out in the rain," he said, picking her up off the sofa and affectionately ruffling her head. Then they walked Doris and Digger across footpaths to look at the barns. Work outside had come to a standstill because of the torrential rain, but enough progress had been made for the builders to make a start inside. Hettie was impressed. She could see it was going to be quite something when it opened. She took particular interest in the barn that would eventually become the equine block.

"I like the partitions Cynthia has at Flintend," Al said. "I keep meaning to ask her who she used. Does the yard there work well, do you think?"

"Yes, very well," Hettie replied. "I'll ask her and let you know." It would give her a reason to call him, she thought. With the puppies all grown, and Dora here, they were speaking less often now, and she was missing it. In fact, things had felt awkward and distant between them since the weekend of the wedding. She wasn't sure if he was cooling off or if she was overthinking. He hadn't flirted at all today, though, she thought miserably. He hadn't even made a lewd comment when he showed her his bedroom.

They trudged back to the gatehouse in their wellies with Digger and Doris running circles around them. They had left Dora and Pig in the run to make mischief together.

"Watch those two." Hettie laughed, nodding her head at the dogs. "I don't think Doris has come back in season, but then, I didn't notice last time. And much as I love those puppies, I'm not sure I want to do it again yet."

"He's been done," Al mumbled. "Flossie came into season. The poor little sod was beside himself, howling all night."

Hettie didn't comment; it had been a sensitive subject when she'd last brought it up.

"When do you hope to open the practice?" she asked instead.

"Not this year," Alexander replied. "Early next, hopefully, although it's hard to say. There's still all the equipment to source and staff to employ." He was irritated by this small talk—it felt awkward and insufficient. But he didn't know what he wanted anymore. He had never spent the whole night with anyone before Hettie, and he wasn't sure what that meant. He missed talking to her every day, and that irritated him too. But without the puppies to talk about, calling her daily felt pathetic. He wished he could forget her, occasionally wished he had never met her, but most of the time he wished he could keep her close forever. And that thought was scaring the shit out of him. He doubted that she was thinking about him as much as he thought about her. Their rare conversations were stilted and awkward, and she had definitely been backing off that night of the wedding. He reminded himself that it had been Hettie's decision to move hundreds of miles away. He thought about Jennifer's comments on unrequited love and cursed himself for his weakness. Shagging Hettie hadn't killed his obsession. If anything, it was worse. But if she didn't want him, so be it. There were plenty more fish in the sea.

"How long are you back for? What are you doing tonight?" he snapped as they approached the house.

"Just one night. I'm working on Monday," Hettie said. "And I'm not doing anything tonight."

"Ted and Anju are down. We thought we'd go to the Fox. You're welcome to join us if you want to. Or we could go somewhere else," he added the last comment hurriedly, as he remembered what had happened the last time they had been in the Fox."

"That would be nice." Hettie smiled. "What time are you going?"

"About eight. I could pick you up."

"No need." Hettie laughed. "I'll be at Mum's. It's only a five-minute walk. Send me a text when you get there."

"Talking of Digger's bollocks," Al started tentatively.

"I wasn't!" Hettie protested.

"No, all right." Al grinned. "I was trying to find a segue."

"A what?" Hettie looked at him, bemused.

"A smooth transition from one subject to another. I am trying to tactfully ask what you, er, we are doing about contraception?"

Hettie blushed. "I'm looking after it," she muttered. "You've got nothing to worry about, I promise."

"I'm not worried," he said. "But you told me you weren't on the pill…"

Hettie rolled her eyes.

"…and then, well, I never asked again. That was irresponsible of me."

"Well, you've asked now," Hettie said briskly. "And I've told you that I'm looking after it."

"So, what, you are on the pill?"

"You want the details?" Hettie asked incredulously. "Or do you not believe me?"

"It's both our responsibility," Al said stubbornly. He had thought about it a lot lately, what with being around baby Charlotte, and then baby Sophie, along with the happy accident with the puppies, and poor Digger having his balls off. It had all made him wonder why the hell he hadn't considered it before. For all he knew, he could have a dozen kids running around out there, and that thought made him very uncomfortable. He had always assumed that the woman he was shagging would be taking care of it.

"So?" he asked again. "I'm a vet, Hettie. I can cope with medical jargon." He grinned.

"I take the morning-after pill," Hettie snapped. "For fuck's sake, can you leave it now?"

"The morning-after pill?" Al looked confused. "But that's not, like, regular contraception, is it?"

"No, it's not. It's irregular contraception, for people who have irregular sex." She almost laughed at the look on his face.

"You should have told me," he said.

"I did, if you remember. It didn't go down too well."

"Fair point." He nodded ruefully.

He Googled "morning-after pill" later that day when Hettie had gone to see Grace. He read that the side effects could cause dizziness, nausea, headaches, breast tenderness, and abdominal pain. *Christ*, he thought as he shut the website down.

"I can't believe how chubby she's got in six weeks!" Hettie said to Grace, who had passed baby Sophie to her as soon as she'd walked in. Hettie didn't usually hold babies, as it rarely ended well. But Grace hadn't given her much choice, virtually throwing the baby at her as she ran to extract a screaming Georgia from her position on the floor where she'd fallen off her scooter and got her head wedged between the table leg and the wall.

"Tea?" Grace asked, leaving Sophie in Hettie's arms after Georgia had resumed her scootering.

"Lovely," Hettie answered, staring in fascination at Sophie's chubby little rosy face.

"She's such a good baby." Grace smiled contentedly. "Anyway, gossip to catch up on!" She grinned, returning to the table with two cups of tea.

"We only spoke two days ago, Grace!" Hettie laughed.

"This is Draymere; there is always new gossip," Grace declared. "But first I want to hear all about the wedding. Al is crap with details, and you haven't been much better. I still can't believe you and Alexander ended up going to a wedding together. Can you marry him, please, Hettie, and be my sister-in-law? Then you'll have to come back here." She laughed at her perfect plan.

"Sorry, Grace, I'm not planning to marry anyone. And Alexander might have something to say about your little scheme. But I can show you some pictures of the wedding on the computer. Jennifer sent a link in her thank-you e-mails."

"Are there any of you?" Grace asked excitedly, opening her laptop. "I know you described your outfit, but I would love to see it."

"One or two," Hettie murmured unenthusiastically. "They were taking them as we arrived. I look rather hot and bothered. Here, you take Sophie, and I'll find them for you."

They looked at pictures of the bride and groom and the bridesmaids, the family shots and the arty romantic poses. "She's a pretty girl." Grace said, "Lovely dress. Poor flowers—it really was hot, wasn't it?"

"Boiling," Hettie agreed.

"Oh my God." Grace suddenly gasped. "Hettie, look at you. You look absolutely beautiful! Alexander scrubs up bloody well too, doesn't he? Almost makes me wonder if I picked the wrong brother! I don't mean that," she quickly amended, turning to

Hettie. "Whoever takes Al on will have her hands full. He must have made a pass at you in that dress! Goodness, Hettie, your description didn't do it justice. And from what Ted tells us, Alexander is far from backward in being forward! Oh, you look so lovely together. That bag, and your hair! And Granny did all that? I might have to give her a call! Are there any more?"

"Not really, not of us." Hettie was glad that Grace had kept her eyes firmly fixed on the screen throughout her enthusiastic discourse. Grace clicked on through the pictures.

"The garden looked beautiful, all lit up, and the food was amazing. Free drinks all night. God only knows what it cost them." Hettie tried to lead the subject away from her and Alexander, but Grace clicked on a picture of the dance floor.

"Is that you? Dancing with Al? It is! And look at his face! Hettie! What aren't you telling me?" Grace turned round with a frown.

"OK, we flirted." Hettie blushed. "But don't get carried away with your plans, Grace. Like you said, he'd make a pass at anyone. But he does scrub up pretty well." She grinned determinedly.

"Oh, please, please marry him!" Grace cried. "I can't bear the thought of ending up with Fiona bloody Harding or one of her ilk as a sister-in-law."

"But you'd wish him on me?" Hettie asked, mock offended. "Your philandering brother-in-law who is, to quote you, 'a bit of a handful'?"

"No, probably not," Grace admitted glumly.

"Anyway." Hettie clicked the web page off before Grace could read anymore into the photographs. "Let's hear your gossip."

"Oh, yes!" Grace exclaimed quietly. "I was riding out with Siobhan—she's not so bad, actually, if you don't mind waiting half an hour for her to finish a sentence. Anyway, her old boss, Julian Greaves, you must know him. Hardacre Farm, you know, the dealer who was flogging his horses off cheap when you gave Rose to Jodie. Not a nice man, from what I hear. Well, he's been arrested! For messing with a fifteen-year-old girl! Her father beat him up, and the police got involved. And then they arrested him! Isn't that awful? It's the talk of the village, of course!"

Hettie felt sick. This was exactly why she'd left in the first place—so she didn't have to hear his name, or anything about him. Or any village gossip at all, come to that. She concentrated on keeping her breathing even. "Yes, that is awful," she said flatly. "I used to know him, years ago. Rode some of his horses. Rose came from him, actually." If he was back in the news, she thought miserably, and Siobhan was spreading gossip, it was only a matter of time before Grace heard about Hettie.

"Oh, Hettie, what a terrible thought! I've never met him, but James knows him, I think. He's even older than James! And the girl is only fifteen!"

They were distracted by James arriving home with Artie and Fred. *Saved by the boys,* Hettie thought as they burst loudly into the kitchen.

"Hettie, I'm off the lead rein!" Fred shouted excitedly.

"Hello, Hettie," Artie said shyly. He stood behind Grace's chair and tickled Sophie's cheek.

"Another cup?" Grace asked Hettie, standing up.

"No, I'll leave you to it. Mum's expecting me back for dinner." She stood up herself, hugging Grace and Fred and shaking Artie's hand. "Lovely to see you boys looking so grown-up." She smiled at them fondly.

"Come back tomorrow, Hettie, if you get a chance," Grace called over her shoulder as she passed Sophie to Artie.

Hettie was cross and fed up by the time she got back to her mum's. And she'd gone right off the idea of spending an evening in the Fox, where the gossip would be at frenzy levels. Or in the company of Alexander, who "wasn't backward in being forward." Not that she hadn't already known that, but it still hurt to hear it. She sent a text to tell him that she couldn't join them after all. Bert called round, and she spent a pleasant hour chatting to him, and then he stayed on for dinner with them. It was delicious as usual, but Hettie couldn't enjoy it because she was still feeling sick about Grace's gossip.

Alexander called at the hall to pick Ted and Anju up. He wasn't in the best of moods himself; Hettie had cancelled on him, and he'd had to clear two puppy piddles and a poop off the sitting room rug before he could get out the door.

"Hettie showed me the photos of the wedding!" Grace cried when he came in. "Didn't you both look gorgeous!"

"I haven't seen them," Alexander said abruptly.

"Oh, I want to see!" Anju said. "Will she bring them tonight?"

"Is she going with you tonight?" Grace asked, surprised and very intrigued by this interesting new fact.

"She was, but she's cancelled," Al said as casually as he could manage.

"The pictures were on the computer," Grace told Anju. "My laptop is on the table, but I think Hettie shut the page down."

"Can I look?" Anju asked Alexander.

"Yes, if you really want to," he replied dismissively. So they went to the kitchen, and Anju found the page on Grace's history and brought the pictures up.

"Who is this Jennifer, anyway?" Anju asked as they flicked through the pictures.

"A mate from uni," Al muttered. Ted flashed him a grin, which he chose to ignore.

"Bloody hell, look at the two of you." Ted laughed when the picture of Alexander and Hettie appeared.

"What a gorgeous dress," Anju enthused. "Did she say where she got it from, Grace?"

"A vintage boutique. Cynthia's mother found it for her. Doesn't she look gorgeous?"

"Bloody gorgeous," Anju agreed, "and you don't look too bad yourself, Al."

Al didn't answer. He found himself mesmerised by the picture of the two of them together.

"Do you or James want to come out with us?" Alexander asked, pulling himself out of his trance. He didn't want to go by himself and play gooseberry to Ted and Anju.

"God, no!" Grace laughed. "That place will be a hotbed of gossip about Greaves, and I won't be able to resist joining in."

"What about Greaves?" Al asked sharply.

"Oh, yes, I was telling Hettie. He's been *arrested,*" she whispered. "Some story about him messing with a fifteen-year-old girl and her father beating him up."

Alexander gritted his teeth. "You two go on," he said, looking at Ted. "I'll follow you later. I'll borrow James's Landy. There's something I've remembered I need to do."

"Hello, Mrs. Redfern." Alexander smiled politely when Anna answered his knock on the door. "I wonder, is Hettie in?"

"Oh, yes, of course, Alexander, come in," Anna answered. "Hettie, visitor for you!" she called over her shoulder. "Come on in. We're in the living room. Bert's here too."

Hettie shot upright in her chair when Al walked in. "What are you doing here?" she asked. "I told you I couldn't come."

"I thought I would call by and see you instead," Alexander replied smoothly. "Evening, Bert. Mrs. Redfern, is this one of your pictures?" He nodded at a picture of Hettie and Natalie as children hanging over the fireplace.

"Anna, please," Anna answered. "Yes, that one is. Years old now, as you can probably tell!" Hettie was a chubby toddler in the drawing, with a mass of unruly curls around her head and a mischievous look on her face.

"Her smile hasn't changed." Al grinned. "And the drawing is wonderful. My mother draws too."

Hettie and Bert were struck speechless by this strange turn of events.

"I know. We used to bump in to each other when you children were little. She always had a sketch pad with her—very talented lady."

"As are you," Alexander cut in smoothly.

"Can I get you a cup of tea, Alexander, or a glass of wine?" Anna beamed at him.

"Tea would be lovely, thank you very much, Anna." He sat down on the chair next to Hettie's.

"I'll come an' carry cups." Bert struggled up out of his chair.

"I am trying to get him to have that hip replaced." Anna nodded at Bert as he finally managed to get up.

"I can't be doing with hospitals," Bert muttered as he hobbled across the room.

"Anna is right." Alexander sided with her. "You've got years in front of you yet, Bert. Get that hip replaced, and you might even get back on a horse. They do an incredible job these days, I hear."

Anna smiled at him, delighted, and Bert muttered something unintelligible.

"Wow," Hettie said dryly when they had left the room. "To what do we owe the honour of the full Melton charm offensive?"

"Grace told me about Greaves. I've come to see how you are."

"Why should I be bothered?" Hettie glared angrily at him.

"It's no good giving me your Doris look. It's why you're not coming out tonight, so you must be bothered." He smiled as he spoke. Hettie glared at him again.

"I'm sick of bloody gossip," she hissed. "No doubt my name will come up. It always bloody does. That's half the reason I left this sodding village in the first place."

"Come back to mine, after we've drunk our tea," Alexander said quickly as the sound of the kettle boiling reached them from the kitchen.

"Why?" Hettie asked suspiciously.

"Because I want you to. Because I want to spend the evening with you."

"Do you promise not to bring up this gossip again?"

"No, I don't," Alexander answered shortly. "But if you don't come with me, I'm staying here, and I'm bringing it up wherever we are."

Hettie glared at him again as her mum and Bert returned.

"Hettie tells me you've done a picture of Doris." Alexander turned his charm back on as he accepted his mug of tea. "I would love to see it, if you've got it to hand."

Hettie glowered into her tea.

"Ted and Anju are having a drink at the Fox, if you wanted to join them, Hettie," Al said loudly as he put down his empty mug. "Catch up on the gossip? Or we can stay here if you prefer?"

Bert gave him an odd look, but Anna smiled. "That's a good idea, Hettie. Why don't you two go out?"

Hettie got up. "OK," she said, trying to keep her voice neutral, although she was livid at being manipulated like this. She thought about feigning a sudden illness but wasn't convinced that he would let her get away with it. Things might get embarrassing. And her mum would get upset if he mentioned *that* name.

Hettie slammed the door of James's Land Rover so hard that it rattled ominously. Alexander grinned. "Tantrum, Hettie?"

She shot him a hard look. "I don't appreciate being manipulated like this," she hissed.

"No, I don't suppose you do." He sighed. "But you cancelled on me, and you shut up like a clam when something is up. You didn't leave me much choice."

"What about the choice to mind your own bloody business?" Hettie shot back.

"I think I would like you to be my business," Al said softly.

That stumped Hettie. She liked the sound of those words, but she wasn't ready to stop being angry yet.

"I saw the wedding pictures." Al carried on talking. "Grace showed us on the computer. I didn't know there were any."

"Jennifer sent a link in her thank-you e-mails. You must have got one," Hettie muttered.

"Oh, I don't check my e-mails very often." Alexander laughed.

"I thought I'd shut the website down on Grace's computer. She was reading far too much into the pictures of us together."

"We went back to the hotel and shagged four times, Hettie. How the hell can she read more into it than that?" He was laughing even more now.

"She wants to marry us off." Hettie enjoyed her chance to shut him up. "So you don't end up with Fiona bloody Harding. I think those were her words."

"Bloody Grace." Al swore, and he did stop laughing.

"Bit different, then, when it's your business we're discussing?" Hettie said smartly.

Alexander didn't answer. They pulled up at the gatehouse, and he sent a text to Ted.

Sorry mate been sidetracked

Not going to make it tonight

"Wine, coffee, tea?" he asked. Hettie deliberated: A glass of wine would go down well right now, but she needed her wits about her with him tonight. Was there any chance they were going to end up in bed? She doubted it somehow, not with the way this evening was turning out.

"Coffee," she said, making a fuss of Digger and Dora, then following Al to tell him there was a puddle on the floor.

"I'll be glad when this blasted rain stops." He swore, grabbing a cloth and some kitchen towels from beside the sink. Hettie took them off him and left him to make the coffee while she cleaned up.

He set the coffees down and turned the expensive-looking music system on before taking her hand.

"Right, you," he said, sitting on the sofa and pulling her down beside him.

"Is this a well-rehearsed seduction routine?" Hettie asked archly as he put his arm around her. She had to admit, it felt lovely to be curled up close to him.

"No," Alexander said seriously. "I have never seduced anyone in this house."

Hettie relaxed against him, and Digger jumped up to join them. They both laughed at Dora's frantic scrabbles to follow on her stubby little legs, until Al took pity and picked her up.

"You'll have a puddle on the sofa next," Hettie told him.

"Oh, well," he said carelessly, pressing a kiss against the side of her head. Hettie felt the familiar stir of desire and became tense again.

"So, as I see it," Al stated flatly. "This bloke, *he who can't be named*, was seeing you when he was my age, and you were…how old? And he was married, and it all came out. And then all sorts of shit and vicious gossip started flying about and has been ever since. And you've still got a major problem with that, and with him, as he recently attacked you. A problem that was big enough to make you leave Draymere. But you won't talk about it, and you wouldn't go to the police."

"I can't do this, Al," Hettie said stiffly. "You're asking me to talk about things I don't even discuss with Nat, or my mum, come to that."

"And you don't think people should know the truth about him?" Alexander said stubbornly.

"I think people should learn to mind their own bloody business," Hettie said heatedly again.

"Are you including me in people?" Al asked.

"No, I'm not." Hettie sighed. "I'd like to be your business; I'd like that a lot. And I can understand how you think this might have something to do with, you know, the other weekend—"

"Did it?" he interrupted.

Hettie was really uncomfortable now. She carried on without answering his question. "But this is too personal, just, too *much.* I can't tell you anymore than you already know, and you summed it up pretty well yourself."

"OK," Al said, resigned. "I'll tell you something about myself, then, something that *I* have never told anyone else. I didn't talk to my mother for fifteen years." Hettie gasped and sat up, but he pulled her back down against his side and carried on. "She left us, fifteen years ago. I thought for another man, but turns out it was more complicated than that. We've only recently reconciled. I spoke to her this summer. I hurt her a lot by refusing to talk to her. I couldn't forgive her. I'm not proud of that, or how I've allowed it to shape the way I think about people sometimes."

Hettie picked up his hand from her shoulder and pressed it against her mouth. "I can't imagine life without a mum," she said sadly.

"Well, you managed without a father," Al said bluntly, trying to shake off the shame he felt at talking about how he had behaved.

"That was different," Hettie said, kneeling up and kissing his lips softly. "I never knew him, never even met him. And Mum did just fine on her own. We never felt like we were missing out on anything."

Al put his hands around her ribs and kissed her back, enjoying the taste of coffee on her mouth. Their connection was instant, and the heat of the kiss grew quickly.

"I'm trying to let you know that I understand," Alexander told her. "And you don't have to talk to me. But holding things inside, bottling them up, well, it's not always the best idea."

"I do know that," Hettie mumbled. "But I'm not ready yet. It's taken me a long time to bury it; it's how I coped. I'm scared to take the lid off that, if I'm honest."

"Shall we christen my new bed?" Al asked, hugging her to him. "No shagging," he whispered. "Not until we've got condoms. I don't want you taking those after pills again, but I'm sure we can think of plenty of other things to do." He grinned sexily and kissed her again.

Hettie, melting with lust and set free by his words, grinned back and grabbed his hand. Picking Dora up with her other hand, she pushed her gently outside. And then they ran, laughing like teenagers, up the stairs.

CHAPTER TWENTY-FOUR

At Flintend there was tense excitement in the lead-up to Cynthia's biggest competition of her career. She had qualified her top horse, Brigadier, for a four-star event, and they were all nervous with anticipation.

Hettie had been in high spirits ever since she got back from Draymere. Her weekend had turned out rather well. She smiled secretly to herself, blushing at some of the memories. And she was talking to Alexander every day again. If she hadn't called him by ten in the evening, he invariably called her to find out why not. It had finally stopped raining, and he told her work on the barns was moving ahead at speed. Alexander was riding exercise again as well. Holly was off work with a broken bone in her foot, having been trodden on by Jack. And Grace was still feeding and fully occupied with Sophie.

"Don't fall for any of the grooms," Hettie said, half in jest.

"Siobhan's not my type." Alexander laughed. "And Bev would eat me alive. Have you seen her poor husband?"

Hettie laughed too, but worried after the call that he hadn't dismissed Jodie. She wasn't used to being jealous, and she wasn't enjoying it much. Grace's words had made her think about the number of other women in Alexander's life, and she couldn't shake the niggling worries about what he was doing when she was miles away. Even more confusingly, she wasn't sure if she had a right to worry about what he was up to or not. They were obviously more than friends now, but whether that made them a couple or not, she didn't know.

Natalie called when the gossip about Julian Greaves found its way to her ears. She told Hettie that she should go to the police to back the girl's story up, to prove that Julian had been at it for years. They had a biting argument. Hettie hung up, then felt guilty and called her back. It wasn't as if she hadn't thought about it; it was proving impossible not to. She kept looking at Harriet and thinking uncomfortably that the girl had only been a little older than her. Harriet was so young and naïve. But Hettie had let too much time go by to start making accusations now. So, swept up in the excitement of Cynthia's competition, she managed to push it to the back of her mind. Word filtered through to her from Grace that the charges had been dropped: against Julian and against the girl's father who had been arrested for assault. Julian had taken off somewhere, but nobody knew where.

Celia visited Draymere again, and for the first time, all three of her sons welcomed her at the hall. She stayed for a week, and Alexander joined them for dinner every day. He showed his mother the gatehouse, and during discussion about the restorations, Grace asked Celia if she would be offended if they did some redecorating at the hall.

"Mon dieu, non! Change it all!" Celia cried passionately. "All of this is Grandmother Melton's work. William was keen to keep with tradition when we lived here."

There was an edgy silence. It was unusual for Celia to mention their father's name.

"Wonderful," Grace cut in brightly. "I will talk to Imogen before she gets taken over completely by the London set and becomes too expensive for us!"

Ted introduced Anju, and Celia, who got on with everyone, was immediately enchanted. They spent a long evening perusing Celia's drawings, and Alexander picked half a dozen to frame and hang in his house.

"Is this Barry?" James asked, showing his mother a drawing of a Labrador.

"No, it is not," Celia answered in her lilting French accent. "He was not one of ours; he came from the village, but I cannot remember his name. A lady I used to meet walking. Anna, she was called. He belonged to her daughter, I believe."

"Hettie?" Alexander blurted in surprise.

"Goodness, is that Dog?" Grace asked. "Well, I never. What a small world it is."

"Anna was an artist too," Celia continued. "We used to talk for ages."

"If that is Dog," Alexander muttered self-consciously, "I know Hettie would very much like to have it."

"Take it, take it!" Celia cried, adding the picture to his pile. "There is no point in art if it can't be shared."

"Hettie worked for us on the yard," Grace explained. "In fact, Dog is buried at Draymere, up by Corner Wood."

"The pretty girl I met when I came last year! Of course she was Anna's daughter; I can see the likeness now! And she told me her mother was an artist. I cannot believe the penny did not drop. If Anna still lives in the village, you know, I might call on her. It would be nice to reminisce," Celia mused.

On the Sunday of Celia's departure for Oxfordshire and Ted and Anju's return to London, the family gathered again for dinner. Celia sat at the table with Sophie in her arms. The usually placid baby had become fractious with teething and refused to be put down. Artie, Fred, and Georgia were seated around her, and Celia kept them entertained with her undivided attention.

"I don't want Mamie to go," Fred said.

"Neither do I!" Grace agreed fervently. "But poor Mamie needs a rest from us all, I would think."

"Do you need a rest, Mamie?" Fred asked her seriously.

"No, I certainly do not!" Celia exclaimed. "You beautiful children make me feel twenty years younger. I cannot get enough of you." She beamed at them all and tickled Georgia's tummy with her free hand.

"You should move nearer; you should move back," Alexander said abruptly, staring doggedly at his plate.

"Yes, you should," James agreed.

"Ah, I am not sure I should do that quite yet," Celia responded quietly, laying her hand over Alexander's on the table when she noticed his fist clenching around his fork. "Cette discussion n'est pas à l'avant des enfants," she whispered.

"What did you say?" Fred asked loudly.

"Something about not in front of the children," Artie told him matter-of-factly. Celia laughed delightedly.

The three brothers and Grace had deliberated at length over whether to tell Celia about their father's will. Alexander had been adamant that it would only cause more hurt. James and Grace were inclined to agree. Ted argued that keeping secrets hadn't served any of them well, but he found himself in the minority and eventually backed down.

Alexander called Hettie as he walked back to the gatehouse after seeing Celia off. He was feeling out of sorts and frustrated that Hettie wasn't nearer. These bloody telephone calls weren't enough. His mood wasn't improved when he heard what sounded like a party going on in the background when Hettie answered his call.

"Where are you?" he barked.

"In the pub!" Hettie shouted back. "Hang on. I'll go outside."

Alexander waited moodily as he listened to Hettie leaving the pub and lighting a cigarette.

"Right, that's better. I can hear you now," she said brightly.

"Are you pissed?" Alexander asked, cursing himself for the sullen tone of his voice.

"No, why?" Hettie responded defensively.

"You sound pissed, and you're smoking. You smoke when you're pissed." *And you flirt outrageously too*, he almost added.

"I've had two glasses of wine!" Hettie told him archly. "Did you call to have a go at me, or was there something else?"

"I'm missing you," Alexander managed to mumble petulantly.

Hettie grinned from the bench outside the pub, and a tingling thrill went through her. "I'm missing you too, Alexander Melton," she said back.

"It doesn't sound like it. Sounds like you're having a party." He was slightly less moody now.

"Sunday lunch at the pub, that's all. The girls are in London with Pieter. Cynthia wanted to take everyone out before next weekend's competition. A thank you in advance to all the people she's called on to help with the animals while we're away."

"Who's everyone?" She had told him about Cynthia's crowd and that they all seemed to have paired up with each other at one time or another.

"Alexander Melton, are you jealous?" Hettie teased with delight. At least she wasn't the only one suffering moments of insecurity.

"No. Yes. Should I be?" he asked reluctantly.

"No, you should not." Hettie laughed. "You have spoiled me for anyone else."

Alexander grinned.

Hettie wanted to ask if the same applied to him, but she couldn't make herself say the words out loud. "I wish you were here," she said instead, and she really, really meant it.

"When will we see you again?" Alexander asked. The question was meant to be flippant, but his voice came out oddly gruff.

"I've got a week off coming up," Hettie told him excitedly. "Not for another fortnight, and I haven't made any plans, but I'll definitely be home for some of it."

"Let's go away." Alexander surprised himself with the suggestion. The words were out before he even processed them.

"Together?" Hettie checked.

"No, separately, of course," he growled sarcastically, uncomfortable with the thought that she was about to turn him down.

"Oh, my God, I would love that! Where would we go?" Hettie's legs felt weak with excitement at the idea.

"Somewhere with a big bed." Alexander grinned, feeling happier than he had since she had left the previous weekend. "Text me with dates, and I'll sort something out."

"I wish you were here even more now," Hettie moaned weakly.

"You'll have to be patient, Hettie Redfern." Alexander chuckled down the phone.

Alexander told her about his mother's visit and the picture that might be of Dog, but he didn't mention his mother's reluctance to move back to Draymere. Hettie told him about their plans for the upcoming trip to Lincolnshire and that they would be staying with the sister of Jonathan Finchley, who was one of Cynthia's crowd. She didn't mention that Jonathan was the most persistent in his efforts to get off with her.

"I might try and get there for cross-country day," Alexander said. "If I can get away."

♦♦♦

Juliette Finchley-Brown and her family welcomed them warmly when they arrived on the Thursday before the event. They lived in a large, sprawling house, created by the conversion of interlinking barns, and had more houseguests arriving on Friday to watch the event. Pieter and the girls were coming on Friday too, meeting them at the venue ahead of Cynthia's dressage test. Hettie was in her element. The Finchley-Browns had land and horses and picturesque bridle paths for Hettie to explore when she took Brigadier for a gentle hack after his long journey. When Brig had been settled, she went with Cynthia to walk the cross-country course, and listened in awe as Cynthia discussed each tricky-looking fence with the other competitors. Riders Hettie was used to reading about in *Horse and Hound* came over and chatted to Cynthia. Hettie was starstruck. Back at the Finchley-Browns', she checked on Brigadier and led him out of his stable for a walk and a nibble of grass. Alexander called while she was standing in the field with Brig munching contentedly at the end of the rope. He told her he was hoping to come up on Friday night if he could find somewhere to stay, although with Burghley on, he wasn't having much luck. Hettie relayed this information to Cynthia, and Cynthia asked Juliette if she could squeeze another body in.

"Yes, of course, if you don't mind sharing," Juliette told Hettie, who blushed and said that was very kind of her.

"About bloody time!" Cynthia remarked with a wink. "But don't let him wear you out. I need your full attention!"

Cynthia was uncharacteristically tense. Competing didn't usually unsettle her, but Burghley was a big deal.

"I promise you will have my undivided support and attention," Hettie reassured her. "The next three days are all about you and Brigadier."

"Nice," Alexander said appreciatively when she told him they would be sharing. Hettie, aroused by his single word, wondered if this was such a good idea after all.

"Don't forget I'm working." She laughed. "And I have promised Cynthia my undivided attention."

"As long as you promise me your undivided attention when we go away together, I think I can live with that," Alexander suggested.

"I promise." Hettie laughed breathlessly.

They came off the phone frustrated. Alexander wondered fleetingly if he could call on anyone else, but no one other than Hettie seemed appealing.

Cynthia's dressage test was without fault. She left the arena grinning from ear to ear and slapping Brigadier's neck. "Team Cynthia" cheered loudly from their viewing point, and when Hettie retrieved Brigadier to take him back to the Finchley-Browns, there were delighted hugs all round.

"That's the best you've ever ridden it, Mum!" Harriet praised. She had been watching her mum practice the test repeatedly for weeks, so she knew better than any of them.

Cynthia stayed at Burghley with her family for lunch and to walk the course again while Hettie took Brigadier back to the Finchley-Browns. She fussed over the horse, telling him repeatedly what a star he was. She checked and double-checked that everything was in place for the next day and, having helped herself to lunch as instructed by Juliette, took her sandwich back out to the stable to sit with Brig while he munched his hay net. She was stranded now, with nothing more to do and no transport to get back to the event. So she led Brig out for more grass, tidied Juliette's kitchen, and stacked the dishwasher for something to do. She called Alexander, but he didn't pick up. She sent him a text with Cynthia's scores and added, "can't wait to see you," with a kiss at the end.

Pieter arrived back on his own. "They are walking the course again. I'm dropping off bags and going back to pick them up. Cynthia was concerned that we had abandoned you. We saw Juliette shopping at the trade stands."

"Not at all!" Hettie protested. "I've been quite happy here with Brig." She made Pieter a cup of tea and showed him where

Cynthia's room and the bathroom were. "I don't know where Juliette has put the girls, er, or anyone else," she told him awkwardly, not exactly sure what the situation with Pieter and Cynthia was. They told everyone they were separated but acted much like a married couple, as far as she could see.

Alexander pulled up outside as they were coming back downstairs. Hettie recognised the engine noise of the Aston, and her stomach did a somersault as she ran to open the door and hugged him hello. She would have kissed him too if Pieter hadn't been there. Alexander returned her hug, but his smile was reserved. "Just the two of you here?" he asked as he watched Pieter descend the last few stairs.

"Yes, Cynthia's still there. Did you get my text? Didn't they do brilliantly? Come in, I'll show you round. Do you want coffee or tea or anything?"

"Coffee would be good," Alexander answered coolly. "And yes, they did, a very good score."

"Isn't she amazing?" Pieter joined in happily, shaking Alexander's hand. Al wondered darkly who exactly he was talking about. Maybe he had underestimated Pieter. Was the quiet charm a ruse? He tried to shake his dark musings as Hettie made the coffee.

"Do you want another?" she asked Pieter.

"No, I must get back before I'm missed." He smiled at them both. "I'm under strict instructions to keep charge of the girls."

Alexander scowled at his coffee.

"You know, my company has asked me to go back to South Africa," Pieter said softly as he picked up his car keys. "I haven't mentioned it to Cynthia yet. I was waiting until after Burghley. I simply can't imagine moving that far away from them all," he finished sadly.

"Oh my God!" Hettie cried. "You can't do that! The girls would be devastated, and so would Cynthia!"

"Surely you can't leave the girls?" Alexander barked, knocked out of his sulk by this news.

"I may not have any choice, if I want to keep my job and if we all want to continue to live the life we have become accustomed to." He gave a sad, heavy sigh. "I should not have troubled you with it. I am sorry. But I find myself in something of a dilemma. I will speak to Cynthia, of course. Next week, when all of the excitement has died down. Please don't mention this to anyone before then."

When Pieter had gone, Hettie grinned and sat on Alexander's lap. Now she did kiss him enthusiastically. Alexander's shoulders relaxed at the desire the kiss conveyed, and he kissed her back with equal fervor. She chuckled against his mouth when they eventually paused.

"Come and see Brigadier the Burghley horse." She grinned. "Before we get embarrassingly interrupted by the Finchley-Browns." Alexander stood up, despite the fact that at that particular moment he wouldn't have given a flying fuck who interrupted them. He slapped her backside lightly with frustration as they walked outside. Hettie grinned at him wickedly over her shoulder.

"I know," she said. "This could turn out to be a frustrating weekend."

"No *could* about it," Al muttered. "But I'll keep reminding myself that I'm getting a whole week of you to myself soon."

"The whole week?" Hettie squeaked. "Where are we going?"

"I haven't decided yet. Does it matter?" Alexander drawled, pulling her into his arms again outside Brigadier's stable.

"No, it doesn't matter at all," Hettie told him breathlessly, standing on tiptoes to kiss him. "A whole week? Can we do that?"

"You texted me the dates for a week. I thought that was what you wanted." Alexander pulled back to look at her questioningly.

"The dates for the week I'm off, yes. I didn't mean we had to go for the whole week. How would that work?"

"What do you mean, how would that work?" Alexander was impatient now. "Are you saying you can't spare a week? And what were you and Pieter doing when I turned up?" He ran his hand proprietarily across her ribs and cupped her breast and whispered this last comment against her cheek.

Hettie pushed him away. "What do you mean, what were we doing? What do you think we were doing?"

"Nothing," Alexander mumbled, running his hand across his face. "I didn't mean anything. I take the question back."

Hettie gave him a hard look. "I'm going to let you take it back," she said, opening Brigadier's door and walking into his stable to untie his hay net. "Because I'm working, and now is not the time. But as we've only been together twenty minutes and we're close to having a fight, I'll ask you again: How would a week work?" Her shoulders were tight, and she bustled around Brig with more energy than was actually required.

Alexander sighed. "I'll be better when I can keep an eye on you." He gave an apologetic half smile to indicate that it was a joke. Hettie glared at him again.

"And what about Grace? And James and my mum?" Hettie carried on as she filled Brig's water buckets. "What are we meant to tell them, I mean, if we are both away for a week at the same time? Are we going to pretend we're not together?"

Alexander's head shot up. "Why the fuck would we do that?" he barked.

"I don't know." Hettie put the bucket down and shrugged weakly, not meeting his eyes. "I mean people will talk. They'll make assumptions that we're together." She forced herself to look at him.

"And why the hell would we care it they did?" Alexander was genuinely confused by this turn in the conversation. "If you don't want to spend a week with me, Hettie, for fuck's sake, just say so."

"No, I do," Hettie started, but at that point they were interrupted by Cynthia and the girls coming to see Brigadier.

"Alexander, good to see you!" Cynthia boomed. "I hope you're not distracting my groom! You are a very distracting man, you know!" She grinned and kissed his cheek. "I have already told her no shag marathons tonight. I need her on form tomorrow. Wasn't this boy a star? That's the hard bit done; tomorrow I can just hang on and kick!" She winked at Alexander. Hettie blushed, Alexander laughed, and Harriet went the colour of the red brick barn wall.

More guests arrived through the evening, including Jonathan, who eagerly attached himself to Hettie's side, despite her attempts to brush him off.

"This is the woman I'm going to marry, sis," he announced loudly to Juliette, "as soon as she works out that she wants me."

Hettie tried to laugh but caught Alexander's glare from the corner of her eye, and then she was annoyed that she was worrying about that when she should be enjoying the atmosphere and the endless horse talk. Juliette had cooked a huge beef stew and a cauldron of rice. Everyone was helping themselves and finding places to perch. Cynthia was revelling in the limelight of being the star attraction. Pieter, sitting with Alexander, beamed at her happily every time she looked his way. Alexander avoided looking at Hettie, who was circulating frantically and trying to avoid being left with Jonathan. She turned down all offers of alcohol, slipped out twice to check on Brigadier, and tried repeatedly to smile at Alexander. But he was deep in conversation with Pieter every time she looked. Harriet and Jessica had joined the other young people eating in the snug, and judging by the number of times Harriet had blushed, Juliette's son, Adam, was making quite an impression.

Unlike Cynthia and Hettie, Pieter and Alexander had gratefully helped themselves to the generous amounts of alcohol on offer. Their conversation had become increasingly deep and meaningful.

"But I still love her, you see," Pieter said plaintively.

"Have you told her that?" Alexander demanded. "Good God, man, if you want her back, tell her!"

"Ah, but I thought I could live with the affairs, you see. That it was a price worth paying to call Cynthia my wife, but I couldn't in the end."

"Tell her that as well," Al said obstinately. "Although from what she's told me, you were both as bad as each other."

Pieter laughed sadly. "I let her think that. I thought if we had an open relationship, she would feel free to tell me when she had played away, and she would always come back. In practice it made it so much harder to bear, knowing the details. I invented a few to keep up with her. How pathetic is that? I didn't want to clip her wings, you see. Harriet, well, she wasn't planned. I promised Cynthia that life wouldn't change, that we could marry to give the baby a stable life and carry on with our lives. I forgot to factor in that I was actually head over heels in love with her."

"Good Lord." Alexander was stunned. "So you didn't actually have an affair?"

"Oh, the last one was real enough," Pieter confessed. "But I suspect I only did it to get a reaction out of Cynthia. My heart wasn't in it, and I got more of a reaction than I had bargained on." He looked thoroughly glum.

"You really need to speak to her," Alexander told him, "before you make any decisions about your future." He added decisively, "My mother moved away when I was not much older than Harriet. Very different circumstances, but I struggled to come to terms with it."

Pieter looked morose.

Hettie came back from her final visit to Brig. "He's fine," she told Cynthia. "Slightly befuddled about why I keep popping up! How are you feeling? Have we done everything we need to do tonight? If there's nothing else, I'm going to turn in, get an early start in the morning."

"I'll bet you are." Cynthia laughed, nodding toward Alexander.

"No chance of that," Hettie said firmly. "I think Al and Pieter are going to talk the dawn in."

Cynthia laughed again. "Isn't it nice that they get on so well? Yes, you go up. I won't be far behind. One small whiskey, I think, to get me off to sleep."

Hettie steeled herself to interrupt Alexander and Pieter; this was feeling rather awkward now.

"Er, Al, I'm going up." She touched his shoulder. "Early start in the morning. I wanted to check you know where you're going?"

"In with you, aren't I?" he asked bluntly.

Hettie blushed. "Yes, but do you know which room that is? Third door on the right as you go up the stairs."

"Next to Cynthia. I can show him," Pieter said.

"Thanks." Hettie smiled. She thought about kissing Al's cheek but decided that might look wifely and presumptuous. "Night, then," she said brightly.

"You're not going to bed, Hettie?" Jonathan shouted from across the room. "I haven't even had a snog!"

Hettie blushed and shook her head as she walked out of the room.

"What room have you put her in, sis?" Jonathan shouted at Juliette.

"In the blue room, with Alexander," Juliette drawled, nodding toward the table where Alexander was sitting and smirking meaningfully at her brother.

"Thank God for that!" Jonathan barked, grinning and nodding at Alexander. "I was beginning to think I'd lost my touch! You didn't tell me she was taken, Cynthia."

"I didn't want to spoil your fun," Cynthia shot back, winking at Alexander across the room.

"I am so glad you two have got it together," Pieter told him drunkenly. "It was obvious you were besotted with each other, but it took you long enough."

"It's not quite as simple as that." Alexander sighed.

"Ah, love never is." Pieter laughed.

"I'm not very tolerant. I'm not a nice bloke like you. In fact, I'm not tolerant at all. I think I do want to clip her wings." Alexander sighed heavily.

"No, you don't." Pieter smiled, laying his hand on Alexander's arm. "You want to believe she loves you as much as you love her."

Alexander cleared his throat, embarrassed by Pieter's use of the L word, and was almost relieved by Jonathan's arrival beside him.

"Jonathan Finchley." He grinned, holding out his hand. "My apologies for trying to pull your missus."

"Alexander Melton. No apology needed," Alexander said smoothly, shaking his hand. "Not unless, of course, you succeeded."

"Far from it!" Jonathan laughed. "Not even close. Melton, you say? Any relation to Ted?"

Hours later Alexander finally made it to the bedroom. He smiled at the sight of Hettie spreadeagled across both sides of the bed, with her faded pyjama bottoms and T-shirt on. He quietly undressed and tried to edge her gently over as he climbed in. She stirred slightly and cuddled up to him without waking up. It took him a long time to fall asleep, with Hettie's warm body curled against his front, the edge of the bed millimeters from his back, and his head full of thoughts, only some of them blue, but all of them about her.

Hettie woke up twenty minutes before her alarm. It was still dark outside, and it took her a moment to remember where she was. Alexander was sleeping beside her, right on the edge of the bed. She smiled and allowed herself a moment to study his shadowy profile. He looked bloody gorgeous asleep, without the too-familiar frown in place. His smile was worth waiting for, though, and she loved it when he laughed. She resisted the urge to wriggle against him; it wouldn't be fair when she had to get up and go out. And she could guarantee she would freeze again if a quickie was on the cards. She sighed at that thought. Alexander moved in his sleep. The urge to kiss him awake was almost irresistible, but she made herself climb carefully out of the bed and fumbled in the dark for her clothes.

"I'm awake," Alexander mumbled. "Turn the light on if you like."

"I didn't mean to disturb you," Hettie whispered, moving round to his side of the bed.

"You always disturb me." He grinned, taking her hand and pressing it against his lips. "But I like waking up with you, I think."

Hettie grinned back and kissed his forehead, running a hand through his hair.

"Is that all I'm getting?" he whispered as she stood back up.

"Morning breath," she said apologetically.

"Sorry," Alexander mumbled sleepily.

"I meant me, not you!" Hettie laughed. "I'm sure you taste delicious."

Alexander grinned and pulled her down beside him. "You need to get to work," he said before he rolled her onto her back and kissed her.

"I do." Hettie moaned when he stopped.

"You taste beautiful in the morning, by the way," he told her, running his hand over her stomach to her waist as he kissed her neck. "Now get up. It's Burghley cross-country day, and I need more space in this bed."

Hettie leaned up on her arms. "I can't wait to get you for a whole week," she said crossly.

"I know how to get my own way now." Alexander grinned, moving to take up the whole bed. "Deprive you of sex."

Hettie slapped the duvet where she could see the shape of his leg, but she grinned too. Her alarm went off.

"Turn the light on," Alexander said, propping himself up on the pillows. "I want to watch you get dressed."

"The opposite of a strip tease, then?" Hettie joked nervously, but she turned the light on and dressed self-consciously while trying to look unbothered.

"Thank you." Alexander grinned. "But we might have to work on your embarrassment levels. You've got a gorgeous body, Hettie. I enjoy looking at it. Maybe I'll take you somewhere hot. Have you got a passport?"

"Of course I've got a passport," Hettie said, glowing pinkly. "I'm not a complete yokel."

"Come here and kiss me good-bye," Alexander ordered. "Good luck. You'll be great," he added when she had finished kissing him.

"I'm bloody nervous now," Hettie said. "And all I've got to do is watch. Come and find us when you get there."

Team Cynthia had the most nerve-racking, tense, but exhilarating day. When Cynthia and Brigadier galloped over the finish line with a clear round and only a couple of time penalties, they erupted with glee. Cynthia punched the air and grinned from ear to ear. Hettie launched herself into Alexander's arms, and he swung her around enthusiastically. Cynthia was interviewed by the BBC, with Pieter and the girls beside. Hettie led Brigadier away to sponge him down.

"You look like you enjoyed that!" the reporter said.

"Better than sex!" Cynthia cried. "Oops, sorry. I forgot I was on the TV."

CHAPTER TWENTY-FIVE

Alexander found a rustic château on the outskirts of a village in the south of France. It had a private swimming pool and a shady terrace for eating al fresco. The balcony off of the bedroom boasted a view over fields to the sea in the distance.

"Wow," Hettie said down the phone to him as she looked at the pictures on her computer.

"I think we should fly," Alexander told her, "and hire a car when we get there. I could drive, but we'll waste half the week traveling."

"Have you seen the price of this place?" Hettie squealed. "And a flight as well? Alexander, I haven't got this sort of money."

"I said I would take you away," Al said stubbornly. "I haven't asked you to pay for anything."

"I can't let you do that," Hettie told him. "I've got to contribute something."

"Oh, I'm hoping you will." He chuckled sexily.

"So you're paying for me to come and sleep with you?" Hettie bristled.

"Don't talk tripe, Hettie," Alexander told her. "I'm offering to pay, and I can afford to. I'm certainly not going to stay in some hovel to avoid wounding your pride."

"Well, I'm still paying something toward it," Hettie said. "But that house is beautiful, and if you want to throw your money around…how much are the flights?"

"Hettie, shut up," Alexander suggested.

Grace got thoroughly overexcited by the news that Hettie and Alexander were going away together.

"I knew it!" she cried, delighted. "When I saw that photo of you two! I knew there was something brewing."

"Don't raise your hopes." Hettie laughed. "I'm crap at relationships, and we probably won't even be on speaking terms by day three."

Her mum made a big fuss too when Hettie tried to drop the information casually in a telephone call.

"I'll need my passport, Mum. It's in my room. Alexander said he would come by and pick it up."

"Oh, it will be lovely to see him again. Tell him to come for dinner! I'll invite Bert too. It will give me a chance to get to know Alexander better."

Hettie sighed. Much as she loved her family and her friends, she sometimes thought it would be easier to be completely anonymous. And she had only told three people about the holiday so far. Cynthia had been easy. "You lucky girl!" she had said with a laugh and a wink. "What I wouldn't give for a week with that man." It was nice to hear Cynthia laughing again. She had been unusually quiet since coming down from her Burghley high. Hettie suspected that Pieter had mentioned South Africa to her, but she couldn't offer support, as she wasn't meant to know.

Alexander did go to dinner with Anna and Bert, despite Hettie telling him not to. She was irritated and unsettled by the thought of them eating dinner in her house without her there. It felt like an invasion of her privacy. Alexander laughed at her annoyance.

"We had a very nice evening," he said innocently. "We barely even mentioned you."

Hettie wasn't sure if that made her feel better or worse. "You remembered to pick up my passport, I hope," she said crossly.

They planned to meet at Stansted Airport, to fly budget airline to Nice. Alexander had eventually agreed to let Hettie pay for both flights, and she had managed to dissuade him from picking her up—a round journey of nearly three hundred miles—when she could easily get a train from Norwich. She was secretly flattered that he had offered, though. The Landy was off the road with a gearbox problem, which sounded worryingly expensive. She had resolved not to think about it until after her holiday.

On the evening before her departure, Pieter arrived at Flintend. As soon as he came into the kitchen, Cynthia stopped what she was doing and, glancing nervously in his direction, turned to Hettie.

"Pieter and I have got some fairly momentous news, Hettie. I'm not sure if you will think it's good news or not, but can we have a word?"

"Of course," Hettie replied warily.

"The thing is," Cynthia told her, "Pieter has been asked by his office to return to South Africa, and, after much discussion, we—the girls and I—have decided to go with him. I'm sorry to put it so bluntly," she added in response to the look of shock on Hettie's face. "But I should add that we would very much like you to come too. We'll be shipping the horses out, lock, stock, and barrel. The company said they would pay all expenses, including yours if you come. Which I very much hope you will."

"What about Granny?" Hettie asked randomly as she struggled to get her head around Cynthia's announcement.

"Granny?" Cynthia barked. "She's already told us she's coming out this winter and staying until the UK warms up, and Pieter's parents already live there, of course. What a strange thing to ask. You must have more questions than that."

"Sorry," Hettie mumbled. "It's a shock. I'm really pleased for you both. It's wonderful news, really. I couldn't be happier for you."

"Does that mean you'll come?" Cynthia asked.

"Cynthia," Pieter cut in, laying his hand over hers. "Give the poor girl a chance to collect her thoughts. We realise we've dropped a bombshell, Hettie, and whatever decision you make will have a big effect on your life. We weren't sure whether to mention it before your holiday or not. But we hoped a week away and some breathing space would give you a chance to think it over in peace. If you do decide to come, you would have your own accommodation. And a good salary—better than you're getting now. But equally, if you decide it's not for you, we would give you a redundancy payment and do everything we could to help you secure another position."

Cynthia tut-tutted with annoyance.

"This winter, you say? You'll be going that soon?" Hettie asked, still struggling to take in the full impact of what they were saying.

"As soon as we can get organised," Cynthia replied. "Before Christmas, certainly. We get a relocation team to work out all the details, and they have already found us a couple of properties, with stables and acres of land. They're amazing places, Hettie. It would be an incredible adventure."

"I've never been further than Ibiza before." Hettie laughed nervously.

"All the more reason to get out there and see the world!" Cynthia proclaimed.

"Cynthia, stop it," Pieter said, quite forcefully for him. "Hettie will need to think about this. Take the week, Hettie. Think things over. Ask us any questions you want to. Take your time. It's your decision. But do know that we would be very pleased to have you."

"Twice yearly flights back to the UK, paid for as part of the deal. Or anywhere else you want to go, of course. You might catch the travel bug once you start," Cynthia added, pulling a face at Pieter.

Hettie's head was spinning. Go to South Africa, could she do that? This year, before Christmas? The idea was thrilling, but to leave home and England? Only see her mum twice a year, be in a foreign country at Christmas, thousands of miles from everyone? And what about Alexander? *Oh, God.*

"I am going it have to think about this," Hettie said slowly. "Don't think I don't appreciate what you're offering, and what an amazing opportunity it would be. And I am really flattered that you are asking me; a lot of people would snatch your arm off for the chance. But, well, there are other things to think about. My family and…the dogs!" The thought suddenly occurred to her. "Will the dogs be coming too?"

"It is possible to take them." Cynthia was guarded. "Bringing them back to the UK isn't always so easy; there are quite a lot of hoops to jump through. But if that's a deal-breaker, I am sure we could find a way."

"Can I tell you when I get back from France?" Hettie asked. She wanted to think about this, and she needed to talk to Alexander, although she wasn't sure why. They were hardly in a long-term relationship.

"Of course you can," Pieter answered smoothly before Cynthia could launch into her hard sell again. "Tell us when you have made your mind up. Take as long as you need."

Hettie lay awake half the night with her thoughts going round in circles and woke up with questions for Cynthia and Pieter over pancake breakfast. Harriet and Jessica were on cloud nine. *Probably because they've got both their parents back,* Hettie thought, happy for them.

Pieter drove her to Norwich station. "I hope Alexander is not too cross with us." He laughed uncomfortably. "Now, Hettie, I know Cynthia is very keen for you to come, and she will keep putting the pressure on. But talk to Alexander and your mum before you make up your mind. Do what is right for you. Don't worry about us. We will be fine. And make sure you have a lovely holiday!"

"I'm so glad you and Cynthia are back together." Hettie smiled, kissing Pieter's cheek as she climbed out of the car.

Alexander was in ridiculously good humour. He hugged her tightly in greeting and was affectionate, amusing, and attentive throughout the flight. He didn't even make a fuss about the lack of legroom in their seats, telling Hettie with a grin that being short sometimes had its advantages. She decided to leave it a while before mentioning South Africa and to enjoy her holiday without thinking too much.

"Starting as you mean to go on?" Alexander grinned when Hettie ordered three mini bottles of wine from the trolley.

"Yup. I'm on holiday." She grinned back.

The little château was exquisite, French chic in style and unpretentiously furnished with rustic wood and cottons and linens in cool pale hues.

"Heaven," Hettie breathed, throwing open the balcony doors from their bedroom and letting the breeze waft through. "You have brought me to heaven."

"Can I take you to heaven again?" Alexander asked, coming up behind and wrapping his arms around her waist.

So they christened the bed before they had even unloaded their bags from the car, and spent a glorious hour making love with the breeze from the sea kissing their flesh and gently lifting the linen curtains. "We don't need one," Hettie whispered, reading his mind when he moved above her and hesitated. "I went to see the doctor, and I've gone on the pill."

"Thank you." Alexander grinned and entered her so slowly and tenderly that the pleasure brought tears to her eyes. "You are very special to me," he whispered as Hettie lost herself to sensation.

I think I'm in love, she thought.

Bags unloaded from their hire car, they dressed in cooler clothing.

"Nice." Alexander grinned as Hettie came back downstairs in her white sundress and sandals.

They ambled into the village to find the stores. Alexander confidently selected bag loads of food and wine, conversing with the shopkeepers in easy, fluent French.

"That's why you brought me to France!" Hettie laughed as they left the first shop. "You wanted to show off your bilingual skills." Alexander grinned.

They ate a late lunch of olives, French bread, and cold meats on the patio, washed down with a silky French wine, as the sun dropped lower in the sky.

"I'm going in the pool," Hettie said, standing up, "before it gets too cool. I'm going to get my bikini on."

"You don't need a bikini; we're not overlooked." Alexander stood up as well, and, reaching toward her, he pulled Hettie's sundress slowly over her head. "Beautiful," he growled appreciatively, running a finger under the lacy top of her bra, which made Hettie reach hungrily beneath his T-shirt and led them to end up making love again, on the thick Provence rug covering the sitting room floor.

They skinny-dipped at dusk, canoodled giggling in the pool, and stood together under the waterfall shower before dressing for dinner. After walking in the balmy evening to a restaurant nearby, they held hands over the candlelit table.

Hettie got the giggles. "This is stupidly romantic. I feel like I've woken up in a cheesy chick-lit novel, but I'm having a brilliant time."

"So am I." Alexander grinned, dropping his hand under the table and letting it rest at the top of her thigh.

Hettie closed her eyes and sighed. "Shall we get the bill?" she asked weakly.

Hettie couldn't remember another time when she had been as relaxed and happy as she was over the next few days. The hours passed in a haze of swimming, sightseeing, and laughter, interspersed with good food, a plentiful supply of wonderful wine, and very, very good sex. They fell asleep sated in each other's arms and woke to start over again. It came as a shock when she realised that they only had two full days left. They had learned a lot about each other, chatting easily, tongues loosened with wine, sunshine, and happiness. That magical holiday time when reality is suspended was fast coming to an end, Hettie realised with panic, and she hadn't given South Africa a second thought. Let alone come to any decision. She snuggled close to Alexander in the bed. It was early evening, but they had ended up there yet again after a late-afternoon swim.

"I've got some news," she prevaricated, "about Cynthia and Pieter. They're back together."

"Good." Alexander smiled, stroking her shoulder with his arm around her. "I take it he's not going to South Africa after all, then."

"No, he is. They both are, and the girls and all the horses." She paused. "They want me to go with them."

Hettie felt him stiffen beside her. "And are you going to?" he asked, his voice flat and devoid of emotion.

"I don't know yet; they've given me some time to think it over. It's a big decision for me."

"A big decision," Al mused. His voice had taken on a menacing tone. He took his arm away from around her and swung to sit up on the edge of the bed with his back turned. "Do let me know when you've made your mind up."

"Don't be like that, Al," Hettie said quietly, rolling onto her side and stroking his now rigid back. "I wanted to talk to you about it. I was hoping you could help me make up my mind."

Alexander stood up and rounded on her. Even in his very apparent rage, Hettie couldn't help but appreciate the magnificence of him, standing in front of her in all his naked glory.

"You wanted to talk to me?" he growled. "To help you make your mind up? And exactly how long have you been storing this little secret? You let me pay for this fucking holiday without so much as a word, and all the time you were planning to fuck off halfway around the world. Wasn't Norfolk far enough away from me?"

"Stop it, Al." Hettie shook her head. "They only told me on Friday." She pulled the sheet up to cover her nakedness and hunkered down into the pillow. Everything was spoilt now, she thought miserably.

"Don't cover yourself up," Alexander shouted, pulling the sheet away, furious with himself for the effect his anger was having on her but unable to fight the red mist. "And don't expect me to believe you hadn't made your mind up before you got on that plane." He hated the way he was behaving, was disgusted by the words coming out of his mouth and the obviousness that his fury was scaring her. But his head was thumping with the awful realisation that she was going to leave. He had opened himself up to feeling again, only to have it hurled back in his face.

"Stop shouting and talk to me," Hettie tried bravely, sitting up on the bed and hugging her legs in front of her. "You don't want me to go? I don't want to leave you either, but—"

"And there's the but," Alexander snarled. "Do what you fucking want, Hettie. I can see you have made up your mind, and whether you fuck off or stay is of no concern to me." He was pulling his clothes on as he spoke. "I'm going out," he snapped. "Alone."

"No, don't go out," Hettie said. She jumped out of the bed and positioned herself in front of the door. "Talk to me, please. Tell me what's going on in your head. We've been having such a lovely time. You don't need to do this. We can work it out." She felt shaky and nervous but determined to stand her ground. This felt like make-or-break moment, and she wasn't going down without a fight.

"Get out of my way, Hettie," Alexander said quietly, refusing to look at her. He was scared by the level of his anger, scared that if he didn't get away from that room, he would do something awful.

"I'm not moving," Hettie said with a tremor in her voice.

"Don't force me to make you," Alexander said desperately, closing his eyes.

"You won't hurt me." Hettie lifted her chin and waited for him, totally naked but no longer even aware of it.

Alexander didn't know what to do. He badly needed to clear his head of the onslaught of emotions that were hitting him. If he walked over there and tried to get past her, he didn't possess the conviction she had that he could do so in a controlled manner. He looked at her, his eyes dark with anger and something close to despair at the sight of her standing there naked—and so fucking beautiful. *She's leaving,* he reminded himself. *What the fuck does it matter what you do?* "Get back in bed, then, and let me fuck you again," he dared her.

Hettie froze. "I'm not really into angry sex," she said firmly.

"So you're moving to South Africa, and now you don't even want to fuck me," Alexander stated coldly. He moved over to her. Taking hold of her shoulders, he kissed her hard. Hettie accepted the kiss but her lack of responsiveness increased Alexander's feeling of total revulsion at the way he was behaving. He pushed her easily aside and walked out of the door.

Hettie sat on the bed and cried when he had gone. She started packing her suitcase, trying to formulate a plan about how she could get to the airport without a car or the number for a taxi, with virtually no understanding of the language. She rubbed her eyes and hunted around to see if Alexander had left his cigarettes lying about. Despite her belief that Alexander wouldn't hurt her, the fight had shaken her up more than she wanted to admit. She hadn't expected the South Africa conversation to be an easy one, but his reaction had knocked her sideways. She tried to think calmly. How would she feel if it had been him telling her he was moving to another country? Pretty devastated, but would she be angry? She thought back to what he had told her about his mother leaving. They both knew he had issues, but was there ever going to be any chance of getting around those issues if he completely lost it and walked away the moment they hit a problem? She poured herself a glass of wine and resolved not to leave before he came back. If he came back, that was.

Alexander walked fast and got as far as the village bar. He hesitated outside, but carried on walking. Beating himself up with self-hatred, he walked for nearly an hour before he had calmed down enough to turn around and head back to the château.

"I'm sorry," he said, and he looked it. He sat beside Hettie on the sofa. She was curled up with a glass of wine and one of his cigarettes and looked at him with red-rimmed eyes. He opened his arms and shrugged an apologetic invitation. Hettie sidled over to rest her head on his chest, and he wrapped her tightly in his arms. He sighed brokenly. "I don't know what else to say."

"We're a pair, aren't we?" Hettie sniffed.

"You haven't done anything." Alexander stroked her hair. "I behaved like a total prick."

"Yes, you did, actually." She smiled sadly against his chest. "They only told me on Friday evening," she told him again. "And I really haven't made my mind up yet."

"Do you want to go out and get some dinner?" Alexander asked, still unsure if he could deal with this conversation.

Hettie shook her head. "No, I want to be here with you." *Forever, if I could*, she thought.

"OK." Alexander sighed. "Talk to me about South Africa, then."

"Are you sure?" Hettie asked, sitting up. "If you lose it again, Al, much as I love you, I'm out of here."

The word was used flippantly but hovered large in the air between them.

"You love me, then?" Alexander spoke lightly, half in jest, pulling her back against his chest and pressing his face against her hair.

"I suspect I'm falling, unfortunately." Hettie sighed.

"Is that so very terrible?" he asked.

"I don't know. You tell me. I'm rubbish at relationships. I'm not sure I want a man in my life; it all gets so bloody complicated. And look at us—it's either heaven or hell. I think we've both got issues."

Alexander didn't answer.

"So, South Africa," Hettie said. She might as well go for it now—flip the coin, see what landed. If he turned on her again, she would accept the offer. There was no way she wanted a relationship that made her constantly worried about doing something wrong. She'd been there before, and it wasn't fun. "They're going soon, before Christmas, Cynthia said. They want me to go, all expenses paid, my own accommodation. It would be a huge adventure, an amazing opportunity. I could even take the dogs, I think, although that sounded complicated. I would have to find out more. You'd know about that with Digger, I guess. But it's pretty bloody scary. I've never been anywhere before. A couple of weeks in Ibiza and now here—that's it. I think I'm a homebody at heart, which sort of makes me think I should push myself. I don't like the thought of being so far away from my mum, or Nat and my mates and, well, you, if I'm honest."

"How long for?" Alexander asked. "A year, five years, forever?"

"I don't know." Hettie sighed. "They're going for the long haul, possibly forever. But I know I couldn't do that. Maybe a year, I don't know. Even that sounds like a really long time when I actually let myself think about it."

"Until you meet someone out there and fall in love and stay forever." Alexander tried to make his voice sound light, but the thought was killing him.

"If you ask me not to go, I won't," Hettie told him.

Alexander laughed dryly. "You know I can't do that, Hettie," he said. "Especially given how I just behaved. It would be an adventure; I can see that. I should have been pleased for you instead of acting like a total jerk."

"I don't think I can go," Hettie said. "I'm not brave enough."

"Hettie, you are the bravest person I know," Alexander told her. "It's one of the things I love about you."

There was that word again. Hettie felt a warm rush of joy.

"And what if you met someone else?" she asked in a small, tight voice. "I don't know if I could bear that." She leaned up and kissed him slowly and deliberately. "Let's not talk about it anymore tonight."

Alexander scooped her up and carried her upstairs. And if anything, the heartfelt, tender lovemaking that followed was their most erotic experience yet.

CHAPTER TWENTY-SIX

There had been a subtle change in their relationship by the end of the holiday: a new, respectful reserve between them. They continued to enjoy each other's company, still laughed a lot, and still frequently ended up in bed, but a careful politeness prevailed. South Africa wasn't discussed in depth, but the subject came up at random moments if something occurred to either of them.

"I wonder if I could go for six months," Hettie said almost to herself one morning.

"If you couldn't take Doris and Pig, I would have them for you," Alexander muttered at dinner. Hettie appreciated the obvious effort he was making not to say anything that might put her off, but it was making the decision even harder.

On the flight home, Alexander swore loudly when he jammed his knees into the seat in front of him. The flight attendant raised her eyebrows, and passengers in nearby seats studiously looked away. Hettie lifted his hand and kissed it; she was pretty fed up, herself.

"So what will I do if I stay?" she asked him an hour into the flight. "Come back to Draymere, and do what? I'll be out of a job. I know James and Grace would have me back, but could I work for Siobhan? Or should I find a job somewhere else?"

"You could work for me at the practice," Alexander said nonchalantly, as if he had only just had the idea. "We'll need someone when the stables are built."

Hettie laughed softly. "Really?" she said, raising her eyebrows at him. "I thought that was phase three of your plan, and possibly not happening for years." She pulled his arm around her shoulders and snuggled up against him. "Anyway, do you really think that's a good idea, or is it your way of keeping me near and 'keeping an eye on me'?"

Alexander smiled ruefully. "I think you should go," he said quietly. "You would have a fantastic time. I think you would love it. You're not really ready to move back to Draymere, are you?" He paused. Hettie thought she might cry. "They have telephones in South Africa—we can talk on the phone. I'll get a Facebook account so I can look at pictures of you." He tried to smile, but it didn't entirely come off. "I can visit—it isn't that far. You should go," he finished decisively. "But not for too long, and then you should come back and be with me."

Hettie stared at him; his magnanimous words were filling her heart. She put her hand against his cheek and kissed him deeply, for long enough to make the flight attendant raise her eyebrows again and the passengers sitting nearby studiously look away for the second time.

"But don't—" Alexander began heavily when the kiss finished.

"I won't," Hettie interrupted. "I've already told you: you have spoiled me for anyone else."

Hettie accepted Alexander's offer to drive her back to Flintend, even though she already had her train ticket. She didn't want to say good-bye to him.

"Stay tonight," she suggested. "Cynthia won't mind."

"Ah, the lovers return!" Cynthia cried when they found her out on the yard, and they were engulfed in an enthusiastic welcome from Doris, Pig, and SpongeBob. "Look at you both; you are disgustingly tanned. I take it a good time was had by all?"

"Absolutely perfect," Hettie told her.

"Well, I'm bloody glad to have you back. It's been manic here without you. You look well, Alexander," she prompted. He hadn't spoken yet, and his lack of greeting was slightly disconcerting.

"Very well, thank you," he replied tightly, thrusting his hands into his pockets.

Oh, dear, Cynthia thought, *someone's not happy. I hope that means Hettie has decided to come with us.*

"We're making tea," Hettie said to Cynthia, trying to ease the tension. "I'll bring one out for you." She shot Alexander a warning look.

"Don't take it out on Cynthia," she hissed as they walked back to the kitchen. "It's hardly her fault."

"She pisses me off," Alexander mumbled grumpily. "She gets everything her own way."

"She's giving everything up to follow Pieter to South Africa!" Hettie responded with surprise. "When she's just started competing at four-star level here as well!"

"First selfless act of her life, then." Alexander grunted.

Pieter and the girls eased the friction at dinner. Hettie told Harriet and Jess all about her holiday and prayed that the South Africa question wouldn't come up until after Alexander had left. Pieter and Alexander discussed progress on the veterinary practice. Pieter said he would very much like to take another look at the barns now that work was nearing completion. Al bit back the cutting comment that it was a long way to visit from South Africa.

"I take it she mentioned South Africa, then." Cynthia probed Alexander when they found themselves alone outside smoking after dinner. "And as you are behaving like a spoiled toddler, I hope that means she's coming!" She grinned.

"I think you should ask Hettie that, don't you?" Alexander suggested pompously. "But thank you for the almighty spanner you've thrown into our lives, Cynthia."

"Oh, don't be so dramatic, man!" Cynthia scoffed. "I've asked her to come to South Africa and have a wonderful adventure. Surely you can't begrudge her that."

"Ah, so it's a purely benevolent act on your part. Nothing to do with the fact that she's the best groom you've ever had and you don't want to lose her."

"Well, I can't deny that's true." Cynthia was indignant now. "But I could say the same thing about you wanting to keep her here. She's only twenty-six, for God's sake. Surely you wouldn't expect her to give up a chance like this for you?"

"You expected Pieter to give up quite a lot," Alexander shot back.

"Yes, that's true, I did. Not that it's any of your business." Cynthia looked at him pensively. "And look where that got me, Alexander. I practically delivered the poor man straight into another woman's bed."

Alexander shook his head. "You're right," he said. "It's none of my business."

"We're having a row," Cynthia announced with relish when they went back into the kitchen, "about South Africa. Alexander thinks I'm trying to steal you away from him, and I think it's too good a chance to pass up for any man."

"Lucky I've got a mind of my own and can decide for myself," Hettie said tartly. "If my minders can't reach a conclusion on my behalf."

Pieter laughed, and Alexander and Cynthia had the grace to look sheepish.

Alexander left early the next day. He felt guilty about how long he'd been away from Digger and Dora, although he had paid Jodie to house-sit, and she was very good with them. He also had a mountain of work waiting for him at home. It hadn't been the best time to abandon the build and Ewan with everything they had going on at the moment.

Hettie rode out with Cynthia. It was nice to be back on a horse, even if it wasn't feeling quite so easy landing back in reality and saying good-bye to Al, who was still being uncomfortably polite to her.

"I'll come for six months, if you want me," Hettie told Cynthia decisively. "If that doesn't suit you, I'm afraid it's a no. Think about it, if you need to." She smiled at Cynthia. "But I could help you settle in. It would give you a chance to find someone to replace me out there. I wouldn't bring the dogs. Alexander said he would have them."

"I take it this is Alexander's idea," Cynthia said thoughtfully.

"No, it is not," Hettie scolded her. "Surprisingly it's all my own work. I want to see South Africa, and I want to be with Alexander. This is my compromise."

"All right," Cynthia said grumpily. "I'll say yes. Maybe we'll be able to persuade you to stay longer when we've got you there." She grinned.

"No, you won't," Hettie stated. "If I promise Alexander six months, then that's what it will be." *Unless he finds someone else while I'm gone,* she added inside her head.

Autumn swept in wet and wild. The trees shed their leaves, which gusted chaotically and formed untidy heaps on the grass at Flintend. At Draymere the gardeners battled relentlessly to keep the lawns tidy. The clippers came out at both stables to tidy horses' winter coats, and Draymere prepared for the start of another hunting season. Holly had handed her notice in; she was going back to college to train as a beautician. Imogen left as well, as "Imogen Interiors" was keeping her fully occupied. In a return of favours, Alexander had helped her lease some premises and sorted out her self-employment accounts. She was working out of a small shop in Cirencester, selling chic objets d'art and work by local artists, including a series of prints of Anna's paintings of different breeds of dog. The prints were flying off the shelves at two hundred pounds each and about to be produced as a set of greeting cards. Helen managed the art side of the business and staffed the store when Imogen was busy with interior design. They had moved into the flat above the premises together. Imogen's house in London had been sold to Ted and Anju, who were also setting up home together. Imogen was still riding her mother's show jumpers at weekends and looking forward to doing some hunting, but had told her mother that she wouldn't be competing again because she didn't enjoy the pressure. Her mother, having been told off twice by Helen for her overbearing behaviour, acquiesced surprisingly graciously. She was struggling to get to grips with this new, assertive, lesbian daughter.

Siobhan was dating one of the Draymere gardeners, a casual, mutually uncommitted relationship which suited them both very well. She offered Holly's job to Carol Greaves, which gave Hettie a moment's unease when she heard. Carol, with her children all growing up, leapt at the chance to get back out with the horses and earn some much-needed cash. She prayed that if she worked super hard and stayed long enough, she might get the chance of a house on the estate and be able to move her poor children out of their poky housing association flat.

Jodie had joined the local riding club and developed a whole new social life, in addition to riding Rose in most competitions the club put on. When she wasn't competing herself, she volunteered as a steward or a jump judge and, having been pressed into joining the committee, spent all her free time organising events or socials. She shyly asked Grace at breakfast break if there was any chance of the riding club holding their annual show at Draymere Hall in the summer. Grace was enthusiastic and started thinking about which Draymere horses could enter. Grace was in the throes of completely redecorating the hall under Imogen's guidance and revelling in the chaos of a house filled with tradesmen and decorators who kept the children thoroughly entertained while she supplied tea, bacon rolls, and gossip. It was like having a party in the house every day, with the added bonus of a ready supply of smoking companions. No one smoked on the yard since Holly had left. Even Bev had broken the evil habit after Chelsea had declared that the grandson she was expecting wouldn't be visiting their house if her mum and dad were smoking.

Grace asked James if he would consider having the snip, but when he readily agreed (overwhelmed at the time by four young children and God knows how many workmen in his house), Grace backtracked rapidly. She told Hettie tearfully on the phone that she couldn't bear the thought of no more babies. She was still probing relentlessly for more details about the holiday.

"He's been ever so quiet since he got back," she told Hettie now. "You might almost think he's in love."

"Stop it, Grace." Hettie laughed. "He's manic busy with the practice; it won't be leaving him much time for social chitchat."

"You're really mean to me," Grace told her. "I expected some juicy details about how it *really* went—and you know exactly what I mean! Maybe I'll ask Alexander instead."

"Don't you bloody dare," Hettie squeaked. "Not that he'd tell you, anyway."

"No, he wouldn't." Grace sighed. "Getting either of you to talk is like trying to get blood out of a stone. God knows what you talk about when you're alone."

"There wasn't much time for talking." Hettie let the delicious little snippet drop. If she were honest, she would love to tell Grace exactly how wonderful their week had been. And how much she was missing him now. But her relationship with Alexander was complicated and fragile, and she didn't want to get in too deep. In her experience, it would mean too much sympathy offered and too many questions asked when things went wrong.

"Sex all week!" Grace crowed delightedly, falling on the snippet. "Did you actually see anything of France?"

"Of course we did." Hettie backtracked. *See,* she reminded herself, *you've already said too much.* "How is gorgeous Sophie?" She tried to change the subject. "Have you decided who she's going to hunt on this season?"

"Ha-ha!" Grace took the joke without offence. "They used to put the babies on horseback, you know, in little baskets, back in the good old days. Not actually out hunting, I don't think. These days, social services would have them off you. But anyway, before you change the subject again, I need to say something serious. I know I said Alexander would be a handful for any woman, but I wanted to elaborate on that. It wasn't a nice thing to say, and I wouldn't have said it if I had known the situation—"

Hettie interrupted. "Grace, there's no need to say anything. I know who Alexander is, and I'm not under any illusion—"

"No, I'm going to say this," Grace returned, determinedly. "Hettie, he's a really good man, and deep down he's got a heart of gold. He's been an enormous help to me at times. He's weirdly insightful into how I am really feeling. Especially strange considering his total lack of communication—a Melton trait, I'm afraid. But they are all good men, really." *Apart from William, of course,* she thought to herself. "So what I wanted to say is that although yes, he might be a handful, I wouldn't want my comments to put you off. He had a difficult time in his teens..."

"I know about Celia leaving," Hettie said quietly.

"What? Alexander told you?" Grace was shocked. "I can't believe that. He's never spoken about it to anyone. My God, Hettie, I was right. You would absolutely be the right woman to handle him."

"Grace, stop it," Hettie admonished with a groan. "You're off again, and I'm not sure Alexander would appreciate the idea of being handled...not in that way, anyway." She blushed as she said it, and Grace burst out laughing.

"Well, I don't think he's been near any woman except you since the thing with Imogen ended. So whatever you say, Hettie, I'm convinced he's smitten."

And Imogen didn't happen, either, Hettie thought smugly. He had told her that on the second night of their holiday, after several glasses of wine. Her annoyance at being played for a fool had been easily outweighed by relief at the news and delight at knowing that she didn't need to feel guilty or jealous about Imogen.

Alexander was busy, ridiculously busy. But he was also lost inside his head with thoughts about Hettie: her leaving, and what the hell his emotions were doing. He was haunted with brooding shame at his reaction to her news. Every time his mind was free to wander, his thoughts ricocheted back to the same relentless questions: Was he like his father? Or, almost as alarming, was he like Cynthia? Did he want Hettie—for good and forever? And if so, did that mean he expected her to be there all the time, follow him around like Digger? The thoughts were uncomfortable, and interspersed with even more unwelcome questions about whether she wanted him. She had moved away, after all, and now she was going even further. Leaving the country, in fact. When he spoke to her on the phone or saw her in person, there was no question in his mind. But in the quiet moments, on his own, the doubts circled like hungry hyenas waiting for a kill. For the very first time in his life, he wanted to talk to someone about it. He was worn out with the constant loop of insecurities. He called his mother and asked when would be a good time to visit.

"À tout moment!" she told him, predictably. So he made plans to visit the following day.

♦♦♦

Cynthia was overstressed and fractious about the amount that needed to be done to ship a family, ten horses, and three dogs halfway around the world while simultaneously trying to keep on top of her regimented training and competition schedule. Pieter, the girls, and even the dogs were keeping out of her way. On Thursday evening, Jessica came out to the yard in tears to find Hettie.

"Mum says I can't take Starlight," she sobbed, burying her face in the neck of the pony in question. "I didn't do my homework, and the school sent a letter."

"Mum's stressed." Hettie gave her a cuddle. "Mums get like that sometimes when they've got a lot on their mind. Do you want me to have a word with her, ask what you could do to make it better?"

Jessica nodded and hiccupped, wiping tearful snot from her face with the sleeve of her school blazer.

"Right," Hettie said to Cynthia when she found her on the front drive, smoking a cigarette and looking red eyed herself. "This has got to stop."

"I'm an awful mother," Cynthia wailed dramatically.

"No, you're not," Hettie said. "But it was a bit mean, telling Jess she couldn't take Starlight. Did you mean it?"

"No, of course not," Cynthia muttered. "I think I'm losing the plot. This was all meant to be an adventure, and now I'm wondering what in hell we're doing it for. Putting ourselves through this much agro when everything is fine as it is."

Hettie sighed. "Cold feet?" she asked. "Well, it was bound to happen. But to be honest, I thought it would be me or the girls. You're the one who just gets on with life and leaps at every opportunity that comes your way."

"Do you think we shouldn't go?" Cynthia asked, doggedly trying to disguise the tremor in her voice.

"I think," Hettie replied, "that you and Pieter should get away this weekend. Away from the house and the girls and the horses. We can cope perfectly well. Granny can help me here. Spend some time together, talk things through. Come up with a plan you can work toward instead of battling on without giving yourselves time to think about anything except the never-ending details."

♦♦♦

Alexander went to his mother's house—a nondescript, standard-issue modern terrace on a housing estate, surrounded on every side by identical houses that overlooked each other's gardens. He hadn't pictured his mother living somewhere like that at all.

"I can't for the life of me think why you wouldn't give this up for Draymere," he said indignantly after hugging her in greeting. Although once inside the house, it didn't feel quite so bad. His mother's unique French style had transformed the boxy rooms into something quite welcoming.

"It's not about giving this up," Celia reminded him patiently. "Now come and have some coffee in the conservatoire."

The garden was actually beautiful, a little haven of colour with eclectic flowerbeds and pots overflowing with grasses and flora. Mismatched aging benches and chairs sat on the brick patio, scattered with vibrant cushions. Celia had hung several bird feeders from branches, and a flock of bright siskins flitted away as they entered the conservatory. Celia fetched a carafe and a plate of freshly baked biscuits.

"You're spoiling me," Alexander said appreciatively. "You have made the garden beautiful," he added, aware that his earlier comment might have been rather rude.

"I love my garden," Celia said simply. "And I love the birds. I try to draw them, but they rarely stay still for long enough."

Celia was obviously delighted that Alexander was in her house, and he was amazed and relieved all over again by her capacity for forgiveness. She had never once remarked on his refusal to see her over all those years, and he was infinitely grateful that he could spend time with her now. He wished she would move back to Draymere so they could all be a family again.

"Now tell me about your holiday with Hettie," Celia said, helping herself to another biscuit. She had guessed correctly that Alexander needed to talk about something. Even after their long separation, she could still read his face as well as she had been able to when he was a child.

"The holiday was almost perfect," Alexander said honestly. He had determined to be ruthlessly candid. If anyone knew about heartache and what an obstinate idiot he was, it could only be his mother. "We got on really well. France was beautiful, the sun shone, and we laughed a lot. I've become really close to Hettie, I think."

"You think?" Celia raised her eyebrow. "I am sensing a 'but,' Alexander."

Alexander sighed. "All right, I know I've got close to her. But she's going to South Africa, so now I don't know if she feels the same about me. And to make matters worse, I behaved appallingly when she told me."

"How appallingly?" Celia was startled.

"I ranted and raved, shouted a lot, said some awful things. I had to leave before I did something worse. I saw red. I can't control myself when I'm like that. Am I like Father, do you think?"

Celia tried to disguise the terrible guilt she felt at his words, but she couldn't help believing this was all her fault. It didn't take much to work out that this reaction to a woman he loved leaving was down to the fact that his mother had done the same. She laid her hand over his and tried to concentrate on the difficult question he had posed.

"Would it be so bad, if you were like your father?" she asked quietly. "He was a good man, honest and loyal, and he loved you all very much."

Alexander stared at her in amazement. "He drove you away from us!" He almost shouted the words. "How can you say that? He was always angry, incredibly judgemental, and seriously unforgiving. A lot of that sounds like me, and I am ashamed of all of it."

"No, Alexander," Celia said sternly. "I can't let you get away with that. It was never a case of saint and sinner; we were both to blame. And if he drove me away, it was me who gave him the stick. I hurt him terribly by that. All the more so because he couldn't tell me that he was hurting. I always thought he would relent and allow me to come back. I still believe he would have done if he hadn't taken to drink. But to understand your father, you need to understand his upbringing. Grandmother Melton was a very cold woman. I do not believe she ever showed him a moment's affection.

He was sent away at a very young age to an all-boys' school. He was an only child with no siblings to lean on. He simply didn't learn about love or affection. But your father had many admirable qualities; he was handsome, brave, and strong. So yes, Alexander, I see that in you. But I also see a vulnerable boy who would welcome love and affection, if he would only allow himself to do so. I fear terribly that your reluctance to do that is more my fault than your father's."

"But he left you no choice!" Alexander protested.

"It felt that way to me, I admit," Celia said gently. "But would I make the same choice again? I don't honestly know that I would—if my legacy is a son so scarred by my actions that he cannot embrace love when he finds it."

"I didn't say I loved her," Alexander muttered.

"Exactly what is worrying me." Celia smiled sadly. "What are you so scared of, Alexander, that you can't even mention the word?"

"I'm scared of everything about it!" Alexander exclaimed. "Scared that I'm not a nice person, scared of my rages, scared that I will love her and she won't love me back. Scared of her leaving, scared of driving her away with my behaviour."

"Sounds like love to me," Celia said lightly to cover the obvious pain the raw confession had caused her son. "But you are talking to me about it, so in that way you are very much not like your father, and I am so very happy that you are able to do that." She blinked away the tears that threatened. "I would like to meet this girl," she added brightly, "who has captured the heart of my handsome middle son. Can I visit when she is next at Draymere?"

"Of course." Alexander smiled. "She should be coming home the weekend after next. Everyone would love to see you."

"Don't overthink it, Alexander," Celia told him. "Love is not black and white. It is simply two people finding happiness together and working to share their lives. If there is a chance, you should go for it. What is the worst that can happen? You could get hurt, of course. But if you turn your back on loving someone, pain becomes a certainty."

CHAPTER TWENTY-SEVEN

Hettie was unenthusiastic about meeting Celia; she had found it hard to think kindly of Alexander's mother since his revelation. But the happiness in Alexander's voice when he told her that Celia was coming to stay with him, the same weekend that Hettie was home, cautioned her to keep her feelings to herself. She was also annoyed that the gatehouse wouldn't afford them any privacy with Celia in residence. She couldn't wait to tell Alexander that she wouldn't be going to South Africa until after Christmas now. Cynthia had come back from her weekend away refreshed and in better humour. Between them, she and Pieter had decided on a more achievable plan for their move: Pieter would go in November, take up his new post, and get things ready for the family to join him early in the new year. He would come home for Christmas and to help close Flintend before they all travelled back together. Hettie was relieved about the new plan. Leaving before Christmas had been stressing her out, and this way she would get to spend Christmas week at home with her family and Alexander.

Alexander was pleased. "Come to Draymere for dinner on Boxing Day," he said to Hettie impetuously. "Do you want to hunt? I'll let Siobhan know."

"That's a strange reversal," Hettie said and laughed. "But yes, I would love to." It felt odd but flattering to have Alexander including her in family plans, and she grinned at the phone.

"And will you be home for the ball?" he went on. "If so, I'm claiming the last dance."

Hettie's grin got even bigger at the thrill of pleasure his words gave her.

"Of course," she said. "Every dance. I wouldn't want to share them with anyone else."

She had a lot to squeeze in to her weekend at home. It was Hannah's birthday, which meant a night out with the girls; she needed to spend time with her mum; she wanted to visit Grace and catch up with Jodie, Holly, and Bev; and then there was Clare and Charlotte to visit. She also needed an update tour of the barns, of course, and now she had this bloody meeting with Celia. She needed a week to fit it all in, but she was travelling by train, which meant arriving late on Friday and leaving early on Sunday. She had got a quote for the Landy, but it was far more than she could afford. The wedding and holiday spending had caught up with her, and travelling home this weekend was costing nearly a hundred quid. She reminded herself that she would be back in only seven weeks, for a longer visit, and tried not to remember that it would be her last trip to Draymere for six months.

Alexander picked her up from the station. "Stay with me tonight?" he asked her. "Mother's not turning up until tomorrow." He grinned.

"Love to." Hettie grinned back. "But I need a shower and a drink. I left straight from the yard."

"Yeah, I can smell that." Alexander laughed. "Anyone would think you were trying to put me off, turning up stinking of horses and then needing a drink before you'll go to bed with me." He said the words lightly, but they both knew there were undercurrents in his statement. "Lucky I'm not easily deterred."

Hettie smiled and leaned across to kiss his cheek as he drove. "Don't ever think I want to put you off," she told him seriously.

It was tricky getting to visit everyone with no car to drive, and Alexander was put out that Hettie was going clubbing on Saturday night. Although knowing that might be the case, she had warned him in advance of her plans. "Give me a call when you want to go home," he told her grumpily. "I'll pick you up, if you like."

"It might be really late," Hettie warned him. "And your mum will be at yours. We can get a taxi; it's not a problem."

"I want to pick you up," he said stubbornly.

"You did that months ago." Hettie grinned at him.

"I believe it was you that picked me up, actually," Alexander shot back, poker-faced.

"Depends which time we're talking about." Hettie laughed. "I'll admit to the very first, but as to the others, it's anybody's guess, really. I don't think we could be accused of conducting a very conventional romance."

"I can do conventional, if that's what you want," Alexander told her. "I can ask you out on dates and pick you up from your mum's. We could go to the pictures, go dancing, or visit the zoo. That's what they do in the movies, isn't it?" He smiled, and Hettie loved the way his eyes crinkled at the edges when his smile was relaxed and genuine.

"When I get back," she said, holding his hand,"I want to do all that."

She managed all her social calls on Saturday; she asked her mum to drive her to Clare and Ewan's. Anna was always happy to spend time cuddling a baby, and Charlotte was ridiculously pretty with her curly blond hair and rosy cheeks. She looked like a perfect little angel. Clare told them that really wasn't the case; Charlotte had developed a will of iron and didn't believe in sleeping but loved charming visitors and random strangers. "Especially men!" Clare rolled her eyes. "She is almost embarrassing when Alexander calls round!" Hettie, pleased that she had managed to avoid the onslaught of questions about her relationship with Alexander that Clare would have hurled at her if Anna hadn't been present, cunningly decided to drag Anna along to Bev's as well. She popped to see Jodie on the yard and got through the embarrassing introduction to Carol Greaves without either of them mentioning that they had met each other before. *Although "met" might not be entirely the right word,* Hettie thought with a shudder.

Hettie persuaded Clare to come clubbing with them after Clare had initially declined on the grounds that she still couldn't get into her prepregnancy clothes, and if she didn't sleep when Charlotte did, it would take her a month to recover.

"Rubbish. You look gorgeous, Clare—a proper yummy mummy. If you drink enough, you'll sleep through anything. And you can drink now that you're not feeding! That should be reason enough to get out and party."

The four of them met at Hannah's for preclubbing drinks, and both Clare and Hannah got very drunk very quickly, which made Jade and Hettie the responsible adults by default, so they eased off the booze at pleasantly merry. When Clare threw up in the early hours, there was a collective decision that their night was probably over.

"I'm getting so old," Hannah wailed drunkenly. "I used to be able to boogie in the dawn."

"You still could if you didn't neck a bottle of vodka before you left the house," Hettie told her as she held her up outside the club and called Alexander. "I'm afraid Clare's puking," she explained apologetically. "You might want to bring a bucket."

Al was really sweet and patient, ferrying them all around, making sure Hannah and Clare actually made it to their front doors. He chuckled dryly when he got back to the car.

"Poor Clare," he said. "I could hear Charlotte screaming upstairs."

Hettie snogged him gratefully when they got to her mum's. She wished she were going back to the gatehouse with him.

"This feels like being a teenager." She giggled. "Snogging in the car because our mums are in."

"Shall I park somewhere more secluded?" Al asked huskily.

"Yes, please," Hettie whispered.

The meeting with Celia the following day started off well enough. Hettie walked down from the hall where she'd spent the morning with Grace. Celia was very welcoming and annoyingly likeable, asking about her mum and wanting to know all about Hettie's trip to South Africa. Alexander made coffee while Hettie thanked Celia politely for the lovely picture of Dog and remarked on what a coincidence it was that Anna and Celia knew each other.

"Not so much of a coincidence," Celia said. "We were both raising children of similar ages not far from one another."

What raising you did, anyway, Hettie thought darkly. *My mum was actually with me.* She was thrilled with the picture, though. The sketches of Dog and Doris were in a drawer at her mum's house waiting for a permanent home where she could hang them on the wall.

Alexander suggested he drive to the barns, as it was tipping with sleety rain. Celia glowed with pride as he showed them around.

"It changes so much every time I see it." Hettie was amazed. "It actually looks like a veterinary practice now!"

"More equipment to source, and we need to employ nurse receptionists, but we're bang on schedule for opening at the beginning of February." They were also hoping to poach Tom from the practice in Norfolk to come in as a partner with specialist knowledge of surgery, but he didn't mention that, as they had only recently approached him.

I'll miss the opening, Hettie thought sadly. *I hope these nurse receptionists aren't too attractive.* "Show me where the stables are going again," she said out loud.

"We can take small animal inpatients from day one, but the equine and large animal side will be developed when we've got more funds under our belts," he explained to Celia. Hettie was pretty much up to speed with their plans. "But we're planning to get another partner on board before then—someone with experience in specialist surgery, who can train me and Ewan up."

It all sounded so exciting now that it was finally happening. Hettie wondered if she had been hasty in turning his job offer down. She wasn't sure how she would feel if someone else got the job in her place. "This could be so nice," she mumbled, looking around the potential stable block. "Maybe I should think again about that job offer." She smiled sheepishly at Al.

"But you're going away!" Celia cried. "On your exciting adventure." Celia didn't mean anything by her statement. She was genuinely pleased for Hettie, despite knowing that Alexander was struggling to deal with it. But Hettie, sensitive to how much Celia might know, took her words as criticism.

"I'll only be gone for six months," she said tartly. "It's not as if *I'm* abandoning him for years."

Celia visibly paled.

"Hettie!" Alexander barked with shock.

"Sorry," Hettie murmured, tight-lipped. "I wasn't thinking."

It wasn't mentioned again, but the drive back to the gatehouse was awkward. To Celia's credit, she made a number of valiant attempts to restart the conversation.

"I should probably go straight home," Hettie mumbled when they arrived. "Mum's doing a roast."

Alexander offered to drop her back, so Celia got out, telling Hettie how lovely it had been to meet her. She sounded so genuine and affectionate that Hettie was ashamed of her earlier comment.

"That was a bit cruel," Alexander said mildly, looking at Hettie on the back seat in the rearview mirror.

"Not as cruel as abandoning you for fifteen years," Hettie retorted. Knowing she was in the wrong was making her defensive.

"That wasn't all her fault, I—" Alexander started to explain.

"Al, you were fifteen! She was the adult. Don't you dare blame yourself!" Hettie almost shouted, alarming herself by the words coming out of her mouth. The statement was almost exactly what Natalie had raved at Hettie over the years. And her mum had repeated the same words in more gentle tones.

"Let me finish," Alexander said patiently. "She tried to keep in touch constantly. She never stopped writing or checking up on me. I've had nearly two hundred letters from her over the years. And I only read them six months ago. So when I say it wasn't all her fault, it is actually true."

"You didn't make her leave in the first place," Hettie said stubbornly.

"No, that's true, but my father did."

They drove in silence for a while. Hettie knew she should back down, but she didn't really believe that any decent mother would leave her kids, whatever the circumstances. Alexander mused that he couldn't blame Hettie for feeling the way she did, even though that comment had been out of order. She knew only half the story. It also felt weirdly flattering to have Hettie fighting his corner.

"I hope you are comfortable back there." Alexander grinned, changing the subject.

Hettie blushed, remembering the previous night. "I'm not sure," she replied, meeting his eyes in the mirror. "A bigger car would make life easier."

Alexander hugged his mother when he got back to the house. "I am sorry Hettie said that. In her defence, she only knows half the story." *And that isn't fair. Why the hell am I still protecting Father?*

"She's a tiger." Celia smiled, hugging him back. "And what mother wouldn't want a tiger protecting her son?"

Emotion and stress were running high at Flintend as Pieter prepared to leave. But the thought of her dad's departure had refocused Harriet's mind from the worries she was having about leaving her friends. Cynthia had finished competing for the year, the horses were being allowed to wind down, and she told her clients to start looking for new trainers. She would stop teaching in December.

Alexander visited Norfolk twice in November. He had meetings with Tom and was glad of the excuse to travel up there. He booked a room in the hotel on both occasions; he was no longer comfortable accepting Cynthia's hospitality. Hettie was pleased that he stayed there. It gave her a chance to escape the tension, and she was happy to spend her free time alone with Alexander. She also thought the family might benefit from having her out of the way. She told Alexander that if the equine clinic job was still on the table when she got back to England, she wanted to be first in the queue.

"Panicking?" he asked, pulling her closer as they lay together in bed.

"Big time," she said into his chest. "Don't hire anyone pretty."

Alexander smiled. "I don't want anyone but you." He surprised himself by meaning it.

Celia was going to stay at Draymere for the whole of December. The decorators would be finished by Christmas, but the house was full of boxes crammed with household clutter. Celia would help Grace sort the house out, keep the grandchildren out of her way, and generally make herself useful in the lead-up to the ball and Christmas. "You are an angel sent from heaven!" Grace declared.

"At least she's not staying at the gatehouse," Hettie said when Al told her on the phone.

"Hettie, stop it," Alexander said. "I want you to like my mum."

"I only meant I want us to have the house to ourselves," Hettie protested. But they both knew that wasn't completely true.

Hettie acknowledged that the prospect of leaving Alexander, not to mention England, was overwhelming her. The mood at Flintend wasn't helping, either. Alexander resolved to speak with his brothers again about Celia and their father's will. All these half truths were making life complicated. He needed to share the whole sordid story with Hettie before she took against his mother for as many years as he had.

Draymere Hall emerged even more beautiful. Imogen's clever design encompassed classical, timeless elegance befitting of the hall with all the comfort and practicality of a busy family home. Grace clapped her hands in delight when the Christmas tree lights went on in their newly decorated sitting room. Her house looked like something out of a classy magazine. By contrast, Flintend was becoming increasingly sad and decrepit, as furniture went into storage and oddments were packed into boxes. Cracks in the plaster, dusty corners, and worn, faded carpets left the house and its residents in melancholy moods. The family was planning to spend Christmas Day with Granny, so they hadn't bothered with festive decorations. Even the horses were packed up and moving to a livery yard several miles away to await relocation. Hettie dreaded to think what it would cost to keep ten horses in livery, never mind the expense of flying them halfway across the world.

"The good thing with having an empty house," Hettie said to Cynthia one morning, in an effort to instill a more positive mood, "is that there is nothing to damage or break. Maybe you and the girls should host a Christmas-stroke-leaving party." The Briggs-Johnstons met the idea with enthusiasm. They chose a date and invited friends via texts, Facebook, and phone. Hettie took the girls to the pound shop, and they filled several baskets with cheap decorations. They spent a happy evening scattering them chaotically through the house.

Alexander laughed and said, "I see your signature style at work" when Hettie sent a photo of their efforts.

The crass decorations and chaotic state of the house induced a student party mood among the guests, who were well supplied with booze by Cynthia and arrived with more of their own. The party was a roaring success, but as Cynthia and Hettie met heavy-eyed and hungover in the kitchen the following morning, they surveyed the state of the house with something close to despair.

"Oh, my God," Cynthia groaned.

"It's not so bad," Hettie tried. "It won't take long to sort out." But she didn't sound very convinced or convincing.

"I've had enough of this," Cynthia said grimly. "It's like living in a bloody squat. I think me and the girls should move in with Granny until school breaks up. The horses are gone, and you might as well go home yourself, Hettie."

Hettie wasn't going to argue with that. She had wondered what the hell she was meant to do over the next week with the horses all in livery and all their tack and equipment neatly packed into shipping crates. The stables had been emptied, scrubbed, and disinfected; as per usual, organisation on the yard was way ahead of that in the house.

"I'm gonna grab a wheelbarrow," Hettie said, "and muck this place out. When that's done, I would be very happy to take you up on that offer." She had caved in and borrowed the money to get the Landy mended off of her mum. It went against the grain, but she needed to get loads of stuff back to Draymere, including the dogs, and the Landy couldn't be abandoned at Flintend for six months. She was hoping the Meltons might let her park it in the corner of one of their barns.

Alexander asked her to spend her extra week with him at the gatehouse and was cross when Hettie stalled over her answer. She wanted to be with him, but the risk of her freezing up without alcohol inside her was becoming an issue, and she *really* didn't want to spend the Christmas break on bad terms. Alexander was trying hard to be tactful and patient about it, but he wasn't patient or tactful when she called him back to say she would be staying at her mum's.

"Why the fuck won't you stay here?" he raged. "You can't have anything planned. You didn't know you were coming back until three hours ago."

Hettie dithered and offered excuses that sounded pathetic even to her. Alexander wasn't appeased, so under duress she agreed to stay at the gatehouse for a couple of nights.

"Forget it," he snapped. "I'm withdrawing the invitation."

It needed sorting out, Hettie knew, this *problem* of hers. But who the hell should she see about not being able to shag unless she was pissed? A GP? A counsellor? The idea of talking about it made her shudder with horror. But the alternatives of being unable to have unplanned sex or, more appealing, becoming an alcoholic didn't feel great either. She knew she ought to speak to Alexander if she was serious about their relationship. Not explaining it to him was just unfair. He took her reluctance as rejection, and that was already becoming a problem. But when she thought about the reality of saying the words to him, breaking up felt like it would be the easier option. Staying with Alexander for the week made sense. She could settle Doris and Pig in, spend more time with him, and *maybe* they could talk. Decision made, she arrived at the gatehouse without forewarning him. If there was going to be a row, it might as well be face-to-face. Alexander wasn't in. She hadn't thought of that, but she let herself into the garden and managed to gain access through Digger's dog flap. Her entrance caused untold excitement and mayhem as Digger, Dora, Doris, and Pig embarked on a gleeful reunion. Dora piddled on the rug. *Oh, shit,* Hettie thought. *That isn't a good start.* On the plus side, Alexander's absence would give her the chance to have a couple of glasses of the wine that was open in the kitchen, and she could delay the dreaded discussion a little longer. She sent Al a text to tell him she was there and ran herself a big bubble bath. A relaxing soak in Alexander's luxury bathroom was a welcome indulgence after the dank en suite shower at Flintend.

Alexander had left a meeting with Ewan at seven. He was in a black mood because of Hettie's refusal to stay with him, so he took himself off to the Fox for whiskey and company. The place was almost empty, so instead of finding distraction, he brooded into his scotch. Hettie was definitely making a fool of him—saying one thing but behaving in a completely different way. Since their holiday in France, she had only been home once, and even then had spent most of the time with her mates. Twice he had chased all the way to bloody Norfolk. Now she was going for six months and couldn't even bear to spend a week with him. Being at Ewan's hadn't helped. They were such a normal family. He wanted that, he realised with surprise. As he downed his second scotch, Dan the farrier came in. Al's mood got even blacker. Having wound himself up into a simmering rage, he needed to clear his head, and he bitterly justified his actions as he drove to Fiona's. Why the hell was he making an effort when Hettie so clearly was not?

He felt disgusted with himself before he even entered Fiona's house. Rather than clearing his head, the sight of her smiling seductively as she ushered him in increased his rage. But he was angry with himself now, not Hettie, not Fiona. She poured him a glass of wine and made a few snide remarks about him always expecting her to be at his beck and call. Ironic given the fact that she was undressing as she spoke and he had barely uttered two words. He heard his phone go off as Fiona began to undo the buttons on his shirt. Relieved by the interruption, he got up and read the message from Hettie. "I've got to get going," he told Fiona casually. She screamed in fury as Alexander readjusted his clothes and walked out again.

Hettie was on his sofa in her pj's, watching TV and holding a glass of wine amid a huddle of dogs. She was glowing from her bath, and still-damp curls framed her face.

"Hello, Mr. Melton." She grinned. "I changed my mind. Woman's prerogative, I believe."

Alexander felt his gut twist with self-rebuke. She looked so fucking beautiful sitting there smiling, and she didn't have a clue about what he had nearly done. His guilt escaped in anger.

"Got pissed enough to want me, then?" He glanced pointedly at the bottle.

Hettie faced him down. "Not pissed," she said. "Only a couple of glasses of wine to celebrate coming home, but I was going to—"

"I'm going for a shower," Al interrupted her abruptly and left the room.

"Shall I come with you?" Hettie tried, but he was already gone, and she didn't get a reply.

CHAPTER TWENTY-EIGHT

They made love that night. Alexander was tender and attentive as ever, but Hettie could sense that their row was still bothering him. She tried to talk to him afterward, but he kissed her quiet, and she thought for a very brief moment that his eyes were filling up. The magnitude of that thought, and of what her leaving might be doing to him, made her stop thinking about conversation. She had been careless of his feelings when she refused to stay with him. She must be more careful in the future. Remember his insecurities, and not make it all about her. As his silencing kiss renewed her desire, Hettie pushed Alexander onto his back and knelt up over him. It was so much easier to show him how much she wanted him than it was to say it with words.

It was brilliant living at the gatehouse, Hettie decided when she woke up in Al's huge bed, looking out over the scenic, frosty grounds of Draymere Hall. Alexander had gone, but she had slept very late, and it was a working day for him after all. She wandered contentedly downstairs and put the kettle on. Doris, Pig, and Dora were there, but Digger must have gone with Al. Maybe he was at the barns. She would have her cup of tea and give him a call. She could walk the dogs over to see him there. The gatehouse landline rang.

"The gatehouse," Hettie trilled, grinning down the phone. She was enjoying playing lady of the manor.

"Who is that?" a female voice replied sharply.

"It's Hettie, Alexander's…friend. He's not here at the moment, I'm afraid." A woman's voice had thrown her; she had assumed it would be Al on the phone.

"Well, well, well," the woman droned. "He's a quick worker, your *friend,* Alexander. I'll give him that."

Hettie didn't answer straight away. She didn't like the tone or implication in the woman's voice, and her heart sped up with impending dread.

"Who am I talking to?" she asked eventually in a dull, flat voice.

"Fiona Harding, of course," the woman returned imperiously. "Alexander left his wallet at mine when he called round to shag me last night."

Hettie felt physically sick. Her hands were shaking, and she wanted to hang up. *Last night?* Her mind screamed, *He couldn't have been shagging you last night; he was here shagging me!*

She heard Fiona laugh bitterly down the phone. "More than a *friend,* then, I take it from your silence. Oh dear, have I upset you?"

Fiona was seething with bitterness. The fury and hurt at how Alexander had behaved last night fuelled her satisfaction in this chance to get revenge. She had been calling Alexander's mobile all morning, but he wasn't picking up. Of course, he never picked up. She knew she was a bloody fool to keep accepting him back into bed the minute he showed up at her door, but she just couldn't help herself.

There was still no reply from Hettie, so Fiona turned the knife. "You didn't honestly think that you were more than a bit of fun for Lexi, did you? You are one of many conquests, you know. An insignificant one, at that. I expect he's had every trashy groom who ever worked at Draymere." She spat the words viciously, impotent with despair that her feelings for Alexander were never going to be returned. Hettie fucking Redfern was *in his house.*

Hettie hung up the phone. *Would Fiona say that if it wasn't true? Please God, don't let it be true.* Doris whined at her feet. The phone rang again, but this time she didn't pick up. When it stopped, her mobile went off, jangling out its inappropriately cheerful ring tone. Al's name came up on the screen. Hettie answered with shaking hands.

"Where are you?" he barked. "I called the landline."

"I'm at the gatehouse," Hettie croaked, and her voice caught in her throat. "Fiona called. You left your wallet at hers when you called round to shag her last night."

There was a moment's pause before Alexander spoke. The hesitation told Hettie everything she didn't want to know about the truth behind Fiona's words.

"Stay there," Al shouted. "I'm coming back."

Hettie hung up on him.

Alexander cursed his decision to walk to the barns that morning; he didn't have a car to get back now. He sprinted down the footpath with Digger on his heels, determined that if she had gone, he would follow her. He would talk to her in front of her mother if he had to. *You fucking, fucking idiot,* his mind raged. He didn't know what he would do if she refused to talk to him.

Hettie hadn't gone. She was devastated, she felt sick, but she needed to hear the truth from Alexander before she decided to leave. He had never promised fidelity. She wasn't sure that either of them had promised anything much. She would have made him promise or left him if she'd known how much this could hurt.

"Don't touch me." Hettie spoke quietly and shook her head when Alexander, breathless from his sprint, moved to approach her. "Just tell me if it's true or not."

"It's true that I was with her yesterday evening, but I didn't shag her." He drew his hand across his face in distress. Hettie was pale and shaking; he couldn't bear that he was the cause of that.

"Why would she say you did, then?" Hettie asked. She wanted Alexander to tell her Fiona was lying, that Fiona was spreading evil untruths again. But his answer took too long.

"Because I would have if I hadn't got your text. Because that is why I went round there." Alexander's answer was expelled in a painful breath.

Hettie thought she might actually throw up. Rage prickled her spine. He might not have promised her anything, but to leave Fiona and come to her and do what they had done last night?

"I am so very, very—" he started to say.

"You don't need to be," Hettie spat. Her eyes were flashing dangerously. "I assumed too much. I totally misread the situation."

"No, you didn't." Alexander tried to approach her again. He badly needed to hold her, to take her in his arms and make all this go away. Make her understand that Fiona was *nothing* to him. Less than nothing. And that she had become everything.

"I'm going to Mum's," Hettie told him, drawing herself up. "I would hate to cramp your style, and I won't be second helpings." Her voice broke on the final sentence.

Alexander closed his eyes and tried to keep his breathing even. "If you leave, I will follow you," he said. "I will follow you to your mum's. I will follow you to South Africa if I have to, and I will keep following you until you listen to what I have to say. If you decide after that you don't want to see me again, I will get out of your life for good."

"I trusted you!" Hettie shouted. "I trusted you not to hurt me. And all the while you were fucking Fiona Harding, and God knows how many other women as well. I *knew* I didn't want a man in my life, but I let you in, and look what you've done!" She rounded on him, screaming, "You're a fucking bastard, Melton! You're worse than Julian Greaves. At least he only fucked with my body. You've fucked with my heart." She saw her words landing on him like blows but couldn't stop. "At least I found out now!" she shrieked. "You know, I was going to talk to you about why I couldn't stay for a week, about why I need to be pissed to have sex. I was worried that I'd hurt you, worried that you might get the wrong idea about why I get like that. I was going to *make* myself tell you—you of all people! The biggest bastard I've ever met. I thought you might be the one worth working it out for. What a fucking joke that is. Why would you even have cared about that when there's a queue of women eager to jump into bed with you when I can't provide what you want? Maybe Fiona was right about needing a trip to the clinic. You're a slut, Alexander. Well, congratulations, you have solved my dilemma. I can get back to the drunken one-night stands. I'm sure there are plenty of blokes in South Africa who will be happy to oblige. In fact, fuck waiting that long, I'll start tonight—follow me if you like, Alexander, but you're not bloody watching." As quickly as her anger had erupted, it was spent. Hettie's shoulders dropped, and Alexander wrapped his arms around her. She closed her eyes. She didn't have any energy left to resist. She was exhausted, washed out, and empty.

"I'm going to make us a cup of tea," Alexander said. "And then we'll talk."

"Oh, what's the point?" Hettie groaned.

"I need you to listen to me."

"Outside," Hettie said. "I want a cigarette." She would hear him out before she left. "But there's nothing you can say that will make this better," she warned.

"No, I understand that." Alexander's voice was emotionless. "But I need to say it, anyway. Facts first: I was with Fiona yesterday evening, and that was unforgivable. But I didn't sleep with her, and prior to that I hadn't seen her for months, not since before the puppies were born."

"But since I left for Norfolk?" Hettie questioned. She didn't really want to know the answer, but like biting on a toothache, something made her ask.

"Yes, one other time," he admitted. "Not long after you'd gone. I saw that photo of you riding on the beach, the one you sent to Grace. You looked like you were having such a good time without me. I was in hell. I couldn't cope with that. I saw her then. And there is no queue of other women. One other girl that I used to hook up with occasionally in London."

"Only me and Fiona, then?" Hettie spat. "Lucky us for winning the dubious prize of becoming your *special girls*. This is pointless, Alexander. I'm getting angrier, and I've got absolutely no way of knowing if you're even telling the truth. Fiona Harding, for God's sake! Of all the women on the planet!"

"I figure I haven't got much to lose right now," Alexander responded wretchedly. "I can't make you believe me, but this is the truth, the whole truth, and nothing but the truth. I don't like Fiona, I don't like her at all. That doesn't make me a nice person, but it's also true."

"You liked her enough to go looking for a shag with her last night," Hettie spat.

"Until I met you, disliking the women I slept with was par for the course," he went on. "Ted accused me of only fucking women I hated, and he was almost right. It had more to do with using sex to stop me feeling anything. Which is exactly what I was planning on doing yesterday." He rubbed his face. "You turned my life upside down, Hettie," he almost whispered. "It's because of you that I got back in touch with my mother. Because of you I let myself start feeling again, after years of being a heartless bastard. I know I've fucked up, more than once, but I spent all those years trying not to let emotions get the better of me. Hating Celia for sleeping with another man and leaving us. I came close to hating everyone. And then I found you. Then I found out that my father had forbidden Celia from living in

Gloucestershire, banned her from any contact with us on the threat of writing us out of his will and giving Draymere away. I thought a lot about the pain his bitter grudge had caused. I thought about my own behaviour, how I had behaved toward you. Assumptions I'd made, how willing I was to believe anything bad about you. You know, I saw you in that car park with Greaves a second before Natalie found you, and my instant assumption was that you were out there willingly. I can't forgive myself for that."

You weren't to know, Hettie thought. *You weren't the only one with secrets.*

"That last night at Draymere," he went on, "I didn't walk away because it meant nothing to me. It was completely the opposite: it meant too much. More than I could deal with, more than I thought I was worth. I don't know if any of this makes any sense to you."

Hettie's head was full of confusing thoughts. She wanted to believe what she was hearing. But the jealousy and anger, the images in her mind of him and Fiona together, were drowning out everything else. "But why last night?" she asked, tears threatening now. She was a fool to still be there, she thought. If she had any kind of self-respect, she would have packed her bags and left.

"Because we'd had a fight. Because you're leaving in a month and you didn't want to stay with me, because I'm still fucked up and full of insecurities and I was acting like an idiot. Because you needing to drink before you sleep with me messes with my head, and I know you don't want to talk about that, but I'm trying to be totally honest."

"So it was my fault?" Hettie knew that wasn't what he was saying, but she wasn't going to listen to him talk as if she had driven him to it.

He shook his head. "Absolutely not."

It was getting cold standing outside, and this was getting them nowhere.

"I'm going now," she told him. "And I've listened to you, so there's no need to follow. I wish we'd had this conversation before I heard it from Fiona. But you tell me, Al, how exactly do I get over this?"

"I don't want you to leave," he said. "If we keep talking, we can get through it. If you go now, I'm scared you will never come back."

"And I'm scared you'll be in Fiona's bed before I'm off the drive," Hettie spat. "So suck it up, Alexander. I'm going home."

Alexander bombarded her with phone calls and messages over the next two days. He had flowers delivered to the house with the message, "I'm sorry. I don't want to lose you. I know flowers are pathetic." Hettie swung between fury and grief. She took two of his calls, but they only made her feel worse. "I trusted you!" she railed at him. "And look what you did." She read all the text messages—more apologies, pleas that they meet—but she only replied to a few. She barely left the house, only going out to walk the dogs on the far side of the village so she didn't bump into him. No one knew she was home, so it was easy to hide at her mum's.

Anna was trying to be patient, but having Hettie descend on her early, in the blackest of moods and with two noisy dogs in tow, wasn't a nice surprise. Alexander was ringing the house at all hours of the day, and Hettie kept ordering her to say she was out, which Anna desperately wished was true.

"She says she's out again," Anna finally flipped, speaking loudly in front of Hettie. "I don't know what's going on here, but I wish you two would bloody sort it out or call it a day."

"I'm sorry, Anna." Alexander was contrite. "Tell her I won't call again."

"For fuck's sake, Mum," Hettie raged when Anna passed on his message. "What the hell did you do that for?"

"Don't you swear at me, Henriqueta!" Anna shouted back. "You're behaving like a brat." She collected her coat and took herself off to Bert's for some peace.

Alexander stopped texting, calling, and sending flowers, and Hettie felt even worse. But she sort of knew she had earned it. He had told her that if she didn't want him, he would get out of her life. She was eaten up with the thought that he might have gone back to Fiona to stop feeling again. It took twelve hours of resistance before she sent a text asking if that was the case.

No, never again, his text replied. *Do you fancy the pictures tonight?*

Hettie wished she could laugh at that. She couldn't even smile, but she did answer, *OK.*

Alexander picked her up. They watched a cheesy Christmas comedy. They conversed politely and sat side by side in the cinema without actually making contact. Neither of them laughed at the film. Alexander drove her home and didn't try to kiss her, but he did ask her if she would go out for dinner with him the following night, and Hettie said yes. She visited Grace the next day. She had forgotten Celia was staying, which was embarrassing, but she spent a nice couple of hours playing with Sophie and Georgia and catching up with the boys.

"How's it going—you and Alexander?" Grace whispered when Celia was out of the room.

"He's being a handful," Hettie said moodily. Grace didn't pursue it.

Alexander had booked a table at the restaurant. "Did you take Fiona out to dinner?" Hettie asked sullenly as she sat down.

"No, I didn't," he replied.

"Where did you meet her? Have you slept with her at yours?"

"I went to her house. That's the only place I've ever been with her. She has never been to the gatehouse, as far as I'm aware."

"Would you have told me if Fiona hadn't called the house?"

"I honestly don't know the answer to that." Alexander sighed. "I was still wrestling with the dilemma when you found out."

"So I might not know if it ever happened again?"

"It wouldn't happen again." He said it with finality.

"Until I pissed you off, made you doubt me, left you for six months."

"It wouldn't happen again," he stated firmly.

Hettie stopped talking and looked at the menu.

"Zoo tomorrow?" Alexander asked when he dropped her off. Hettie was frustrated that he still hadn't attempted to kiss her. She wouldn't have let him, of course, but it would have been nice to get the chance to turn him down.

"OK." She sighed.

Alexander picked her up again, and they drove to the wildlife park. He took her hand as they walked. "I've totally bolloxed your Christmas, haven't I?" he said sorrowfully.

"You've bolloxed more than that," Hettie said. "You told me you weren't interested in anyone else. You let me believe we might be…oh, I don't know, together. Or maybe I just read too much into it. I've always been crap at relationships."

"No, you didn't," Alexander said. "I wanted us to be together. I still want that now. I want you to forgive me. I have never wanted anything more in my life."

"Could you forgive me if it was the other way round?" Hettie asked, but she already knew the answer.

"No, I don't think I could," Alexander answered truthfully. "To be honest, I'm still struggling to forgive you for sleeping with anyone else before you met me. I'm praying that you are a better person than I am."

"Well, we both already know that's true," Hettie shot back.

"Will you come back to mine?" he asked her when they got back to the car.

"I won't sleep with you," Hettie said hurriedly.

"I'm not asking you to," Alexander replied as fast. "I'm inviting you back for a coffee." He took her acceptance as a positive sign, but he was under no illusion that Hettie couldn't still decide to walk away from him and his fucked-up behavior. To be honest, it felt like he deserved her to.

She told him she felt like a fool when they sat down with their coffee. A fool for being there, a fool for spending time with him. But she couldn't work out which hurt more, walking away from him or accepting he slept around.

"Used to sleep around," he corrected her.

"Last week." Hettie looked at him. "Hardly a lifetime ago."

"Tell me about Julian Greaves," he said. "I want us to make this a new beginning. No secrets, everything out in the open. We've got to be worth a try, Hettie. I have never felt about anyone the way I feel about you. I've aired all my dirty laundry now, and I know it's not pretty, but you are still here. So if you are even considering sticking with me, we should get all of our shit out of the way now."

"You think that will make us even? Trading secrets? The problem with that, Alexander, is that you are still making your dirty laundry."

"And you are still keeping yours under lock and key," he responded evenly.

"All right." Hettie lifted her chin. "Maybe that will make *you* walk away and solve the problem for both of us."

"Try me," Alexander said.

So Hettie told her grubby story of meeting Julian Greaves, riding his horses, and being flattered when he gave her attention. She told him that she became obsessed with Julian, couldn't wait for school to finish so she could be with him. "That's the bit that no one understood," she said. "Not Mum, not Natalie. It wasn't all his fault, you see. I never did anything to put him off. I went to *him* after an argument with Mum. She wanted me to stop going there. I didn't want to stop. I didn't want what happened next, but I'd let things go too far by then to tell him that."

"How old were you, Hettie?" Alexander asked, moving from his chair and sitting down next to her on the sofa. Digger jumped up between them.

"I was fifteen, but only weeks from my sixteenth birthday. Old enough to know better, hardly a child. I was confused, infatuated with him, in a way. Scared, hormonal, upset. I was a bloody mess, to be honest. It was a blessing in disguise that Carol found us in the tack room. It gave me my out, or at least I thought it had at the time. Mum was distraught, of course. Natalie was furious, especially when Greaves started putting it about that I was sleeping with him to get rides on the horses. Julian wouldn't leave me alone. He sent really sick messages, and I think he was following me; everywhere I went, there he was, shouting and ranting at me, even out in public. Mum spoke to Bert about moving Rose to the field next to his house at Draymere, but looking back, I should have left Rose there. It added fuel to the gossip that I had been using Julian to get something for free. I don't know, maybe I had. Mum and Natalie wanted me to go to the police, to tell them that I was only fifteen when it started and to stop Julian stalking me. But how could I do that? I had been running to Hardacre and flirting with him for months before anything happened. I was getting rides for free, I was competing every weekend, and I loved being around the horses. I accepted Rose off of him, for God's sake."

Alexander put his arm around her shoulders, and Hettie didn't shrug him off.

"So I went off the rails," she went on. "There were constant rows at home. Julian kept telling me that no one else would want me now that they knew what a slut I was. And people *were* shocked. There was whispering and gossip at school, and everywhere else I went as well. I failed all my GCSEs. I got pissed most nights of the week and set out to prove to everyone that I was as bad as they thought I was. You probably don't want to hear about that bit." She glanced at him ruefully. "It was getting the job at Draymere that saved me in the end. I'd stopped trusting anyone—men in particular. And I stopped believing in myself at all. Being around the horses again, and being good at something, gave me the chance to get back on my feet. The lasting legacy, of course, which you already know about, is that I've never had pain-free, sober sex. I thought it would be different with you. I've never wanted anyone like I want…er, wanted you. But that wasn't the case. That wedding when we were anticipating all evening made me overthink it again, and there it was, the demon returned."

"Wanted?" Alexander asked.

"Out of all of that, that's the bit you picked up on?" Hettie asked him incredulously.

"No, I picked up on all of it, every single word," Alexander told her. "I'm treading carefully because I don't know what you need to hear from me, if anything at all."

"I need to hear that you might still want me, now that you know everything," Hettie said in a small, weary voice.

"That's easy," Alexander said, pulling her close. "I will never stop wanting you, Hettie."

CHAPTER TWENTY-NINE

Alexander and Ewan were called to London to meet their investors a week before Christmas. They would be gone for two nights. Hettie stayed at the gatehouse to look after the dogs. She missed his presence in the house, but easily filled her days socialising, Christmas shopping, and clearing up behind the puppies. Alexander called constantly. Since the Fiona incident and her revelations about Julian Greaves, he had been overattentive and affectionate. He told her repeatedly that she was special to him, that he cared about her, and that nothing she had told him would ever change that. Hettie walked for miles through the familiar frozen countryside, using the time alone to resolve her conflicted thoughts. The exercise and solitude helped to ease the ache inside her that craved a return to the passionate, physical side of their relationship. Despite his demonstrative touches and affectionate embraces, the gulf of fractured trust remained between them.

Hettie chose her outfit for the ball with care. She wanted to look her absolute best; she wanted to radiate self-confidence and glamour to hide the wretchedness she was feeling inside. If she was absolutely honest, she also wanted to show Alexander exactly what he risked losing by sleeping around. She wasn't going to think twice about the reaction her outfit caused him this time. Fiona Harding and Carol Greaves would both be at the ball. Occasionally that thought overwhelmed her, and she came very close to bailing out. But she hardened her resolve: *she* hadn't done anything wrong this time, and Julian Greaves *was* a bastard.

The past needed to be conclusively put to bed. *To coin a phrase,* Hettie thought wryly.

Alexander was agitated to be away from Draymere, knowing he had left Hettie to stew and simmer. He had wanted her to come with him but accepted her refusal in good grace, while fear trickled through him that he had lost the only woman he had ever loved. He swung between black moods—from overwhelming dread to anger at himself, at Fiona, and even at Hettie for making him feel like this. Turning on the charm for the investors was gruelling and exhausting. His mood only lifted was when he was on the phone to Hettie, but the stilted politeness of their conversations left him tense with impotent anxiety.

Alexander had prepared a speech for his return, and he ruminated on what he would say throughout the train journey home. Ewan, frustrated by the monosyllabic responses he got to every attempt at dialogue with Al, had a rare, exasperated outburst.

"Alexander, I hope you are fully on board with this venture. This might be a sideline for you, but my future career is at stake. I've got a mortgage, a wife, and a daughter to think about. Not to mention a good mate who I've now persuaded to give up his well-paid job to throw in his lot with us. I don't know what the hell is eating you, but I need to be able to trust you. If you're thinking of walking away, I bloody well need to know."

Alexander's head shot up. "Christ, no, of course I'm not. What on earth gave you that idea? I've put hours of time and thousands of pounds into this. Of course I'm committed."

"You run so bloody hot and cold," Ewan muttered. "It's impossible to know where your head's at."

"I'm sorry, Ewan." Al sighed. "I think I've fucked things up with Hettie, and to be honest I can't seem to focus on anything else at the moment. But I am fully committed to the practice; I would never let you down like that. I'm disappointed you could think that of me."

"It's hard to know what to think when you switch off on a bloke, Al. Your default problem-solving mode is to clam up and stop talking. I wouldn't even know that you and Hettie had something going on if Clare hadn't told me you'd gone on holiday together. And I see you practically every day. I didn't realise it was serious, Al. I'm sorry that you're having problems. Isn't she off to South Africa in the new year, anyway?"

"She is, and I want her to marry me when she gets back." Alexander said the words stubbornly, as if stating it with enough conviction would make it happen.

"Bloody hell!" Ewan gasped. "Does she know that? You'd better unfuck things pretty fast, then."

Hettie wasn't at the gatehouse when he got back. Only Digger and Dora were there. A note on the kitchen table read:

Gone back to Mum's, everything fine here. Hope you had a good trip. See you at the ball.

He scrunched the note in frustration but resisted the urge to call her and rant in pointless, unjustified annoyance. He sent a text instead.

Thanks for looking after the dogs. I will pick you up for the ball—7:30 at your mum's

Hettie's message came back almost immediately.

No need I can catch a lift with Bert

I WILL PICK YOU UP

He tapped out the words determinedly, then breathed a sigh of relief when a further rebuttal was not forthcoming.

Hettie couldn't believe it was a year since Dog had died. And more than two years since Alexander had arrived back at Draymere and shattered her nice, simple life into a jigsaw of confused fragments. Good or bad, she wasn't sure, but what a ride it had been, she thought with a rueful smile. His assertive text caused her a treacherous prickle of excitement. Without doubt, it had been long past time to burst the protective bubble of a life she had created. Hell, maybe she hadn't really been living at all. But she had been safe, and life with Alexander felt far from safe at times.

She dressed carefully. The Wonderbra was back in action, and her expensive rose-gold sandals were getting another outing, but the dress was new. Close fitting, red, and strapless. If she was going down, she was damned well going to do it with aplomb. She left her hair down and let her copper curls fall over her naked shoulders. Hettie was painting on a second coat of red lipstick when she heard Alexander pull up outside, and she peered surreptitiously from behind her bedroom curtains as he unravelled himself from the car and strode down the front path. The beauty of him in his dinner suit almost made her moan with appreciation.

"My God, woman, you are gorgeous," Alexander growled, bending to kiss her cheek as she let him in. "The most beautiful thing I have ever seen."

Hettie grinned. The giveaway darkening of his eyes confirmed that her outfit was having the intended effect.

"I bought you a present, if you'll accept it," Al muttered, unusually self-conscious, withdrawing a narrow De Beers box from his pocket.

"Guilt gift?" Hettie asked ungraciously, then kicked herself for her mean-spiritedness when she saw Alexander's face fall.

"No, love gift," he said softly, opening the box to reveal a rose-gold necklace with a round pendant medallion, inset with a circle of polished and rough-cut diamonds. "It's a circle of trust," he said, taking the necklace out and moving around behind her. "We just need to join the dots, between us." He fastened the necklace, lifting her hair, his fingers brushing her neck. "Wear it for me tonight, please." The pendant rested prettily above Hettie's cleavage, which was rising and falling more rapidly than she wanted it to be. Alexander grinned and ran his thumb over the diamonds, grazing the skin of her breast.

"You bastard," Hettie mumbled, laughing and shaking her head as she spoke. "But thank you. The necklace is beautiful. I will wear it tonight."

Hettie was on the Melton table, which felt bloody weird. Especially as the grooms' table, housing Bev, Jodie, Siobhan, and Carol, was in her line of sight. But it was great to be with Grace. Ted and Anju were good company, and Alexander was being ridiculously attentive. So much so that it was starting to wear her out.

"Alexander, I haven't turned into a bloody princess. I've got the hump that you went sniffing around elsewhere. Stop treating me like china," she hissed at him when he asked her if she was all right for the umpteenth time.

"Fair enough." He grinned. "I'm going to snog you in public later."

Hettie rolled her eyes and laughed, but she didn't argue. The wine was making forgiveness seem so much easier; she was even beginning to wonder what she had made such a fuss about. It wasn't as if he had actually *slept* with Fiona.

When the meal and the toasts were over, the lights dimmed and the DJ took position.

"First dance?" Alexander asked with a grin.

"First dance, last dance, and every dance in between," Hettie told him firmly. "If you think I'm letting anyone else get near you in that suit, you've got another think coming."

"I'm going to request 'Lady in Red,'" Alexander said as he led her toward the dance floor.

"Cheesy!" Hettie crowed delightedly.

At the Melton table, Ted and Grace raised surprised, hopeful eyebrows. James held up crossed fingers on both hands.

The evening proceeded in a happy blur of laughter, dancing, and company. Hettie abandoned her sandals when the DJ started pumping out the disco classics.

"Be careful with that dress," Alexander whispered after a particularly energetic jive to "Footloose." He traced a finger across her cleavage before pulling the fabric gently upward. "Anything below that line is for my eyes only." Hettie grinned at him wickedly, so he picked her up and snogged her in public as threatened, amid raucous cheers from the surrounding dancers.

"Thank God for that!" Anna whispered to Bert.

When they left the floor, Siobhan and Carol approached them. Hettie grabbed Alexander's hand, and he squeezed it in reassurance.

"Carol has got something she'd like to say to you," Siobhan announced.

"I'm not sure now is the time…" Alexander started, but Hettie silenced him with a shake of her head and a squeeze on his hand.

"No, it's OK. Say what you need to, Carol." She lifted her chin and stared at Carol defiantly, wishing she still had her sandals on to give her extra height.

Carol glanced nervously at Alexander. "I wanted to apologise, was all," she said tremulously. "For what, you know, happened. And for not being brave enough to put a stop to it. I hope you can forgive me, and I wanted you to know that if you ever decide to prosecute the bastard, I would be more than happy to give evidence for you."

Hettie was knocked for six, and Alexander pulled her closer. "Well, er, thank you, Carol," she mumbled in confusion. "But, God, well, it wasn't your fault. I mean, what could you have done?"

"I could have spoken out sooner. I should have spoken out sooner. I knew what was going on, and I kept quiet. I will never forgive myself for that."

Hettie's eyes filled with tears. She moved away from Alexander and took Carol's hands in her own. "Please forgive yourself," she said intently. "It's all in the past."

In the early hours of the morning, the DJ rolled out the slow songs. Hettie kissed Alexander's neck and pushed her hips against him as they smooched to Van Morrison crooning, "Have I told you lately that I love you."

"Have I told you lately that I love you?" Alexander asked her.

"No, I don't think you have." Hettie pouted comically.

"Then I love you, Hettie Redfern. And I think I always will." He pulled her close. "Take away my sadness, fill my heart with gladness, ease my troubles, and forgive me."

Hettie sighed and held him tightly. "And I love you, Alexander Melton. I think I always have," she whispered. "Now can we go somewhere private?" She flashed him a wicked grin.

Alexander didn't need asking twice. They stumbled to the gatehouse, hand in hand, leaving a trail of footprints on the frosted Draymere lawns.

NOT THE END, BUT THE BEGINNING

Also by Sam Russell

Coming soon… *A Bed of Brambles*
Draymere Hall Volume II

www.russellromance.com

14001925R00218

Printed in Great Britain
by Amazon.co.uk, Ltd.,
Marston Gate.